Praise for *The Air We Br...*

"[*The Air We Breathe*] thoughtfully examines ~~xenophobia during war~~ time, the manner in which political events impinge on personal lives and related attendant issues. . . . The book's most winning aspect, however, is the manner in which [Andrea] Barrett keeps the narrator's identity a mystery."　　　　　　　　　　　　　—Tim Follos, *Washington Post*

"[Barrett's] gift for story, for mining America's past, and her ability to construct a specific moment in the quest for knowledge are remarkable."
　　　　　　　　　　　　　—Karen Heller, *Philadelphia Inquirer*

"Barrett's writing has a quality of reflective mildness, a restraint which some might call quiet. . . . There is an elegance of tone, but an enormous amount happens."　　　　　　　　　—David Mehegan, *Boston Globe*

"Barrett enriches her story with science . . . In fact, her style, always stylish and exact, is at its most compelling when she's describing her characters' engagement in their scientific studies."　　　　　—*Atlantic*

"A careful researcher and an even more deliberate writer. . . . This expertly paced and thoughtfully written book is ample testament to her gifts."
　　　　　　　　　　　　　—Corrie Pikul, *Elle*

"This novel is like an elegant ghost story, narrated by a chorus of not-quite-innocent spectral bystanders."
　　　　　　　　　　　　　—*Washington Post Book World*

"An evocative panorama of America . . . on the cusp of enormous change."
　　　　　　　　　　　　　—*Newsday*

"*The Air We Breathe* is 'slow food,' to be consumed morsel by morsel, as Barrett creates a world where the science is, mercifully, deeply embedded, and the writing unusually good." —Liz Else, *New Scientist*

"Richly detailed. . . . A marvel of intelligent design, and a truly original cautionary tale, from one of the most interesting and unconventional of all contemporary American writers." —*Kirkus Reviews*, starred review

"A deft and quietly wrenching tale of human misunderstanding."
—*Library Journal*

"Vivid and engrossing." —*Publishers Weekly*

"What matters in this novel are the casual bonds formed by people thrown together by fear and tragedy, and how tightly drawn those bonds can be, and how lasting." —William Thornton, *Historical Novel Society*

"I first read [*The Air We Breathe*] about 2008 . . . It was impressive then, but more compelling now. Just as *Breathe* described characters' worlds within larger worlds, COVID changed my experience of Tamarack Lake."
—Jerry McGovern, *Adirondack Daily Enterprise*

"Barrett is among the best novelists writing today, and warrants special attention." —Rob Neufeld, *Citizen Times*

"A poignant reminder of how deeply Barrett can penetrate a character's core." —Rebecca Donner, *Bookforum*

"Barrett's work often focuses on the excitement of scientific discovery, and there is also a strong if labored conflict between the curiosity of the poor immigrants and the willful anti-intellectualism of the power holders."
—*Booklist*

THE AIR WE BREATHE

The Air We Breathe

A Novel

ANDREA BARRETT

W. W. NORTON & COMPANY
Celebrating a Century of Independent Publishing

For information about permission to reproduce selections from this book,
write to Permissions, W. W. Norton & Company, Inc., 500 Fifth Avenue,
New York, NY 10110

For information about special discounts for bulk purchases, please contact
W. W. Norton Special Sales at specialsales@wwnorton.com or 800-233-4830

Manufacturing by Lakeside Book Company
Book design by Chris Welch
Production manager: Anna Oler

Library of Congress Cataloging-in-Publication Data

Barrett, Andrea.
The air we breathe / Andrea Barrett. — 1st ed.
p. cm.
ISBN 978-0-393-06108-6 (hardcover)
1. Tuberculosis—Patients—Fiction. 2. Immigrants—New York (State)—History—20th
century—Fiction. 3. Communicable diseases—New York (State)—New York—Fiction.
4. Adirondack Mountains (N.Y.)—Fiction. I. Title.
PS3442.A7327A35 2007
813'.54—dc22   2007022428

ISBN 978-1-324-06599-9 pbk.

W. W. Norton & Company, Inc.
500 Fifth Avenue, New York, N.Y. 10110
www.wwnorton.com

W. W. Norton & Company Ltd.
15 Carlisle Street, London W1B 3Bs

1 2 3 4 5 6 7 8 9 0

For Heather

Men are like plants; the goodness and flavour of the fruit proceeds from the peculiar soil and exposition in which they grow. We are nothing but what we derive from the air we breathe, the climate we inhabit, the government we obey, the system of religion we profess, and the nature of our employment. Here you will find but few crimes; these have acquired as yet no root among us.

—J. Hector St. John de Crèvecœur, *Letters from an American Farmer, Letter III, "What Is an American?" (1782)*

In the first place, tuberculosis is largely a disease of the poor—of those on or below the poverty line. We must further realize that there are two sorts of poor people—not only those financially handicapped and so unable to control their environment, but those who are mentally and morally poor, and lack intelligence, will power, and self-control. The poor, from whatever cause, form a class whose environment is difficult to alter. And we must further realize that these patients are surrounded in their homes by people of their own kind—their families and friends—who are also poor. It is this fact which makes the task so difficult, and makes the prevention and cure of a preventable and curable disease a matter of utmost complexity.

—Ellen N. LaMotte, *The Tuberculosis Nurse: Her Functions and Qualifications (1915)*

THE AIR WE BREATHE

1

IMAGINE A HILL shaped like a dog's head, its nose pointed south and resting on crossed front paws. The main buildings of Tamarack State Sanatorium for the Treatment of Tuberculosis, including the two long brick wings where we used to cure, are set where the eyes would be. There's a siding at the base of the hill—four posts, a metal roof, space for a cart and the portable steps—where the train makes a special stop and where, on arrival day, we'd each looked up to see the sanatorium windows staring back at us. We all remember looking down for the first time, after getting settled in one of those wings, to see the new arrivals sagging down the steps or being passed on stretchers through the windows of the train.

Back then we lay on our porches in orderly rows, the two chairs assigned to each room still separated by shoulder-high panels and sheltered by canvas awnings. Fields surrounded us—they still do—and also a river, three ponds, and the road curving down toward the village. After the cities from which we'd come, this looked to us like wilderness. Rivers,

mountains, wild geese honking. The air meant to cure us pouring anti-
septically through the woods. The Adirondacks were new to us, and we
were shocked to learn that Canada was so near. The snow shocked us too,
along with the dark winter days and the heavy mist that sometimes blan-
keted the fields. A fox, hunting, would brush his tail through the surface,
leaving a track we followed with our eyes. Ducks escaping the fox would
burst into the air as if they'd been shot. The sight made us think that our
own lives, hidden similarly, might still be launched on their proper paths.

We weren't a big group even then—sixty women and sixty men, if
every spot was taken—and a single arrival shifted scores of relationships,
as did a single discharge, or a death. On the porches we gossiped as
eagerly as we drew breath. Twice each week, if the mist didn't block our
view, the train pulled up to our unmarked siding and we inspected who
might join us next.

IN LATE JULY OF 1916, the train from New York City brought us Leo
Marburg. Tall, thin, with black hair worn too long and big hands with
spatulate fingertips, he paused on the boarding steps until a porter passed
him like a sack of wheat to the driver of our cart. The driver, without asking, draped Leo over the pallet in the back. Leo forced himself back up.

"I'm not that sick," he said. Up on the hill, our windows blinked at
him. "Let me sit beside you."

He eased himself down and around until, with the driver's grudging help,
he was on the bench and looking out over the horses. The cart climbed from
the siding and up the track, the buildings dotting the lower slope wavering
slightly in the suffocating haze. Staff cottages, laundry, incinerator, power
plant; he recognized only the stables, the others he'd learn later. The mountains were cool, he'd been told in the city, the air crisp and restorative. So
what was this steamy batting wrapped around him?

Inside the door of our central building, Leo found it hotter still. The linoleum floor felt sticky; the hands of the nurse to whom the driver delivered him were hot and moist, and she treated him, Leo thought, like a bag of raw sugar being taken off a ship. Plop into a wheelchair, plop went his carpetbag into his lap; plop on top of the carpetbag went a pamphlet bound in olive paper: *Rule Book*, this said helpfully.

"Read it," said the nurse.

Before he had time to glimpse more than a few of what seemed like hundreds of rules, she pointed out his Patient Number, inscribed in white ink on the booklet's cover, and then a page where he was meant to sign his name. Above it was a statement saying he'd read the rules and agreed to abide by them. *I understand that I am occupying a bed badly needed for someone else, that I am fortunate to be here, and that only by obeying the rules conscientiously can I show my value to the community.*

"Sign," she said. We'd all been through this, and all, like Leo, had felt uniquely prosecuted.

She pushed a pen at him, prodded his hand, said "Good" when his hand obeyed her request, and then rolled him briskly down the corridor and into the lift that rose to the infirmary. What had he signed? As if to make up for his slowness, she recited rules as they whisked along. No talking, during his initial period of total bedrest. No smoking, no laughing, no singing, no reading, no writing. Do not get out of bed for *any* reason, bathroom privileges come later. Do not think gloomy thoughts. Eat what's put in front of you. Rest. Think only of resting.

How was this better than Brooklyn? When the lift opened he saw metal beds, in which lay long lumps not talking, not moving, not singing. Then he was inside a bathroom with a dark red floor. Toilets to one side, washbasins on the other. An adjoining room held a huge white tub, in which the nurse proceeded to boil him. That he'd had a bath before getting on the train meant nothing to her: *All* new patients must be bathed on admission, she said firmly. This was a rule. So too was the astonishing temperature of the water, the disinfectant she poured in a copious stream, the harsh green soap with which she washed his hair. He tried not to wince as she scrubbed at his arms and back. Not to choke as she rested the heel of her hand on his head and gently, but quite firmly, pushed his head under the water.

"Take a breath," she said, and then he was under, panic rising in him so swiftly that he could see, before it happened, his body bursting from the water, leaping upright, shaking off droplets like a dog. He stood there, naked and breathing heavily.

"That's not going to do us much good," she said calmly. "I still have to rinse you off. But I can use a pitcher if you'd prefer."

He squatted back down, squeezing shut his eyes while she poured water over his head. Count, he thought, as the acrid water streamed. *Onetwothreefourfivesixseven* . . . He had always hated being underwater, but how could she have known that? When she was done she draped him in towels and inspected his bag, first pulling on white cotton gloves. Piece by piece she pincered out and laid on a metal table two pairs of flannel pajamas, a shabby woolen robe, a sweater, pants, a few shirts, underwear, books.

"Why didn't you bring warmer clothes?"

"I packed exactly what the tuberculosis nurse in Brooklyn told me to," Leo said.

She shook her head and made a note on her clipboard. "We keep telling them—these are *completely* insufficient. Put on those pajamas for now." While he dressed she bundled up his belongings. "No books, you won't be reading for quite a while. We'll issue you appropriate clothes from the storeroom. The other things we'll fumigate and put away. I need the address of your next of kin, so we know who to contact if that becomes necessary." She stood with her pencil poised.

"I *have* no family in this country," he finally said. "Why else would I be here?"

"If you don't appreciate how lucky you are to be given this chance to cure," she said, "and to be supported by the state while your health improves, there are plenty who'd be glad to change places with you." How many times have we heard that? "You have *no* family?"

"None," he said.

She shook her head. "Another one. Where do you all come from?"

If he'd had a place to go, he might have walked away. "I'm grateful to be here," he said instead. He was twenty-six years old, and the nurse had just touched everything he owned. On a machinist's hand he could count the friends—Vincenzo, from the sugar refinery; Meyer, from the boat— who knew or cared where he was.

She stowed him in an empty ward, the top sheets of the beds around him pulled so taut that the edges hovered above the blankets. All of us, he later learned, started out here, wedged between those cotton sheets in one of the white enameled beds, each separated from its neighbor by a small white cupboard. He learned to eat, propped up very slightly, from a white tray on a wheeled stand that swung over his chest. He learned to use a bedpan, to brush his teeth and wash his face in bed, to cough always into a paper handkerchief and expectorate into a waxed-paper sputum cup, casting cups and handkerchiefs into a paper bag pinned to his stand. He learned that his meals, which came on trays, would almost always be cold but would be garnished by a bit of folded colored paper, a Daily Thought: *Resting is done with the mind as well as the body. Getting well depends on YOU.*

On Thursday, his weekly bath day, he squinted with fear when an orderly came, heaved him from his bed onto a stretcher, and rolled the stretcher into the bathroom, but the tub was now off-limits to him; instead he was sponged gingerly and then patted dry, covered with blankets, and inserted back into bed. Food came endlessly, more than he'd seen since childhood. The nurse followed the food cart, taking his temperature and his pulse, and the minute she left—"Coughing can be *controlled*," she scolded—he hacked and heaved and rattled in ways that he couldn't, before, have imagined. In the early evening a resident doctor made rounds, peering briefly at him and then making notes on his chart. If all went well, the doctor said, and he rested thoroughly and ate everything, he might be allowed in a few weeks to walk once a day to the bathroom, to sit in a chair for fifteen minutes, to read or write for another fifteen.

~

DURING HIS CONFINEMENT to the infirmary, weeks spent staring out the window while time clotted like blood in a bowl, Leo thought often about the Lithuanian forest of his earliest summers, dark and leafy and crowded with men who cut down trees and lashed them into rafts they sent hurtling down the river. Because he'd been a Russian citizen, people he met in this country usually thought he was Russian. But in fact his father's people were Baltic Germans and his mother's were Polish, and divided; her parents were converts. When he was small, and his mother was still alive, he'd lived near her parents, in Grodno. Every summer, though, he'd spent six weeks in a forest called Białowieża, near the rest of his mother's family, who were Jews. In Grodno he learned to speak as his mother did: Polish to her parents and her parents' friends; Russian to his father, who worked for the government, and his father's friends. His mother's other language, which she spoke in the forest, he lost when she died.

The forest, which he lost as well, remained in his dreams. When his father sold the house and started moving them from village to town to marshy plain, always south until they finally settled in the outskirts of Odessa, Leo retreated in his sleep to the woods where his cousins had taught him to use an ax. His father married a plump Ukrainian with bright yellow hair and narrow eyes, and then he had brothers and sisters who looked like buttercups. He shot up, gangly and dark, amazed at the black hairs sprouting from his knuckles. The year he was thirteen, soldiers murdered Jews in nearby Kishinev and his father stormed around the house until the new wife seized Leo by the shoulders, thrust him in front of his father, and said, "This one makes you feel like that. The son of that Yid."

"She was Catholic," his father said. "My wife."

"Pfff," the new wife said. "Once a Jew . . ."

So he was Jewish, then? Yes to his stepmother, no to his father, yes in Odessa, no in New York. His father hadn't defended him, and everything that happened in the years just after Kishinev, after he'd run away from home, was jumbled. In Odessa, a stray boy knowing several languages hadn't been unusual; the city was filled with strangers born in Italy and Germany and Turkey and Sweden, all busily trading and making money. He'd found work in a cooperage run by a Greek; later with a French wine merchant who offered him room and board. He was clever, the merchant said approvingly. And had clever hands. With the merchant's help, he studied chemistry at the polytechnic institute, learning along the way about fermentation and the making of wine. For a while he worked at a winery, but later, as the strikes and the riots continued and his friends fled one by one, the balance had tipped for him as well. At twenty he felt like a middle-aged man; what was there to keep him at home? His mother was dead and his father was dead to him. He left for America convinced that here, he might be anyone.

Instead, somewhere between his first days on the Lower East Side and his move to Williamsburg and the sugar refinery, between the job in the char house, which he'd hated, and the one he'd made for himself, as the head chemist's assistant, his lungs had rotted and all his prospects had disappeared. Working one day at the refinery, he'd walked from the room upstairs, where he'd been testing effluent from the melter, down four flights and past the hall that led to the char house, across the floor where the graders were working, and into the corner laboratory next to the dock, where the head chemist was analyzing a sample from the ship. He'd given Karl his results, said good night, and stepped outside.

Near the door was a bin of raw sugar, the last load left to be tested. He'd leaned over to look at the color and rubbed a pinch between his fingers. Then he'd coughed—the same cough he'd had all spring, no more—and watched, astonished, as blood sprayed over the pale crystals.

Everything after that had also caught him by surprise, and that itself had been surprising. Despite his six years in New York, despite all his jobs and the people he'd met and the evening classes leading up to his citizenship hearing, he still hadn't expected the way that, once the government was involved, one step led to the next and the next, until he was cornered and forced up here. A nurse came to the flat where he'd boarded in Brooklyn. Someone who had seen what happened at the refinery had told someone else, who'd told someone who worked at the clinic. What a fool he'd been, not to spit over the side of the dock, not to hide his cough! A mouthful of blood on a mountain of sugar, and then this.

In that nurse's hurry to fill out her forms, she'd dropped Leo's diagnosis into the conversation as casually as if he already knew it and then walked from one end of the flat to the other, winding between the boarders' trunks and beds, examining the clothes hung on nails on the walls and the wash on the line in the courtyard. In the kitchen, saying nothing, she counted the plates and the cups. Back at Leo's side again, she started with the questions: How many people live here, what do they do, where do they sleep? When he explained about Tobias and Rachel and their two children, the four other boarders and the sleeping arrangements, she said, "Children, and you contagious." From a pamphlet she handed him—*Circular #2: Advice for Patients Suffering from Pulmonary Tuberculosis (Consumption)*—he numbly read a paragraph:

> Be hopeful and cheerful, for your disease can be cured, although it will take some time. In the treatment of your disease, fresh air, good food, and a proper mode of life are more important than medicines. Take no medicine that is not ordered by your physician. Don't

waste time or money on patent medicines or advertised cures for your disease: they are worthless. If you are offered admission to a sanatorium, accept at once. Until then, stay in the open air as much as you can; if possible in the parks, woods, or fields. Never sleep or stay in a hot or close room; keep at least one window open in your bedroom at night. Have a room to yourself, if possible.

As if a person like him would have a bedroom, or a window. As if his part of Williamsburg had a park. The nurse made him spit in a cup, ordered Rachel to keep his clothes and dishes separate, and referred him to a floating day camp for consumptives. There, during the hours he used to spend at work, he lay on a reclining chair on the rear deck of a ferryboat that had once crossed the East River between Brooklyn and lower Manhattan. The breeze blew through the open decks; meals appeared on a long table built in the center, where once there'd been engines and boilers; doctors examined them in rooms along the sides. Men on the lower deck, women on the upper; all of them immigrants, all of them poor. On and off the boat stepped officials from the Board of Health, visiting nurses, social workers, all trying to find placements for the patients. Prying into their backgrounds, investigating their living situations, checking their clothes for lice. After a month he chose not to remember, a woman with lopsided lips had handed him a train ticket and told him to pack his bags.

THE NURSE WHO'D admitted him to Tamarack State was right: he needed more clothes, and he came to miss the heat he'd so hated when he arrived. The leaves turned color, far earlier than he expected; the rain and wind poured through the long windows, kept open day and night; he was constantly cold, he was freezing. Some of us had relatives who arrived on visiting days with extra clothes or treats, but he had no one, and nothing he'd brought was right. He learned to be grateful for the worn but heavy garments grudgingly doled out to the indigent patients—which, he learned, included him. What he couldn't learn, despite being chided again and again, was to stay still. He spoke to anyone near him, tossed, turned, sneaked out of bed to pick up a magazine he saw on a table at the end of the ward, and then read it, surreptitiously, beneath the covers. The nurses barked at him and Dr. Petrie came to speak to him.

"Why can't you behave?" our assistant director said. "Don't you understand how sick you are?"

"I *hate* this," Leo said passionately, glaring at the doctor's small figure. With his crisp dark hair and pointed beard and small oval spectacles, Dr. Petrie resembled the inventor Charles Steinmetz, minus the hunchback. Not quite five feet tall, Leo guessed. No doubt with problems of his own. He yielded his left wrist to Dr. Petrie's thumb and first two fingers.

"Your lungs," Dr. Petrie said, his gaze averted while he counted the beats of Leo's heart, "have little pockets of infection scattered through them, which your body is trying to wall off. Right now the scar tissue around each pocket of germs is fragile, like a spider's web." He dropped Leo's hand. "If you move suddenly, or take a deep breath or stretch your arm—like you just did, when you reached for your pillow: *don't do that*—you break the scar tissue and let the germs escape. And then they make new spots of disease, and we have to start all over again. You seem like an intelligent man. Can't you understand that?"

"Of course I can," Leo said, "but until now no one's bothered to explain the point of lying here like a corpse."

With half a smile, Dr. Petrie said, "We'll try to keep you better informed."

By mid-September his temperature was down, his cough had improved, he'd gained six pounds, and the nurses let him walk to the bathroom and sit, for a little longer each day, on a cure chair on the infirmary's porch. Not since first running away from home had he been so alone, for so long.

One day an orderly took him in a wheelchair down the lift, through a tunnel, and into the X-ray facility beneath the dining hall. In the gloom he stood stripped to the waist, bending and turning as the technician instructed, holding his breath and then exhaling, perfectly aware what an X-ray was from his studies in Odessa, but unfamiliar with this particular apparatus. That the technician was a woman struck him as odd, as did the purple glove on her left hand and the angry sores on her right.

His radiographs, Dr. Petrie told him later, showed a small cavity near the top of his left lung.

"Am I going to die?" Leo asked.

"Much of what happens now depends on you," the doctor answered. Always, they pretend it's up to us. "Curing is a full-time job. But you've made good progress, and there are signs that the cavity is already beginning to shrink. We're going to transfer you to the men's annex next week. You'll be allowed a little more movement, once you're there. But you'll still have to be very careful."

ON A WEDNESDAY morning in October, an orderly took Leo down in the lift from the fourth floor of Central, wheeled him through the corridors and across the covered walkway, and deposited him on a porch off his new room, on the second floor of the men's annex. Two cure chairs nearly filled the sliver of open space: one of them waiting for him. Company, Leo thought, as eager to meet the figure lying in the other chair as he'd once been to meet a woman. His heart raced as he introduced himself.

"Ephraim Kotov," the man responded, waiting patiently as Leo arranged himself and struggled with his blankets. Beyond his toes and the wooden railing, Leo saw forest stretching to Canada, ranks of trees marching up hills and down, nearly black where they were shadowed by clouds, and the color of his childhood in between.

"In Minsk I was Kotovachevsky," his new roommate continued, "but here I am cut-off. Kot-ov." He held out his hand. "A little joke. Welcome."

"Thank you," Leo said, reaching across for Ephraim's palm.

Ephraim, who like the rest of us had been speculating about Leo during his weeks of isolation, said, "That was Hiram's chair. Yours now, though; he passed last week. Do you play chess?"

"Not well," Leo admitted.

"Too bad. Hiram was good at it."

Leo stretched his legs, wondering what else Hiram had been good at. What he'd liked and disliked, how he'd died. Should he apologize for taking Hiram's place? He looked back at the forest, seamed here and there with a birch. Below, a train pulled into the siding and tiny figures moved across the platform. For them, he must be a speck in the dog's right eye. "I came here from New York," he said. "You too?"

"From an apple farm near Ovid," Ephraim answered. In response to Leo's puzzled gaze, he added, "One of those little towns in central New York, near the Finger Lakes, named after classical places and writers. Troy, Ithaca, Homer, Virgil . . ."

"A Jew from Minsk, in the middle of farm country," Leo said with a smile. "How did that happen?"

Quietly—conversation has always been forbidden during rest hours—the two men leaned toward each other and, breaking the first of many rules, settled in to talk.

2

IN THE VILLAGE of Tamarack Lake, which is two and a half miles west of us, private cure cottages line the roads fanning up the hills from the water. While Leo settled into his room, Naomi Martin delivered the afternoon trays at the cottage referred to as "Mrs. Martin's house"—her mother's house, not hers, eight rooms rented to invalids who needed constant care and feeding. Three times daily she served the boarders in the dining room, in between ferrying treats to the porches where they cured. What had been a weekend chore and a summer job had turned, since her high school graduation in June, into a full-time misery. Day after day, she was trapped in the house that still, after a decade, she refused to think of as home.

Home, as she'd often told her friend Eudora, was the house where she'd been born: yellow-gray stone with two chimneys, a center door with a fanlight, and a front lawn cut in half by a flagstone walk. Tulip trees and holly had dotted the lawn, while peonies and iris thickened each year in the perennial beds. The town of Chester was small and quiet but Philadelphia was close enough for shopping and special trips. Everything ran smoothly; they'd had help. A man—George, she thought his name might have been—took care of the grounds, the carriage, and the horses; also they'd had a maid named Katie, and a cook. After the accident, when the help left, her mother took over the kitchen herself and learned to make meals from a book.

What Naomi remembered of the accident was this: a spring day in 1903, when she was five and her brother Thomas was almost four months old. In the big tub, at the end of the day, in water that Katie had boiled in kettles on the stove, she'd been splashing happily. Outside, her mother was still dividing the irises. Inside, she made a mess and Katie dried her roughly and scolded her, then left to boil more water for Thomas's bath. She went to her room and brushed her hair. Her mother came in—she called her "Mama" then—and took off her gardening gloves and came upstairs to bathe Thomas, which she liked to do herself, in his special china basin. Katie poured water into the basin and turned away to get more towels. And her mother, talking to Katie about the garden and thinking, perhaps, about her plants, dunked Thomas into the basin without checking the temperature first.

Blue eyes, or brown? Brown hair, or black? After a while, she couldn't remember. She remembered Thomas's cries, and her mother's screams, and Katie sobbing. Her father's feet pounding up the stairs and the things he said to Katie and her mother. Katie, the next day, slamming out of the house after Naomi's father dismissed her. She had an uncle who was a doctor and another who was a pharmacist and neither of them could do anything; she remembered their faces. Not the funeral, though, which she wasn't allowed to attend. And not her father, after a while: or not the way he was before the accident. When she thought of him she saw him *after*, that year when he stopped going to the law office, started drinking all day, stopped telling her stories or talking to anyone else.

The house began to fall apart, the lawn turned into a meadow, fruit rotted on the ground and weeds sprouted everywhere. One day her father ran away, and later, when someone found him in Texas, her mother divorced him. His brothers, Naomi's uncles, took the house. Lawyers and bankers came and went, also the women who'd been her mother's friends. Her mother went to Philadelphia again and again until the night she came home with her face set and made Naomi start packing. Later there was the train heading north and the gray-haired woman who met them at the station: Elizabeth Vigne, Eudora's aunt. The cure cottage, a big wooden pile made of rooms added to other rooms, porches stacked on other porches, was theirs if they wanted it; Naomi's mother accepted the job and they went to work.

She'd been eight when they reached Tamarack Lake, with nothing but some clothes and the recipe book that would make her mother's table famous. By now, prospective boarders in places as distant as Atlanta knew about "Mrs. Martin's house," and that had been, her mother said, their salvation. Naomi thought that almost anything would have been better. Live in the woods, live by the ocean, live in another country or on a boat: anywhere but this diseased place. Up and down the hills ran the cottages, lumpy with porches, packed with the sick. Some catered to Cubans, some to vaudeville players, some to insurance workers. Their house catered to the rich.

This afternoon, she was hoping to pry a favor from Miles Fairchild, the wealthiest of her mother's boarders. Early in his stay he'd taken over their largest room, gaining with it a red armchair, a walnut bed, and paneled bookshelves near the fireplace. His radiators always worked, while his cure chair, as she was reminded when she stepped onto his porch, offered an excellent view. The lake shining at the foot of the hill was green and calm and shaped like a mitten, sprinkled here and there with boats. Nested in soft kapok cushions, Miles might have enjoyed the couples courting in sailboats, children dangling handlines from rowboats, a great blue heron rising from the reeds and flapping slowly, just above the water, to the park at the distant end—but instead, he was reading. The umbrella fixed to the back of his chair he'd angled to shade his pages, shielding his eyes from any brightness.

She straightened her shoulders and moved toward him with her tray. A red ribbon held her hair in a way she knew made her look her best. Her sleeves were turned back to expose her wrists, her apron was fresh and neatly ironed, and as she set his rice pudding down, she willed him to look at her. He was thirty-seven, nearly twenty years her senior, but not yet dead; during the last month he'd gained weight and grown restless in a way she thought she might turn to her advantage.

"Lovely," he said, glancing first at the dish but then at her, shifting his legs and closing his book as he did. "Thank you."

"Extra whipped cream," she announced, stepping back and framing herself against the view. When his eyes followed her figure, she added, "What you said last night . . ."

At dinner, as she handed around the roast chicken and parsnips, he'd asked if anyone knew where he might hire a car and driver. He was starting a new project, he'd said, obviously pleased with himself. Something involving the inmates at Tamarack State, where he planned to visit one afternoon each week; he needed a chauffeur. She'd continued walking around the long white table, poking the platter between dark shoulders while her mother managed the gravy boat, nodding silently when a boarder thanked her, still saying nothing as she set the platter down on the sideboard and straightened the vases. Even before she pushed through the swinging door to the kitchen, though, she'd started scheming.

"Yes?" Miles said now, his spoon poised over the dish.

"I thought I might drive you to Tamarack State," she said. "I'm an excellent driver; I already run most of the household errands but I'd like a chance to work on my own. To earn some money."

Over the last six months, she explained, as he looked dubiously at her hands, she'd been thoroughly trained to drive by Eudora's brother, who worked at the Tamarack Garage. She'd also learned a number of basic repairs, including how to change a tire and use the instruments tucked in the toolbox on the running board. "So you won't need to worry about breaking down," she concluded. "Also I know every road in the village, and most of what's between here and Lake Placid. I can bring you wherever you want, at any hour."

"Wednesdays are when I'd need you," he said. "At least at first. You're free then?"

Pushing aside her mother's endless demands, and also the fact that the Model T in the carriage house wasn't actually theirs, she said, "I can be." The car, like all but their most personal belongings, really belonged to Eudora's aunt, along with four more of Tamarack Lake's most reputable cottages. Each was managed by an ambitious woman who, like Naomi's mother, didn't have the funds to buy a place of her own.

Last year Eudora's aunt had coerced all five managers into buying identical Model Ts, the loans to be paid off in monthly installments added to the house rent. The car, meant to please prospective boarders who might be swayed at the thought of a doctor fetched more swiftly, had unexpectedly offered Naomi a scrap of freedom when her mother refused to learn to drive it. Yearningly the boarders, their own cars left at home, stroked the black fenders, but they weren't allowed the exercise of turning the steering wheel and it sat until Naomi saw her opportunity. Within the month she'd appeared at the Tamarack Garage and persuaded Eugene to give her driving lessons. Soon she was picking up groceries and dropping off laundry, fetching packages from the station and sometimes driving a boarder to church or to visit a friend: all with her mother's grudging approval. If she occasionally took a few minutes for herself during one of those errands, that was no one's business but hers.

She smoothed her hair and turned toward Miles. "You'd be doing me a favor," she said. "For me to have some time in your company, away from my work here . . ."

"You do work very hard," he observed. "I see you working all the time."

She shrugged, smiling, as if she were the sort of person who would never complain. A few more minutes of conversation, an easy negotiation about her wages, and they were agreed. With a smile she left his room, slipped out the front door without her mother noticing, and walked down to the garage to tell Eugene what she'd just done. A small job now might lead to something larger later; who knew what would happen once Miles was cured and back home running his business? She imagined herself in a city, typing in a handsome office; perhaps she could follow Miles back to Pennsylvania. Any road out of the mountains seemed appealing.

⁓

AT OUR END OF THE ROAD, on the bulletin board in the dining hall, Miles had several weeks earlier persuaded Dr. Richards, our director, to pin this notice:

> ### GROUP FORMING NOW
>
> For the purposes of educational discussion and study. Male patients competent in written and spoken English are welcome to join in this exchange of work experience and other knowledge. Meetings to be held Wednesday afternoons, from 4 to 6 p.m., in the central solarium. I will give the opening talk or two. Please join us in this educational experiment.—*Miles Fairchild*

"Miles Fairchild," one of us had said then. "Who's that?"

"Who's the *us*?" asked someone else.

No one knew, although we saw that he'd done his research; the time he proposed fit into the only possible spot in our routine. Every day, then as now, we woke to a bell at six-thirty. After that, it was wash, dress, and breakfast at eight; doctors' rounds and procedures until ten; rest cure until lunch at twelve; back to the porches after lunch to rest until four. We ate dinner at six and then cured again from seven to nine, with lights-out at nine-thirty. Our only free time, very precious, was that slot between four and six: which twenty-two of us offered up on the Wednesday following Leo's release from the infirmary.

The sun was shining that afternoon, but the air streaming through the open windows already had a bite to it and we entered the solarium to find a slight man, with the same concave chest that many of us had and one shoulder drooping slightly lower than the other, standing in front of the fireplace with his jacket buttoned against the cold. A decade or so older than most of us, he wore a gray wool suit that looked new and expensive despite its old-fashioned cut. While we filed in he turned his head away from us, studying the framed documents above the mantel. Perched on the window seat nearest him was a slim girl—sixteen, we guessed; really she was eighteen—with flossy dark hair, an olive complexion, and deeply set blue eyes. She examined us as we settled hesitantly into the rows of chairs.

"Good afternoon," the man said, turning back to scan our faces. "My name is Miles Fairchild, and this"—he gestured at the girl—"is my driver, Naomi Martin. Thank you for letting us join you today."

Pacing confidently back and forth, with the sun glinting off his face, he said he wanted to start by giving us a little background about himself. He was thirty-seven years old and had been sick on and off for some time. A little more than a year ago, both his regular doctor and a consultant in Philadelphia had advised him to seek a cure in the Adirondacks. Since then he'd lived at Mrs. Martin's boarding cottage in the village, which he was sure we knew.

A small slip, but we noticed it; we seldom went to the village, although it was so near. Who had money to shop? That Miles didn't grasp this suggested how little he knew about our lives.

"Recently my health has improved," he continued, "which has made it possible for me to think how I might be of use to others. Being sick is lonely, in addition to everything else. Boring, too. All of us need conversation, and instruction—which is what I hope to offer. It's my idea that we'll teach each other, thereby widening our horizons."

As he spoke he moved from the window—nearly brushing, several of us noted, the skirt of his dark-haired driver, who nonetheless looked away from him—and then to the fireplace; to the window and back again, as regularly as a shuttle. We might, he continued, while we pondered his use of the word "thereby," be in a public institution while he was in a private cure cottage; our means might be strained as his were not; perhaps we hadn't attended school for long: none of this mattered. We all knew things of value, which we might share. At his home outside Doylestown, Pennsylvania, he, for instance, now managed the cement plant he'd inherited from his father.

For a moment, while he described his smoothly running plant, we thought we knew where he was going. His quarry, with its abundant limestone and shale; his grinding mill and his talented chemists and engineers; his vertical kilns, so technologically advanced. His special formulation for use in cement guns.

"I was one of the first to see the potential of Akeley's invention," he explained. "After the Cement Show of 1910, when the perfected cement gun was exhibited, others hopped on the bandwagon—but my engineers had already begun to modify the device, and we've since developed varieties of gunite that exploit the qualities of our cement and also make the best possible use of the double-chambered gun. Our materials have been used in the construction of dams and water tunnels, to resurface worn buildings and coat the steel columns for new . . ."

We listened with interest while he spoke in this vein. But after a while—oddly, we thought; what kind of speaker turns away just as he's captured his audience?—he paused, drew a deep breath, and said, "But that's only my work, and that's enough about that. Since I was a boy, all my free time has been spent collecting and preserving the fossils of extinct vertebrates, and that's really what I want to tell you about."

Suddenly he was describing weekend trips to New Jersey or western Pennsylvania, longer trips to Kansas, winter nights spent sorting and cataloging his finds. Not just a hobby but his passion, his chief recreation, he said, and he was sure . . .

When he paused again, it wasn't to ask if any of us had ever worked in a cement plant, as several had, nor to see what we, who'd had only Sundays off before arriving here, thought of having a "chief recreation," but to ask if we knew what a fossil was. Most of us didn't—a type of rock, some thought—but no one wanted to admit it. A few were curious what Miles would say if no one interrupted him. How long will a person keep talking about himself before noticing that no one is listening?

Quite a while, as it turns out. A truth some of us had already learned from each other. Once Miles said the word "paleontology," he was over the falls, into the rapids, and out of sight, his concave chest lifting as he waved his arms while a clump of hair, gray and fine, bobbed over his forehead. Rock formations, strata, epochs, eras: "It doesn't matter what you know or don't about such things," Miles said dismissively. "I'll fill in the details later. My best trip was two years ago, when I spent the summer digging up dinosaur fossils buried in the western Canadian cliffs. So exhilarating!" he exclaimed, while we exchanged glances. "I brought a map of the strata to show you."

Millions of years ago, Miles said, unfolding a small square covered with curving lines, giant creatures different from anything now living roamed the earth. In the oceans were ichthyosaurs and plesiosaurs; through the air flew pterosaurs; on land, dinosaurs crashed through tropical forests. Only their spoor, their tracks, and their bones remain now, turned to stone. In Alberta, in western Canada, the Red Deer River cuts through the prairie to form an enormous canyon, exposing these bones in the cliffs. The site has been widely explored since Tyrrell's first excavations in the 1880s and . . .

See, we do remember. At the time, though, we stared blankly. *Ornithomimus*, bird mimic; *Trachodon*, which had webbed feet and a bill like a duck—what were we to think? On a steep cliff lay the *Ankylosaurus*, bearing a club on its tail. Miles explained that he, a friend from Doylestown, and that friend's son (this would be our first hint of the Hazeliuses) had volunteered to act as assistants to a dinosaur-hunting expedition directed by a famous Canadian team.

Our flatboat, Miles was saying, floated between the cliffs. Day after day, a speck below the prairie, the mosquitoes attacking in such great swarms that we wore gloves all the time, along with nets that fit over our hats and tucked into our shirts. The boat could carry ten tons of bones, and we dug up nearly that many. Humerus as big as a person, femur the size of a tree (here Miles thumped his upper arm and his thigh); skull like a rowboat, claw like a foot. The endless labor he described—dig, chip, wrap, lug, pack, store, ship—we understood better, the work of moving tons of something from one place to another. We'd dug tunnels for subways, poured concrete for buildings, hauled bricks and grain or cut out shirt collars by the thousands, salted down millions of fish. What we couldn't understand was what this person, speaking with so much enthusiasm and so little understanding, wanted with us.

UNTIL THE PREVIOUS WEEK, when he'd suddenly emerged as someone she could persuade, Naomi had thought of Miles mostly as a middle-aged man who received an inconvenient number of packages from bookshops far away, and whose linen required extra care. In the car she'd been surprised by his questions and his apparent interest in her; now she was further surprised by how much he knew and how passionately he spoke about his fossils. Old bones—who would care? Yet he seemed carried away by what he was trying to tell us. With her back to the window, facing us, she saw the same things he saw: our worn, mismatched outfits and slippers and our clumsy, nearly identical haircuts, shaped by the barber who visited monthly and cut us all at once. Our faces, which, betraying the countries where we'd started out, were unlike those she'd known before and, to her, looked dull.

One face, framed by a wheelchair, stood out from the others and caught her attention: Leo Marburg's. His flossy dark hair, so similar in color and texture to her own; his narrow, unusually long and deep-set eyes, also like hers; his bony hands and his soft rounded nose. This was her first sight of him, but none of us noticed if she stared or blushed, looked away and then looked back, and she made almost no impression then on Leo. He was listening intently to Miles and, at the same time, looking around our main solarium, which he hadn't seen before.

Two glittering rows of windows, front and back, kept perfectly clean and, except in the most bitter weather, always partway open. Six electric chandeliers, hanging from the ceiling; a piano, several round tables, plain wooden rockers and a great many lightweight bentwood chairs. The scrubbed-clean fireplace, never lit, and above it two of the framed instructional placards that dotted all our public rooms:

I.

Like the snakes in Ireland, there is no remedy for pulmonary tuberculosis in the sense of a specific medicine or form of treatment directly applied to the exciting cause—the tubercle bacillus. Innumerable supposed specifics have been proposed and tested, but all have been found wanting. The only treatment which has successfully stood the test of time and experience is the indirect one of developing and maintaining the resistance of the individual to the toxaemia of the infection. We name it the "hygienic-dietetic" or "open-air" treatment. In brief, it consists of (a) breathing pure out-door air night and day; (b) an abundance of nourishing food; (c) rest in the open air, all the time if the patient is febrile, and at least a portion of the time if afebrile; (d) proper disposal of the sputum to avoid reinfection; (e) combating all symptoms or conditions which interfere with the main treatment.

II.

The tubercle bacillus is an infinitesimally small, slender rod, in length from one-quarter to one-half the diameter of a red blood corpuscle. It is frequently more or less curved, and sometimes it has an irregular knobbed appearance. It may occur in chains or in small clumps. It is a long-lived tough parasite that may retain its vitality for several months but does not multiply outside the body, except when grown upon a favorable medium. It reaches the lungs in two principal ways: (1) directly through the respiratory passages, by inhalation, and (2) indirectly by way of the gastro-intestinal canal, by ingestion.

A, b, 1, 2, d. Naomi saw those placards too, before she turned toward the garden with its patio and central fountain. From May through September water pulsed up through pipes disguised as reeds and fell into a scallop-shaped bowl. Above the bowl rose a nearly life-size woman's figure, carved from white marble. Her open arms and upturned palms pushed aside the folds of a cape to expose the enormous cross, which had two horizontal bars rather than one, incised on her gown from belt to collar. HYGEIA, read the plaque at her feet. FOUNTAIN OF HOPE. The fountain in her mother's garden was smaller but also sported a carved inscription: *Hope Springs Eternal*. Pleasant phrase disguising what, in Naomi's view, was her mother's true self: a woman who used to have money and didn't anymore; and was proud of succeeding despite that; and hated everyone because she'd had to. The girls she hired to work in the kitchen smirked at her behind her back.

Some of us were smirking at Miles: more talk, words like a river. We listened or dreamed or dozed, with no idea where the river might lead, thinking instead of a child's face, a woman's touch, a three-legged brown dog. Jaroslav, who had once worked as a cameraman at a movie studio, was imagining a sequence in which, against a black background, an eggshell lit from above and to the left, decorated with red geometric shapes and the thinnest gold lines—one of his mother's treasured Easter eggs—would tumble delicately end over end. Albert was thinking about his father's last letter and the passage he hadn't been able to understand, not because his father's hard pencil left such a light trace but because what he remembered of his father's Norwegian vocabulary was fading, as had his knowledge of his mother's Serbian. The rest of us were occupied similarly, which wasn't unpleasant, exactly.

Finally Miles stopped, at a few minutes after six, making us late for dinner. We were split up differently then, the women and the men in separate wings, the dining hall among the few places where we met. Even there, a wide corridor patrolled by two attendants separated our territories. No talking was allowed across that borderland, no joking, no flirting, no winking nor passing of notes. Soon Miles would learn to capitalize on this separation, but that night our group still consisted only of men, arguing among ourselves about the afternoon's session.

By the time we reached the dining hall, half of us had already decided we wouldn't attend again. This Miles person, someone said—who was he? A bored boss with too much time on his hands. Someone else, annoyed by the clicking sound of Miles's fancy shoes on the wooden floor, agreed. But Leo and Ephraim and several others said we should give Miles another chance; parts of the talk had been interesting, and it was a break from our routine. How many of those did we get?

Still arguing, we entered through the big double doors, each pinned for an instant by the gaze of everyone else. We had tables for six, then, ranged in even rows on either side of a central passage, and that made it easy to see at a glance how many were present; the dining room attendants used to count us at each meal. Ephraim entered the room last, pushing Leo's chair. And Leo—this was his first public appearance, except for the meeting—looked calmly around and waved, which made some of us laugh.

Ephraim wheeled him to Hiram's old place and then went to the food line. Alone at the table, Leo studied the room. Clarice, who was serving that night, brought Leo a plate: a privilege that came with the wheelchair. Stewed chicken, egg noodles in gravy, applesauce, string beans, a biscuit with butter. When Ephraim sat down with his own full plate, he saw that Leo was picking at his. "You know you have to finish that," Ephraim said.

"She brought me too much," Leo complained.

"It's the standard portion," Ephraim said. He pointed to the sugar bowl, where the Daily Thought was propped. Leo read from the pink rectangle: *Food is life. Eat three times as much as you think you need: once for the fever, once for the germs, and the final time for yourself.*

"I thought once I got out of the infirmary I'd be done with some of these rules," Leo said.

"Actually there are more rules here," said Ephraim, "but they aren't written down. We're expected to pick them up from each other, to regulate ourselves."

"Aren't we fortunate," Leo said, which made Ephraim laugh out loud.

3

A PIPE BROKE THAT afternoon in the village, leaving all the houses on the street below it temporarily without water. Despite Mrs. Martin's apologies, Miles, who'd been looking forward to his evening bath, felt unreasonably annoyed. In place of his excellent porcelain-lined tub, his robe warming by the radiator as he soaked, he had only the familiar curves of his cure chair, a book he'd ordered with great excitement but had since lost interest in, and the glow of a lamp that, as good as it was for reading, made invisible all that his porch screens normally revealed. Beyond its circumference stars, trees, rooftops vanished, people vanished along with their dogs, leaving him cut off from the outside world and yet completely exposed. From the street, he knew, the porches dotted the sky like movie screens, revealing every action. He crossed his eyes and waggled his fingers by his ears; let anyone walking by Mrs. Martin's house, and rude enough to look, see that. Behind the porch—men were working invisibly, still trying to fix that broken pipe—a tool clanged against the buried iron.

How did they work in the dark? Headlamps, perhaps, or miner's lanterns shining down on the water where it gushed. In the same way he'd meant to illuminate for us, earlier, the excitement that for almost thirty years had shaped his life. On his best days he still felt it: the pure delight that had swept him when, as a boy of eight, his friend Edward Hazelius had shown him a magazine article about a vanished world. Text running in double columns with colored illustrations: the artist had depicted an inland sea, covering what was presently Kansas and swarming with paddle-finned plesiosaurs, gigantic turtles, mosasaurs, and giant clams. Above the water, pterodactyls flapped while the horned *Monoclonius* lumbered on the shore. New creatures, he read with wonder, were being discovered every month, altering our ideas about the history of the earth. Instantly, he and Edward had seen their path.

For years after that, Miles had walked daily from his own family's stone mansion to the peculiar concrete home designed by Edward's father and built with cement from Miles's father's plant. The Hazelius house boasted rooms shaped like wedges of pie, others shaped like pillows or teepees, all of them studded with the colorful tiles that Edward's father had brought back from different parts of the world or manufactured in the tile works behind the house. The library was filled with natural history books and magazines, and near the fireplace, which was framed by tiles depicting the branches of knowledge, the boys devoured everything they could find. Edward's father ordered books for them, while his ancient great-aunt Grace, who lived in a separate wing of the house, fanned their interests. Although she seemed to Miles like a dinosaur herself, wrinkled and knobbed, she'd traveled in the Dakota Badlands long ago, excavating fossils with the help of her sister and accumulating the treasures now filling her rooms. The teeth of saber-toothed cats, the jaws of a primitive camel; where, Miles wanted to know, had she found these things? Neither he nor Edward knew sign language and she was deaf, so they wrote out their questions. She answered in a precise and tiny script, revealing secrets so interesting that the boys imagined lives spent hunting fossils.

Perhaps this was more appealing because they knew what really lay before them—both were only sons, the cement plant waiting for Miles as the tile works would fall to Edward. In college they dutifully studied the chemistry, physics, and engineering their futures would demand, but they also went to geology and paleontology lectures and read surreptitiously. During the summers they made field trips, camping out in Kansas or Nebraska and walking formations each day. Sun, sky, powdery earth, the feel of fossil bone and the sound of Edward's piercing whistle when, from an adjacent ridge, he signaled a find: the trips jumbled in Miles's mind but specific moments were captured whole, as if they'd tumbled intact into the tar pit of his memory.

How hard it had been to leave those trips behind! During their junior year, Edward met a girl named Chloe in the fall and married her—recklessly, Miles judged; she was seventeen—in the spring. That summer Miles went to Wyoming alone, but once he graduated and returned to work at his father's plant, he too stopped traveling. Still Edward was only a few minutes' walk away, settled into the mazelike house with Chloe and their new baby, Lawrence, and although both men were busy they met almost daily to trade news from the bone-hunters' world.

Throughout their twenties they'd continued to share books and conversations. Chloe usually went her own way when they gathered; even after Lawrence's birth she wore surprising clothes and continued to act, in Miles's opinion, like a girl. She showed no interest in the family business, which expanded under Edward's direction into the manufacture of ceramic materials used in ships and automobiles. When their second son, Charles, was born, Miles bought a crib worthy of one of the heirs to such a firm. Chloe took both the crib and Charles with her when she ran away.

For a while, then, there was no discussion of the Carnegie Museum's acquisition of a nearly complete *Apatosaurus* or the newly named *Alberto-*

saurus; both men were focused on Lawrence, who didn't speak for almost a year after his mother left. They hid her note from him: *Lawrence can manage without me now,* she'd written. *If I stay here any longer I will die. I have taken Charles, he's too young to leave behind.* The hats she'd left on the closet shelf gathered a yellow haze of pollen before Lawrence cut them apart with the garden shears.

In their efforts to comfort the boy, and to shape a daily routine around his gaping loss, Miles and Edward drew even closer. Miles visited the Hazelius house each day, ate dinner with the pair each night, helped Lawrence with his studies and answered his questions. Still unmarried himself, he taught Lawrence everything he could and felt rushing back to him, when he showed Lawrence a set of bones or a model, the delight he'd felt at a similar age. Dinosauria, he would tell Lawrence, lit up again as he'd been as a boy. Later revised to two great orders by Seeley: Ornithischia, the bird-hipped dinosaurs; Saurischia, the lizard-hipped.

"Ni-*this*chia," Lawrence would lisp.

He was tall for his age and loved the outdoors. When he turned eleven, Miles and Edward started taking him on fossil-collecting expeditions during their summer vacations. Miles, who by then had had enough trouble with his lungs that he'd ended two romances and given up the idea of marrying, found that camping outside helped him, and also that Lawrence flourished in the sun and the dry air. By the summer of 1914, Edward was able to arrange positions for all three of them as volunteer assistants to a collecting expedition run by a famous team of paleontologists.

Two large flatboats set off early that June, each with a center-mounted tent that sheltered cots and a cookstove and food, tools for excavating the fossils and sacks of plaster of Paris. The professionals on the first boat, searching out the fossils in the cliffs and leaving behind markers and instructions, floated so far ahead that Miles didn't see them often, but he'd found it thrilling simply to follow, digging and lugging as ordered.

The two Canadian students in charge of them—Ewan and Alistair, disciples of the famous pair—praised them occasionally.

At first, Miles and Edward and Lawrence were allowed only to do the heavy digging. Once they'd proven themselves, though, they were granted the privilege of chipping away the matrix from the bones and helping apply the plaster bandages. Hot, heavy work, which Miles loved. Shoveling rocks and dirt, fetching water, cooking porridge or washing his shirts in the river: all of that was also fine. Each day brought a new discovery. The sun burned, the mosquitoes pierced their clothes. Huge hailstones fell so hard that their tents were knocked down and their arms, where they'd held canvas over their heads, were beaten black and blue. The work was so exciting that they didn't mind.

Miles, who'd turned thirty-five that summer, felt as vigorous as he had in college and lost the cough that had nagged him all winter. Lawrence, who quickly proved that he could lift as much as Ewan or Alistair, row as hard and shoot as accurately, seemed happy too. Sometimes the three youngsters would go off hunting together, leaving Miles and Edward to nap, sunburned and pleased with themselves, under the canvas awning on the boat. Their group of five men, Miles thought, formed a perfect society, sharing equally in all the tasks and teaching each other, during the long stretches when they were floating down the water, whatever they knew. Ewan taught celestial navigation, which both Miles and Edward had always meant to study. Miles taught Ewan and Alistair a way to treat fragile shale so it wouldn't splinter. Ewan and Alistair taught Lawrence how to steer the flatboat, and as Miles stood at the bow, looking back at Lawrence handling the huge steering oar, he knew that he and Edward had, even without a woman's influence, done a fine job.

Those days floating down the river, between the fossil-laden cliffs; how delicious they'd been! He'd followed his father into the cement plant, rising through the ranks until he was ready to take over, but that was his duty: this, he loved. In early September, they finally reached the tiny town where they had to unload the specimens and prepare them for shipment east. Only then did they learn about the war.

Miles couldn't blame Ewan and Alistair for running off to join the Canadian forces as soon as they heard; nor could he blame them for leaving him and Edward to manage the crating and shipment of the tons of specimens. But he couldn't forgive them for encouraging Lawrence. One day Lawrence was on the boat and the next they found, where he should have been, an excited, apologetic note, more well-meaning than his mother's but equally devastating. No one could track him down. Only after months, during which Miles and Edward took turns blaming each other—who had had the idea for the trip? Both of them, they finally agreed—did Lawrence write from France. Having lied about both his age and his citizenship, he'd succeeded in getting shipped off with a Canadian battalion dotted with other eager, illicit American volunteers.

Night after night Miles and Edward talked about what to do. They weren't powerless; they could have forced Lawrence home. But his letters sang with hope and a desire to prove himself. *Let me stay*, he wrote. *Let me do this. It's what I have to do, what I want to do.* Chloe had disappeared completely—she never wrote Edward and no one knew where she was, only that she'd run off with some stranger—and in her absence the men talked as any two parents might. In the end they agreed that they had to let him stay.

⁓

IN ALBERTA, Miles had felt so well that he'd considered once more trying to find a suitable wife and then, with her assistance, selling off the cement plant and devoting himself wholly to working with fossils. The feel of the bones under his hands, their hot, crumbling, dusty surfaces and the sense that he was holding the earth's history, stroking the hidden parts of an animal no one had ever seen or could see, seemed like the only thing that had ever made him happy. In the days before they'd docked the flatboat and learned about the war, he'd stretched out on the deck at night and imagined changing his life. Just for once, he'd thought—during those months when he'd felt so strong and well, before the war started, before Lawrence left—he would leave his duties behind.

Instead, his lung complaint returned and he'd ended up at Mrs. Martin's house, pampered and stuffed with her wonderful food, but bored beyond words. He had books shipped in by the carton, a dozen magazine subscriptions; Edward wrote weekly and he wrote back, but none of this was a substitute for real conversation. One day, after a restless night during which he recalled the pleasures of teaching Lawrence, a plan for Tamarack State had drifted into his mind. Immediately, he recognized that this was what he needed. Most of us were younger than Lawrence in terms of what we knew, even if we were older in years; he assumed that if he could teach Lawrence, he could teach us.

How mystifying, then, that only twelve of us came to his second session, most looking for that promised "exchange of work experience." Failing that, we hoped for more talk about gunite; after Miles's first presentation, Ephraim had mentioned that one of his wife's cousins had worked with a cement gun while lining a siphon supplying water to New York, and that had made Miles's work seem more interesting. Instead we got a talk about the process of excavating bones. On he went about the needed skills, the special tools, the patience. Special whisk brooms with stiff, flexible bristles were apparently helpful, and also some little awls, which were used to follow bits of bone in from the surface while being careful not to disturb the bone itself.

Still pacing back and forth, wearing a suit cut like the previous week's but brown instead of gray, he described in detail the process of freeing one particular specimen and encasing the blocks in plaster-and-burlap jackets. Twenty or thirty minutes into this, Naomi slipped off the window seat and went outside; three-quarters of us envied her, although Leo and Ephraim continued to listen. Afterwards, at dinner that night, more of us decided to drop out.

AT THE THIRD SESSION, on October 25, only six of us were present besides Miles and Naomi. A few minutes after the session started, we were joined by Eudora MacEachern, whom we knew then only as one of the ward maids. When she stepped inside the doorway, we learned from the way she smiled and the swiftness with which Naomi leapt from the ledge and moved to greet her that she was also Naomi's friend.

While Miles spoke, Naomi and Eudora leaned against either side of the doorframe exchanging quiet comments and looking, Leo thought, like two animals similar in general health and sleekness but different in their natures: a hawk and a heron, say, or a coyote and a dog. Eudora—about twenty, he correctly guessed—stood on the left, tall and large-boned, strongly muscled but not at all fat, her light brown hair framing hazel eyes and pale skin that flushed easily. Leo had glimpsed her many times, when he and Ephraim went out to the porch for morning rest hours and she came in to make the beds and mop the floor, but in this context he finally saw more than the long blue cotton apron, the combs holding back her hair, and her chapped hands.

"My mistake," Miles was saying as Leo examined the two young women. "I didn't understand, at first, how little context most of you have for the work I've been describing. That was foolish of me. Let me try again."

We turned, hoping for something to grasp, but soon learned that by "context" he didn't mean anything to do with our lives. He meant history. The *Megalosaurus*, he said, had been discovered in 1824 by William Buckland, an Englishman who'd lived with his family among a menagerie that included a hyena and a dancing bear. Gideon Mantell, accompanied by his wife, had stumbled upon the *Iguanodon*, after which Richard

Owen, examining those and other finds, invented the name for the order. In London, in 1854, Waterhouse Hawkins filled the Crystal Palace with models of those prehistoric creatures, also mounting in Philadelphia the first skeleton of the *Hadrosaurus*.

Twenty minutes, forty minutes, an hour. During the first two sessions, Miles had forgotten to take a break for our snack, even though food had been laid out invitingly. We'd been too timid to complain, then, but this time, with a smaller group, Ephraim rose early in the second hour and pointed at the laden table.

"Oh, of course," Miles said, slightly flustered. "Let's take ten minutes. Please enjoy your refreshments."

We stood back while Miles poured a cup of hot chocolate and went over to the window, apparently drawn by the row of pigeons who'd settled along Hygeia's shoulders and head, spacing themselves at intervals so precise they might have used a measuring tape. Except for Leo, the rest of us crowded around the food. Leo moved toward Miles to ask if he knew the work of the Russian paleontologist Vladimir Kovalevsky.

Miles's face lit up. "Darwin's Russian correspondent!" he said. "His work on fossil horses inspired Huxley. Such an interesting thinker. How do you know of him?"

"He studied in Odessa," Leo said. "As did I, briefly. He's still much discussed there, because of his influence on Dollo—do you know, in this country, about Dollo's law?"

"Of course," Miles said enthusiastically. "Here, we paraphrase it as: 'No major evolutionary change is ever reversed.' During the evolution of the hoof, the toe bones, once lost, don't reappear."

"The phrasing's different in Russian," Leo said, "but the meaning's the same. What's lost is gone for good."

Miles looked at him thoughtfully and asked a few more questions. As he did, Leo grew more animated, pushing his fine dark hair away from his face. He was the first to take his seat, and when Miles began to speak again, returning to the subject of his own finds, Leo listened eagerly to his description of a giant creature with skull-frills of bone. He barely noticed the evening nurse who ducked inside the doorway and tapped Eudora on the arm.

THOSE BONES STICKING out like a ruff, Eudora thought as she followed the nurse down the hall. She'd never know, now, why a creature might have those sprouting from its skull. But this was the nature of her job as a ward maid: she was pulled constantly from one task to the next, never hearing the ends of conversations. Anyone—nurses, doctors, orderlies—could ask her for help, and everyone did. Without complaint she fetched files, retrieved lab results, made beds, damp-mopped floors, wiped down walls and furniture with a cloth wrung out in disinfectant. There were ward maids who hated those interruptions, but to her they felt as natural as her childhood.

Still she could remember the feel of watching from her crib as her older brothers and sisters swept into the kitchen, all four shouting and arguing before disappearing again, their mouths filled with something delicious their mother had made. Once she could walk, they'd treated her like a pet. Ernest might carry her off on his back, to serve as a lookout for one of his and Eugene's games. Or Helen might dress her in Eugene's cast-off clothes, blacken her eyebrows, tuck her hair under a cap, and declare her a tramp, only to have Sally remove the cap, tie her to a tree, and turn her into a princess awaiting rescue.

In a single day she might be used as a mascot in four different imaginary worlds, never completing a single game but delighted by so many adventures. When she grew tired, or when Eugene, who was very strong, accidentally grew too rough, she could retreat to her father's taxidermy shop and hide among the drying animal skins, the knives and chisels and trays of glass eyes. Or she could run to her mother's fragrant kitchen, where a beefsteak kept her eye from turning purple after she'd fallen into one of Sally's traps. She'd grown so tall, she often thought, and gained such muscles in her arms and legs, from the effort of keeping up with her rowdy siblings. Later, when she started helping out at her Aunt Elizabeth's cure cottage, she'd learned to divide her attention a dozen ways without diluting it. She liked her own swift adaptations to the constant change and the exhilaration of successfully juggling all the boarders and their requests.

Someday she'd find more ambitious work that made use of that adaptability. For now, though, this suited her fine. She chatted with everyone on her floors while carefully folding closed the brown paper bags pinned to our bedside stands, slipping them into the covered tins, and wheeling those to the incinerator out back. Picking up clean sheets and towels at the laundry and delivering the dirties was nothing; wheeling us to the laboratory or the X-ray facility, when the orderlies were overworked, she relished for the surprising confidences that emerged on these short journeys. She liked the pay envelope, too, and the chance to meet people from so many different backgrounds and places.

In fact she liked almost everything but the cleanup after what the nurses called "a situation." Sometimes that meant a patient had died. Other times it was something like this: Raymond, sitting up to take his temperature and unexpectedly throwing an enormous hemorrhage. The nurse, easing Eudora into the now-empty room, said, "You're so good at this," as if the flattery would change the task. "No one else is as thorough as you are, and we're shorthanded this evening."

Clean rags, cold water, boiling water, disinfectant. She *was* good at this, she knew; she had just the right touch, swift and light but exceedingly careful. Never spreading the tainted blood past the site of the spill, never flicking it onto herself, never letting water drip from the used rags onto anything else. Each rag quickly sealed in the covered bin and then, after the linen on both beds was changed, the floor mopped, and the furniture wiped, the bin whisked away for the rags to be burned. She could turn out a room in an hour.

Six o'clock came and went as she worked, and she missed her chance to hear the rest of Miles's story. But at least, as she found when she put on her coat and went outside, Naomi had waited for her.

"Do you want a ride home?" Naomi asked. She looked over her shoulder at Miles, bundled into the back seat in a heavy wool jacket. "I mean, if you don't mind . . ."

"It would be my pleasure," Miles said. "Your friends are mine."

"That would be wonderful," Eudora said. "Snow's coming, I think. And it's been a long day. I enjoyed your talk—what I heard of it, anyway."

She and Naomi tied her bicycle onto the back of Mrs. Martin's Model T and then cranked the engine. Just as it was turning over, Miles asked if they needed help.

"Thank you," Naomi said patiently, "but we're fine—I do it myself, all the time. Eudora's only helping because she wants to learn to drive on her own."

Eudora sat beside Naomi, up front, so she could watch the dials and gauges. The wind blew, the clouds chased each other across the moon, and the car flew between the trees and then around the enormous curve that, from our perch on the porches, obscured for a long stretch anyone arriving or departing. While Miles watched the clouds, Naomi tried, for the third or fourth time, to explain to Eudora how to set the spark and the throttle levers.

"Start over," Eudora said. Why did she find this so hard to remember? Otherwise she was very good with machinery.

"Look," Naomi said, tapping the levers on the steering wheel as they came to a rise. "If you're in high gear when you get to a hill, push the spark lever back till it's at the second or third notch, and open the gas to seven or eight notches. As soon as you hear the engine start to labor, use the clutch to put it in low gear and then move the levers like this. It's simple."

"I'll remember this time," Eudora said, even as she felt the details slipping away. In the headlights, which brightened as they picked up speed, soft fat clumps of snow began to rush at the windshield. She turned her head toward the back and said to Miles, "I missed the end of your story. Would you mind telling me more about that dinosaur?"

Eagerly he leaned forward and, as Naomi shifted gears and told Eudora to listen as the sound of the engine changed, repeated what he'd told us. Naomi steered along the edge of the lake, where some geese who should have headed south earlier were huddled by the benches in the park, and then drove into the village, past the lights and the people walking through the wet flakes. Miles completed his story and then said, shyly, that he thought the afternoon had gone well.

Eudora agreed. They passed two doctors who worked at the private sanatorium up by the tobogganing hill; three boarders from Mrs. Martin's house, standing in front of the theater; the mayor, walking his dachshund; one of the druggists talking with the director of the second-best funeral parlor. The dachshund, Eudora saw in the light pouring out from the theater, trotted along on his dwarfed legs as if he were exactly as important as the mayor.

They passed the village train station, so much more welcoming than the siding at Tamarack State, and then pulled up at Eudora's house. Inside, she knew, her parents would be sitting at the table, waiting dinner for her, listening to the empty rooms. If she was lucky, Eugene might have come over from the garage, in search of a home-cooked meal. If not, she'd be on her own, caught in her parents' silence. What did they do all day, now that she was working at the sanatorium and everyone else was gone?

"That was a treat," she said to Naomi, opening the car door. "Thank you."

As she was about to walk back and untie her bicycle, Miles cleared his throat and said through the open door, "I wonder if you—I mean this for both of you—I know you're both busy but you did seem interested in what we were talking about . . . Would you like to join in our sessions? Officially, I mean, not just listening on the side like you've been doing."

Naomi hesitated just as Eudora said, "I'd be delighted."

~

MILES WAS DELIGHTED that they'd said yes. Later that week, tucked into his bed at Mrs. Martin's house, he wrote to Edward Hazelius:

I hope this finds you well. I am doing well myself, very comfortable in my fine room. Just now I am in my excellent bed, the windows open and the alpaca shawl you so thoughtfully sent on my shoulders. The electric lamp shines down on my tray, which neatly holds my pen and papers; the covers are snugged over my legs; what more could I want?

Well, my health, of course. And to be back in my own house and, if not back at work, at least planning travels with you and Lawrence. Our last trip has been very present to me these weeks, as I go through my journals from that summer and talk to strangers about our work. The experiment I described to you continues—our group had its third meeting this week— and although I meant to speak only at the first meeting, and only as an example to the others, I've found myself surprisingly caught up in the plea-sure of sharing what I know. Also I've been stimulated by the realization of how very little the Tamarack State inmates know about the world around them. In education (or lack thereof), background, and training they are not dissimilar to the hands at your plant or mine.

Because of this I'm often forced to backtrack, defining terms as I describe aspects of where we went or what we found; even the simplest principles of sedimentary deposition are beyond them. But this week I made real prog-ress, I think. There is one inmate who seems particularly alert and whose face I use as a sort of living barometer; when I have his attention, I know I'm speaking well. This week he asked me about Kovalevsky! That a man in his position should know that name . . .

Sorry—that blot marks the entrance of my very vigorous landlady,

Mrs. Martin, come round with our evening glasses of hot milk and some fresh gingerbread. A crisply starched apron; her hair perfectly coiffed and a smile on her face—you could not find a better housekeeper, and there are reasons this is the most expensive cure cottage in the village. As always we get what we pay for. Her daughter, who helps her out, has offered to drive me weekly to the sanatorium.

I see, speaking of getting sidetracked, that I have once more succumbed. This happens to me so commonly now that I wonder if my daily fevers have not impaired my mental functions. Though more likely it is the result of spending so much time in bed, so lazily: I hate this. The inmates at Tamarack State must hate it as well but their opportunities for self-improvement, unlike mine, are minimal. Their so-called library is shocking, ill-sorted shelves of castoffs donated by the villagers: old encyclopedias, new inspirational tracts, dime-store romances, gardening manuals, anthologies of sentimental verse, memoirs of unknown military figures, outdated almanacs. I could weep when I think of the orderly reading rooms we established in our plants. If our public library can deliver good and useful books on a weekly basis and encourage a program of systematic reading among the workers, why can't that be done here? And if, in our well-run cafeterias, up-to-date magazines are available for the workers' perusal, why must these inmates rely on tattered copies of Yiddish- and Russian- and German-language newspapers brought up weeks or months later by visitors from New York? Why isn't there a daily English class? (The speech of many is far from perfect.) Or any of the other amenities we introduced in our plants?

What I am trying to do is modest but I know it's right—if they return to society better fitted to be happy and productive workers, the sort we would be pleased to hire, I will feel most satisfied. I am with Taylor in his philosophy of management: "Men, not materials, are the finished product of a factory."

And not only men: women as well. I did something bold this week, Edward. Attendance at the second and third sessions dropped a bit, and *so I asked the housekeeper's daughter, the one who's been driving me, to join our group formally. Also I asked a friend of hers, a ward maid who'd come by to see her and stayed to listen. Both have agreed, which pleases me. I think I'll issue a general invitation to the women's annex, to make the group truly coeducational. The men and women are kept largely separate, meeting only for meals, prayers, or the occasional moving-picture show. They should welcome this chance for further interaction.*

In your last, you said nothing of Lawrence—I worry about him all the time. I haven't had a letter from him in a month, have you? Often at night I have trouble sleeping (so would you, if you spent half of each day lying about) and then I see our trip again in my memory. I remember the way we grew so thirsty, after working in the rocks all day, that when we got back to the boat in the evening we dropped our heads to the river and drank like horses: you and me and Lawrence side by side. I remember the little boy who told us the Sioux legend about the giant monsters who'd once roamed the land, and how the Great Spirit struck them down with lightning bolts. Their explanation for dinosaur fossils, both of us realized at once. When the little boy said that the bones still lay on the ground where they fell, as no Sioux would touch them for fear they might be similarly destroyed, Laurence said: "I will touch them!" Brave boy. Where did all of that go?

There is little news; my health is much as it has been, neither worse nor, unfortunately, any better. Write when you can, your letters cheer me greatly.

4

EACH WEDNESDAY MILES continued to make the drive between the village and Tamarack State, puzzled that he hadn't drawn more of us in but sure that he'd succeed in time and comforted by the presence of Naomi at his side. The two women he'd courted seriously in the past had been ample and tall, while Naomi was as small as a child: the top of her head barely reached his nose and her figure was very slight. Sitting close to her in the car, though, always aware that she'd approached *him*, he saw that he'd missed the beauty of her eyes, her fine skin, and her wide, mobile mouth. Nor had he noticed, before, how sharply she observed those around her. On their rides, as she navigated the bumps and turns or steered around a frightened rabbit, she had something to say about all the other boarders at her mother's house. This one looked worried, those two had quarreled, that one's cough had changed. What, he wondered, did she say about him? Imagining her talking to Eudora, he began on Wednesdays to dress more carefully, tending to his fingernails and smoothing lotion on his hands.

One afternoon, aware of her perched on the window seat as he listed geological periods, Permian, Devonian, Carboniferous, he stopped mid-sentence and started talking, instead, about how each of us possessed at least one gift. No matter how poorly we'd been educated, no matter how deprived our lives, we each had something worthy of sharing. "That's why I started these sessions," he said, walking toward the window. "I believe that absolutely. Look—"

Swiftly he bent down, tugged away from Naomi the tablet of drawing paper she always had with her, and on which we'd seen her sketch our surroundings and sometimes our faces, and held it up. Leo and Ephraim side by side, an excellent likeness of both.

"A perfect example," Miles said. "Naomi's gift, one of Naomi's gifts, is the way she can draw anything."

She frowned and took the tablet back, flipping the pages to a drawing of roosting crows and wondering what else he thought he knew about her. He was *studying* her, she thought. As if she were a rock formation hiding a big skull. All month she'd felt his gaze following her as she dropped off laundry or picked up his library list, and often, now, despite the months when she'd been invisible to him, he looked at her intently and wanted to talk. His glances had prickled her skin as she sketched and she was almost sure he'd been eavesdropping on her and Eudora earlier, in the hall. She should have asked him for work simply, bluntly, instead of trying to charm him—why had she done that? On their last few drives she'd spoken little and answered his questions tersely, trying to act more like an employee than a companion, but he'd sensed nothing. Oblivious, like all the antiques: her mother, Eudora's parents, Mr. Baum who sold her fabric and buttons, the fat geese who ran the village with their swollen middles and scrawny necks. All of them sure they knew how the world worked, unaware that their advice was useless and that they had nothing to say to her. What did they know about what she felt, what she needed, how the world was shimmering beyond these mountains, waiting for her to grasp it? They'd forgotten everything important about being alive.

"And so," Miles was saying, having swerved back to his original subject, "when you consider the comparative paucity of the fossil record . . ."

Arrayed before him, we looked up obediently: more geese, Naomi thought. But we weren't as stupid as she believed. We were people trying to learn something in a situation that offered little else, and at a time when we needed the distraction. That November, while Naomi was already trying to undo what she'd set in motion, also brought President Wilson's reelection. Despite his campaign promises, no one really believed he'd be able to keep us out of the war much longer. November was the news from France, the battles at Verdun and the Somme just grinding to their end. It was rain and a new cook in the kitchen and two orderlies leaving; it was Morris and Pinkie back in the infirmary and Sam—age twenty-six, beloved first of Pearl and then of Celia—dead. November was the sky dropping down over our mountains like the lid of a cooking pot, until even the description of a three-horned herbivore was more pleasant than our own thoughts.

A shifting group of us kept showing up for the sessions with Miles, but each week we managed to stretch the length of our refreshment break a little further, taking pleasure in talking, then, about whatever we wanted. One afternoon Ian, who roomed a few doors down from Leo and Ephraim, looked around at those of us holding cups of hot chocolate and slices of bread and butter topped with jam, and started talking about his brother, who had a wonderful job making children's toys. For three years, he explained, his brother had worked at the plant that produced Erector sets, stamping steel into miniature girders, each tiny element precisely made and glowing with its nickel coating, the girders fitting so neatly together that a boy might construct a miniature bridge or a battleship. Instead of working as a collier, as he'd have been doing if he'd stayed in Wales, he was aboveground, not black with coal dust, enjoying the routine of a well-run factory.

"I run an excellent factory myself," Miles said, leaning into our circle. "At my plant . . ."

Ian smiled, nodded, and then, as if Miles hadn't spoken, continued. "I was hoping to work there myself, before I got sick," he said. "My brother was sure he could get me a job."

"You'd be right to leap at that," Leo said.

The rest of us nodded, having many times admired through shop windows the gleaming parts bedded in sturdy wooden boxes. Those boxes, Ian continued, were exactly what he'd hoped to make; in Flushing he'd worked as a cabinetmaker and he had just the skills required. Several of us, longing to purchase the least expensive sets for our sons, wondered if Ian could get a discount and moved closer as Ian asked Naomi if he might have a few sheets of paper. He drew girders and angles and connecting strips, wheels and tiny motors, along with sketches of some of the models that boys from across the country submitted for the yearly contests. A windmill, a dredge that actually dug. A streetcar with wheels that moved.

For several more minutes we chattered, ignoring Miles's attempts to interrupt us. At supper we wondered if our discussion had irritated him, but to our surprise an elaborate Erector set turned up in our library that weekend. The three of us who unpacked it and spread out the pieces were impressed to see an electric motor and extra gears.

"If we'd talked about books," Frank said, "would he have sent up a crate of those?"

"Records?" asked Pietr, who loved opera.

"He wants something," Abe said flatly. "He must. But what?"

"Why does he have to want something?" Pietr said, setting the lid of the box aside. "It's a toy, and that's all it is. But still—we've got enough parts to build almost anything."

Together he and Frank and Abe made a simple building with a smokestack, rather like our power plant, which they left on the library table next to the open box. Soon after that the building disappeared, replaced by an arched bridge. Then a skyscraper rose and melted away, replaced first by a railroad car and then by an ambitious but inaccurate attempt at a battleship. Eudora stopped by the library after work one day and found Leo standing over that ship, which was now missing part of its deck. In his right hand he held a shiny hexagonal ring the size of a dinner plate.

"What did you make?" she asked.

"Model of a benzene molecule." He hung the hexagon over her extended wrist. "Did you take chemistry in school?"

"Two years," she said. "Not as much as I would have liked, but that's all girls can take here. I remember benzene, though—six carbon atoms?"

"Kekulé's structure," he said. He'd built it almost unconsciously, his hands fitting the girders together into what for him was a common shape.

"Peculiar name," Eudora said, turning the angular ring on her arm.

Leo pushed what was left of the ship across the table, remembering the scarred oak tables that had filled his old schoolroom, the smooth-bellied glass vessels and the sinuous tubing pulled fine as thread, the purring, nearly invisible flame of the Bunsen burner. Head-clearing tang of acetic acid, eggy stink of sulfur; he couldn't think without pain of his dabbles into aromatic substitutions, pleasurably simple and yet so complex. During the few years of his studies in Odessa, the chemicals spritzing up from the bench had burned holes in his shirts. How hard he'd tried, during his first years in New York, to find work that made some use of his training! And how completely he had failed. One menial job after another, only the sugar refinery offering even a hint of possibility. Up here, where Miles's descriptions of his cement gun and his fossil dinosaurs could seem equally interesting, or equally pointless, now that he knew he'd never be a chemist or find work he loved, he was doing his best to appreciate whatever came his way. Apparently his hands hadn't resigned themselves, though.

"Where did you learn that?" Eudora said.

"In school," he answered, wondering how long he'd been silent. "A while ago." Briefly, and with more cheerfulness than he felt, he described his training in Odessa and his struggle, after emigrating, to find work.

"You ought to talk to Irene Piasecka," she said. "The woman who runs the X-ray laboratory."

"A woman took a radiograph of my chest," he said. "Was that her?"

Eudora nodded. "She wasn't raised around here either."

The gleaming metal shape he'd made, which she now held in front of her like a dish, was perfectly useless but had at least drawn her attention. "Keep that, if you'd like," he said.

IN THE BASEMENT, two floors beneath them, lay Irene's domain: a long, dim, cool room, windowless and below the ground, smelling of ozone and the flagstone floor, the chemicals used in the darkroom and tarnishing silver. Dr. Petrie used to sit for hours at the end farthest from the X-ray apparatus, gazing at Irene's face across the low table and, in the light of a single lamp, talking about his patients—us—and about the young men he'd once loved, both of whom had died. Ephraim, Leo, Pietr, Zalmen, Polly, Nan, Lydia, Abe—all of us had stood perfectly still, comforted by Irene's voice, while she peered inside our chests. Sadie had talked obsessively to Irene about the dogs she bred, which she'd had to leave behind; Ladislav had talked about his childhood haunts, some of which Irene had also known; we liked the X-ray room, we felt at home. No point in describing how it is now.

On the day Leo gave Eudora the model, she headed down into the basement to visit Irene. Inside the door she dropped the hexagon onto her coat and then forgot about it. From Leo, as from Naomi and everyone else, she'd purposefully kept any suggestion of how much time she spent here. Evening after evening she approached Irene, who welcomed her if she wasn't too busy. Over the last few months she'd learned what a Crookes tube was, how electrodes worked, and, although she'd never held a camera before, how to negotiate a darkroom and develop film. She'd helped Irene make pictures that once, she learned, had been called skiagraphs—images of shadows—but now were roentgenograms, or radiographs, a projection of something that blocked or absorbed the X-rays. Bones and teeth cast a strong shadow; organs and tissues left shadows lighter or darker depending on their densities. "In your imagination," Irene had said, "you have to see the three-dimensional shape creating the one-dimensional shadow. That's why it's so hard to interpret the images correctly. Why they can be ambiguous."

This made sense to Eudora, who was fascinated by the shadows of our organs. Inside the lungs of those she cleaned up after, bacilli were madly reproducing: what did the shadow of that invasion look like? In her high school biology class she'd seen bloodless drawings of human parts and also, in heavy old jars at the back of the room, preserved organs—brain, liver, and, yes, a small pair of dog's lungs, still attached to bronchi and trachea—afloat in cloudy solutions. What she wanted to learn, though, was how lungs and heart, stomach and diaphragm, fit together within the cage of a person's ribs. Before she started visiting Irene, her only hazy sense of this had come from the innards strewn about her father's taxidermy shop.

There'd been times, as she was helping out her Aunt Elizabeth, when she'd wondered if she might like to train as a nurse. Since working at Tamarack State, and discovering both how comfortable she was around us and how little she was disturbed by the blood and mess of illness, she'd begun thinking about it more seriously. In the meantime she was grateful to Irene, who let her spy on our insides without judging her ignorance. Another person might have refused to teach her anything about X-rays because she knew so little physics or chemistry, declined to show her diseased lungs when she knew so little about healthy ones, been reluctant to let her develop an X-ray image before she'd handled a camera. But Irene, whose own path had been haphazard, didn't seem to mind Eudora's unsystematic approach.

Over the course of several nights, she'd told Eudora a little of her history. In Kraków, she'd been raised by her father, after her consumptive mother died. At university she'd studied chemistry and married a photographer but been widowed after only three years. Still in her twenties, she'd decided to come to America to join her sister and her husband, an energetic Czech. For a year, until she too was diagnosed with a mild case of tuberculosis, she'd shared a house with them in New York. Then, at the suggestion of her brother-in-law, who'd finished his medical training by then, all three of them had moved to Colorado Springs, which was filled with people curing in the mountain air.

Not long after Roentgen's discovery of the rays, she'd been drawn into the excitement. With some borrowed equipment she made plates of her brother-in-law's chest, and then of her own; once she saw the scars left by her own disease she couldn't stop experimenting. Her brother-in-law, equally astounded by the discovery and the new possibilities, had been eager to take advantage of the medical applications while she, with her background in chemistry to guide her, quickly learned to make the most of the equipment. Together they'd built a little studio.

"A wonderful room," she'd told Eudora. "In the back of Joe's medical office; one of his patients donated the money to build it in memory of his son. Eventually I had my own darkroom, my own induction coil and a tube stand and battery; I ordered them from an advertisement in *Scientific American*. Later I replaced that apparatus with a much stronger one. I made my first fluoroscope, and my first plateholders. I looked into my own hands, the chests of my sister and her friends, cats and frogs and the trout we caught in the river." She'd had work, she continued, almost as soon as she'd set up the apparatus. Joe had encouraged his associates to bring in patients with broken bones, and soon others came as well, people with old fractures that had healed poorly, those suspected of having kidney stones. It was practice, she said, that she could have gotten in no other way.

In the glow of the darkroom's ruby light, taking notes as Irene mixed the chemicals and floated the film in one solution and then another, Eudora had listened intently and tried to remember everything. Once or twice, when she'd had to ask a question, the hint of irritation she saw on Irene's face reminded her of how patient she'd been so far. "Sometimes," Irene had said a few days ago, "the best way to learn is just to experiment on ourselves."

Which was how Eudora had reached this evening, finally about to see the inside of her own chest. She'd unlaced and stepped out of her shoes, removed her blue apron so the buttons wouldn't interfere, and slipped off her blouse. Dressed only in her skirt and stockings and camisole, she stood motionless in the darkened room between the two upright poles of the tube holder. Irene adjusted the height of the crossbar. Inside the suspended wooden box, hidden except for the rounded surface gleaming through the glass port, the powerful new tube—a high-vacuum Coolidge tube with a tungsten target that Irene had recently acquired—warmed up.

Irene, who'd been peering at the coated cardboard of the fluoroscopic screen, moved behind Eudora and opened the port so she could replace one lead diaphragm with another. "That should work better," she said.

Returning to the screen, she lowered her goggles and peered through the dark red glass. "Lift your arms. When I tell you to, take a deep breath and then hold it. Ready?"

"Ready," Eudora said.

"Lovely," said Irene, before falling silent for half a minute. "Release it—good. Now just breathe normally for a bit."

What, Eudora wondered, was she seeing?

"Excellent lungs," Irene said approvingly. "If you give me another few minutes I'll take a radiograph."

In the darkroom, earlier, she'd shown Eudora how to load the metal holders with the floppy sheets of nitrocellulose film. The glass plates she'd used before weren't available anymore, she said; they were made in Belgium. But the film had its own advantages, which now, as she moved Eudora away from the tube holder, took some measurements, and positioned another stand, Eudora began to see. The film holder slipped weightlessly, easily, into the frame on the stand.

"Hold your breath again," Irene directed. Something whirred and she looked intently at her timer. "I like this tube, it's so much easier to use. The exposure time is far shorter, too—but it almost makes me unnecessary. The old gas tubes were so idiosyncratic that it took a real knack to get good images using them, but these—I could train you to use this in a couple of months. You can step away, now."

The red goggles lay on the table; Eudora picked them up and peered through them but could see nothing. As she handed the goggles back, Irene said, shyly but also with a note of pride, that in her early days she'd done so many experiments that she'd been asked to meetings, and published papers, and consulted for doctors all over the country. "I made a reputation in Colorado," she confided, "almost by accident. But it was enough that, when the doctors here decided they wanted someone to set up and run an X-ray facility, they contacted me despite my lack of medical training."

"They didn't mind that you . . . ?"

"That I'm a woman?" Irene curled her lip. "They probably did mind. But not enough to keep them from hiring the best person they could for the pitiful salary they offered."

Interesting, Eudora thought. Those little spurts of anger, so seldom released. "Is that when you hurt your hands?" she asked. "When you were setting up the equipment here?"

Irene tucked her gloved left hand—we'd all been curious about that glove, which she never explained but which was always present, and always some shade of violet—into her pocket, holding out her naked right hand for Eudora's inspection. The skin had the color and texture of leather and three nails were missing completely, while the other two were thick and misshapen, veiled by overgrown cuticles. She stretched out her stiff fingers before closing them into a fist.

"I think I did most of the damage in Colorado," she said, "during the late 1890s and the early years of this century, when we didn't have any idea that the rays might be harmful. I used to test different Crookes tubes by holding my left hand between the tube and the fluorescent screen and then adjusting the anode until I got a good image."

Before long, the skin on her left hand had dried and cracked, and then the hand had swollen as if she'd burned herself. Later the skin came off completely along with her fingernails and the little hairs. But this, she explained, had happened to everyone; it had seemed like a bad sunburn and everyone assumed that the effects of the Roentgen-ray dermatitis were temporary. They'd used petroleum jelly to protect themselves, and gloves. Later, when news began to spread about some who'd worked with the machines, she'd covered her hands with tinfoil and also built some different shielding for the beam. Perhaps those efforts had saved her right hand from the worst damage.

"Probably I was too late for this one, though," she said, freeing her left hand from her pocket and turning it front to back as if inspecting the dark violet cloth for holes.

"Can I see?" Eudora asked.

Irene shrugged. Until then, she'd shown only Dr. Petrie what lay beneath the glove. "If you want." Slowly, pulling from the tip of each finger, she peeled off the glove, taking with it three of the fingers as well.

"Surgical cotton," she noted, holding the glove out for Eudora's inspection. "I stuff the finger holes to look like a normal hand, so people don't have to think about what's underneath."

Raw-looking stumps where the three middle fingers had been amputated; open sores on the little finger, which was also missing its top joint;

dark thickened patches, like calluses, in places where no callus would ever be. On the back of the hand and thumb, Eudora saw crusty growths, but nothing anywhere resembling normal skin.

"For years," Irene said, looking down at her hand, "I corresponded with a woman in San Francisco, another early experimenter with X-rays. Before I came here I learned that her hands, which had been very bad for some time, had gotten much worse and that she had a kind of cancer. She had her fingers amputated, then her left hand at the wrist, then at the elbow, and finally at the shoulder, but by then the cancer had already spread to the nodes in her armpit. A year later she died. Almost the same thing happened to Mr. Edison's assistant. The last time I saw him he'd lost his whole left hand. Before he died the doctors had taken one arm off at the shoulder, the other at the elbow."

She looked down at her ungloved hand as Eudora tried to imagine the whole thing gone, and then the arm: impossible. "Not long after I came here the trouble with my own hands began," Irene continued. "I had first my index finger and then these other two amputated. It's happened to so many of us—doctors, people who manufactured and tested the tubes, other technicians: how can I complain? I can still remember the first exhibition of the rays I saw, at a county fair. A line of us, walking one at a time before the open fluorescent screen: on one side people clothed in their flesh, on the other the bones revealed. After that, all I wanted to do was learn how to control those rays, so that I'd be able to see inside."

"Does it hurt?" Eudora asked.

"More than you can imagine," Irene said calmly. "It keeps me from sleeping. At night I walk around my room with one hand or the other held up above my head, wrapped in wet bandages or slathered with different ointments. Even Dr. Petrie doesn't know what will happen next, what part will have to come off."

She peered sharply at Eudora and then reached for her glove, adding, "But we never do know what will happen to us, really—and nothing like this will happen to you, the equipment is perfectly safe now. That's what the lead lining in the tube holder is for. And the diaphragm. Why don't you move over here and take a turn yourself?"

Following her careful instructions, Eudora exposed a film of Irene's chest. They skipped dinner, nibbling instead on some chocolate and crackers Irene kept in a drawer, and then Irene said that, although it was late, they might go into the darkroom and develop the images. When they were done they inspected the films with Irene's viewing box.

"Hold the narrow part up to your eyes," Irene said.

Obediently, Eudora grasped the handle and brought the black pyramid over her face. The bottom, covered by a sheet of glass, formed a rectangle eleven by fourteen inches, the same size as their largest sheets of film. The top narrowed and then flared out again into a shape like an eye mask, its rim padded with black fur that tickled her skin.

"Now press the film against the glass, and face the electric light."

At first, as Eudora turned her head and the box uncertainly, she saw nothing. Then she found the light and the film lit up, the shadows varied and subtle. Sternum, diaphragm, and encircling ribs, also a thickened central area, which meant nothing to her inexperienced eyes. When she asked what that was, Irene took the box and held it to her own face. Then Eudora saw what she'd looked like: a chimera with a woman's body and a woman's mouth, eyeless above a flared black snout that shimmered and refracted light and seemed, as it moved this way and that, to be sniffing for food.

Irene returned the box. "Look at that thickened area again," she said. "Can you see it?"

"Yes."

"Good—now follow my hand." Reaching around the bottom of the box and into the illuminated field, her finger moving like a submarine through the shadows, Irene pointed out Eudora's backbone and the outlines of her heart.

After Eudora had studied the film a bit longer, Irene took it away and replaced it with the image of her own chest. "See the faint shadows clustered between the ribs? Those are tubercular scars, from when I was sick; that's a classic presentation."

Again Eudora inspected the image closely. After a few minutes she removed that film from the glass, replaced it with the first one, and then exchanged them again, memorizing the differences.

"You seem to have a gift for this," Irene said. "Do you know who Madame Curie is?"

Eudora nodded. "The Frenchwoman who discovered radioactivity with her husband."

"*Polish*," Irene said. "But the Curies have long been heroes of mine, especially Marie. I've always remembered what she said about coming into her workroom at night and seeing her jars glowing on the shelves. That's what made me study chemistry—I wanted my own life to be like that. Hard work but then, afterwards, something I'd made glowing in the dark."

Not once during the evening had Eudora thought of the metal hexagon lying on her coat, but now she remembered what Leo had said about his own years studying chemistry. For a second she wished he were here with her, listening to Irene.

With her gloved hand Irene tapped the image of Eudora's chest and said, "In the end, though, I decided to stick with Roentgen's rays. They're mysterious and powerful enough for me."

"For me too," Eudora echoed, thinking: Compared to what?

"Madame Curie has embraced the X-rays now," Irene said. "Even though she never studied them before. When the war started, she taught herself what she needed. Then she got various manufacturers to donate parts, and got rich women to give her their automobiles, and she turned them into mobile radiological units. Little curies, the soldiers call them. Each one is fully equipped, the dynamo driven by the automobile's motor.

She takes them to the field hospitals and helps the surgeons locate bullets and shell fragments. The soldiers think she's a saint. When she can, she leaves fixed radiological stations behind. And she trains technicians, scores of them—she's trained over a hundred people so far."

"Who?" Eudora said, struck by the idea.

"Anyone willing," Irene said. "Nurses, of course, and engineers—but also soldiers and others with only an elementary education. Photographers make excellent X-ray technicians, they're already familiar with glass plates and film and how to use a darkroom and develop the pictures."

"Could I do that?" Eudora asked.

"Anyone could," Irene repeated.

5

SOMETIMES WE SPLIT into factions, half of us disagreeing with the other half over how to relate these events: should this come first or that, should this be emphasized more, or less?

Show them, one side insists. *Morris, Edith, Denis. Before they're gone.*

We can't, the rest of us argue.

Why not? It would mean more, if they stood out.

Less. It would mean less.

Eventually we reach some agreement and move on. We can't show everyone, and some—Irene was long overdue—have to show up before others. Days and nights that aren't interesting, we skip. We do our best.

Skip our fifth session then, which was only Miles saying more of the same. And although we love our movies—we don't have much to look at here, beyond our own rooms, our slivers of porch, the walkways connecting the buildings, and the view which, although beautiful, is hemmed tightly by mountains and trees—skip November's movie night, during which there were no raging quarrels and no new romances. Skip that weekend, too, which, without the gossip that usually followed a movie night, was unusually dull. By Monday we were already back to our routine, lying cold and damp on the porches. Reading, most of us: plodding through whatever we'd found, longing for something better. Ephraim looked up from the pages of the novel he'd been struggling with for a week and said out loud what he'd meant only to think: "Why would someone *write* this?" Beyond the railing, branches drooped.

Leo looked up. "Bad?"

"Worse than bad," Ephraim said. "But I'm at fault here too—why am I reading it?"

"Why have we been playing with an Erector set?" Leo said, making a face. "Grown men—I get so bored that parts of me aren't even awake enough, anymore, to know what the other parts are doing."

"I built that little model of a skyscraper," Ephraim admitted.

"*You* made that?"

Ephraim nodded, wadding up a piece of paper and tossing it into the basket between their chairs. "When I was first in New York," he said, "I was determined to work in one of those buildings someday, high up in a room with big windows, looking out on the city—"

"What did you think you'd be doing in there?"

Ephraim laughed. "That was the trouble—I didn't even know enough to imagine the work."

Leo waited for more—he was always interested in Ephraim's stories—but instead Ephraim blinked, bent his head, and returned to the novel he'd just denounced. A line from a long-ago physics class appeared inside Leo's head: *A body in motion tends to stay in motion; a body at rest tends to stay at rest.*

With that, his own head bent as well. Secretly pleased that he'd uncovered something better from the latest box of book donations, secretly ashamed that, having found something delightful, he hadn't yet shared it with his friend, he returned to H. G. Wells's *The World Set Free*. The first few pages had been dull but soon the pace had picked up, and now he was caught up in a futuristic world—1940, 1950, was it possible he'd live that long?—in which a new energy derived from atoms liberated people from all toil and, after one last terrible war, rendered war pointless.

He turned the pages, following the skilled bomb-thrower who, grasping the pitcher-like handles of a spherical atomic bomb, bent his head to the cold metal surface and bit off a little celluloid tab. Air rushed in, the reaction began; the thrower crouched in the flying machine and hurled the bomb down onto the target. The ground welled up in a great volcano that would seethe and seethe—forever?

That page he read again. *Those used by the Allies were lumps of pure Carolinum, painted on the outside with unoxidised cydonator inducive enclosed hermetically in a case of membranium:* what kind of chemistry was that? Yet so many astonishing things had been discovered in the few years he'd been away from his studies that even this might be true. Herschel, one of his companions at the polytechnic in Odessa, would know; he'd gone to England instead of America and found work as a chemist at a dye works in Manchester, from which he used to send enthusiastic letters. Once he'd described a meeting at the local literary and philosophical society, to which he'd gone expecting the usual reports on bird migration or new mining techniques. Instead a physicist named Ernest Rutherford had discussed the inner structure of the atom, which he'd proved was not a solid ball at all but a tiny nucleus tucked inside a whirling cloud of negative charge. It was so exciting, Herschel wrote, that he'd wept—which Leo, reading the page on the stone jetty at the sugar refinery, his hands black with carbonized bone from the char house, had wanted to do himself. That nucleus, it seemed, played a role in Wells's new world. Absorbed, he continued to read, while Ephraim moved his eyes back and forth across the lumpy print, dreaming of Rosa and his girls.

WHEN MILES ANNOUNCED, at the end of our sixth session, that he was finished speaking and that it was time for the rest of us to take over, we talked for a while about who should address the group next, and in what order. Several of us wanted Leo to talk—we all longed to know more about him—but a majority felt that those who'd been confined to Tamarack State the longest should get to talk first. Finally we voted that Ephraim should begin, followed by those who'd been here more than a year. Later there'd be time for Leo and any other new residents who joined us. And so, on an afternoon when it was snowing heavily, white flakes blowing in sheets across the field, Ephraim left the boring novel on his porch and came down to tell us a story.

Sixteen of us were in the solarium that day, including the five women who'd responded to the invitation Eudora had hung in the women's annex. Dr. Petrie, who'd dropped by out of curiosity after hearing some of us discuss the sessions, was also there; he meant to stay only a few minutes but he settled into a chair and listened intently, occasionally pushing a hand through his wiry hair. Most of us knew that Ephraim had been an apple farmer, but not how he'd become one. And although he'd spoken often of his daughters and his wife, he'd said little, until that afternoon, about his past or his daily life on the farm near Ovid.

"I lived in Minsk when I was very young," he began, "but almost all I remember from there is the smell of the air. And our crossing."

His Yiddish he claimed he'd learned not in Minsk but on the Lower East Side, where from the age of eleven he'd lived surrounded by people from the place his family had left behind. Like most of us, he had worked too hard, been paid too little, eaten poorly, spent hours arguing about politics but never seen anything change. After following his father and his brothers into a sock-knitting factory, he'd taken evening classes that got him nowhere; gone to the Yiddish theaters and seen plays that made him homesick but also infuriated him with their sentimentality; dreamed about escaping from his cramped flat, his cramped life—and never, until he met Rosa and her family, thought to leave the city.

We'd lived some version of that life, if not in New York then in Utica or Binghamton, Syracuse or Rochester, and we nodded; we knew how that went. While we thought about our old lives, Eudora, whose bedroom shelf was now adorned with the gleaming model Leo had given her, thought about why he'd made it. She was trying to imagine what she'd be like if, in one country, she'd been highly educated, fluent in several languages, knowledgeable about music and theater and chemistry, while in another, across the ocean, she'd been turned into someone barely fit to blast rock for a subway tunnel. Compared to Leo or Ephraim, she thought, she might have lived inside a shell. Her mother and her aunt had left England as tiny girls in the care of their parents, wanderers themselves; the gray-haired man with the deeply lined face who occasionally showed up at the house for a week, talking about a year spent in Siberia or six months in Tibet, and then looked at her mother and Aunt Elizabeth as if they were unusual rhododendrons—that was her grandfather, Max Vigne. Sometimes her grandmother Clara arrived with him, and sometimes not, but no one ever said why. On her father's side of the family were stories about his mother, Nora MacEachern, who'd traveled from Ireland to Canada to Tamarack Lake, where she nursed consumptives and later trained Aunt Elizabeth to do the same. Nora's brother, Ned, was born in Ireland too and before he built the Northview Inn had once traveled, as a cook on a ship, up near the North Pole.

But all that had happened so long ago. By the time she was born her relatives seemed to have lived in Tamarack Lake forever, their names—Kynd, Vigne, MacEachern—as much a part of the scenery as those who'd been here for generations. Walking through the shops downtown, she'd see an advertisement for one of Aunt Elizabeth's cure cottages, a sample of her father's work, or one of the placards, dusty now, which Ned had proudly hung when his nephew joined the business: *Ned Kynd and Michael MacEachern, Taxidermy. Art and Craft.* Everyone rooted in this small place from which she, despite her ambitious relatives, had traveled no farther than she could reach on her bicycle.

New York was his home, Ephraim continued while Eudora mused, and he'd been too ignorant to imagine a different kind of life. His whole self had been formed there, among the pushcarts and tenements and tiny stores that many of us knew well. He'd only managed to leave because of Rosa. "We met in a café," he said, his whole face lighting up.

A sigh passed through the room as we remembered cafés, sitting in freely chosen places with our chosen friends and lovers. Or perhaps the sigh came from the obvious feeling with which Ephraim had spoken Rosa's name. Of the husbands and wives and lovers we'd left at home, some waited patiently but others had abandoned us; is it surprising we turned to each other? Some of the women now among us had joined the sessions not for the talks but because this was a place where we could mingle. More men had returned in their wake and among our group were now several couples—cousins, as we call them here; Polly and Frank, Nan and David—delighted to have a new meeting place.

Ephraim, who'd never chosen a cousin, went on to describe Rosa's brothers and their friends, socialists who, in the old country, had marched in protests, distributed leaflets in factories, seen comrades exiled to Siberia—a place so enormous, they claimed, that this whole country could fit inside it with room left over. In Siberia, Leo remembered, the chemist Dmitri Mendeleeff had been born and raised and taught by his mother, who ran a glass factory and later managed to get her son across the thousands of miles to Moscow so he could go to school. Later, long before Leo was born, Mendeleeff had taught science for a few years at a school in Odessa.

"Rosa's brothers told me that the climate of Siberia is horrible,"

Ephraim continued, "but at least a man has room to breathe there. I don't know if that's true, but they convinced me that what we all needed was *space*."

Why, he'd finally asked himself, had his parents settled in exactly the same place as everyone else who'd left the Pale? We knew the answer: family, familiar foods, the streets filled with languages we understood. Rosa's brothers, Ephraim learned when he asked her to marry him, had answered the advertisements of a Jewish relief society that helped resettle families on farmlands far from the city. Free land, the brothers said. Land we will work together, crops we will sell in common. Fresh air, open space, no landlords or bosses; Siberia with a better climate. Ephraim had joined the group made up of Rosa's extended family, three other families, and a few young men, and with them headed across the state, to the land near the Finger Lakes the society had set aside.

"I was twenty-one when we moved," he said. "In the city, when someone said 'farm' to me, all I could imagine was the countryside around Minsk, which was filthy. But Ovid was beautiful. So beautiful—I felt like a fool when I saw it. I hadn't known before there were places like that."

Outside the sky had darkened while he spoke and we saw coming up the hill the headlamps of the night attendants, shining in the distance and then, as they reached the big curve in our road, winking out of sight. Leo, who'd chosen a seat at the end of the second row so that without being noticed he could watch Eudora at the opposite end of the front row, barely noticed the spectacle. The room smelled of scalded milk, warm chocolate, the felt in our slippers, and the disinfectant used on the floors, a trace of which clung to Eudora's hands. The down on her cheek was visible as she turned to Naomi, who was whispering in her ear.

He'd managed, in the library, ten minutes of sensible conversation with her, after that first awkward discussion of his benzene skeleton. Enough to learn a few scant facts: she lived in the village, her aunt ran a cure cottage, she was the youngest of five. School—she'd liked school, and missed it. Didn't he? Answering her, he'd responded to what he felt beneath the ordinary words: long, calm waves, which to him seemed to carry her real nature like music through the air.

He might, he imagined, tell her about his mother. About the forest he still dreamed of, or about the school where, briefly, he'd thrilled at the sight of Mendeleeff's periodic table and the possibility of unknown elements that might fill the gaps in the array. Three had been found with exactly the atomic weights and properties predicted: germanium, scandium, gallium. Eudora bent her head, the clean line of her nose tilted toward Naomi's tablet of paper, and reached for Naomi's pencil. They were writing notes, Leo saw, half charmed and half annoyed.

Ephraim said that the deep narrow lakes had surprised him, as had the gentle, fertile land, the old farms, and the villages with their cobblestone buildings. In those surroundings they'd tried to shape a different kind of life—a commune, or so he supposed he'd have to name it. None of them had known anything about farming. In Russia they'd kept shops or traded goods; in New York they'd cut sleeves and collars and cuffs and pulled bales of fabric through the streets; in Ovid, they were supposed to grow apples. What did we know, Ephraim asked, about apples? But they'd made do, some going to work as laborers for the farmers in the area while others cleared the woods, began to build, planted vegetables and the first small trees in the orchards.

After the first crops failed, the relief society sent teachers and charities sent food; the colonists worked part-time for their neighbors and learned more as they did. Within a few years all the married couples had houses of their own and only the young men still lived communally, in the big dormitory that had been the colony's first building. Even then, though, they'd continued the tradition established in their first days. At night, after the day's work was done, they met in the common room of the dormitory for lectures and debates. Concerts, sometimes; several of the men had brought fiddles, others had concertinas or flutes. They'd read books out loud—together they'd assembled an excellent library—and argued over them; they'd taught English to the older people who hadn't learned well, and Yiddish to the children who knew only English.

"Learning circles," Ephraim said, "workmen's circles—some of you will know what I mean, do you remember these?"

Again we nodded in recognition, laughing when Ephraim, inspired by his own words, had us rise from our wooden chairs and rearrange into a loose circle the two stiff rows in which we'd sat for weeks. Naomi fussed with her tablet as she stood up, tugging free the top sheet and slipping it under the others. Dr. Petrie joined instantly but Miles seemed ready to protest, clamping his hands to the seat of his chair until, seeing the rest of us move, he shrugged and moved as well. When we sat again Ephraim was among us instead of before us, describing how such circles had been part of daily life in Ovid, and how much he missed them. We might not have raised apples, but we knew what he meant.

Some of us remembered going to the Educational Alliance as children, learning English and American history and using the shower baths and the gymnasium, while others remembered adult classes there and elsewhere: a George Eliot circle, a mechanics circle. Those clubs and classes had changed our lives, but until Ephraim spoke, we'd forgotten how much we missed them. Everything here existed in lines. Our chairs lined up on the porches, our tables lined up in the dining room, the beds lined up in the infirmary, and the pictures of our lungs lined up in the files downstairs—isn't it natural we'd forget what it was like to gather as equals and teach ourselves? For weeks we'd been like students peering up at a teacher, but now we entered as a group into the experience of one of us. For the first time we felt ourselves both inside and outside, here and there.

"We were poor," Ephraim said, "but we made a good life."

"But when," Miles interrupted, "did your crops finally turn a profit? When did your colony become self-sustaining?"

"That was the fly in the ointment," Ephraim said with a wry face.

They'd had houses, he explained, and a school and some scraps of culture, but they hadn't made money. For a while they'd struggled on, until finally—we should have thought of this ourselves, he said—two Jewish industrialists from Syracuse, not so far away, had come to visit the colony and, after seeing the problems, decided to build a canning factory that would employ some of the colonists and provide a market for their produce.

"We canned apples," Ephraim said. "We made applesauce and apple butter. All of us made the same wage and the owners marketed the goods; we turned a profit the first year the factory was running, which was a kind of miracle." A few people left but most stayed, and as the cannery grew, some of the Ovid natives came to work there, while others attended the night school for adults.

"We ended up being part of the town," Ephraim concluded, "and actually I know quite a lot about growing apples now. I never could have imagined this, but I've turned into a farmer."

"Not quite," Leo said, and everyone laughed.

"He's funny," Naomi whispered to Eudora. "I like that about him."

Eudora nodded but, having seen Naomi's drawing pad as we rearranged our chairs, turned away before her friend could say more. She'd noticed Naomi flirting with Miles during their shared rides down the hill after the Wednesday sessions. A finger brushing the back of his hand, a gaze held a second too long—none of it, Eudora suspected, meant in the least. She'd done that herself when she was younger, testing her new powers as her father might test the edge of a knife. The instant Miles had responded and shown signs of finding her attractive, Naomi had drawn back, amused and, or so Eudora thought, a little repelled. Now her attention seemed, annoyingly, to have bounced to Leo. Following her friend's covert glances, Eudora had also followed the moving pencil as it touched the pad; the page Naomi had hidden was covered with drawings of him. Leo in profile, Leo in three-quarters view, a study of Leo's left ear.

The rest of us, who hadn't seen those drawings, ignored the two young women and enjoyed our new seating arrangement. Miles had fallen silent after his question about money and seemed to be studying us; we ignored him too. Bea pushed her heavy red hair off her face and said, "Imagine what we could make of this place if it was just us, if all the doctors and administrators were gone and we had the land to raise food on, the laundry and the dining facilities to use; if somehow we could take care of each other . . ."

For a minute, that idea hung before all of us. Then everyone was talking at once as Ephraim leaned forward in his chair, orchestrating the discussion and answering what questions he could; this was wonderful. We forgot to take our break, we forgot what time it was. When the dinner bell rang, Dr. Petrie, who'd stayed for the entire discussion, shook Ephraim's hand and said how much he'd enjoyed himself. Ephraim beamed, and then brought him over to Miles.

"I had my doubts about this," Dr. Petrie said to Miles as the rest of us began heading to supper, "but I think what you're doing here is a very good idea, as long as everyone's health is up to it. I can see why Dr. Richards supported you, and I hope you'll continue."

"It did go well," Miles said. "Not quite what I expected, but . . ."

His gaze was so openly assessing that Dr. Petrie ran his hands over his shirtfront to see if he'd lost a button. "Why don't you join us again?" Miles asked. "Perhaps there's something you'd like to talk to us about."

"I can't talk about medicine, or treatments, or hospital policy," Dr. Petrie said. "That would be *quite* against regulations."

"I can see that," Miles said. "But perhaps there's something else you're interested in, that you'd like to share. Some travels? Something you've been studying?"

Dr. Petrie considered the question. "I was in France last year. Touring battlefield hospitals, helping out where I could."

"I have a dear friend in France," Miles said. "A kind of nephew. I'm always eager to learn what I can about conditions there. If you'd share your experiences, I'm sure the others would also like to be instructed."

Dr. Petrie said he'd think about it and moved away. Leo, who'd been eavesdropping, turned to Ephraim and said, "I hope he keeps coming. Our little learning circle expands . . ."

"Did you think it went all right today?"

"It went fine," Leo said, patting his friend's arm. "We all enjoyed it."

And in fact we had. We had a sense, then, of what our circle might be. What we might be. Suppose Bea talked about her union work and Kathleen about teaching music, Albert about the intricacies of forming incandescent lightbulbs and Pietr about his method for blanching celery? How much we might all learn! It was embarrassing that we'd needed Miles to get us started, but still here we were, and we were headed—well, someplace, though no one knew where. But after Ephraim spoke, we all felt pleased with the way we'd decided to spend our Wednesday afternoons.

6

YEARS AGO, a man came to Tamarack Lake from New York
in the hopes of improving his health, married the under-taker's
daughter, worked in a bank, and then built the village's telephone
exchange. Resigning his position when he had a relapse, he began in 1912
to write a history of his adopted home. From deeds, contracts, old letters,
newspapers, the reminiscences of guides and visitors, he reconstructed
who started the bank, built the churches, organized the schools and the
hospital. He wrote about when the last guest came to the Northview Inn,
when the boathouse fell into the lake, what happened to Dr. Kopeckny
and the first sanatoria. Who donated money to those institutions, and
which doctors worked where. Comfortable in his retirement—he sold
the exchange at a fine profit—and cared for by his wife, he worked at his
project for years but never mentioned us.

Sometimes we thumb through those pages, looking for traces of our
lives and places where our histories overlap. Fires, accidents, holidays;
holidays always bring complications, both down in the village and up

here. Someone ends up in the infirmary, after having grown too melancholy to eat; someone wanders into the pond and nearly drowns; friends quarrel savagely. That Thanksgiving, which wasn't any different, also had the disadvantage of interrupting our Wednesday sessions just as we were getting used to taking charge of the talks for ourselves.

It didn't help that the sanatorium staff, resentful at having to work that day, made it clear that they felt burdened. In the village, those caring for patients also felt that they were having the opposite of a holiday. More cooking, more shopping, more cleaning at the cure cottages and boardinghouses and hotels. The butcher worked overtime, extra porters unloaded extra trains, drivers took extra shifts. At Mrs. Martin's house, Miles would spend the afternoon eating turkey with chestnut stuffing and giblet sauce, sweetbreads, tongue in aspic, duchess potatoes, and Mrs. Martin's Nesselrode pudding served with boiled custard, quite unaware that in the kitchen, Daisy and Darlene were telling Naomi they were ready to quit. At the same time Eudora, across the village, would be wishing that she had someone to grumble to. She'd been looking forward to her days off. Irene had loaned her two textbooks, which she'd hoped to spend some quiet hours reading. Instead, as had been the case since she was old enough to wield a knife, and especially since her older sisters had married, her mother called on her to help with their elaborate meal.

Not simply a turkey but also a ham, cornbread stuffing with oysters and mushrooms, clear soup with homemade dumplings, roasted squash glazed with maple syrup, potatoes mashed and scalloped and baked, heaping dishes of corn and carrots, tiny onions creamed and dusted with nutmeg, three kinds of pie. Even with the whole family eating steadily, all five brothers and sisters along with Sally's and Helen's husbands and babies, the food left on the table when they were done would have fed another household. Eudora cooked, served, ate, cleared, washed and dried dishes and put them away as if she didn't have a job of her own; as if she were still a girl.

In between chores she talked with Ernest, home from New York for the holiday, and with Sally, whom she hadn't seen in weeks. By the time she finished in the kitchen everyone had moved toward the sofas and armchairs, preparing for the naps that followed her family's holiday feasts as reliably as dessert followed the roast. One by one they nodded off, until the house felt as dead as the Northview Inn, which was slumping into the ground. Once every few months her parents would open the inn's main door, look at the flies and the holes in the floors, bite their lips, and then do nothing with what they'd inherited. When Eudora's father, who'd known the place in its heyday, spoke about the guests with their guns and their guides, his uncle presiding over a dining room filled with sportsmen from New York and Boston, it was as if not thirty but a thousand years had passed.

When her father woke—he was snoring now—he would, she knew, return to his taxidermy workshop, hinting how much he could use her help. She'd give in and sit with him, watching the whole night disappear as the day already had. Rebelliously, she hopped on her bicycle and headed away from the lake and her family, toward Mrs. Martin's house. Naomi might, she calculated, have finished serving dinner herself and be free for an hour or two.

It was colder outside than she expected; she'd forgotten her gloves. She passed Eugene's garage, the firehouse, and the telephone exchange where, in an unused room two floors above her, the amateur historian wrote the pages from which we were always absent. She passed the library, the theater, two of the churches, the bank, and the electric light company. Climbing the gentle slope of the hill, she passed the rows of cottages, each tier larger and more elegant. At Mrs. Martin's house, which was near the top, she stopped and dismounted, leaning her bicycle against the tall hedge.

Up the neatly tended pathway, up the steps to the paneled door. She tapped a brass dolphin against the plate and considered the enormous wreath, dripping with gilded pinecones and berries and gold bows stiffened with wire, that had just been hung. Stuffed chickadees with bendable wire legs and feet—her father's work, she saw, as clearly his as the owl in the solarium at Tamarack State was the work of Uncle Ned—dotted the branches. What would it be like to live where her family wasn't in evidence everywhere? Again she dropped the dolphin against the plate.

To her dismay, Mrs. Martin herself opened the door, with the discouraging news that Naomi was in the kitchen, making cinnamon rolls for tomorrow's breakfast and busy—absolutely busy—for the rest of the day. Stepping outside and pulling the door shut behind her, she added, "But it's just as well; I've been wanting to talk to you." She crossed her arms over her chest. "Cold, isn't it?"

Then why not ask me in? Eudora thought. Gesturing toward her bicycle, she said, "The exercise keeps me warm."

"Good," Mrs. Martin replied. "Because I know it's convenient for you to accept a ride home with Naomi on Wednesday evenings, when she's bringing Mr. Fairchild back from the sanatorium, but I was hoping you could get home under your own power for a while."

"Of course I *could*, but—" Eudora said, and then stopped, realizing that Naomi hadn't told her mother about their driving lessons.

"I want Naomi to have some time alone with Mr. Fairchild," Mrs. Martin continued. "When they can talk without interruption." Blandly, as if there were nothing odd about what she'd just said, she added, "How are your parents?"

"I don't *interrupt* them," Eudora said. "Why would I? My parents are fine."

"Good," Mrs. Martin repeated. "I thought your father was looking a trifle run-down." Gazing steadily at Eudora, she added, "Miles is a wealthy man. A kind one too. I see the way he looks at Naomi. If she gave him a little encouragement—surely you want what's best for her? You've always been her friend."

"I still am," Eudora said stiffly, stepping back. "Would you tell her I came by?"

She pulled her bicycle from the hedge and pedaled down the hill and back along the village streets, wondering, as she overshot the turn to her house and continued westward, how Mrs. Martin could understand so little about her own daughter. Always she seemed to miss what was most obvious, including the fact that in the past two years, Naomi had come close to running away half a dozen times.

Ahead Baker's Ridge loomed, black against the graying sky and already casting the village into shadow. Eudora pedaled faster, remembering how Mrs. Martin's clumsiness had helped bring her and Naomi together. Although her aunt employed Naomi's mother, they might not have become real friends if she hadn't found Naomi weeping stormily one afternoon under a spruce near her Aunt Elizabeth's house. Mrs. Martin had visited the school that day, delivering one of her lectures on home economics, and at first Eudora suspected that Naomi was weeping with annoyance; the lecture had been very dull. Instead, Naomi confessed that her mother's newest boarder, a Mr. Elliot, had that morning pulled her into his bathroom as she'd dropped off his clean towels and then stood there, beaming and naked.

"And then," Naomi had said—but Eudora, transfixed by that image, had heard nothing for a minute.

"It's not as if this is the first time either," Naomi added. "Other men do things like this, like they think their weekly fee covers me along with their meals. Whenever I try to tell my mother she claims I'm exaggerating, or if someone really did say or do something he didn't mean it, it was just a passing weakness brought on by fever."

"They touch you?" Eudora said. They'd been, she thought now, thirteen and fourteen then.

Naomi shook her head impatiently. "They don't really *do* anything— they're so feeble, most of them, I could push them over if I had to. But just listening to them, and the way their eyes crawl over me when I'm serving meals—and then this." She leaned back against the tree and gestured toward the house. "I was going to see if your aunt would talk to my mother about it."

"Maybe," Eudora said, thinking of her aunt's firmness with her housekeepers, "that's not the best idea."

Instead she'd talked to Naomi herself, the two of them circumnavigating the lake as Naomi complained about her mother and her chores at the house. Eudora, who had similar chores, was surprised to learn how much Naomi disliked them. At her Aunt Elizabeth's cure cottage, where she helped out after school and on weekends, she'd found that she liked being useful. Her oldest sister, Helen, had married and had twin daughters by then; Ernest had already moved to New York and Eugene had started sharing quarters above the garage with his two friends. Sally was about to move to Plattsburgh, leaving her—always the baby, the one everyone forgot—with no one to talk to and nothing to do. Her father stayed in the shop out back, struggling to keep up with the changing fashions in taxidermy, always a few years behind. Her mother lived in the kitchen, cooking as if all seven of them were gathered at the table, surprised each time the dinner hour brought only Eudora and, blinking and covered with sawdust, her father. Only at her Aunt Elizabeth's did she feel she was learning something new each day.

"My aunt tells me to look closely at everything around me," she told Naomi. At the far end of the lake, the wooden park benches were spattered with rain and so they kept walking. "Get to know the boarders and their habits, so I can anticipate what they need. Get to know the house and *its* needs. She says a house like hers is alive, it's like a giant organism."

"Not *our* house," Naomi said. She laughed and startled a handful of frogs in the reeds, who woke and plopped indignantly into the water. "Ours is just a business. Everything my mother does, including the way she uses me, is about *efficiency*."

Naomi, Eudora soon learned, shared her own curiosity about the outside world and was equally stubborn, and equally independent. Tiny, vigorous Miss Olafson, who was fluent in five languages and who taught first Eudora and then Naomi, pressed armfuls of extra-credit reading on them and encouraged their habit—broken only last year—of reading together. Tromping in the woods or bicycling together for miles, they'd talked without stopping. George Eliot's work had propelled them up and down mountains, while Tolstoy had pushed their bicycles to Lake Placid and Samuel Butler had helped them skate in circles. From the characters revealed in books they moved on to themselves; what they were good at and what they hated, what they might do someday. Naomi was fascinated by the swirl of voices and conflicting desires that Eudora, within her large family, calmly negotiated, while Eudora was amazed by the way her new friend drew.

"The pictures just come," Naomi said. "My hand decides. I can be thinking about one thing and my hand will pick up a pencil and draw something entirely different."

My hand: she said this as someone else might say, *My dog.* Eudora would have found this ridiculous except for the likenesses of people and objects she'd seen pour fluently from Naomi's pencil while they talked about something else. As a child she too had loved to draw, but her gift had abandoned her abruptly and it astonished her to see someone do without thinking what she could now do only with difficulty. Equally startling was the way that Naomi referred to the other selves jostling rebelliously inside her. The person whom Eudora knew was not, Naomi claimed, the Naomi who slaved for her mother at the house, the Naomi who'd once lived near Philadelphia, or the Naomi who stood by a frozen creek on a bitter winter's night, baring her throat and chest to the rays of the moon.

Those were the moments when Eudora had most fiercely wanted to understand what it felt like to be Naomi. She herself had two hands that did what she asked and were strong and competent, one self that sometimes wanted different things but was always, clearly, her *self*. How dull, compared with Naomi's dramas! And how little, she thought—she'd reached the top of the ridge, where the wind cooled her face and a delicious downhill ride awaited—she knew of those dramas now. She could just barely admit to herself that, since starting work at Tamarack State, and particularly since getting to know Irene, she saw Naomi much less.

NOT UNTIL AFTER supper the following day did Naomi escape from her mother's house. Exasperating to be trapped for so long; more exasperating to learn only at lunch that Eudora had come by to see her yesterday. Why, Naomi thought furiously, did her mother think it was reasonable to withhold a message overnight? Through a cold mist she walked down the hill and through the village, moving between the streetlamps' cones of light and the dark wedges by which they were separated. At the far end she turned up the flagstone walk leading to Eudora's parents' house.

"Come join us," Mrs. MacEachern said, opening the door and welcoming her in. "We're just finishing supper—I know Eudora will be glad to see you."

Naomi moved through the cluttered hall and into the crowded, pleasantly untidy dining room, so different from her mother's crisp arrangements. A piece of oilcloth over the table, in place of starched white linen; gingham napkins and a pair of shaded lamps; mismatched silverware and big crockery bowls. She sat in the chair Eugene pulled out for her, accepted the plate Mrs. MacEachern passed her way, and, although she'd already eaten one meal, savored the turkey hash and sautéed greens and cornbread with fresh butter. Eudora's mother was every bit as good a cook as her own, with less fuss and, as far as she knew, no recipe books at all.

Around the table were Eudora and her parents, Eugene and two of his friends from the garage, Sally and her children but not her husband, who'd gone out to visit someone else, and Ernest, whom Naomi almost never saw. When she and Eudora were still girls, he'd bolted from the workshop out back and, without discussing his plans with anyone, gone to New York City. Six months later, back for a visit, he announced that he'd found a place as an apprentice in the taxidermy studio at the Museum of Natural History and had no intention of returning home to live. Since then he'd done well enough that he now had several people working for him.

If she had an older brother, she thought—older, not younger; she never thought of Thomas—whom she could ask for help and who could show her the world, everything would be different. Leaning over, she asked Ernest what he was working on now.

"An elephant," he said, and laughing as her eyes widened. "For a diorama, a complete African scene to go in one of the first-floor halls— it's great fun, really. Fascinating."

She listened as he described the huge, heavy pieces of hide, bark-tanned for half a year before being hoisted, dripping wet, over a form coated with wet clay that would capture the shape of all the wrinkles. Seven years ago, when he'd left, he'd been a quiet, clumsy, somewhat lumpish boy whom everyone ignored. Now, as he leaned back in his chair, his legs spread and his arms relaxed, he exuded an easy confidence that made her wish she knew him better.

Before she could ask him anything else, though, Sally and her children rose and said it was time for them to go. In the confusion of farewells, Eudora made an excuse to her parents and handed Naomi her coat. Suddenly they too were outside, and alone.

"See why I came over to your house yesterday?" Eudora said as they headed for the lake. Her hair turned gold each time she entered the cone of a streetlight. "Our house, at the holidays . . ."

"My mother didn't even tell me you'd come by until lunchtime today," Naomi said. "I wish I'd heard you knock."

"She didn't tell you until *today*?"

The mist lightened as they reached the lake and a few stars appeared through the clouds, followed by the nearly full moon. Talking as swiftly as they walked, they caught each other up on the day's events until, at the cove opposite the Northview Inn, Naomi paused and reached into her pocket.

"My mother's contribution to the household this morning," she said. "I had to take it down before Darlene and Daisy could see it."

Eudora tilted the heavy piece of paper, trying to catch the moonlight. "I can't read it," she said. "The usual?"

"Close enough," Naomi said, taking it back. Largely from memory, she recited what she'd found posted above the sink:

THIS WEEK'S HOUSEKEEPING NOTES

1. *Spiderwebs*—I have noticed unusual numbers of these in the corners of the ceilings, especially in the stairwells and in the hall where the kitchen meets the pantry.

2. *Tray service*—With four of our guests on trays at present, we need to be particularly careful that the last person served receives food as hot and attractively arranged as the first (Darlene, this applies especially to you).

3. *Laundry*—as always, I remind you: the water must be *scalding*, especially for the last rinse.

4. *Christmas supplies*—By the end of the day all seasonal decorations, inside and out, should be up and attractively arranged; all meals should be served on the Christmas linens; bud vases for the trays should be in combinations of green, red, and white.

"Your mother," Eudora said, less amused than Naomi had expected. "Yesterday . . ."

She paused, looking uncomfortable. Then she continued, "She said the oddest thing to me before I left. She asked me to stop riding home with you on Wednesday evenings—because of Miles, she said. Because she wants you and Miles to have time alone together. She seems to think he's interested in you."

Naomi groaned. "Miles," she said. "If she had just let me get a *real* job I never would have asked him for work."

"Your mother's not the one who's been flirting with him," Eudora pointed out.

"I haven't been *flirting*," Naomi said. "Not really."

Eudora scuffed her feet through the damp leaves as if they deserved her full attention. In the silence Naomi almost believed her own words. The idea that her mother, characteristically alert to anything that might advance their lives, was pushing her and Miles together made her wince. "Whatever he's thinking," she said, "I'm certainly not interested in him."

"He's not so bad," Eudora said. "At least he's trying to do *something*."

Naomi made a face and changed the subject, baffled that Eudora hadn't grasped her dismay. Not a single person understood—she didn't understand herself—how she could want and want and want. She wanted not to keep living in Tamarack Lake, under her mother's thumb. Not to end up with some local boy, because no one else was around. And not to choose someone like Miles, just because she could make him tremble by flashing her stockings when she crossed her legs. Both she and Eudora had let the boys they'd known in school take them out to moving-picture shows, skating parties, hayrides. Some they'd kissed, but Eudora never liked to talk about that, and when Naomi tried to tell her about the time she and Liam O'Connor had done a little more than that in the woods last summer, Eudora wouldn't listen.

But that had just been Liam, sweet and as dumb as a big yellow dog; Naomi had wanted to see what he'd do. Liam, the Dalton brothers, Mrs. Flaherty's husband, Miles: what a waste, Naomi thought. What she really wanted was to know what being with someone *felt* like. What it was like to be in love, and with someone who didn't act like a dog at the end of her leash.

Into her head flashed a picture of Leo Marburg, so intriguingly different from her despite his similar hair and eyes. His life before Tamarack State was a blank; no one visited him and he never mentioned brothers or sisters or parents or a girlfriend. Did he have a family? He had to be poor, or he wouldn't be here. And smart—beyond the questions he asked Miles, he seemed to read a great deal and Eudora had shown her the toy he'd made from the Erector set. He'd been in this country for six years; he came from someplace overseas. When she was close to him she felt the way she used to feel in Chester, early in the morning, when she couldn't imagine what the day would bring but was thrilled to get up and meet it.

He was lonely, she thought, and he had no idea how attractive he was. He seemed mystified by the way people moved toward him, often resting their hands on his arms as they talked. Sometimes she'd caught him looking her way, seeming to study her as she studied him, and she'd imagined rising, while whoever was speaking droned on, and slipping out into the garden as he followed her. There was a nook outside the solarium door, near the chimney and across from that fountain, and he pressed her into it, not clumsily like Liam but tenderly, moving his hands along her back as if he was investigating . . .

". . . and Eugene said he'd ask you," Eudora said. "What do you think?"

Naomi stopped. "About what?" She'd missed half a conversation, and the huge boulder, perched as casually as if a giant had dropped a pebble on the thumb of land protruding into the lake, loomed before her as if some other set of feet had carried her there.

"I've been talking for five minutes—what were you thinking about?"

"Just . . ." Naomi gestured toward the lake, the stars dimly reflected in the water but the distant shore invisible and the mountains lost as well. "Don't you get tired of this?"

"Of what?"

"I don't know. Work. Our families, everything. How empty it is here."

"It's home," Eudora said.

"Not for me," Naomi said. "Not really." She struggled to explain herself more clearly. "When I was tiny and we lived in Chester," she began, "I used to wake up in my room almost wild with excitement, so anxious to run out into the garden, down to the river, everywhere, so thrilled to talk to the fishermen or the neighbors. If I found a flower that had fallen from one of the tulip trees, that was enough to make the whole day. A pinecone. The sight of the neighbor's gray horse. Why is it different now?"

"Is it different?" Eudora asked.

"Mostly—you don't feel that? I can see the world around me, I can draw everything in it. But now I'm *outside* it, on the edge somehow. It's like being trapped on the wrong side of a window. If I could scratch through it, maybe I'd know what everyone else wants and feels."

"You *know* what I feel," Eudora said, stopping to look directly at Naomi, her expression wounded. "I tell you everything."

Naomi shook her head. "You don't," she said. "No one really does, do they? That's what I mean. You tell me lots of things but not what's most important to you, what's hidden inside. Everyone else I know does the same thing. We're all like that and some days I can't stand it, I just can't *stand* it."

Her eyes were wet, her voice was loud, she was flinging her arms about and Eudora was looking at her as though she'd hit a dog with the Model T—why was she saying this, why would she even *want* what she'd just said? Suppose Eudora knew what she really thought about Miles, about Leo, about Ernest or the men she passed on the street. Suppose Eudora, so helpful to the patients at Tamarack State, knew what she did to some of her mother's boarders? The young women, especially—how she turned her back when they wanted to confide something sad, how she dawdled over their fretful requests. It was unbearable the way that, despite all their money, they acted like their lives were over and they had nothing to look forward to. Unbearable that they confused her with the hired help and spoke to her in the same tone.

Eudora didn't know that she sometimes stole from them. Little things, something small and part of a set, so that for months they'd go on searching for a cuff link, an earring, a lone calfskin glove. A single turquoise stocking, which wouldn't be missed for weeks. Or letters, which she took just often enough to baffle them. The boarders left their mail in the basket on the sideboard, trusting her to deliver it to the post office. Once in a while she took a letter for herself, which was how she kept track of what they thought. Or she'd slip an incoming letter from the pile she brought home and then listen, her face blank, while they fretted about how their families never wrote.

Eudora reached for her hand, her face concerned. "What is it?" she said. "What am I missing?"

They'd reached the boulder and were heading back now, to the village and their families and their jobs and their lives that would never, Naomi thought, ever change except to grow still more confining. She drew the cool air into her lungs and tried to focus on the bare trees lining the path, so common that they'd given the village its name. Each limb lined with twigs, each twig dotted with tiny stubs from which the smallest, softest, pale green needles would sprout in the spring, darkening throughout the summer and then lightening again once the weather changed until they'd turn a beautiful yellow and, before Thanksgiving, shower to the ground. On the ground they looked like a golden veil. A hundred times she'd drawn tamaracks, which were pleasing in every season. Not once had she told Eudora or anyone else how she loved them.

"What is it?" Eudora repeated.

"Nothing," Naomi replied. *Everything*, she thought.

7

During that long Thanksgiving weekend, the rearrangement of our chairs, which Ephraim had undertaken so casually during his talk, seemed to shake something loose in us. As we considered Miles's assumption that each of us might know something interesting, we also began to imagine what we might polish up to share on a Wednesday afternoon. Old hobbies, new curiosities, hard-won skills. Books we'd loved in our earlier lives. Some found a new appetite for reading or conversation, some started journals, some began to think about their futures as well as their pasts: you might call this hope; it is always disturbing. Briefly the air around our porches seemed to flicker, as if the railings were electrified. On the ship from Hamburg to New York, Leo remembered, the sky had also felt like that.

His old friend Vincenzo, who worked in the char house at the sugar refinery, where Leo had started, sent him a letter that week. Three workers with Hungarian names had been dismissed after a warehouse fire, Vincenzo wrote angrily. On no more evidence than their friendship with a former crew member from one of the German merchant ships being held in the harbor. Dark thumbprints edged the sheet of paper, which was filled with large black words slanting toward the lower right corner. *That's how it is now—you're better off out of it. Anyone born overseas falls under suspicion whenever anything happens. Sometimes I wish I was up there with you. Do they feed you well?*

Leo touched the grubby sheet thoughtfully, a reminder of the days he'd spent packing bone black into the enormous filters used to purify the sugar solution. He and Vincenzo had worked side by side, so filthy they could be distinguished only by their teeth and eyes. Without Vincenzo to guide him—without Vincenzo, who'd shared his lunches of bread and cheese, shown him the cheapest place to have shoes resoled, taught him the best times at the public baths, and introduced him to the head chemist—he wouldn't have survived.

He'd taken the job when he was starving, after weeks of searching for a position in a hospital or a university, anyplace with a laboratory. In Russian, or German, or sometimes in Yiddish, depending on the look of his prospective employer—he'd known only a little English when he'd landed—he explained the particulars of his education and his training. After a while he learned not to be surprised that no one understood. Not to be surprised that they thought he was stupid. By the time he got to the refinery, he'd learned to be grateful for anyone who'd offer a hand. New York was nothing like what he'd imagined but, crowded into the shared room at Tobias and Rachel's flat, swilling the same cheap food and beer as his companions while working the same hard jobs, for long stretches he'd convinced himself that he was getting somewhere. He lived like the Irishmen and Sicilians and Ruthenians and Poles he met, the Finns and Jews and Germans, absorbed into the crowd—until, in the middle of a sentence or a task, he'd start thinking about something he'd read or studied, some experiment that had once captivated him completely. Then he'd stop listening to whoever was around him and withdraw his attention, feeling for those minutes utterly alone. Once more he was a boy, stirring sugar and potassium chlorate in a white porcelain bowl and trickling sulfuric acid over the mixture, stepping back as the smoke spewed and a cone of carbon rose in the dish.

Someone would bark at him, disgruntled to find him daydreaming, and then the boy who'd done that experiment disappeared. In place of his clean hands, his ambitions, and the alert, chattering, clever friends who'd studied physiology or the nature of the chemical bond, he had comrades who joined the preparedness parades in the streets. Along with them came employers who contributed to the cost of the gigantic electrified sign—ABSOLUTE AND UNQUALIFIED LOYALTY TO OUR COUNTRY—hanging over Fifth Avenue, and strangers who narrowed their eyes at the sound of his name. In Brooklyn, Vincenzo reminded him, people were changing their names. The explosion of Black Tom Island, which had occurred while he was in the infirmary and had been blamed on German spies and the German-Americans who sheltered them, had made the situation even worse.

Yet still, Leo thought, he wouldn't have left the city on his own. How had Ephraim's Rosa and her brothers found the courage? For them, as for him, New York had been home since getting off the boat. Only after the city ejected him had he understood that he hadn't really *believed* in the rest of this enormous country. West of the Adirondacks, Ephraim claimed, New York State continued for hundreds of miles, green rolling land, rivers and valleys, town after town, and beyond the border Pennsylvania, Ohio, Nebraska . . . who could imagine Nebraska?

Leo read the letter again and then, reluctantly, went to bed, where he slept poorly. A few days later, he received a second, even more unexpected, letter. Opening his copy of our sanatorium newsletter, *The Kill-Gloom Gazette*, he watched, bemused, as a small white envelope with no address and no stamp slid from the stenciled pages and landed in his lap. Inside was a note in blue ink:

I love your dark hair, I lose myself in your eyes,
your hands are beautiful. I dream of touching them. The rest of you,
too. I dream about you. I dream about touching you.

No signature; no salutation. Perhaps it had been meant for someone else? After trying to ignore it for a day, he showed the contents first to Ephraim and then to the rest of the dinner table. One of the patients who helped produce the weekly paper must be responsible, someone said.

"A female patient, I hope," Ephraim said, which caused a few smiles. Ian suggested the fat woman who collated the visitors' list, while Frank said it might be the girl who'd written the poem about the dying chrysanthemums. Or perhaps the sad woman—Abigail? Adelaide?—in her early thirties who delivered the newsletters without meeting anyone's eye.

Leo put the note aside but still couldn't make himself throw it out. Something about it stirred him, not the content but the cryptic delivery, which lured him into spending more time in our excuse for a library. The women had separate borrowing hours, so it wasn't as if he'd meet anyone there. Still, he sat where he was visible from the hall, reading old copies of *Scientific American* magazine while wondering if the note writer, passing by, might see him and make a sign. Who would be drawn to him? His pale face, thin legs, shrunken shoulders; the weight and strength he'd lost: he'd been proud of his body when he was younger, but now he was sure that if someone were ever interested in him again, it wouldn't be because of the way he looked. Still, his last romance—they'd all been brief—had ended more than a year ago, and since then there'd been only work and sickness. It was just possible, he thought, that the person who wrote him was someone he might like. He sat in the library, reading an article about the geometry of snowflakes and inspecting the photomicrographs, while waiting for the note writer to show herself. Because of this, he missed the visit of Ephraim's friend.

VISITING HOURS: late afternoon, twice each month, the same slot of time during which we met for our sessions but fortunately not the same day. The first Tuesday in December brought a scant crowd, which we'd expected; many would wait for the third Tuesday, when we'd be closer to Christmas. Benny's sister came, bringing a potted plant. Ian's mother came up from Albany. Polly was visited by her former fiancé, who'd broken off their engagement when she became ill but now, having heard from a mutual friend that she was cousining with a welder from Yonkers, was interested again. Two young men from the private sanatorium across the village called on Lydia—she'd sneaked over there one night for an illicit dance—and Otto's nephew arrived with a box of homemade gifts from his family in Utica.

Ephraim, unusually, had a visitor that afternoon as well. At his insistence Rosa seldom came to see him; their daughters home in Ovid needed her, as did her parents, and he counted on her to keep the family going until he was cured. His own parents had once traveled up from New York, and a few young men from Ovid, who had other business nearby, had also kindly come by at different times, but Felix hadn't been among them and so Ephraim was surprised to see him now.

Nearly a decade younger than Ephraim, Felix was the younger brother of Rosa's brother-in-law: high-spirited, hot-tempered, impatient with apple-picking and pruning. The Work Committee had moved him to the cannery but he hadn't liked that either, although he'd shown a great aptitude for fixing the machines. Finally one of the foremen, tired of disciplining him but wanting to make the most of his talents, had sent him off to Syracuse, where the brothers who'd established the cannery also owned a foundry. Just before Felix arrived there, the works had been converted into a shell assembly plant. He'd been assigned to the cleaning shed, where along with sixty other men he brushed off shell casings and cleaned out the protective grease with rags dipped in gasoline.

Ephraim had never known him well, but it was pleasant to sit with Felix on one of the benches in the garden outside the solarium. With his back sheltered by the high wall and the sun beating down, he was warm enough to open his jacket while Felix tossed crumbs to the sparrows clustered around the fountain. Most of his earnings, Felix was explaining, he sent back to Ovid—*home*, Ephraim thought, imagining the soft brown mole on Rosa's thigh—and soon he'd be eligible to move into the foundry itself, where he might gain some useful training.

He crumbled another stale biscuit and dotted a trail from the ground across the tip of one work boot and back to the ground again. "Will the birds follow that?" he asked.

"Watch," Ephraim said. "They're as tame as we are; they know we can't do anything to them. Sometimes they take food right out of our hands."

As a sparrow charged his boot and snatched the crumbs, Felix continued describing his plans—exactly, Ephraim thought, as if planning ever did anyone any good. Until recently, Felix said, his job had been fine, but the plant had contracts from Russia and England for millions of shells and the owners were pushing the workers to their limits. A fence had gone up around the plant; some union organizers had been arrested. Now guards searched them all for what they called "incendiary literature" before they went in, and also for actual matches: Felix's shed, packed with workbenches on which the men kept pans full of gasoline and mounds of soaked rags, was uncomfortably near buildings filled with detonators, shrapnel, and powder. Each week the quotas increased, and also the grumbling, the late night meetings, the complaints filed with the gang foremen.

"I'm worried," Felix said, tapping his toe until the sparrow darted away. "That something's going to happen."

"What would happen?" Ephraim asked.

Instead of answering him directly, Felix reached into the canvas sack he'd brought—a clean shirt and food for the train trip, Ephraim had assumed—and drew out a tin box the size of a loaf of bread.

"What's this?"

"My friend Joe had it in his locker, and when he got suspended for gathering some of the workers together and talking about a possible strike, he slipped it to me before the guards came down to search his belongings. He said we'd all be fired if anyone saw it, and asked if I could find a safe place to hide it until some big meeting he's going to this summer. I took it out with my dirty overalls that night, but then I couldn't figure out what to do with it. Nothing's private in the place where I stay."

He opened the box and showed Ephraim the articles clipped from the Socialist papers, the IWW pamphlets, a copy of a Russian-language anarchist monthly, two compact coils of copper wire, a piece of unglazed white ceramic tile about the size of a playing card, and three pencils that did not, upon closer inspection, exactly look like pencils. Ephraim ran his hands over the wire and then turned one of the pencils around. "And this is . . . ?"

"I wasn't sure, at first," Felix said. "But I read the papers like you do, I see what you see: spies have set fires with things like that. The wire, though, and the tile . . . maybe it's just stuff Joe confiscated from some of the workers."

"Why give it to you, then?"

Felix spread both hands in the air. "I don't know. But when I asked him to take the box back, he said he couldn't, and he made me promise to keep it safe until the summer meeting. You know what's going on with unions all over. Things are going to be bad at our plant for a while."

He looked at Ephraim, and then looked away. "The thing is—I told Joe I'd bring the box up here and leave it with you. You're so far away, no one would look here for something like this. You don't have anything like a labor movement, no strikes or demonstrations. Just sick people, and a lot of woods."

He flushed as Ephraim frowned at him. "I know I should have asked you first."

"I don't see why you'd pull me into this," Ephraim said. Framed by the garden walls, the woods meant to insulate him from both germs and worry slipped slightly out of focus, signaling more snow.

"Because," Felix said, looking over Ephraim's shoulder, "I'm a little bit more involved with the union organizers than I should be. And who else could I ask? You're family."

It was obviously wrong, Ephraim thought, and clearly risky to keep the box. Yet it was equally impossible to refuse Felix's request. He *was* family, as well as a member of the Ovid community, and Felix wouldn't ask this of him unless it was important. At the same time he wouldn't want to be beholden. Casually, as if nothing had just happened, Ephraim turned away from the trees and said, "You'll come back for it?"

"More likely Joe will," Felix said. "Or another friend of his. Someone will come for it, though."

Without transition they talked, then, about Felix's parents and Rosa's sisters, about Ephraim's daughters and Rosa herself, and finally about Ephraim's progress and when—"Only a few more months," Ephraim said. "I feel sure of it"—he might be released and allowed to come home.

⁓

LEO LEARNED ABOUT the visit only after supper, when he and Ephraim returned to the room together. As soon as they were out on their cure chairs, Ephraim handed over the innocent-looking box and told Leo to look inside. Just as Ephraim had done, Leo stirred the papers—most no worse that what appeared in our own library after each visiting day— looked over the coils of wire and the piece of tile, and then picked up the peculiar pencils, listening as he did to Ephraim's account of the visit.

"How involved do you think Felix is?" Leo asked.

"I don't know," Ephraim said. "He always exaggerates, but still—I wish I knew what he was up to. And I wish he hadn't brought this here. He's a good boy, though. Not such an odd duck as me, at any rate."

"Well, but it's not him, necessarily," Leo said. "Just—everything's getting so peculiar. Now some stranger is supposed to come here someday and ask for this—I wouldn't have let Felix do that." He frowned, thinking of all the shabby items—old guns, worn knives, homemade explosives, smeared pamphlets—he had glimpsed during his last year in Odessa. People had been arrested for nothing more than being near such things.

"You would if he was family," Ephraim said, reminding Leo yet again of what he lacked.

❧

MILES TOO WAS disturbed that week. Two letters made their way to him by different routes, the first enclosed in a small, heavy package. From Doylestown, his friend Edward Hazelius wrote:

Bad news, my friend. Not Lawrence, thank God: though it is weeks now since I've heard from him. Still this is the ruination of so much that mattered to us. Virtually all of the excellent duck-billed dinosaur bones that we shipped east with the rest of the expedition's finds, and which were destined for the museum in London, are lost. The steamer bearing them from Halifax was torpedoed by a U-boat and now lies at the bottom of the sea. Some but not all of her crew were saved by a passing merchant ship. All the fossils are gone. When I think of our efforts, all our chipping and brushing and plaster bandaging and the work to get these into the wagons and onto the flatboat, not to mention the efforts of those who for two years have been restoring the bones and preparing them for shipment—I can't believe it's all been lost in an instant's vandalism.

I wish we would just fight—don't you? It is inevitable that we enter this war, every day we put it off only makes our position more false. It makes me ashamed to be an American and if I were younger I would do what Lawrence has done, I would run up to Canada and enlist right now and hope to take my revenge on those who sent our beautiful duckbills down. I am sorry to be the bearer of this bad news but I knew you would want to know. Lawrence fights for something; there is that.

I am sending along—it's an early Christmas present, I have an excuse—an odd thing that might comfort you. You will remember my great-aunt Grace, who showed us our first fossils. Last month, cleaning out the attic, Mrs. Smithson found some crates of books that Grace had stored there years ago. All are copies of a tract written by Samuel Bernhard, who was my great-great-grandfather. Do you remember flipping through this same book when we were boys? I didn't understand the family connection then.

As wrongheaded as the book seems now, I cherish it as one of the things that got us interested in the field, and I thought you might like a copy of your own. May it cheer you during your long evenings in bed. I'll be thinking of you reading it as I travel through Arizona (which is where I am going for the Christmas holidays; a tiny excursion, much diminished by your absence).

You will have heard from Mr. Maskers that there have been some small incidents at your plant as well as mine. Nothing to worry about, it is just the usual unrest. The troublemakers have been fired.

Inside the package was a brown book, smelling of leather and mold. Miles felt nothing when he looked at it. No wave of nostalgia, no stab of recognition. Why would he want this old tract, more theology, really, than paleontology? Edward's great-aunt he could hardly remember; her face had vanished, and when he thought of her now he remembered only her narrow, wrinkled hands, cupping fossils or writing with her darting, vertical strokes. He wanted not reminders of his past but Arizona, the bone quarries, mountains, crisp air. Travel, freedom, work. In the absence of those he wanted, at least until he got the second letter two days later, news from Lawrence.

I haven't written to my father. What would I say? I'm alive. I can't tell you what this has been like. What I have seen. What I have done. Nor can I tell you where I am now. Dirt above me, mud below, live men sleeping next to me and dead men crumbled all around, as thoroughly mixed with the soil as if they were designed all along to be fertilizer.

A white mist hides us completely this afternoon. I can hear but not see the men around me. I can see this paper only when I hold it close to my face. The air is still, the mist doesn't move. Mist, gas, fog, smoke—I can't tell the difference anymore until it's too late but before it came I was watching a dead plane, caught in the tree next to me. The man inside, charred quite black with his arms and legs burned off, looked like a cigar. I miss you and think often of our time together in Alberta.

8

SHORTLY AFTER MILES got those letters, and with no under-standing of how they might affect us, we gathered for our usual Wednesday session. We were looking forward to it more eagerly than usual; it was Dr. Petrie's turn to speak, and we thought we might learn something new about him. He knew parts of us that we didn't know ourselves: not just the calcifications in our lungs, the tubercular lesions on our bones, the sores and infections we concealed from each other beneath our clothes, but also what we looked like when he gave us bad news. What happened to our faces when he said, gravely, that we must resign ourselves to another six months or a year inside these walls. For all he knew about us, though, we knew almost nothing then about his personal life.

Back then, he wouldn't have told us, for example, why he was so short. It wouldn't have seemed right to him that we should know about his own case of tuberculosis, which had infected his spine when he was a boy, permanently stopping his growth before he reached five feet tall and deforming his vertebrae. Although the pain sometimes made him absentminded and curt, he concealed the cause, just as he dressed to disguise the curve below his neck and the lump where his shoulder was misaligned. That day, in fact, he entered the room rubbing his shoulder but stopped as soon as he saw Ephraim noticing.

Christmas was only a few weeks away, and the staff had hung huge garlands from the rafters and decorated an enormous tree. The resemblance between the cloth wrapped around its base, and the green tartan scarf of the same pattern pushing out Dr. Petrie's pointed beard, distracted some of us. He smiled above the scarf, released his shoulder, and started our eighth session by saying he wanted to discuss what he'd seen in France during the spring of 1915. The French government, he explained, had asked him to visit their military hospitals and evaluate their plans for the treatment of tubercular soldiers.

"Miles has been telling me about his young friend Lawrence, who's off fighting with the Canadian forces," he added, "and that made me think again about my own time there. I've been meaning to write this down." He looked at something in his lap. "I know these talks are meant to be informal. But I never could speak without notes, so I hope you won't mind if I read from these."

Usually he stood over us as we lay passively in bed; he asked and we answered; he wrote down, with sharp and vigorous strokes, what our bodies revealed. On his rounds his manner was so strong and reassuring that we often forgot how tiny he was beneath his stethoscope and starched white coat. But here, as he joined our circle as an equal, his hands shook as he fingered his index cards, his voice trembled, and he couldn't hide the fact that he had to point his toes to reach the floor. He was nervous, the rest of us realized. Perhaps because of that, his description of the spread of tuberculosis in France was a little dull.

In a light, dry voice he spoke about the rapid mobilization of the French army and the failure to thoroughly examine all the troops. Many, he explained, suffered from latent or incipient tuberculosis, which in the cold, wet conditions of the trenches had quickly developed into active disease and, in the overcrowded billets, had spread rapidly among the men. Lydia made a face at Nan, who raised her eyebrows in response— was this something we wanted to hear?—but Dr. Petrie didn't notice, instead taking encouragement from the expression of interest on Eudora's face. The sickest had been sent back home, he continued, where there were no trained tuberculosis nurses, very few sanatorium beds, and no special wards in the hospitals. Paris, where the soldiers mingled with the refugees who'd fled the German invasion, was the worst, and few of the French doctors were as experienced as any sanatorium doctor here. He'd visited hospitals and refugee centers and military encampments and prisons, making recommendations and gathering data for his reports. Some of the data he had here, summarized on these cards . . .

We avoided each other's eyes. For the last couple of months we'd been able to read current news about the war, thanks to a doctor in New York who, when Dr. Petrie complained to him about our wretched library, had started gathering up the daily papers and sending them in batches on the train. Now that we had those, what we most wanted was an insider's view of the war, but this wasn't it. There were charts involved, some tables and figures. Our eyes glazed over even as Miles leaned forward avidly.

When Dr. Petrie finished we murmured politely; Pietr complimented him on his scarf and Olga praised the neatness of his tables. We managed not to say to each other what we thought, or how much better we would have liked learning something about his personal life, but the following week only half of us showed up. Once more we prepared ourselves for a dry set of facts. During that second talk, though, Dr. Petrie surprised us, shedding his nervousness along with the foolish scarf. After a few sentences about the care of tubercular soldiers, he was suddenly describing the early days of that May, when along with every other available physician and scientist in the country he'd been rushed to an enormous makeshift hospital to help treat the victims of the first German gas attacks.

He spoke about his hurried journey, the sidewalk cafés crowded with little tables and the men walking with bareheaded girls, soldiers and sailors from Siam and Senegal mingled with *poilus* and Tommies. "Plane trees," he said, looking at the wall across the room as if they were painted there, "and the gardens, the thatched roofs, the pears espaliered on the walls—you should see what they do with fruit trees over there."

He described the fields, which like those back here were filled with clover and alfalfa and rye but dotted unfamiliarly with brilliant poppies. As he made those leap before our eyes we began to see what he'd seen—it was beautiful, he said, the undamaged parts of France were so beautiful—and so we also saw the desolation as he neared the front, the shattered trees and the churned-up ground, the twisted wrecks of automobiles and, once he reached Boulogne, the far worse wrecks of men.

Near Ypres, he said, the Germans had released a poisonous gas, which had killed thousands of French troops and wounded thousands more; a few days later more had been released, this time against a Canadian battalion (here Miles drew a sharp breath); other attacks had followed swiftly and no one knew how to care for the casualties. Those who hadn't died in the trenches or dropped as they tried to run away had collapsed in the primitive treatment posts just behind the front.

"When I saw those men," Dr. Petrie said, "I—nothing could have prepared me for the shock."

His feet fluttered against the lower rung of his chair. Gas warfare, he said indignantly, was the exact reverse of everything he'd spent his life learning to fight. He knew more acutely than most what those victims were suffering and he thought that we, so alert to the difficulties of living with imperfect lungs, might also sense what those men had been through. We did, we were fascinated by what he said but shaken too, and most of us would have been glad if he'd stopped then. But something about what he'd seen made him keep talking and us keep listening. We took no break, instead sitting horrified in our circle as he continued.

"There was a cloud," he said. "A green cloud half a mile deep and four miles long moving slowly toward the trenches, with the wind."

During the first minutes, the survivors told Dr. Petrie, the cloud caused simply a cough and a dry mouth. Before long, though, the gas—a corrosive poison, Dr. Petrie noted—stripped the lining from the bronchial tubes and the lungs and caused an instant inflammation. Men coughed up cupfuls of foamy yellow fluid; some coughed so hard they ruptured their lungs; men frothed and drowned in their own fluid before his eyes. A few who'd had some high school chemistry recognized the smell as chlorine and remembered that the ammonia in urine would neutralize its effects. Those few had told everyone they could to piss on their socks and handkerchiefs and stuff them in their mouths. Through the clouds rolling over them, they'd seen German troops bending over cylinders while peering through the single gleaming lenses of their hoods.

But truthfully, Dr. Petrie said, most of the soldiers he saw in the hospital had told him nothing; they'd choked and gasped and coughed and heaved and died. With the other visiting doctors and scientists he'd run around, uselessly trying to ease the men's sufferings. By the time he saw them they were drowning, lying motionless and slowly drowning, their faces first blue and then finally black. He had thought then, he said—by now he'd crushed the index cards in his hand—that a nation that could in cold blood implement such a foul method of warfare should not be permitted to exist, should itself be strangled and made to suffer.

Across the circle from him, Miles, who had grown very pale, gripped his knees. "They *should*," he whispered.

Anyone might have said something here; a number of us had relatives, or had once had relatives, either in that sprawling chunk of Europe now called the Central Powers or nearby, in places overrun by them. *We* hadn't done this, not us, not people we knew—but then, who? Leo and

Ephraim, startled by Miles's muffled comment, exchanged glances. Dr. Petrie took a long, raspy breath and then continued.

"Since I couldn't help directly," he said, more quietly than before, "I tried to learn what I could from the deaths of those men, in the hope of helping to develop suitable protection. At the autopsies I attended I saw the lungs push forward the instant the chest was opened, running with frothy yellow fluid, the sight as bad, perhaps worse, than the most grossly tubercular lung, and this made me wonder if—"

Miles's hands slipped from his knees. His lips, turning as pale as the rest of his face, opened, and he fell to the floor in a faint.

AFTERWARDS DR. PETRIE could not believe what he had done. Our circle of wan, unhealthy faces gazing at him so earnestly—what had he been thinking, talking to us about ruptured lungs? Now, when we're all thrown so much more closely together and have so little privacy, he will sometimes admit that back then he'd been lonely and that, although he'd worried about joining our circle on terms of such equality, at the same time he'd been unable to resist the lure of our weekly gatherings. Also he admits that, once he started, he'd simply forgotten his audience. Only when Miles slumped to the floor had he understood what he'd done.

The meeting ended in chaos, most of us stumbling out, frightened and worried, as Dr. Petrie resuscitated Miles with Eudora's help. A few minutes later, he eased Miles into Naomi's car and then offered to drive down with her, in case Miles felt faint again.

"He'll be fine," she said, at the same time squeezing Miles's hand reassuringly. "It's just—your story made him think about his friend Lawrence, I think. Come if you want."

What an idiot he'd been. After stumbling out a string of apologies he sat silently in the back seat, appalled by what he'd done, and then at Mrs.

Martin's house hastily explained what had happened before escorting Miles up to his beautifully furnished room.

"I have no children," Dr. Petrie told Miles, easing him into the clean, fresh sheets and pulling up the blankets. "No family at all. I sometimes think that makes me insensitive to the attachments of others."

Miles reached for a light brown shawl and said, "Lawrence's father gave me this."

What was it made of? Dr. Petrie wondered as he draped it over Miles's shoulders. Cashmere, musk ox, something rare and costly; it was amazingly soft: alpaca, perhaps? Everything in this room, he could not help noting, from the silver brushes to the monogrammed pajamas and fleece-lined slippers, was expensive and elegant, whereas his own rooms at the sanatorium were dreadfully bare and his few luxuries—a heavy robe, that green tartan scarf—had been left to him by grateful patients whom he'd lost.

"Edward hates the Germans too," Miles continued. "As much as you do." Then, while Dr. Petrie shifted uneasily from foot to foot, Miles told him about the torpedoed ship and the sunken dinosaur bones, and he displayed first Edward Hazelius's letter and then Lawrence's painful note.

"I hated hearing about the gas, and what you saw," Miles said, returning the papers to his bedside table. "But it's a relief to know that you aren't neutral about this war either."

"Neutral's an odd word," Dr. Petrie said noncommittally. His time in France had made him furious, but not only with the Germans; everyone was to blame, he thought, the generals especially. Before Miles could assign to him more opinions he didn't truly hold, he turned away. "You need to rest," he said. "Is there anything else I can do for you, before I go?"

With a sigh Miles eased himself back into the soft mound of pillows. "May I come visit you before our next session? I'd enjoy some time to talk alone."

"It would be my pleasure," Dr. Petrie said, noting that his feet were, meanwhile, backing him efficiently from the room. He *didn't* share Miles's feelings about the Germans, and the way Miles had behaved in the car had further put him off. Carrying on about how dizzy and weak he felt; leaning into Naomi Martin's shoulder while she tried to drive and begging for sympathy: he'd hated to see that.

All through the following day he hid in the X-ray laboratory, trying to review our films but still upset at what he'd done and disturbed by Miles's embarrassing display in the automobile. That evening he entered our dining hall at ten minutes past six, when he knew we'd all be seated. In his clean tweed suit, with his high-collared shirt and his tidy, old-fashioned boots, he stood in front of the serving tables, so small despite his excellent posture that many couldn't see him.

"What happened yesterday afternoon," he said, "I—there's no excuse, I'm sorry. I haven't been sleeping well. So much bad news, lately, about the war; it wears me down. When I read certain things in the newspapers, they set off memories that upset me. That's no excuse, though. There's never an excuse for such behavior and I simply want to say again: I'm sorry."

Our weekly sessions were far from secret—anyone might join at any time, and the solarium in which we gathered was visible from the corridor—but still, those who'd never attended had little idea of what we did and were baffled by Dr. Petrie's remarks. Some thought, as the rest of us would learn later, that he was apologizing for mistreating a patient, and that that was why his hands were shaking.

For the next few days, as he made his rounds, he was unusually attentive, lingering longer by our chairs and fussing with the blankets wrapped around our legs, but by the following Wednesday he'd put the episode behind him. Waiting impatiently in his office on the second floor of Central, one floor above the dining hall and two above the X-ray facility, he'd forgotten the look on Miles's face when he awoke from his faint, and he was wishing he hadn't promised to talk with him. Already it was several minutes past three, and the thought of wasting this precious hour, when taking two hours away from his work for our session was already such an extravagance, made him wild.

He'd stopped work precisely at three, wanting to be ready for Miles mentally as well as physically; his pen was capped and lay along the edge of the report he was writing for the next staff meeting. If he picked it up and began again, Miles would certainly appear in mid-sentence. If he sat here waiting Miles would never come, and he would have wasted a whole hour. If he got up and went to the window, scanning the grounds for Naomi's Model T, either he'd see it and be annoyed at their slow progress toward his office, or he wouldn't see it and would grow more anxious. If . . .

Clicking his teeth with exasperation, he sat down—eight minutes past three—uncapped his pen, and returned to the most recent set of autopsy reports. Charlie Goldstein, Frank Mistretta, Alicia Jurik; all had been in the infirmary for extended stays and each had ended by traveling late at night to the undertaker's in the village. Behind them had followed young Dr. Dorschel, who, as Tamarack State lacked a morgue, carried a suitcase with his instruments tucked into their soft padded slots and returned after dawn with his reports. Perhaps, Dr. Petrie thought, he might recommend a raise for his young colleague.

As he read he made notes for his own report on a separate sheet of paper. Tomorrow or Friday he'd sit down with Irene, retrieving all the X-rays for each of the subjects and correlating what they'd previously read from those films with what the autopsies showed to have actually happened. Settling into the report on Charlie, feeling his mind sink into its familiar groove, he was unpleasantly surprised a few minutes later to hear, not Miles's expected if tardy greeting but a conversation taking place just outside his door.

A female voice, which sounded annoyed, a male voice that seemed to be pleading; he couldn't make out the words but the sound was distracting. An entire sanatorium with all its public and private rooms, the scores of sheltered corners both inside and out in which, as everyone knew and pretended not to, acts far more private than arguments took place—and this couple had to argue a foot from his office? Once more he capped his pen and lifted his shoes from the wooden footrest that a grateful patient, long since dead and autopsied, had built especially for him.

IN THE HALL, near two of the wooden chairs lined beneath the row of portraits on the wall, Miles—that was Miles out there—leaned closer toward Naomi.

A row of faces watched them: solemn men, in formal clothes, staring directly into the camera. Miles knew some of them—the governor, state representatives, members of the Board of Health and the Association for the Prevention of Tuberculosis—but at that moment he couldn't have recognized his own mother. His whole frame was trembling. There before him stood Naomi, whom he'd almost let escape. During the drive up the hill, he'd meant to say what he'd been rehearsing in his mind all week, but he hadn't been able to open his mouth and the ride passed silently. Then after they'd parked the automobile and walked toward Dr. Petrie's office, Naomi had announced that instead of waiting for him in the corridor, she was going to see Eudora. Only as she'd turned to leave and as he, choking on all he'd meant to say, had reached toward Dr. Petrie's door, had the words suddenly rushed from his mouth. "I'd like us to spend more time together," he'd said. "In a different way, a more serious way—"

"My mother keeps me very busy," she'd replied, looking toward the portraits.

Shy, he understood. And also caught off guard. He said, "Last week, when you held my hand in the car: that's when I realized you understood about Lawrence. You're the only one who does and when I'm around you I feel—you know what I'm feeling. Don't you?"

"I have to go," she insisted. She raised her hands and held them at her waist, palms toward him. "I promised Eudora . . ."

"You *do* know," he said enthusiastically. "I'm so glad—I couldn't wait anymore to tell you. It's not that I lack willpower, but since last week I have had such a sense of our fragility—do you know what I mean? Our *fragility*. Time is so short, I assume that I'm getting better each day but I could just as well be getting worse. And if I am, I don't want to die without having tried to get what I want. You must have felt this way yourself—why should we wait? Why should we put off saying what we really mean?"

He reached for one of her hands but stopped the instant she pulled back. Of course it was far too soon to touch her; she was young and it must be confusing, even embarrassing, to be talking about their feelings so directly. But the dark cloud that had filled his eyes during Dr. Petrie's talk, the sense of the cold floor drawing him magnetically and the terror of waking without knowing where he was, longing for his mother and Edward and Lawrence but finding no one who loved him, only strangers, pushed him on.

"I don't mean to rush," he said more quietly, "but I want you to know how I feel, and I don't want to waste too much time. It's fortunate that we're in the same household and that we have so many opportunities to see each other. Perhaps, though, we could also have a meal together outside your mother's house, or take a ride together to Lake Placid?"

"I have to *go*," she said, and darted down the hall. For a minute Miles, his body still vibrating, stood staring after her. Her shoulders, so slim and straight in her white blouse. Her waist, so small inside the belt that cinched the folds of her skirt, and below that—it wasn't his fault, surely, that he noticed this; skirts were startlingly short now—her stockings visible above the tops of her narrow boots. So finely put together, so healthy and yet so diminutive that even he might hope to pick her up. Still imagining what it might feel like to circle her waist and lift her off the ground, he tapped on Dr. Petrie's door, already twenty minutes late, and let himself inside.

There Dr. Petrie sat as Miles threw himself, without an apology, into the armchair across from the desk. There he sat, as, except for his time in France, he'd sat for nearly twenty years, listening not only to us but to our benefactors, our overseers, our families, and our enemies, listening as Miles recounted his conversation with Naomi. Once he interrupted to say, "You're not *dying*," but otherwise he was quiet. Dr. Richards had introduced him to other rich men, who like Miles ran important companies or managed huge plants; usually their reserve was impenetrable. Perhaps Miles was sicker than he'd guessed.

Longing to take his guest's temperature and to have Irene look inside his lungs, he said, "Did you really tell her all of that?"

"It all came out of me at once," Miles said, causing Dr. Petrie to imagine, unpleasantly, a spill of dark fluid. "But where's the harm? She needs to know that the differences between us mean nothing at all."

"Oh, dear," Dr. Petrie murmured. Worse than he'd thought. "What is she, nineteen?"

"Eighteen," Miles said. "It doesn't matter. You see the way she is at our sessions, she listens with such attention, soaking in every scrap of information. She wants to learn, I know she does. And she has no money of her own. I could give her that, as soon as I'm better I could give her whatever she wanted. I know I could make her happy."

"You want to *marry* her?"

"Twice before this has happened to me, I was very attached to two other women but both times my health interfered. I didn't think it was fair to ask either of them to wait, or to burden them with my condition. But it's different with Naomi. She's grown up among people like me. She's helped her mother all her life, she understands. And I am"—here

Miles puffed out his concave chest, smoothing his thin lusterless hair with a hand on which, Dr. Petrie saw, the skin had the texture of crumpled paper—"You're the only one I can say this to. I'm in love with her. If she'd let me court her seriously, I think there's a real chance she could come to have feelings for me."

"I don't know what your own physician tells you," Dr. Petrie said, looking down at his legs. His suit was getting shabby, he saw. Miles's trousers were very much nicer, a soft matte herringbone. "But if you were a patient here, you would have heard me say this a hundred times: it's not your job to fall in love, or out of love, or grow anxious or overemotional or have arguments. Your job is to lie still, to breathe the fresh air. And to get better. Really," he said, pushing together his autopsy reports, "really I will hear no more of this. Now if you would like to talk about something sensible, I would be delighted."

Miles looked down at his knees. "Forgive me," he said. "I should keep my feelings to myself."

"Better to keep them firmly in check," Dr. Petrie said. "Best not to have them at all." He looked at his watch. "We only have a few minutes before our session. Why don't you tell me about one of your other trips, before you went to Canada. Where else have you been?"

Obediently, his heart racing, his mind moving kaleidoscopically among images of Naomi enjoying his house in Doylestown, picking snapdragons in the garden, walking beside him to Edward's house with her narrow feet in fresh new pumps that were strapped at the instep and trimmed with bows, Miles smoothed the excitement from his face and, gazing just past Dr. Petrie's chin, talked about Nebraska.

9

W E MISSED THOSE discussions; what we saw was the two men entering the solarium together, Dr. Petrie with his lips in the thin crinkled shape they sometimes formed when he was angry with one of us but trying to conceal it, and Miles flushed and feverish-looking, his hair stuck moistly to his head. They showed up at exactly four o'clock—usually Miles was a few minutes early—and were followed five minutes later by Eudora and Naomi, one pale and worried and the other pink. Four faces, none looking quite normal, arriving at odd times and in odd pairs—usually a sight like that would have fueled gossip not only during our break but for several weeks to come. We were so lethargic, though, that we hardly noticed what was going on.

This was our last session before Christmas, and we knew that several weeks would pass before we had another. Our December movie night had been a disappointment—the drama we saw had made us all uneasy, especially when the courtroom cheered on the cheating young wife as she cast blame for her theft on a Burmese businessman—but even so, we grew bleak thinking about the time until the next distraction, especially since the weather had grown so harsh. The snow, which had fallen generously around Thanksgiving, had melted and then withdrawn itself so that now, although the temperature had not been above twenty degrees for a week, the ground was flinty and dark. The evergreens looked black against the sky, even the ice on the pond looked dark; the birds were silent and the wind droned day and night. We were a day from the winter solstice, Otto had said earlier that afternoon. A day from the shortest, darkest day of the year. That we felt so low, so empty and dull, was the combined result of our disease and of the sun's refusal to climb higher in the sky.

Apathetically we drifted, at the beginning of this tenth session, into the empty circle of chairs we'd left the previous week. Several of our regulars were absent, too droopy even to rise from their beds, but this was less noticeable because we'd also gained a person: Irene Piasecka, who after listening to both Eudora and Dr. Petrie had decided to investigate our sessions for herself. Miles was sitting on one side of Dr. Petrie but the chair to his left was open, and she settled herself and then leaned over to whisper in his ear.

"You don't mind?" she asked. "I've been wanting to see what this is like."

"Of course not," he replied. Late at night, in her laboratory, he'd talked for too long about the mistakes he'd made during his presentation and also afterwards, in Miles's room; she'd listened patiently and tried to persuade him not to apologize publicly. Bad advice, he'd thought then, although usually he trusted her. Now, wondering if his abject little speech in the dining hall had somehow made possible Miles's confession, he thought she'd been right but he was still taken aback by her presence. Was she here to keep an eye on him? Surely it was Miles, beaming across the circle at Naomi, who needed watching.

The rest of us missed both his moist glance and Naomi's refusal to notice it. Irene tilted her head toward Dr. Petrie again and said, "If the talk isn't interesting, I'll leave at the break."

"As you wish," Dr. Petrie said.

But to her surprise, to everyone's surprise, Arkady turned out to be an inspired speaker. Within minutes we were sitting upright, leaning toward him, our heads making the shape of an unfolding flower as he said he'd thought long and hard about what to discuss and had finally decided to explore something that had been on his mind since Ephraim's talk.

Quite calmly and clearly—how had we failed, before, to realize Arkady's strengths as a teacher?—he reminded us that Ephraim's community at Ovid was only one in our country's long history of communitarian and cooperative colonies. "Let me give you some context," he said. And then, much as a teacher at his workmen's circle might have done, he gave swift descriptions of the Shaker communities at Mount Lebanon and Niska-yuna, the Owenite settlement at New Harmony in Indiana, Brook Farm in Massachusetts, and the Fourierist phalanxes in upstate New York, not so far from Ovid. He mentioned Oneida, also upstate, and the experimental colony of Topolobampo, in Mexico, about which he'd been told by a friend.

Irene sighed with pleasure, delighted to hear something, anything, clearly explained; even without having heard Ephraim's talk she could see the connection between his community of transplanted urban Jews and the long tradition that Arkady described. Crisply he detailed still other attempts, considering the differences between the religious and the secular, the communities founded in settled areas and those on the edge of what had then been frontier. "All of them," he said as she nodded appreciatively, "all failed despite the best intentions of their founders and participants."

Except for the rattled quartet, the rest of us, along with Irene, listened intently until it was time to break. Over our milk and hot chocolate, Leo turned to Ephraim and asked if his community had known about all these others.

Ephraim, setting down his slice of buttered bread, said, "We didn't think about it. We were shtetl Jews, then city Jews, before Rosa's brothers got us involved in this—what did we know about Shakers and Harmonists? If we were thinking about anything, it was about the movements in Russia. One of Rosa's cousins—"

But here, before Ephraim could finish his sentence, someone touched Leo's arm. Once or twice, while Arkady was speaking, Leo had looked over at the woman with her frizzy gray hair pinned loosely above her narrow eyes: was she the person who, months ago, had taken his radiograph?

"You're Leo Marburg, aren't you?" she asked. She held out her right hand a few inches higher than was common, all but her index finger curved slightly toward her palm. He grasped that finger with the tips of his own, as she seemed to want, and shook it gently as she said, "I'm Irene Piasecka."

It *was* her, then; the person Eudora had mentioned. Standing, she was nearly his own height. "A pleasure," he said.

"Eudora's told me about you," she continued. Her left hand, he saw, was encased in a violet glove. "Your early education, your search for work in this country—"

Eudora talked about him? She'd arrived too late for him to say hello, and now she was standing with Naomi near the door. Worried that he wouldn't get to talk with her, he shifted his weight and prepared to excuse himself. Then froze as Irene continued, "What she said made me wonder if you'd like to visit the X-ray laboratory and see some of what I'm doing."

Him? She was inviting him? Astonishingly, she added: "You might be able to assist me, when your health permits, and if you're interested."

"I *am*," he managed to say.

"Good," she said. She smiled, touched his arm once more, and in response to Arkady's gesture, headed back to our circle of chairs.

Later, Leo thought, he would find Eudora and thank her. For thinking of him, for arranging this introduction. His head hummed as he returned to the chairs, where the rest of us were also settling. How soon could he visit Irene's lab?

Once more we bent our heads toward the center of our circle. Arkady, picking up where he'd stopped, explained that to him the most interesting thing was not the failure but the ardent idealism that, in the face of so much failure, attempted again and again to form utopian communities. Was this brave, or was it foolish? He talked about some of the people involved in those experiments, what they'd given up and what they'd hoped to gain. As his examples piled up, Leo caught one, lost the next, caught another, and half wished that Arkady would finish so that he might talk to Eudora about his prospects with Irene. Annoyingly, she was sitting three chairs away, where he could neither reach her nor see her face clearly.

She wasn't paying attention either, although for a different reason. Arkady was talking about the same things that the book she'd taken from the village library described less elegantly, but despite her interest, she was too worried about Naomi to concentrate. Throughout the first half of the session Naomi had been drawing furiously, and now, her cheeks still pink, she was once more focused entirely on her pencil, moving it across her drawing pad. Beneath the point a building was taking shape, four wings of equal height surrounding an empty courtyard. A barracks, a prison? A version, probably, of the Fourierist compound Arkady had described—except that a figure, completely out of scale and crowned with Leo's face and hair, filled the courtyard. Why him? But after what had happened earlier, she couldn't blame Naomi for drawing whatever caught her eye. Anyone who wasn't Miles must have offered some relief.

She glanced across the circle but Miles, chewing on his lips, for once wasn't looking at Naomi. His vest was buttoned up, his shirt collar flawlessly crisp, and the color faded from his cheeks. No one could have looked more respectable—and yet he had, Naomi claimed, suddenly, horribly, declared his feelings to her as they stood outside Dr. Petrie's office.

Eudora had happened to look out a window shortly afterwards, and so she'd seen her friend striding through the frozen garden, so upset that at first, when Eudora rushed down to join her, she could only sputter.

"That stick!" she'd said indignantly, after explaining what had happened. "I held his hand after he fainted because I felt *sorry* for him. He's almost old enough to be my father."

For twenty minutes Eudora had paced with her, nodding patiently as Naomi fumed, never reminding her that she might, in first approaching Miles, have played any role in the feelings he'd developed. They'd come in for Arkady's talk, but at the break, when Naomi continued complaining, Eudora had suggested, "Stop driving him."

"Give up the only money I earn, because he's a fool?" Naomi had made an unhappy face before adding, "It would be easier if you were still riding with us, and still practicing your driving."

"I know," Eudora said, "but I'm here so many nights now . . ." Weeks ago she'd stopped the driving lessons with a casual sentence, so eager to spend more time in the laboratory that everything else was distraction. A car, compared with an X-ray apparatus, was no more mysterious than a fork; she could learn to drive anytime.

"So you say." Naomi's hand added shadows to Leo's eyes. "It's fine, though. I can manage him."

Across the circle, Arkady said something about a boatload of naturalists moving down a river toward Harmony. Robert Owen, Arkady continued—it would be months before he understood why he was telling a story about New Harmony; months before he woke from a restless sleep thinking *Nadezhda, Nadezhda* and realized that he'd reproduced for the rest of us almost exactly what his teacher, Nadezhda, had recounted to his workmen's circle five years ago: before he was sick, before she was dead, before he'd realized she knew only slightly more than her students—Owen had promised that a new society would rise from the fertile land along the Wabash. But meanwhile, he said, while Eudora continued to examine her friend and to think just for a moment that despite Leo's unusual looks, Naomi's hand was capturing the least interesting part of him, the settlers at New Harmony had no food, no shelter, no tools, and no materials with which to build. Owen proposed that by reasoned choice we could remake our institutions and the ways we live; that our characters were formed not by but for us, and so could be re-formed by changing the conditions of our lives. By the wide and sluggish river, though, actual people grew hungry and cold, and ultimately, Arkady said, Owen's experiment had failed.

Naomi finished shading Leo's cheekbones as Miles, who so far had said nothing, chimed in, "But *ours* won't." Keeping his eyes on Dr. Petrie, Miles added, "Although we are a small group, I think of this room as a kind of laboratory, and what we do here as something that might change all of us."

"Change," Dr. Petrie said, "is . . ."

"Change," Irene said at the same moment, "follows . . ."

Both sentences got lost in the discussion, during which many of us spoke at once while Arkady, clearly pleased with what he'd started, did his best to orchestrate. Only Eudora and Naomi contributed nothing. Watching Naomi sketch an elaborate border, Eudora thought about the drawings Naomi had given her over the years, some of which had lost their meaning. In that way they resembled the tiny, crumpled leather boot her great-uncle Ned had pressed on her long ago. Hands shaking, eyes milky, he'd mumbled a story: he'd loved the woman to whom it had once belonged, or he'd had a friend who had loved the woman? She hadn't paid attention, although she'd been fond of him. But because she'd been absorbed in something else, she now had the boot but not its meaning, the relic but not the story. If someday she had a daughter of her own and wanted to pass on this bit of family history, the lost context would be her fault. Naomi's drawing, she thought, would lose its meaning in just the same way.

She was wrong about this, of course. Later we'd all know what the drawing meant, and we'd wonder what would have happened if Leo had seen it that day. But as Naomi was drawing and we were arguing and Eudora was remembering her great-uncle Ned, Leo was focused almost entirely on Eudora. If she'd mentioned him to Irene, then she must be aware of him. If she remembered that Irene might help him, then she knew who he was? He was so delighted he could hardly keep from reaching over to her.

Some of us had already noticed how, no matter who was speaking, Leo studied Eudora; how he managed to post himself next to her during our coffee breaks and to sit across from her, so she was always in his gaze. Still it was Irene, new to our circle and alert to Leo after their brief exchange, who noticed his expression most clearly. At the end of the session, as we were trickling from the room, she and Eudora paused by the door. When Leo passed by them, she nodded and said, "I do hope you'll come visit."

"I *will*," he said. "Very soon." He waited, but when neither woman moved, he said a few words to Miles and then reluctantly joined Ephraim and Arkady in the hall.

"You didn't tell me he was so interested in you," Irene said to Eudora.

"Leo?" Eudora said.

"He never takes his eyes off of you."

"Not me," Eudora said, anxious to correct her misunderstanding. "It's Naomi he must be looking at." She looked back over her shoulder, toward where Miles and Naomi, standing near the fireplace, seemed to be arguing.

"It's not," Irene said, shaking her head. "But that's your business, not mine. Would you like to join me tonight? We could spend a few hours reviewing films while we gather material for Dr. Petrie's Monday meeting."

By then she'd seen in Eudora a quality that many of us had missed: whatever absorbed her, absorbed her completely. In the laboratory, Irene had seen pictures memorized, captions inhaled, whole passages from the books on her shelves swallowed and integrated. If she hadn't learned in much the same way, first from her brother-in-law and then elsewhere, she wouldn't have thought it possible that a person could grasp so much so fast. "I can have two supper trays sent down," she added.

Ignoring whatever was going on with Miles and Naomi, and also Irene's remark about Leo, Eudora followed Irene out the door.

10

FOUR DAYS AFTER Arkady's talk it was five below zero, and we were wearing mittens as we trotted through the halls. The library was freezing, also the dining hall, the solarium, and every place but the basement, near the furnaces. Out on the porches, where we had our elaborate layers of newspapers and blankets and hats and sometimes a glimmer of sun as well, we often felt warmer than when we were inside.

Cold awake, cold asleep; we lived in a building designed to freeze our bacilli, which also meant freezing us. Torpid as bears, we waited for the Christmas season to pass, knowing every minute that, at our distant homes and also in the village, celebrations we couldn't share were taking place. We were allowed to exchange only cards, a practice meant to make our lack of funds less painful, but elsewhere both the sick and the well were passing gifts at festive parties. Miles, still proud of himself for telling Naomi how he felt, overwhelmed everyone at Mrs. Martin's house with his generosity. The new novels, the woolen shawls, the handsome lap desks were too much, agreed the other guests, who'd given each other chocolates or playing cards or socks. Mrs. Martin was delighted with her elegant serving platter, but Naomi, who'd driven Miles on his shopping errands and thought she'd seen everything, was mortified to find, next to her plate, a necklace set with shining aquamarines.

"To match your eyes," Miles announced.

Silently she pled with her mother, hoping to be told that it was inappropriate and she should give it back. "Very handsome," Mrs. Martin said instead, with what Naomi knew was envy in her voice.

"I know a good jeweler in Boston," Miles said, looking pleased.

If she'd been able to turn to Eudora, perhaps she wouldn't have felt so terrible—but on the day after Christmas Eudora was back at work, cheerfully scrubbing floors and mopping tiles and helping us tack our homemade cards to the moldings. As soon as her shift was over she sprinted to the basement, where Irene was letting her experiment with some outdated X-ray equipment. Although this had been pushed to the back of the laboratory as soon as the more powerful replacement arrived, for Eudora it was as good as new. With the manual, a handful of textbooks, and two diagrams, she set to work cleaning the knobs and filaments and investigating the properties of the rays.

For subjects she used a group of ancient, moth-eaten specimens she'd smuggled from her father's workshop: two ducks, a chipmunk missing a leg, a tattered osprey, and a little opossum. Stitches showed, seams gaped. Her father had made these as a boy, when he was learning his craft from his Uncle Ned, and by now the osprey had only one eye while the toes of the opossum were as limp and shabby as old gloves and all of them were infested with bugs. She posed them between the tube and the film holder and then varied the distance, the voltage, and the length of her exposures. The bugs disappeared. The images she developed were good, bad, better, worse; sometimes, as she noted in her ledger, the leg wires and the wing bones were perfectly crisp but the neck vertebrae, in a slightly different plane, were out of focus. Sometimes she could see every detail of the skull but sometimes not. She found a pair of scissor-handled stuffers wound by accident into the excelsior filling the opossum and learned that the toes sagged because whoever skinned the creature had discarded the littlest bones. What were those called? One of Irene's anatomical atlases revealed the answer: distal phalanges. On New Year's Eve she stayed very late, eating the apples that Irene kept in a box and forgetting entirely about the date until, halfway down the hill on her bicycle, she looked up at the crescent moon and the sparkling planet near its lower tip, and realized that the earth had completed another revolution around the sun.

Often she and Naomi had made New Year's resolutions together—they would read these books, travel to these places—but not this year. On her bicycle, flying past winter trees so bare they resembled ribs, Eudora had only one wish: *I want more time in the lab.* She remembered Naomi, of course. But the image of her was, at that moment, no more vivid than that of one of her Aunt Elizabeth's former boarders, whose face she remembered warmly but whose last name she'd forgotten.

We weren't thinking about Naomi, either; she meant little to us and when we noticed her it was always as Miles Fairchild's driver, Miles's little friend. That New Year's Eve she was alone in her room, looking out the dormer window toward the same crescent moon but acutely aware of Eudora's absence. She lit a candle and swore that she'd be someplace else before the year ended. With Eudora or without, she would leave her mother's house and find a new place to live, where she could do something interesting. Something that used her talent for drawing, perhaps. She might make sketches for a clothes designer, illustrations for a magazine. Drawings for an architect: did she need to go to school for that? Last week she'd made sixteen sketches of Leo's face, from memory. Profile, three-quarter view, his eyes cast down or looking up; each one better than the last. For Christmas, Eudora had given her a thick pad of drawing paper she'd ordered specially. "You have such a gift," she'd said—but what she'd really meant, what had filled the pause after that, was: *Why don't you draw something other than Leo?*

Because I dream about him at night, Naomi had wanted to say. Dreamed about him, woke up thinking about him, served breakfast thinking about him, started the Model T and ran the errands and sorted mail for the boarders thinking about him every minute. Inside her head they had conversations in which he spoke and she responded, the clarity of what she felt and heard exactly mimicking her memories of actual conversations. How was a person to keep straight what she truly remembered, and what she remembered inventing?

Back in Chester, in the field behind her family's house, there'd been a space she sometimes visited, not far from the hedge where the deer used to sleep. The tall grass was pushed to the ground, the stems bent over and swirled to make a clearing shaped like an egg. When she could find it—it was almost invisible until she was right on top of it—she sat there for hours. The grass beyond the clearing moved in the breeze. The sun came in and the bent grass where she sat was damp and fragrant, sometimes tufted with pale hair. Always she'd fall asleep there, and when she woke there'd be a moment when she didn't know where she was, or even *that* she was: only the smells and the sounds and the movements and the feel of the sun on her skin. After her move to Tamarack Lake, nothing had made her feel that way again until she saw Leo—and that, she knew, was why she was so miserable. It wasn't just the holidays and her mother's frenzy and all the extra work, the special meals and extra decorations and the boarders' private parties. It wasn't just Miles, who'd been clinging to her like a tick. And it wasn't even that she missed Eudora, who swore she wasn't avoiding her but was never around and talked, when she could be found, only about the X-rays.

A few days ago, when the brakes on the Model T needed adjustment, Naomi had arranged to meet Eudora at the garage where Eugene worked and to take a walk with her while he did the repairs. Only after Naomi was already there had Eudora telephoned to cancel. Annoyed, Naomi had waited on the bench by the door, complaining until Eugene said he'd hardly seen his sister lately either. Busy all the time, he said. Ernest, who was back from New York for a couple of days, walked in, leaned over to inspect the brakes, and joined the conversation.

"Runs in the family," he added, handing Eugene a wrench. "When one of us gets interested in something we really get *interested*."

As if she didn't know that herself. Later, while Eugene was fiddling with a cable, Ernest had offered her a cigarette. She'd only smoked a few before and so she puffed at it cautiously while he talked about New York. There was nothing like the city, he said, straightening his handsome shirt. Movies every day if he wanted; the docks and the markets and the people in the streets, men working in caissons beneath the river while others moved through ironwork high in the air—just being there was exciting. And who would have expected that all the hours he'd put in with his father and his great-uncle in their taxidermy shop would have helped him get a job he liked so much!

"You're lucky," she'd said, unable to hide her envy.

He'd given her a look and leaned in toward her, his hair hanging softly over one eye. "Why don't you think about visiting sometime?"

Weakly she smiled and then coughed on the smoke from his cigarette.

ON THE SUNDAY after New Year's Day, which was bitterly cold and completely still, a dead hawk appeared in the low mound of garden centered, like a bull's-eye, inside our circular driveway. From our breakfast tables we couldn't avoid the sight of the corpse among the stiff white stalks. Irene, who hadn't seen the bird herself, heard about it from Leo, who arrived five minutes early for his tour of her laboratory. He chattered nervously while she showed him both her X-ray apparatus and the older equipment Eudora was playing with.

"Since when does it get so cold here that birds fall frozen from the sky?" he said. "You'd think we were in Siberia."

Irene shrugged, smiled, and pointed toward the new Coolidge tube. "Did you ever use one of these?"

"Not that one exactly," he said, "but earlier versions, of course. Where I went to school, we had all the usual gadgets for studying electricity. You must have too—you studied in Kraków?"

She nodded. "A long time ago, though. Everything I've learned about the rays, I learned in this country."

"I learned it back there," Leo said. "What little I know. I was six when the Roentgen rays were discovered; by the time I was in school we took the rays for granted and were more interested in what we could *do* with them than simply in producing them."

"We couldn't imagine such a thing, when I was in school," Irene said. "Twenty years—what a difference that makes."

Leo looked at the cabinets filled with glass plates, the long rows of chest films filed on the shelves that wound around the room, the darkroom, the chemicals and the glassware. "*Ten* years makes a difference," he said tensely. "Two. What really made me feel old were the discoveries Moseley made in Rutherford's laboratory. That's when I realized I'd never catch up."

"X-ray spectroscopy is really astonishing, isn't it?" Irene said. That there should be a way, now, to identify elements by their X-ray spectra and confirm their positions on the periodic table: this seemed as magical as peering through the envelope of human flesh. The papers demonstrating that each element had a specific number of electrons had been brilliantly clear, but still she was startled to think that Leo might understand them.

"You're familiar with Moseley's experiments?" she asked.

He shook his head again. "I was already in New York when he did his work," he said bitterly. "Already no one. No lab, no books, no colleagues . . ."

"Such a waste," she said, meaning Moseley's death at Gallipoli but then embarrassed that Leo might think she meant him. "Why," she couldn't help asking, "did you come to America?"

He rubbed his thumb repeatedly down the inside surface of his index finger, a gesture she hadn't been able to make in years, and said, "Didn't we all come for similar reasons? We thought it would be different here, that we'd have a better chance." Again his eyes wandered around the laboratory. "It worked for you. For me, it didn't."

His hand reached toward but didn't touch three Erlenmeyer flasks drying upside down on a wooden rack, and when she saw the hunger on his face she rummaged in the shelf of books near her desk. Absently, as if the gesture meant nothing, she handed him two worn green volumes.

"My old copy," she said, watching him. "I almost never use the set anymore, it's a little out of date."

He turned the volumes over before setting one down and opening the cover of the other. Surely this wasn't the text from which he'd learned chemistry in Odessa? And yet it was, or a version of it—an English translation of the sixth Russian edition of Mendeleeff's *Principles of Chemistry*. His copy, in one fat blue volume, had been stolen at the docks, along with most of his belongings, on the day six years ago when he'd arrived in New York. But here, as if a piece of his old life had been returned, was the same photograph, Mendeleeff with his open mouth and badly cut hair looking more like a madman than the genius he surely was. Here were the precious words and tables, along with the scores of small engravings showing everything from Lavoisier's apparatus for determining the composition of air to the tall furnaces used in the dry distillation of bones.

Irene was looking at him, he knew, but he couldn't keep himself from reading the beginning of the translator's preface. *In the scientific work to which Professor Mendeleeff's life has been devoted, his continual endeavour has been to bring the scattered facts of chemistry within the domain of law, and accordingly in his teaching he endeavours to impress upon the student the prin-*

ciples *of the science, the generalizations, so far as they have been discovered, under which the facts naturally group themselves.* That was right, exactly right, thought Leo: the *principles* of the science. *Chemistry,* he read, *offers an insight into the unchangeable substratum underlying the varying forms of matter.* He saw the lantern-jawed, goggle-eyed face of his kind young teacher and at the back of his throat he suddenly tasted ammonia.

"I thought," he heard Irene say carefully, in the tone of someone who'd repeated a sentence more than once, "that this might be a good refresher textbook."

"Better than you know," he made himself say. Although the basement was delightfully warm, he was shivering. "This book—this particular edition, I mean, the Russian version—I used to know every page of it. If I could just borrow it for a while . . ."

"Keep it," she said gently. "Since you cherish it so. After you've had time to study, we'll talk about some ways you might help me out here, if you're interested."

When he seized her hand in thanks, she winced and cried out. Eudora, carrying the frozen hawk by its feet, entered the laboratory just then and said, "Oh, don't *squeeze,* you're hurting her!"

Baffled, Leo dropped Irene's hand and stepped back. Irene shook her fingers, as if trying to restore some feeling; Eudora set down the dead bird and stroked her shoulder.

"Not your fault," Irene said. "Not at all, my hands are unusually"—she looked at the hawk, then up at Eudora—"sensitive, that's all. Eudora, I was showing Leo around and explaining some of what I do here. He might come and help out now and then. He was just leaving."

"I'm glad you could visit," Eudora murmured. Nodding, she picked up her latest specimen and headed for the old machine.

"Another time?" Irene said to Leo.

He nodded, embarrassed. "Thank you, again," he said. "And I'm sorry."

THE TEMPERATURE OUTSIDE continued to hover near zero and the sky was its peculiar Adirondack gray. In the library Ian played laconically with the pieces of the Erector set, which had lost their charm but, because of their link to his brother, remained more interesting than nothing. Diagonally across the hall, Dr. Petrie worked on a report for the upcoming trustees' meeting, while below him Clarice and Deborah cooked our supper. Two of the maintenance men, Bronsen and Andrew, their coveralls bulging over scarves and sweaters, swept drifted snow from the walkways, the *whisk, whisk* of straw across the flagstones audible throughout the wings. Inside, irritated by the steady, gentle noise and the memory of days when we too had been able to tidy a piece of our world so casually, we were turning the pages of magazines and rereading old letters, trading gossip and marveling at the news of Rasputin's death, which had happened just before Christmas. We were playing cards or checkers or chess, regretting something that had happened at the New Year's celebration, anticipating the next movie night, wondering what our families were doing at home. Some of us, like Ephraim, were lying on our beds, concentrating only on getting better.

We were trudging off toward the dining hall, lining up and then sitting down, regarding our plates and each other; we were flirting across the invisible barrier separating women and men. Doing what we did each evening, what it seemed that we might always do. While we began our meal, someone asked Leo where he'd been and he mentioned that he'd gone to the X-ray laboratory. He didn't say why, though, nor what he'd been given. When Gordon asked if he'd learned anything about why Irene wore that violet glove, her cry of pain flashed through his mind but still he was able to say, with perfect honesty, "No." Secretive, we thought. As we'd thought before.

Back out onto the porches, into the cold, under the covers, over the cushions: next to each other, freezing. Ephraim and Leo lay quietly after supper, Ephraim dreaming of home and Rosa and his girls, the deep snow blanketing the fields, the deer browsing through the bushes while his daughters, wrapped in layers of flannel, built a snowhouse with the help of their uncles, even as Leo—often this happened to us, this thinking or dreaming in parallel with the companions to whom we were closest—dreamed also of snow and his family. Not the second family, his stepmother's children, but his mother and her parents in Grodno where, during a winter like this, the snow piled up over the windows and the smoke from the train could be seen for miles away. He could see himself, dark hair hidden beneath a knitted cap, moving quietly between the white walls. Crows called harshly to each other from the trees. A hawk flew, casting a shadow, and the world seemed vast; so many things to do and see and he knew he would live forever. The rabbit he'd kept in a hutch out back: what had his name been?

That world had disappeared when his father took him off to Odessa. Then another had opened, only to vanish as well, but now—he turned to his green volumes, which were light enough to balance on his chest, easy to read even when he was wearing mittens. Each page begged to be lingered over. In this edition, he remembered his teacher enthusing, not only had Mendeleeff finally understood all the implications of the periodicity he'd discovered, but he'd also given himself free rein with his footnotes, which were speculative, fascinating, a parallel text taking up nearly half the book. Young and eager to learn the essentials as fast as he could, he'd skimmed over them when he'd read the text in Russian. But now—now he had nothing but time; he'd read every line, he'd take notes. He tilted the pages toward the lamp and slowly read the first footnote, inserted before Mendeleeff got halfway through his opening sentence:

[1]The investigation of a substance or a natural phenomenon consists (*a*) in determining the relation of the object under exam-

ination to that which is already known, either from previous
researches, or from experiment, or from the knowledge of the
common surroundings of life—that is, in determining and expressing the quality of the unknown by the aid of that which is known;
(b) in measuring all that which can be subjected to measurement,
and thereby denoting the quantitative relation of that under investigation to that already known and its relation to the categories of
time, space, temperature, mass, &c.; (c) in determining the position
held by the object under investigation in the system of known
objects guided by both qualitative and quantitative data; (d) in
determining, from the quantities which have been measured, the
empirical (visible) dependence (function, or "law," as it is sometimes termed) of variable factors—for instance, the dependence
of the composition of the substance on its properties, of temperature on time, of time on locality, &c.; (e) in framing hypotheses or
propositions as to the actual cause and true nature of the relation
between that studied (measured or observed) and that which is
known of the categories of time, space, &c.; (f) in verifying the
logical consequences of the hypotheses by experiment; and (g) in
advancing a theory which shall account for the nature of the properties of that studied in its relations with things already known and
with those conditions or categories among which it exists.

He forced himself to take a breath. Perhaps this wouldn't be as easy
as he'd thought? He didn't remember the language being so thorny but
perhaps this was the result of the translation. He took another breath and
dove in again.

On the other side of the divider Abe and Arkady were arguing, fiercely
but amiably, and in very low voices—we were not supposed to talk during
this time, we were supposed to rest completely—about Chernyshevsky,
who Arkady felt had been crucial in shaping revolutionary thought but
who Abe thought was a fool. Sean and Otto, a few spaces down, had

both dropped into a heavy sleep, which meant they'd be up and tossing restlessly all through the night, while over in the other wing Lydia was staring at a magazine, fiercely scanning a column listing new inventions—cotter pins, a peanut stemmer, a device for rolling and finishing shrapnel bars—and considering how to patent her own. Elsewhere on the women's porches, Sadie, Olga, Karin, and Pearl were whispering about their cousins or the men they hoped might become cousins, gazing at advertisements for lipsticks, reading with despair a child's misspelled note from home, watching the sliver of moon creep up on the edge of a cloud, disappear, and slowly reemerge. The stars swung slowly and in the woods an animal shrieked. Irene, alone in the basement, looked up from her desk.

If only, she thought, the moment when her two visitors had surprised each other had been more illuminating. Between the chemistry text, which distracted Leo, and her own squeal of pain, the pair had hardly interacted and she couldn't be sure what she'd seen. She might have asked Leo directly how he felt about Eudora, or at least asked Eudora more about Leo, but she hadn't had the nerve. Leo's gaze, she'd wanted to tell Eudora, might change her whole life, and pretending not to see it wouldn't help. The thing was to acknowledge it; to see what it meant and decide what she wanted. Yet instead of finding out what was going on between these two, she'd been diverted by Leo's responses. He'd once known, she now understood, at least as much chemistry and physics as she did herself; all these months she might have been training him as well as Eudora. Stupid, she thought, not to have seen that.

11

IRENE ALSO DIDN'T see—neither did we, but how could we?—how quickly one of our essential souls might disappear. On the Tuesday after Leo first visited Irene's lab, Ephraim got a frantic message from his wife. Gemma, his youngest daughter, had something that might be meningitis, a piercing endless headache and a fever that wouldn't come down, and although two doctors had seen her and everyone in the community at Ovid was trying to help, she was in grave danger and calling out for her father. *I do not want to disturb you when you are yourself so sick*, Rosa said. *But . . .*

The thought of Gemma crying for him—Gemma, who when he left home for Tamarack State had been too young to speak—made Ephraim's hands curl as if he might still cup her head. Nothing our director, Dr. Richards, said could keep him from leaving. Nor could Dr. Petrie, to whom Ephraim had, otherwise, always listened, convince him to stay, not even when he pointed to his temperature charts for the last three months, his last radiograph, the results of his last sputum count. "You have a new spot, an active one, in your left lung," Dr. Petrie said. "It's essential that you rest for some months. You put your own life at risk by leaving here. Not to mention your family."

"I'll sleep on my cousin's porch," Ephraim said. "I'll take my meals separately. You've taught us plenty about how to quarantine ourselves."

"That wasn't so you could kill yourself," Dr. Petrie said. "I could force you to stay, there are papers . . ."

Ephraim, who towered over Dr. Petrie, shook his head. "You wouldn't."

"I might, to keep you alive."

We don't know if it would have come to that; Ephraim arranged things otherwise. That night, after supper, he lay silently next to Leo on the porch until finally he slapped the arm of his cure chair and rose. "I can't stay," he said. "You have to help me."

"Whatever you want," Leo said. Lying so close to Ephraim's chair, he'd felt the tension building in his friend. *Rosa, Gemma, Rosa, Gemma.* If he himself had someone he loved, a family and a home of his own, he too would go.

He followed Ephraim to the front of their room and held open the carpetbag that Ephraim took from his metal locker. Ephraim stuffed into it two shirts, a pair of pants, three books; because it was very cold that night—the rest of us, still on the porches, were complaining to each other —he was wearing almost everything else he owned.

"People on the outside are going to notice those," Leo said, pointing at the pajama bottoms hanging below the hems of Ephraim's thick wool pants.

Ephraim stripped, handed the bottoms to Leo, and put the pants back on. Leo added the pajamas to the carpetbag along with a knitted scarf of his own and then stood looking at his friend.

"You'll leave tonight?"

"It's the best thing," Ephraim replied. "I'll get a ride into the village with someone I know, then take the first train out from there. If I try to leave from here tomorrow, Dr. Petrie is going to stop me. It's not his fault, he has to do it. But it's not my fault I have to go."

"It's not," Leo agreed. "But I worry about you. I have three dollars—would you take that?"

"Thank you," Ephraim said. "You know I'd do the same for you. There's one other thing, though."

"Should I make up a story about where you've gone?"

"They'll know," Ephraim said. "But I don't think they'll bother to look for me once I'm safely off their hands. They just don't want to be responsible for letting me leave."

He reached into the locker again, pulling from behind some books the small metal box Leo had last seen when the young man had visited from Ovid. "Felix said a friend of his would come for this before summer. Could you keep it until he gets here?"

"Whatever you want. You don't want to bring it home?"

"Better it should stay here," Ephraim said. "This way I know that it will get to the right person."

"I'll take care of it," Leo said, embracing his friend at the door. "You have no idea how much I'm going to miss you."

"I have an exact idea," Ephraim said, smiling wryly. "I wish I could say I'll be back soon, but if all goes well I won't."

"She'll get better," Leo said, quickly stuffing the metal box into his own locker. In Odessa, in the months before he'd left, he'd known wild-eyed men with boxes hidden under their beds, boxes holding pistols, ammunition, knives, foreign currency, fevered tracts; he'd left in part to escape their frenzy and he resented Ephraim's friend for bringing that shadow here. Still, of course, he would do what Ephraim asked. "You'll get better, too," he predicted. "I'll come and see you in Ovid as soon as I'm discharged."

Ephraim waved, scouted the corridor to make sure it was empty, and then without a word to the rest of us—not those who'd known him since the beginning, not those who, until Leo's arrival, had thought of ourselves as his closest friends—he tiptoed along the corridor, down the stairs, and out the kitchen door.

⁓

AFTER EPHRAIM LEFT, the women among us began to play a larger role at the Wednesday sessions. All the first speakers had been men; to make up for that imbalance, a string of women—all of whom had been here longer than Leo, which meant deferring Leo's talk yet again—now spoke as we began our new year. Sophie started, describing the settlement house she'd worked at before she became sick, and how she'd taught English and history to people like us at night. Pearl, who until her money ran out had been in a cure cottage not as fancy as Mrs. Martin's house but still nice enough, and who'd had stretches when she was nearly well, then spoke about her weeks working as an extra on a movie shot here in the village, where the frozen rivers and the gray cloudy sky had stood in for the Klondike. After that, we had some discussions in the halls and over dinner about the direction of our talks.

We'd enjoyed those last two, especially Pearl's lively account of her brief acting career, but how anecdotal and personal did we want these afternoons to become? Did we want to discuss how we treated our children's winter colds, how one of us made a tender brisket and how another turned rags into braided rugs? These matters too were important, some of us argued. And interesting. Yet they also made us miss even more the lives we'd left behind. Better, safer, to steer our talks back toward the territory Miles had first established: science, art, ideas. Celia, who was a good deal older than the rest of us and had lived in Russia until she was twenty-three, offered to discuss the work of Anton Chekhov.

"A Russian writer," she said, one January Wednesday. Still she spoke English with a heavy accent. "Very famous there although not yet here."

Because she'd developed symptoms in her knees and hips, she preferred to speak sitting down, moving only her hands. Against her heavy green jacket, they seemed unusually white. Like us, she said, Chekhov had suffered from tuberculosis, dying of it in his early forties but before then writing strange and wonderful plays, which at first hardly anyone understood. Stuck in sanatoria far from the city, he knew, she said, what our lives were like. "His stories are as beautiful as his plays—I like best a volume called *Khmurye liudi*. In English *Gloomy People*," she said with a smile. "Or *Gloomy Folk*, like us."

When she tried to summarize for us some of the stories she'd treasured, she grew frustrated and said that with all writers, but especially Chekhov, summary ruined everything: beauty lay in the story itself, the particular arrangement of sentences. But she promised that if any of us were interested, she'd try translating a story or two—and in fact Leo, whose own Russian was very rusty, and several of the rest of us took her up on this and later enjoyed the results.

Still, despite those diverting sessions, we missed Ephraim more than we might have expected. His steadiness and his easy sense of humor, which had often lightened our moods, disappeared just when they were most needed. Week after week, the news from the outside world was bad, and we found ourselves talking constantly about the war. In New Jersey an enormous shell-assembly plant blew up, half a million shells exploding while people all over the area trembled at the noise. After we heard that, Lydia, with her great gift for practical invention, brought to her session a working model of a sprayer she'd originally designed to mist fruit trees. If the country went to war, she said, she'd submit the model and her patent application to the War Department, along with notes on how to adapt it to spread an ignitable fog of gasoline.

We tried to imagine such a device and shuddered when we did. Our concentration wavered; how could we appreciate Nan's discussion about the suffrage movement when just before that the German government announced that their submarines would now attack all ships, including

American ships, entering the blockade zone surrounding Great Britain, and when the president severed relations with Germany in response? Passenger ships were being torpedoed, people were drowning: it was as if the German government *wanted* the United States to enter the war, and that, we thought, made no sense at all. In the library we passed sections of our newspapers back and forth and sometimes smuggled them into our rooms.

A week after Valentine's Day, Kathleen, who'd been a music teacher at a progressive elementary school in Utica, wheeled into the solarium an upright piano, which the women among us knew as well as we knew our own cure chairs; it came from our sitting room. We'd spent hours playing it, cursing the sour notes, singing in groups around it, but for the men it was a surprise. Thumping, pounding, singing loudly over her own playing and shouting directions as she played—*Here* you must imagine woodwinds, *daaaah, da-da-da-da da-daaah*, calling and answering like birds . . . Now the strings! All at once, *DUM, dum-dum-dum-dum; DUM*—Kathleen squeezed through that worn old instrument a reduction of Stravinsky's shocking ballet, *Le Sacre du printemps*. The orchestral version, she assured us, was just as chaotic and fragmented as what she rendered for us. More so really—a new kind of music, which she was just beginning to learn for herself from a recording.

We remember that session with particular clearness, and not only because of what Kathleen's playing would later signify. The men were dazzled by her knowledge and skill, while the women, who'd earlier heard her distill Rimsky-Korsakov and Mussorgsky, were fascinated by the music itself, and by our growing realization that life in the men's and women's annexes had been more different than we'd thought.

We questioned each other, and her, intently. We had a wonderful talk. Gleaming beneath it was an intuition that time would later confirm: Kathleen's session was one of the few when we were nearly whole. Except for Ephraim, all the members of our little group were present that day:

Leo, Dr. Petrie, Irene, and Eudora; Celia, in the first stages of translating her Chekhov stories, and Polly, getting ready to talk the following week about poetry; also Sophie, Pearl, and Lydia, who'd already surprised us with their talks. Ian was there, with new advertisements his brother had sent from the Erector plant; Arkady and Abe, now arguing over every page of something Celia had given them to read about a penal colony on Sakhalin Island; Pietr, who'd been in bed for six weeks, talking to David, who was doing so well he dreamed of being discharged; Olga and Nan, who despite having quarreled had each refused to miss a session and so sat on opposite sides of our circle. Jaroslav, who played the violin, was discussing the possibility of duets with Kathleen. Bea was showing off the embroidered slippers she'd been given for her thirty-first birthday to Sean, who was wishing he'd given them to her. Zalmen, Frank, Otto, and Seth, united by their joint plan to settle in Utica and start a tool-and-die shop once they were cured, leaned toward each other while Albert, always dreamy, wondered under the influence of the music how his mother and father had met. We were all there, with our hopes and plans, our clashing and mingling purposes, our delight in what Kathleen had done and—Naomi was sitting near Eudora but Miles was off to one side, alone; how did none of us see it?—our shared neglect of Miles.

WHEN MILES SKIPPED the next session, on the last day of February, we hardly noticed at first. That day Polly told us about Carl Sandburg, a performance as surprising in its own way as Kathleen's. Only Polly's two closest friends, Olga and Nan (they'd made up by then), had known before that Polly wrote poems herself, or that she followed new poetry as avidly as our library and her own very limited budget permitted. From Sandburg's book *Chicago Poems*, she read pieces nothing like those we'd learned in school. No fancy language, no kings and floating princesses or holy grails. These were about the copper wire strung between the telephone poles and carrying our voices. About hoboes and soldiers and factory workers, ships that heaved like mastodons, the windows shining in railroad cars, the mist and the fog and prairie cornfields and, yes, the war—but not what the men who sat safely in warm rooms imagined it to be. These poems described the war as it looked to men fighting it, and we had never heard anything like them. We listened—Polly read well—and then pulled our chairs into a tighter circle to look at some passages more closely. Only as we bent our heads together did we realize that Miles was absent and with him, of course, Naomi.

We learned why the following week, when they returned. As David, who'd arrived at Tamarack State six months before Leo and had once worked in Mexico, explained the implications of the newly published document the newspapers called "the Zimmerman telegram," Miles listened impassively. David read out loud the German telegram as it had been translated and printed in the papers, six weeks after it was sent:

Berlin, January 19, 1917. On the first of February we intend to begin submarine warfare unrestricted. In spite of this, it is our intention to endeavor to keep neutral the United States of America. If this attempt is not successful, we propose an alliance on the following basis with Mexico: That we shall make war together and together make peace. We shall give general financial support, and it is understood that Mexico is to reconquer the lost territory in New Mexico, Texas, and Arizona . . .

It hadn't been even a year, David reminded us, since Pershing took American troops into Mexico in pursuit of the revolutionary general Pancho Villa; hardly a month since those troops had withdrawn; the Mexicans were eager to pay the Americans back. On a map David showed us how easily that territory might be reclaimed. We thought of Canada, just a few miles away, and how we'd feel if the Germans had proposed an alliance with them. The war, we understood then, was here.

Some of us drifted away when David finished speaking, while others continued talking in twos and threes. Only the handful of us clustered around Dr. Petrie noticed how, as Miles made his way toward us, he stepped as if the bones in his feet had been shattered. Six inches, six inches, six. Finally he reached our group and stopped.

"I have to tell you," he began, his eyes fixed on Dr. Petrie's chest. The pause that followed was long enough to silence the rest of us and make us turn toward him.

"To tell you," he tried again.

Dr. Petrie reached for his hand. "You don't feel well," he said. "Please, sit down."

Miles backed a few inches away. "My friend was killed," he said quietly. "My friend in France. I wanted you to know."

"Not Lawrence!" Dr. Petrie said.

Miles nodded. "Gassed," he whispered.

Seth began to cough as the rest of us wondered whether to draw closer to Miles or to leave him and Dr. Petrie alone. We kept our places. Still looking at Dr. Petrie's chest, Miles said that since hearing the news he hadn't left his room, until today.

"I'm sorry," Dr. Petrie said, gently touching one hand to Miles's jacket. Behind him the rest of us mumbled our regrets; this was the first personal thing Miles had ever told any of us other than Dr. Petrie, and we didn't know how to respond. "I'm glad you were able to come here."

"It's what got me out of bed. I missed you. I missed this."

Embarrassed, but also touched, we continued to stand there clumsily. After a minute, Miles took some folded papers from his jacket pocket and handed them to Leo, who was standing closest to Dr. Petrie. "Lawrence wrote this not long before he died," Miles said of the first sheet, gesturing to Leo to pass it around. "You can see . . ."

Not what he saw, probably: but as each of us in turn read the scrawled words we grasped that the letter was terrible. Reluctantly we took the second sheet, this one the letter from Lawrence's father announcing his son's death. Together they were so sad that we didn't know where to look or what to say. Pietr rubbed his eyebrows, Arkady mumbled a word. Seth, still coughing into a paper handkerchief, stepped away. Leo put the sheets in Dr. Petrie's hand, as if he couldn't bear to give them back to Miles himself. Dr. Petrie kept up a steady murmur of consolation but the rest of us were useless. We could not, after all, touch a man like him, and we had no idea how or if he prayed.

TO OUR SURPRISE, Miles returned the following Wednesday and sat mutely, very close to Naomi although not touching her, during Jaroslav's explanation of cinematography cameras. Until a few years ago Jaroslav had worked at a studio in New Jersey, repairing and maintaining their equipment, and although he didn't have a camera he was able, with a few sketches and some strips of paper cut to the width of film stock, to show us how the film spooled on rollers between the two magazines tucked inside each camera box. He diagrammed the sprockets and the corresponding perforations in the film, and also the clever mechanism that moved the film in synchrony with the opening of the lens shutter, exposing it at the rate of sixteen frames per second. Our eyes, he said, when confronted with images shot and projected at that speed, magically converted stillness into motion.

We listened eagerly, some of us taking notes; we loved our movie nights, which never came often enough, and it was a pleasure to know more about what we saw. Polly and Bea noticed, despite their absorption, the way Naomi kept shifting away from Miles's legs, which occasionally tilted in her direction. Zalmen and Abe saw, instead, the way that Miles, despite his recent loss, tried to concentrate on Jaroslav's explanations.

"In its essence," Jaroslav continued, "cinematography *freezes* light, storing it like ice in an icebox. During projection, the light is released again in measured quantities, animating what would otherwise seem dead."

He paused while Sophie, who had recently relapsed, coughed, choked, coughed more violently, shook off Bea's whispered offer of help, wiped her running eyes, and subsided. Then, thoughtfully, he tried to link his subject to what Miles had taught us. "Perhaps," he said, "the reconstruction of living action from still images isn't so different from the effort to reconstruct creatures from fossilized bones."

"That," Miles said unsmilingly, "is a preposterous analogy."

Arkady and Sean exchanged glances and Lydia frowned as Jaroslav paused, his feelings clearly hurt. He hurried through the rest of his presentation and then left the room, in the company of Pietr and Abe. The rest of us filed out more slowly. Often we left our sessions elated, hovering in the corridor or in front of the windows to talk more about what we'd just learned, but Miles's comment squelched us. He was grieving, we knew. His words had been instantaneous, unconsidered—but somehow seemed worse because of that, as if all along he'd found our presentations foolish but no longer had the energy to conceal it. Halfway down the hall, in front of a freshly painted exam room, Nan said to David, "He probably didn't mean to do that."

"But it's who he *is*," David replied. "That's the trouble."

Behind them the solarium had emptied out except for Leo, who'd stepped into the alcove to the left of the fireplace, and Miles, who a minute later came to stand beside him. Leo was gazing out the window, and he jumped when Miles said, "Won't you be late for your supper?"

"I didn't know you were still here," Leo said.

"I can't go anywhere until Naomi's ready. She wanted to talk with Eudora about something, so . . ." He gestured toward the pair outside, walking in the frozen garden. "I wish she wouldn't keep me waiting like this."

Leo, who'd stayed behind simply to watch Eudora, nodded absently.

"It doesn't seem fair," Miles added, clicking his fingernails against the window as if Naomi might hear him. "Especially not now. Last week I got some letters that Lawrence wrote me and never got the chance to send. One of his friends found them and mailed them on. It's so—reading words he wrote months ago, hearing his voice in my head when I know he's gone—I can't explain what that feels like."

"I'm sorry," Leo said, meaning it despite his absorption in the scene below, and his annoyance at the way Miles had treated Jaroslav.

"They're too grim to show anyone," Miles said. "If people here really knew what was going on there, they would want—"

"To stay out of it?" Leo said.

Miles looked at him appraisingly. "To get *into* it. I'm sure we'll declare war any day now, but why have we already wasted so much time? We should have committed ourselves much earlier. If we had, maybe Lawrence wouldn't be dead."

Below Leo, a shadow moved across the drift—it had finally snowed—and from above a bird plunged. Back home, he thought, in the marshes and hollows he'd known as a boy, all the men must have gone off to fight, leaving behind only the birds and the fish and the empty forest. Lawrence wouldn't be dead if he hadn't volunteered; how would it help to send more men after him?

"One thing I can't stop thinking about," Miles said. "Jaroslav reminded me of it, when he mentioned the fossil bones. Lawrence wrote that some nights, when he was lying awake in the mud, he thought of the river we floated down as a river through time. He said for him, our boat journey might have started in the nineteenth century, in his father's world, and mine. When it ended it dropped him into another century and another world."

They looked out the window again, eyes averted from each other, fixed on the women below. Lawrence, Miles continued, had described all too vividly the trench walls where he was stuck, slick and slippery and caving in daily, dotted with bones and body parts: a nightmare version, he'd written, of the cliffs from which they'd excavated the cleanly layered fossils.

"It makes me sick," Miles said, slapping his hand against the window-sill. "Not just his death, but what happened before it, what's in those letters—I think he *wanted* to die. What's wrong with the French and the British, that they can't organize matters better than this? The inefficiency, the sheer waste of life and idealism—when we get over there, when Americans are in charge, things will be different."

"Will they?" Leo said, not thinking how his words might sound.

"Of course they will," Miles said. "If you saw the way my cement plant runs, or the way Edward's factories are organized—we'd never let men rot like this. Not just physically but morally, spiritually. Lawrence and his friends were trapped."

Leo tried to envision Miles's cement plant in Doylestown. Different from the sugar refinery, not chaotic and filthy but well run and organized, workers calmly tending their machines before stopping for useful after-hours classes, encouraged by small rewards to produce more and still more—was that what Miles meant? Those same men, overseas, would climb docilely out of the trenches and march toward the bullets.

He glanced down and saw that Eudora was leaving the garden; the sky had darkened further and he'd missed his chance to speak with her again. "I wish I could help," he said to Miles. "Truly."

Miles drew himself up a bit straighter. "It was kind of you simply to listen. I expect you have to go—"

"—to supper," Leo said. "But I'll see you next week."

~⌒~

LEO TOLD NO ONE about this conversation; only later would the rest of us hear a version of what, at the time, seemed private. His imagination was dark with those images of Lawrence, and he felt more sympathy for Miles than he would have thought possible. He was startled—all of us were—to hear later that, while we were sitting down to supper, Miles had stopped by Dr. Petrie's office. There he spoke not about Lawrence and the letters, but about Naomi.

"Maybe you could talk to her *for* me?" he asked. "Convince her to give me a chance . . ."

"Convince her, more likely, to avoid you completely," Dr. Petrie said impatiently. Hadn't they already talked about this? "I know this is a terrible time for you, it's natural to look for comfort anywhere you can find it—but infatuations are as common up here as colds. You need to find some way to control this. I would never have expected you to take these feelings so seriously."

"I gave her the book Edward gave me," Miles said miserably. "That was terrible of me, but I thought she'd like it because it's old, and a curiosity. But she didn't, and—"

"Look *outward*," Dr. Petrie said. Even to himself he sounded harsh, but nothing was more important than preserving Miles's health. "Stop focusing so much on yourself. Naomi can't console you for losing Lawrence. There isn't a person up here who hasn't lost a friend or a family member. Do you think you're alone?"

Miles slumped once more in the gray chair. "You think I am self-indulgent," he said. "You think I'm ridiculous."

"Not at all," Dr. Petrie said wearily. "I'm only trying to help. Of course you're grieving, you've had a terrible blow. No wonder you feel confused. But sometimes the best cure is to think about other people, involve yourself in their lives. The way you helped Lawrence when he was a boy."

"If you had lost someone," Miles said, "I would be more sympathetic. Or if you were in love."

Later he sent Dr. Petrie this:

I do thank you for your conversation and advice. I take it seriously.
I know I should have written, should now be writing, further letters of
consolation and condolence to Edward. I know I should tell him about the

awful letters that Lawrence wrote to me and maybe I should send them on: but I can't, they're all I have left of him. Nor can I let go of my hopes for Naomi. What else am I to look forward to?

I am taking one bit of your advice at least. Lawrence is gone, I can't help him; perhaps I can help someone else. It has struck me that Leo Marburg seems more than a little lost since his roommate has left us. I have formulated a plan that may assist him, which I hope to discuss with him, and then you, sometime soon. In the meantime I promise not to trouble you with personal matters again

12

ON THE MONDAY following Jaroslav's talk, Leo fell asleep on the porch during afternoon rest hours and woke to the hollow *chock, chock, chock* of someone splitting wood near the barns, a sound that in the last moments of his dream made him see an ax in his cousin's stout arms and his mother, framed between two giant beech trees, smiling off to one side. Rising groggily, already late, he pushed open the door of his room and, turning toward the library, nearly crashed into Miles.

"Sorry," said Miles, who still had his overcoat on, buttoned up to the neck. "I know I'm not supposed to be here."

"That's true," Leo agreed. "We're not allowed to have visitors in our rooms."

"I'm not exactly a *visitor*," said Miles.

Leo drew a breath, remembering all that Miles had lost. "Who are you looking for?"

"You," Miles said, "actually. I want to talk to you about something." As

Leo struggled not to look at the clock on the wall—so little time to work before supper, and so much he wanted to do—Miles added, "I think you should consider coming to stay at Mrs. Martin's house."

"I'm sorry?"

"At my expense," Miles continued. "A room just opened up on the first floor. It's not the nicest one; it's in the front, and modestly sized. But it's clean, and private, and very much nicer than here. Plus Mrs. Martin keeps a marvelous table."

Leo shivered, too cold in the windy corridor to think of the right thing to say. As if he'd leave when Ephraim might still come back and when, two floors below him, Irene and Eudora were working with equipment that might someday be available to him. In the weeks since his visit to the basement, he'd been slowly, painfully, trying to recover what he'd once known. *Thus matter does not disappear and is not created, but only undergoes various physical and chemical transformations—that is to say, changes its locality and form. Matter remains on the earth in the same quantity as before; in a word it is, so far as we are concerned, everlasting.* Somehow that sounded more surprising in English than he remembered it being in Russian. All of it surprised him, really; digging down through the rubble that, during his six years in New York, had buried his mind, he'd felt like a worker excavating a subway tunnel. He'd set himself the task of relearning all of Mendeleeff's book, not because Irene expected it—he knew she didn't— or because he needed more than a scrap of that knowledge to help her out in the laboratory, but because he was looking forward, still, to speaking at one of our Wednesday gatherings and he wanted to draw not on his scattered, broken American self but on who he really was.

"I can't," he finally said, drawing his hands up into his sleeves. "Those places are very expensive, not to mention all the doctors' bills I'd have. I could never pay you back."

"It's not a loan," Miles said. He'd lost weight in the last few weeks and his shirt, which normally fit so tidily, gaped at the neck. "It's a gift. Room, board, medical care—it's what I'd give Lawrence, if he needed it. Since I can't help him any longer, I'd like to be of some service to you. When we're both better, I thought I could offer you work as a chemist at my plant. The work you were trained for."

Leaning forward, his lips trembling, he rested one hand on the doorframe—too upset, Leo assumed, by the very thought of Lawrence to remember the rule against touching the woodwork. "Cement can be interesting," Miles added. "The nature and proportion of the lime, the temperature and time in the kiln and the grinding of the clinker, the exact blending of the different constituents, the lime with the silica and the alumina—everything depends on the skill and accuracy of the chemist. I need good help."

"That's kind of you," Leo said, "truly, but . . ." Once more he caught himself, continuing as patiently as he could. "Unfortunately," he said, "my training's in quite a different area. Fermentation chemistry, mostly. Organic chemistry."

The chemistry, his teacher had explained years ago, of carbon and its compounds—vegetable matter, animal matter, wax and oil and tar and wood, wine and vinegar and starch. Everything alive, which had nothing to do with gray cement. Each day he'd been working through a few of Mendeleeff's pages. Carbonic anhydride, formed during alcoholic fermentation and found in nature near extinct volcanoes and in caves and mountain fissures, had been this morning's lesson. Insects flew into those hollows and died, Mendeleeff wrote in one of his footnotes. Also the birds chasing the insects, and the animals pursuing the birds. A man mining or digging a well in such an area may be suffocated. In a sunny classroom, Leo remembered, he'd once placed a mouse in a bell jar and measured the amount of carbon it expelled before it died.

"Don't you want to think about my offer?" Miles said.

"I wouldn't be any use to you," said Leo. "Anyway I wouldn't leave my friends here." He gestured toward Miles's hand, still grasping the door-frame. "You should wash before you go."

Miles lifted his fingers from the wood. "I'm trying to *help* you," he said stiffly. "Mrs. Martin's house has amenities that this place can't provide. I thought the arrangement might be good for both of us, but I see I was wrong."

He turned and hurried away, the hand that had been touching the wood now held, Leo noted, some inches from his body, just as if he were someone healthy enough to worry about getting sick.

That evening, alone in his room with a newspaper propped against his knees—the czar had abdicated, the czar had abdicated: no matter how many times he read the headline and the columns that followed, he couldn't believe it—Leo reviewed Miles's offer only to dismiss it again. Why would Miles think he'd accept that kind of charity? In Russia, he read, everything was on the verge of changing, the rational and harmonious order so many had proposed for so long about to sweep away the corrupt, the foolish, and the antiquated; every day brought a new astonishment. The people rose up, the czar fell down, a provisional government appeared by what seemed like consensus: how could this be? If only he could talk with Ephraim. Since his friend's departure he'd been trying to imagine the community in Ovid and what might be going on there. What might go on here, if we were left to our own devices. In Russia everything seemed possible but here—here, we seemed blocked at every turn, the conversations of our Wednesday afternoons the one place we were free.

NOW, WHEN THE February Revolution seems like a child's dream and we've seen the consequences of the Bolsheviks' October triumph, when we read daily the terrible news of Russia's civil war and dread what comes next, the optimism of those weeks seems laughable. But it didn't feel that way, then. It felt, Leo thought—many of us thought—as if we were walking into a new world. During the last two weeks of March we had two more excellent gatherings, Pietr talking about the constellations visible from our porches, and then Zalmen and Seth, together describing the design and manufacture of machine tools; these raised everyone's spirits and even Miles, so quiet since Lawrence's death, asked questions at both sessions. Those were the same weeks during which Leo, working steadily, regained his old familiarity with Mendeleeff's work and borrowed other books from Dr. Petrie and Irene, which delighted both of them. Meanwhile Eudora, who cheered Leo on whenever she saw him, nearly finished tuning up the old X-ray apparatus.

Three or four nights a week, sometimes with Irene and sometimes alone, she'd been working in the basement. Finally she understood what Naomi had meant about her hand seeming to draw without conscious instruction; her own hands seemed to understand the tubes and wires without interference from her brain. She couldn't explain to Irene why she did what she did; she couldn't have written down what she was doing or justified her actions according to any rules. Yet as she stared at the apparatus, her hands knew that this part should be moved here and that part there, this connection resoldered. It looked better that way; it made more sense. When the images improved, even she was surprised. It wasn't so different, really, from the implements and appliances in her parents' house, which she'd always been the one to repair. She'd sharpened her father's skinning knives, fixed the telephone when it broke, repaired not only her own bicycle but everyone else's too. Only Naomi's Model T had eluded her—and that, she thought, watching the dead animals yield their secrets under her hands, might after all have been because she'd known it was something Naomi wanted to keep as her own.

Naomi, during those March weeks, found herself watching Leo even more closely. With Ephraim gone, his face radiated a kind of loneliness that she herself had known as a child and, now that Eudora never had

time for her, was painfully feeling again. No wonder, if Leo felt so abandoned, that he'd be driven to spending most of his free time in the library
with the books Irene had given him. Old things, useless things. Anything
to fill his empty hours. She'd examined Irene's frizzy hair and worn face,
her shapeless dress and absurd purple glove, and reassured herself that
however much Leo liked her books, he could not like *her*. If Irene meant
to Leo what Miles meant to her, she had nothing to worry about. How
tiresome Miles was when he caught her alone! He pulled his chair close
and couldn't stop talking: had she enjoyed the book he'd given her, did
she like old things?

Like me, he meant. What did she care about his interests? The book
had left thick brown smudges on her hands and clothes and she couldn't
stand to touch it. If Miles would just give his books to Irene, they could
talk with each other and leave her and Leo alone. She had her own plans,
the thought of which made her able to smile blandly at Miles no matter
what he said.

ON APRIL 3, the day after President Wilson went to Congress and asked
for a declaration of war, Naomi drove up the hill to Tamarack State,
parked near the power plant, and entered the men's annex through the
service door. Although it was spring by the calendar, the ground was still
frozen, the woods thick with snow, and Leo was in the library, as he was
during every free hour. The door to his room was partway open and
Naomi knocked on it twice.

Then as now we live without locks; when no one answered she slipped
inside, hoping that Leo would be alone and eager to see her and perhaps
also, at the same time, hoping that he'd be absent and she'd be able to
root among his belongings without distraction. He wasn't there. She shut
the door behind her and sped through the room to the porch, where she
examined the blankets piled on Leo's cure chair, concealing the layers of

newspaper; the soapstone pig, presently cold; the two volumes of Mendeleeff's book balanced on the little table between the chairs; the second chair, oddly bleak, which had been Ephraim's. Tentatively she stretched out on it and convinced herself she was seeing what Leo saw. Hill, hill, hill, hill, trees and trees and trees. Only the clouds marching from west to east were pleasant to look at. Dark birds rose from the trees, circled around, and settled again; what were they? She imagined Leo, lying a yard away, reaching out a hand to say he loved her.

"Leo?" Abe called.

His chair was a few yards farther down the porch, beyond one of the thin partitions that still, then, marked off territories specific to each room. Silently Naomi retreated inside and inspected Leo's bed, not just the sheets but the blankets, the pillowcases, the movable tray table that slipped over his legs so that he might eat or write with ease. She investigated the nightstand, the lamp, and the stubby pencils jumbled, inside the nightstand drawer, with white quartz pebbles and pinecones. She inspected the slippers beneath the bed and then, moving toward the front of the room, the little cubicle containing the washbasin, the toilet, and the two metal lockers. His clothes were here and the rest of his belongings. Wool pants hung from a hook; she slid her face along the fabric and then sniffed a sweater she'd seen him wear. More clothes, as well as a laundry bag to investigate. She had a few minutes to herself.

And then Eudora walked by the door to Leo's room, as she did most afternoons. Seeing it closed—we were required to keep our doors at least halfway open during our free time, so the nurses and orderlies could spy on us—she knocked twice and, worried at getting no answer, opened it. What she found was not Leo slumped over the sink or hemorrhaging in bed but Naomi, perched on a chair with some clothes at her feet, her hands filled with papers, a metal box on her lap.

"What are you *doing*?" Eudora said. Swiftly, before anyone else could come by, she closed the door behind her. When she turned back she saw Naomi's hand emerging from her waistband. "What do you have?"

"Nothing," Naomi stammered. "I was just—I saw his door was open and I wanted to come in for a minute and see his things. The locker was already open, sort of . . ."

"You know it wasn't," Eudora said, walking over to the chair, as close to slapping her friend as she'd ever been.

"Well, it wasn't locked, anyway," Naomi said, for the first time seeming embarrassed. "Then I saw this box under a sweater and I took it out. I know I shouldn't have, but once I looked inside, I couldn't put it down."

What was it, Eudora wondered, that so drew Naomi toward Leo? As she reached over for her friend's hand, she remembered an October afternoon, not long after Leo had first joined Ephraim in this room. All day rain had been falling and at four o'clock, when the shift changed, the sky had been nearly dark. Along with a few nurses and kitchen helpers and other ward maids she'd stood near the main entrance for half an hour, waiting for a break in the weather and gossiping about the doctors and patients. Leo's name kept coming up. The way he looked: not that he was so handsome, a dishwasher said—not at all, a nurse's aide agreed, he was too bony, and his hands were so large they were frightening—but more that even when he was with a group at the dinner table, he seemed alone. As if, another aide said, he needed not so much company as a companion.

Clarice, who had served Leo his dinner the first night he joined us, and who'd been married twice and widowed once, smiled slyly and said that if he was healthier, and she was younger, she'd be tempted to take advantage of him. His eyes were part of it, someone else claimed, while the rain dripped steadily from the breezeway. But not just his eyes. Eudora, listening alertly, had tried to fit this with what she'd noticed as she tidied his room each day. She hadn't seen that in Leo, herself; both Leo and Ephraim interested her but they were always talking when she came by and she hadn't wanted to interrupt them. Only after Ephraim left had she seen how solitary Leo seemed, and how Naomi's whole body tensed in his presence. Just now she was so rigid that her hand, when Eudora touched it, felt like wood.

"Let go of that," Eudora said, tugging at the open box. Reluctantly, Naomi held it out.

On top of some newspaper articles lay a pencil. Next to it was what looked like its mate, reduced to parts: two slim wooden halves, one with a centered groove running down its entire length, the other with an identical groove that cradled a very slender tube, nipped at the middle like a waist.

Eudora leaned over and pointed at the tube. "Shouldn't the lead go there?" she asked. She picked up the intact pencil and examined the tip, which didn't look right and felt glassier than a normal pencil's tip.

Naomi held out a piece of paper. "This was in there too," she said. "Something Leo drew, I think. Isn't that his handwriting?"

A diagram, Eudora saw, in which the wooden halves of the dissected pencil had been drawn side by side, accompanied by Leo's comments. *Pencil soaked in water until the halves came apart. That's how the lead was removed and the tube inserted. When the two halves are glued back together the pencil appears nearly normal.*

He'd labeled the bottom of his drawing of the slim glass tube, *Chlorate of potash mixed with sugar*; the top, *Sulfuric acid*. A paragraph connected by an arrow to the pencil's tip noted: *Capillary action forces acid down into the mixture when the tip is broken and air is admitted. A very hot flame appears instantly.*

He really *was* a chemist, Eudora thought. But how had he come by this?

"I wonder if it works," Naomi said. She reached over and scratched the tip of the intact pencil with her thumbnail. "I can't believe this would catch fire if I just snapped off a little piece . . ."

Eudora snatched the box away. "Whatever this is, it's Leo's. You shouldn't even *be* here."

As Naomi rolled her eyes, Eudora took the diagram from her, asked if it had been folded, and when Naomi said no, slipped it back in the box. "Was it under the pencils?"

"On top," Naomi said. "Like that." Even now, she didn't apologize.

"What else did you disturb?"

Naomi held her hands up, palm out, in front of her chest. "I just looked at that one thing."

Eudora frowned and returned the box to the back of the locker. Then she closed the door and stood aside as Naomi moved the chair back next to the sink. "Maybe you should tell him how you feel. Either he's interested, or he isn't. Why should you live in this kind of uncertainty?"

"That's not the point," Naomi said angrily. "He has to tell me first, for it to count. He can't just want me because I want him. He has to feel like that by *himself*. To want me worse than anything."

Eudora let that pass, suggesting instead, "What if you did something to help him, which would also help him to notice you? You could bring him some books, maybe, from the town library . . ."

"I'm not interested in what he's *reading*," Naomi said. "Why would you think—"

"—think what?" Leo said, walking in just then.

The fingers on his right hand were stained with ink and his wool pants badly needed mending. His hair was shaggy, like everyone's; our barber hadn't visited yet that month. Naomi took a step toward him, but before she could say anything, Eudora seized her arm.

"I'm so sorry," she said, gripping Naomi just above the elbow. "We were walking down the hall together and then Naomi suddenly got dizzy"—*Me!* Naomi thought, pulling her arm free—"and she stumbled."

Twining her hands in her ugly blue apron, Eudora continued to spin her lies. Because she knew how much of his free time Leo spent in the library now, she'd guessed that his room might be empty and had led Naomi inside for a minute's privacy: "So she wouldn't faint. So we wouldn't upset the patients."

How ridiculous, Naomi thought. If she hadn't fainted when her brother died, when her mother took her from Chester or when she first saw a dead body, why would she start now? But Leo must have sensed that, simply from looking at her. She could feel that she was the opposite of pale, her face hot both from the thrill of being in the room with him and from knowing she had a scrap of him tucked between her waistband and her skin.

"You're welcome to use anything you need," he said gently. "Maybe Naomi should lie down on the bed?"

He was looking at Eudora as he said this, but Naomi could feel how much he actually wanted to be looking at her, how conscious he was of her, so nearby. How much he wanted for her to lie down, for Eudora to vanish, for the door to close behind her.

"Really, I'm so sorry," Eudora said again. She looked at him as if try-ing to distract attention from what Naomi had done, while he looked at Eudora as if, Naomi thought, by not looking directly at her he could deny the attraction between them. She stood there, mutely watching, until Eudora seized her elbow again and hustled her away.

THEY HAD A few sharp words in the parking lot—Celia saw them, from her porch, also Sadie and Pearl and Bea—and then Naomi drove home alone, leaving Eudora behind to whatever she did in that basement with Irene. Eudora's annoyance was nothing, Naomi thought, a misunder-standing she could explain away later. What she wanted to think about was that brief encounter with Leo. She was so excited she stalled the car twice and bumped the fender entering the carriage house. Inside, serving dinner, her mouth responding to her mother's orders and the boarders' comments, her eyes avoiding Miles's face, she mulled over all she'd learned. She'd seen a new part of Leo, and she was sure—his eyes were the same transparent blue as her own—that for the first time, he'd really seen *her*. As if that weren't a big enough gift, she also had what she'd stolen.

She'd meant to take a scarf, or a pillowcase—something that, if he were to miss it, he could imagine had been lost in the wash. She would have, if Eudora hadn't barged in and she hadn't had to act so swiftly. On the drive home, she'd been disappointed to end up with something so impersonal, but in the dining room she reconsidered. She served the hazelnut torte, poured coffee, cleared the dishes. By the time she got up to her room and could examine her treasure, it seemed like the one perfect thing. When she rolled it in her hand she told herself: *It's not a pencil*. Then she stood it alongside the others in the cup, the point hidden and the long seam almost invisible—and it *was* a pencil, no different from any other. She could leave it anywhere without a person noticing; carry it in her pencil case or in a pocket. Holding it made her feel like she could see inside Leo's brain.

LEO, WHO DIDN'T know the pencil was missing, went to supper and, as he had done with Miles, told no one about the visit. Not, the rest of us think, because he wanted to hide it, or because he feared what some of us might say (and it's true that any of us could have pointed out Naomi's growing interest in him), but simply because he didn't think it was important. Eudora he'd been thrilled to see, Naomi he'd hardly noticed; he'd taken Eudora's story at face value and forgotten it the minute she left. The box tucked in the back of his locker hadn't crossed his mind. Weeks ago, right after Ephraim's departure, he'd methodically examined everything in it, dissected the pencil, diagrammed its workings, and then, reassured that he knew all he could about it, put it back and moved on to more interesting matters. When he thought about pencils, he thought about a page he'd found in his Mendeleeff: *If sugar be placed in a charcoal crucible and a powerful galvanic current passed through it, it is baked into a mass similar to graphite.* If the sugar refinery in Williamsburg was hit by lightning, would it fuse into a shiny black mass? He'd turned to the footnote below, which concerned the best sources of graphite for pencils: *In Russia the so-called Aliberoffsky graphite is particularly renowned; it is found in the Altai Mountains near the Chinese frontier . . .*

Why should those sentences, about a part of Russia he'd never seen and a substance interesting only for its unusual molecular structure, have caused such a massive fit of homesickness in him? Yet they had, they'd made him see not only the places where he'd lived as a boy but all of Russia spread out in his mind's eye, taiga and tundra and Lake Baikal, St. Petersburg and Moscow, spots as distant from his childhood homes as he was now from California. Just that afternoon, in the library, he'd found an out-of-date atlas and spent his free hour hunched over maps showing the advance and retreat of Napoleon's army, the location of salt mines, the average number of bushels of buckwheat a field might yield. He'd taken notes, without knowing why. When he'd stopped by his room to find Eudora and Naomi confused and guilty-looking inside, his imagination had been a jumble of maps and politics and molecular structures, against which the women had seemed, for a second, as insubstantial as ghosts.

Then Eudora had solidified enough for him to realize that he'd caught her and Naomi in an awkward moment, some female difficulty perhaps, into which it was best not to pry. A waste, he thought; there was no way, given the situation, for him to ease Naomi gently from his room so that he could talk to Eudora alone, although he badly wanted her advice. The atlas, with its hints of home, had made him think about his mother and the dim hours between four and six when she used to go over his lessons with him. She sat on the green sofa with her skirts spread out, one of his books in her hands, and he stood before her. The sun slanted over her left shoulder and onto the pages and her knees. He recited a stanza of a poem or a bit of elementary German, whatever he'd studied for the day, and she read along in the book, checking his recitation. When he was done she smiled, clapped her hands softly together, and held out her arms to him.

So we might applaud, or at least understand him better, once he'd given a Wednesday talk. In the library he'd finally thought of a topic and he'd wanted Eudora's opinion: what if he talked about synthesis, the glory of chemistry? Surely everyone would be interested in that. All scientists, he imagined saying, analyze complex objects and processes, breaking them into smaller and simpler bits until they can be understood. But chemists also, thrillingly, *make* things. Even as a boy, with a schoolboy's tools, he'd made things himself. He could use examples from his Mendeleeff and the books he'd borrowed from Irene and Dr. Petrie to illustrate the process of linking small, simple molecules into larger, more complicated structures, until from what had seemed like thin air something useful arose, essential even, fertilizer or indigo dye.

13

Before Leo had time to propose a talk, our Wednesday sessions were swamped by our need to talk about the war, which President Wilson had just brought us into. A munitions plant had blown up in Pennsylvania and Miles, who knew the plant's owner, was pale with fury; a hundred workers had been killed, he said, and most of the plant destroyed in what was obviously a reaction against the declaration of war, another example of blatant sabotage. None of us can remember now who was meant to speak that Wednesday. Instead, Miles talked about the need for all of us to do our share, despite being unable to fight, and then Sean and Frank started arguing about conscription.

By the time the session ended Leo was ready for supper, tired of our conversation and also of the way, each time he turned his head, he found Naomi staring at him. Afraid to embarrass her further—what had been wrong with her, he wondered, the afternoon she was in his room?—he tried to avoid her, but no matter where he looked, she seemed to be there.

As he left the room he passed Eudora, who stopped him with a touch and said, "How are you doing with your chemistry books?"

"Pretty well," he said. "I've been working every day."

"Me too," she said with a smile. "You should see what I've been doing in the X-ray laboratory."

"I'd love to, if you have the time."

The supper bell rang just as she was saying, "Why don't you let me show you?" Bodies, our bodies, streamed through the corridor. "It's too late today, I guess," she added. "Maybe tomorrow?"

"If you think it would be all right." He stepped into the stream, narrowly missing Pietr, and as the current caught him said, "Four o'clock?"

The next day they met in the basement. Irene was absent and the laboratory door was closed, but Eudora let herself in with her own key, so at home that Leo couldn't help but envy her. Moving past Irene's apparatus, sternly modern and encased in dark metal, she led him down the rear wall of shelves and into a shadowy corner. Outside, the late afternoon sun was still shining, but here it was dark until Eudora turned a switch.

"What do you think?" she said.

The discarded X-ray apparatus looked almost new in the glare, the metal caps gleaming where the electrodes entered the delicate transparent tube. The tube itself, grapefruit-sized, was stained a yellowish brown by the discharge. A long protuberance sprouted like a stalk from one end, with two shorter ones opposite, like roots. The cup-shaped cathode and the slanted disk of the target glittered inside. She'd remounted the whole arrangement on a new stand and placed, between the apparatus and the spot where she stood to control the current, a wooden screen faced with sheet lead. "That screen seems sensible," he said.

"Irene's suggestion," Eudora said. "The shielding on her appliance is built right around the tube, but this is a decent substitute."

A cable snaked from the apparatus across the floor and toward the Snook transformer. On the wall a wooden rack cradled more handblown gas tubes, each shaped a bit differently but all sprouting cylindrical thumbs. "Also Irene's," Eudora said. "Some are ten years old, while others have never been used. They're obsolete now that she has her new Coolidge tube, but for me—it's a wonderful way to learn. What she can do with a single tube and a rheostat, I can do a little more clumsily by finding a tube with the right amount of vacuum. The ones with the most vacuum need a higher voltage to activate them, and produce more penetrating rays."

"So, a shorter exposure time," Leo said. The tiny singed spots dotting her blue wrapper made him wonder just how well she knew her way around the wiring.

She nodded. "The low-vacuum ones take less voltage and give a less penetrating ray. So those take a longer exposure, but then I get finer detail with soft tissue."

The peculiar sensation he felt as she was talking was, as he'd tell Dr. Petrie later, a compound of admiration, envy, delight, and pure curiosity. He'd been working very hard to relearn his old chemistry, but still he could fit only a few hours of study each day into our rigid routine, and even then he didn't have the energy he'd had before getting sick. She'd obviously accomplished far more, despite having only nights and weekends to spare.

He followed her as she moved away from the machine and toward the shallow, glass-topped wooden box mounted on the wall like a picture frame. She'd designed this herself, she said proudly. Irene's handheld contraption allowed only a single image to be viewed at a time, by a single person. But this—she flipped a switch, lighting up the glass within the frame—let them look at a film together, or at several films mounted side by side.

Among the hanging negatives he recognized the dead hawk he'd seen her bring in some weeks ago: skull, spine, wing bones, heart. Another was clearly a rabbit—he could see not only the tiny bones of the feet but also the shadowy outlines of its ears, veined like dragonflies' wings—while others, empty of organs and threaded through with wire and screws, looked like mounted specimens. "Squirrel?" he asked.

"Opossum!"

"Not a Russian animal," he said as she laughed. Six in a row—or not six opossums, but six images of the same creature, identifiable by the pair of scissors trapped inside. The foggiest images were on the left; the sharpest, to the right.

"Different tube for each image," she explained. "I took that last one with the tube that's mounted now."

"Very nice," he said. Did she know how much she'd already learned on her own, or how inventively she'd arranged her results? His teacher in Odessa, who'd had a great passion for laboratory demonstrations, claimed that the best way to remember ideas was by solving practical problems on our own. Because of him, Leo had learned chemistry not in a lecture room but standing with his classmates at a long bench, surrounded by glassware, happily setting fires and shattering beakers and shooting fumes toward the open skylights. Here Eudora, alone except for Irene, seemed to have been going through the same process, which he now remembered as the most absorbing experience of his life.

Gently, as if any false word or move might disturb her work, he said, "How did you get the scissors in there?"

"I didn't—they're stuffers, not scissors, which probably my father left in there by mistake. He made this specimen when he was a little boy."

Leo leaned closer to the sixth and sharpest image, which wasn't perfect but still impressed him. "You've got this apparatus working as well as a new one."

"Almost," she said. "I think Irene will be pleased."

"You haven't shown her yet?"

"I wanted to wait until I could reliably get a good image, and then surprise her."

"Try it out on me," he begged. Suddenly the idea of standing there, a living demonstration into which she could peer, was what he most desired.

She shook her head. "What if I don't have something calibrated correctly?"

"But you already do. Obviously." He pointed at the last of the opossums. "I've been feeling better—maybe we can see what's healed on the films."

Not since the day she and Irene had taken radiographs of each other's chests had she examined the inside of another person. But she knew more now; she'd arrange the exposure as she had with the rabbit, she thought, a soft ray beautifully revealing the blood vessels and the lungs.

"Fine," she said, gesturing to him to stand with her behind the shield. "Take off your shirt."

She couldn't help looking, while the tube warmed up, at the pattern of fine black hair on his chest. The transformer rumbled, the tube hissed, one end of the tube glowed purplish yellow, and the air began to smell like rain. When the tube was ready, she arranged Leo in front of the film holder.

"Hold your breath," she said, just as Irene had once said to her. She slipped in the film and counted.

The tube was alive, he thought. A breathing thing—that was ozone he smelled—glowing and probing inside him, the rays streaming from the target and out the side of the tube, passing through him to trace his rounded image on the film.

Irene was still absent, but Eudora had developed plenty of films with her watching silently, doing no more than nodding her approval. What harm, then, in developing the image alone? In the darkroom, among the comforting eggy stink of the chemicals, she splashed through the familiar steps and was rewarded by ribs, vertebrae, collarbones. Leo's heart, his diaphragm. She was trembling, she noticed. He was standing very close to her, looking over her shoulder, and she could feel the warmth of his body on her back. On the negative she saw the clouds of his lungs, dotted with the scars of healed cavities and a few more dubious spots.

"I shouldn't try to read this," she said. "Irene will have to make you a better one when you're due for another consultation with Dr. Petrie."

"How could she do any better?" Leo said, his chin near her ear. "The detail—that's marvelous."

"I had a feeling that tube would work well with you." Her cheeks were hot and she moved away. "Let's go see if Irene's back."

Still the space outside the darkroom was empty except for them; still it smelled as if lightning had passed through. The machine, cold now, was only a heap of metal and wood, but Eudora's face was pink and haloed by her electrified golden hair. An idea had developed in Leo's mind as he watched the image of his chest appear, and now he blurted it out.

"Would you—we have a movie night coming up in a couple of weeks, would you join us for that? Would you go with me, I mean, that evening?"

She looked as if he'd slapped her. "You, and—me?"

"*Yes*," he replied, catching himself before he reached for her hand. "I've been wanting to ask you. I thought you knew."

She stood, staring at the film, for what seemed to him like a long time. "I didn't," she said. "Not at all." More silence, more staring at the film they'd developed together. "I lied to you earlier, about Naomi," she said. "About what she was doing in your room."

She hadn't led Naomi in there because Naomi felt faint, she confessed; Naomi had entered the room by herself, hoping to see him, or to learn something more about him. Before Eudora completed her awkward story, Leo realized he knew what she meant and he stiffened with embarrassment.

"She's so drawn to you," Eudora concluded. "She doesn't seem able to tell you herself and I wouldn't have told you except . . ."

"Except what?" Had Naomi, he suddenly wondered, written the anonymous note he'd found inside his *Kill-Gloom Gazette*?

"Except it's Naomi you should be taking to the pictures. Obviously."

"But it's not Naomi I'm interested in. I have no interest in her. None."

Then it was his turn to look at the film on the light box. He waited, listening to the air moving raggedly in and out of his lungs—why was he so conscious of his breathing?—until he could add, "It's you I want to see."

"I can't," she said.

"It's just the movies. You might come see them on your own, I know you like them."

"Naomi's my friend," she said.

He caught himself digging the thumbnail of one hand into the palm of the other. "It's not Naomi," he said again. "It's not ever going to be Naomi."

She ran her finger half an inch above the surface of the film, pausing at two different spots before moving on. "All right," she said—a moment which, later, she'd pause over again and again. "I'll meet you there. But just to see the pictures."

ON THE NIGHT after Eudora X-rayed his chest, Leo slipped stealthily past the nurses' station and then down through the kitchen and out the back door, just as Ephraim had done on the night he left us. Once he was beyond the buildings, the grounds, so vast and dark, absorbed him instantly. Down the slope he moved, over the lawns and through the meadow toward the woods, passing a fox trotting up the hill. The sky was clear, the stars were blazing, a moist breeze drifted from the disk of ice still floating in the center of the pond. As he walked down into hollows and then back up, the air felt cool then warm then almost cold against his cheeks and he smelled rotted leaves, wet dirt, sap moving beneath bark, witch hazel, thawing carcasses. The moon, which was nearly full, lit the trees around him.

At dusk he'd heard a chorus of tree frogs, but now the peeping had stopped and whatever had made the slow, clacking sound—a duck, Arkady had said irritably, although Abe claimed that it too was a kind of frog—was also sleeping. A few bats swooped over his head; moths surged around him; a dead duck lay in a puddle. In the moonlight his feet glimmered oddly through the ground fog. The dirty patches of snow, he found, were easier to walk on than the mud.

At the sugar refinery in Williamsburg he'd felt ancient; the other workers had been eighteen or nineteen or even younger, boys in their early teens skittering through the machines. Up here, where most of us were around his age but where we lived at a middle-aged pace, wrapped in our blankets, endlessly resting, he'd felt younger in some ways, older in others. Now, in the cool piney breeze, he felt how young he really was. Twenty-seven! He might still do almost anything, might even without Miles's help find work related to the chemistry he'd once studied. He might find a good job, start a family. When he'd leaned over Eudora's shoulder and seen her holding his ribs in her hand, something had reacted inside him. There were different kinds of chemical reactions, his teacher in Odessa had once explained. Decomposition, displacement, exchange, rearrangement, union . . .

From a tree an owl called; was he in love? Was that the name for this sense that, like the trees, the cattails, the frogs peeping, the geese arrowing overhead, he was springing back to life? Or maybe he was simply in hope, which might be the same thing. Something had been growing in him all winter, just now poking a green tip through the surface; a sense that almost anything might after all be possible. He felt—this astonished him—*grateful.* Not since he was a boy had he had time to think and study and look at the world and himself; and although throughout his stay up here he'd been sick, sometimes terribly so, and had feared for his body, at the same time these past months had been astonishing. Food, shelter, books, the forest, our Wednesday gatherings. The world, unclouded. Eudora. He drew another deep breath and made a modest plan, one step at a time. Study, tell Irene he was ready to work. Work, and then meet Eudora at the movies. There, perhaps . . .

14

BEFORE THE NEXT movie night, though, we had two more Wednesday sessions scheduled, which we were particularly excited about because Irene had finally agreed to take her turn. The rest of us had been flattered that she continued to come to our sessions; she was older than most, better educated than anyone except for Dr. Petrie, and she knew so much about so many things that we couldn't predict what she'd discuss. Poland, Ian hypothesized before that last Wednesday of April. Madame Curie, Kathleen said; we knew she worshipped the Polish scientist. Eudora, wedged between Naomi and a mute and clumsy Leo—he'd hardly been able to speak to her since their session in the darkroom, and he still hadn't asked her advice about his own proposed talk—wondered out loud if Irene might describe some of her first experiments with X-rays. Dr. Petrie worried that she'd mention their work correlating her films with the autopsy reports. But instead she announced something we hadn't even known she was interested in: the work of a German physicist named Albert Einstein.

In our chairs we shifted uneasily; would this be like our first meetings, when Miles had spoken so abstractly, and at such tedious length, about a subject that meant nothing to us? Right away, though, Irene made it clear why we should be interested. This man, she said, had changed our conception of time and shown that what had once been thought to be absolute was really relative. What could be more important? Here at Tamarack State, time passed so slowly that it sometimes seemed to stop entirely, but outside, she said—outside, where men in trenches were dying daily—clocks were ticking relentlessly and time was speeding down a giant hole.

We could *feel* this, she said—that time did not flow at the same speed for all of us, nor did it flow consistently—but until Einstein formulated his theory of relativity no one had articulated what that meant. Around us the walls glowed with the afternoon sun. Kathleen moved her chair so the rays wouldn't shine on her face; Ian moved to make room for her; the movement passed through our circle of chairs like a puff of wind through wheat. Irene said that while many of us might know the theory already, because she herself still wrestled with the basic idea she thought perhaps some of us did as well. Her violet-gloved hand swooped with her words and one lock of hair detached itself from her loosely pinned braid. Both Celia and Pearl, wondering when she'd tuck it back in, kept losing track of her argument.

"Einstein," Irene explained, "published a crucial paper a dozen years ago, in 1905, when he was twenty-six and working as a patent clerk in Berne."

Deftly she wove the strand of hair back into place, describing how she'd paid no attention to that work until, during her first winter at Tamarack State, a Hungarian physicist curing in the village had been sent to her for a radiograph. While she was struggling to get the best view of his chest, he'd tried to explain his own work to her and mentioned how much he relied on Einstein's discoveries. After she'd confessed her ignorance, he sent over some papers for her to read—but these, she said, had only bewildered her further. Yet the central idea was so interesting, and these days so essential, that she wanted to try to explain it.

"Time," she said, catching the eyes of first David and then Seth, Olga and Sophie and finally Pearl, "is not something out there, something beyond us that flows serenely like a river, without any reference to us or our doings; it is not a fixed reference against which our own lives move. It is not background, it is not—

"It is *not*. That's the strangest part of what Einstein said: time is not a thing but a *relationship*. Things moving in relation to each other. All of us grew up thinking that if everything around us disappeared, our world and even the stars in the sky, time and space would still continue on. Einstein says that time and space would disappear together with the things."

Eudora, rapt until now, felt Naomi poking her elbow and looked down to see a note sliding from Naomi's pad of paper onto her lap. Irritated, she looked back at Irene without reading the note but then felt Naomi's hand again. *I'm bored*, Naomi had written. *Aren't you?*

Eudora frowned, slid the note into her pocket, and turned away, only to find herself caught in Leo's gaze. Him on her right, Naomi on her left; where was a person to find any peace? Already she'd begun to fret about agreeing to meet Leo for movie night. Standing there in Irene's laboratory, his chest revealed on the film they'd made, he'd seemed truly transparent. Nowhere had she seen a speck of interest in Naomi, and when he'd dismissed Naomi's feelings for him so firmly, it was almost as if the feelings themselves had disappeared. But Eudora was surprised to find, in the space opened up by that, her own curiosity as to what might happen between the two of them. When she'd accepted his invitation, she'd been thinking of movie night as an experiment akin to trying out a new tube on the machine, which might yield interesting results, or nothing at all.

By the time she turned her attention back to Irene's talk, Pearl and

Sophie had started taking notes. Sophie had a small brown volume on her lap, which Eudora hadn't seen before, while Pearl was writing on a single sheet of paper folded into quarters. Both were using the stubby pencils kept in our library, which we were forbidden to take. Before Einstein wrote that paper, Irene was saying, he'd worked on other problems, important but not revolutionary; no one could have expected what he'd do next. He'd written about Brownian motion, photons, a method for determining the size of molecules . . .

"I read that paper," Leo interrupted. "In German, a few years ago."

Our heads, as if they were attached to a single string, swiveled together. Miles, who'd been irritable all afternoon, sniffed and said, "German science is nothing to be proud of, these days."

"But you wouldn't really call this *German* science," Irene said, impatient with the interruption. "It's just—science."

She turned back to Leo. Obviously he was ready to start the next part of his training, and the timing was right: there'd always been more work than hands to do it but now, with so many doctors and nurses heading overseas, her laboratory might well end up serving the whole village and she could use him right away. Still, she worried about the consequences of him working with Eudora. She'd seen the radiograph of his chest, and while at first she'd been amazed at the quality of the image and delighted to see the old machine so well restored, she'd also been startled to find Eudora experimenting without her. That the subject had been Leo concerned her even more. Twenty years ago, she and her brother-in-law, experimenting eagerly in the first months after the rays were discovered, had in the process of peering into each other's bodies felt a kind of electricity that had nothing to do with an induction coil.

"I was sure I wouldn't be the only person who knew of Einstein's work," she said, seeing even as she smiled at Leo the small, unhealed spot on his left lung: another cause for concern. "In this paper, he's simply exploring the idea that time is not absolute but flows at different rates depending upon where you are and how fast you are moving."

Someone groaned—Polly, perhaps?—and Ian dropped his head in his hands.

"I know it's confusing," Irene said. "I don't really understand it either although I'm told it makes perfect sense mathematically. But the point is just to think about what it means in the most basic terms: that time doesn't move at the same speed for everyone everywhere. You know this is true; we all feel it."

She paused while we murmured and shifted; unlike Miles, she paid attention to the way we responded to her words and she gave us time to try to absorb them. Sophie and Pearl both wrote down her last sentences exactly as she'd said them. Then she continued, "There's so little time, now, between discovering something and applying it. Barely twenty years from the first hints of the Roentgen rays through the early apparatus to the equipment I have downstairs and the portable units in France. Everything moves so quickly. My fingers"—here she held up her glove—"got lost along the way. The lives of my friends. Time was moving slowly for me as I lived it—I think it moves even more slowly for you—but very swiftly in the world of science. Who knows how it moves for a soldier caught in battle? That's not really what Einstein meant when he spoke of time being relative; he sees things mathematically and he was concerned with something different, the speed of light and the nature of energy. But in our everyday lives, we feel his ideas in a different way. Do you know what I mean?"

Leo nodded, as Sophie wrote *What is the speed of light?* and turned her book toward Pearl, who didn't know. Miles claimed that he'd heard of these ideas years ago and knew of several good books that could explain them far more clearly than Irene just had.

"Excellent," Irene said. "If you have copies, perhaps you could lend them to those who want to read further?"

"They're at home," Miles said. "In my library there. And anyway—"

But he didn't finish whatever he meant to say and Naomi, who had bent over her drawing pad, frowned at him. Earlier that week they'd had an unpleasant conversation about some committee he said he was joining because of the war. He needed a permanent driver, he said, someone he could count on every day; important work, for which he'd pay a weekly salary. When she'd told him he should check for someone at the garage, he'd made a face like a puzzled sheep. Her mother, scolding her after Miles had tattled, had said that the decision wasn't solely hers, and that they'd discuss it further when they had more time. Now, as his voice subsided, she said to him, "If you understand it so well, why don't you give the rest of us the benefit of your *wisdom?*"

WISDOM: WHAT IS THAT? Like time, it's different for all of us; certainly Miles's wisdom wasn't Leo's or Naomi's, Zalmen's or Pietr's or Sadie's. Nor was it ours as a group. The dispiriting note on which Irene's first talk closed was a reminder of how easily things could go wrong even when we were all intrigued by a subject. Miles and Naomi squabbled and then Miles left, embarrassed that we'd overheard him. Naomi, after trying to say something to Leo only to have him back away, followed Miles, while Leo, as soon as Naomi was gone, moved toward Eudora. But Eudora was talking to Irene, and the sight of the two of them laughing gently made Leo feel so left out that the ideas Irene's talk had sparked in his head blinked out one by one.

And then a week later, Irene's second session, which might have been so interesting, went nowhere. Miles caused that as well, circling the room rapidly while the rest of us took our seats and then, before Irene could pass out the diagrams she'd retrieved from her files, brusquely waving her toward a chair.

"I have some announcements to make," he said.

Naomi stood near the window, arms crossed over her chest, as rigid as the statue of Hygeia outside. Her dark hair, mussed by the wind, tangled with her collar.

"I have to miss these sessions for a while," Miles said. "Some weeks, or maybe longer. New . . . duties have fallen on me, which I can't describe in detail. They have to stay secret. But I can't stand by while we are in such danger." Flourishing a creased page of newsprint, he continued, "I want to read this to you. You might have seen it when it was printed, a couple of weeks ago, but I never know what you pay attention to, here."

Bea came close to saying something sharp then; so did Arkady, but we caught ourselves.

"It's from President Wilson's war address to Congress. I want to point out this particularly important part, where he says 'one of the things that has served to convince us that the Prussian autocracy was not and could never be our friend is that from the very outset of the present war it has filled our unsuspecting communities and even our offices of government with spies and set criminal intrigues everywhere afoot . . . Indeed it is now evident that its spies were here even before the war began.'

"That's been proven *exactly* true in the last few weeks. *'From the very outset of the present war'*—the more I read and hear, the more I am convinced. There are a million German aliens living here, probably half of them spies. Since war was declared they've been streaming from our country into Mexico and they may be heading into Canada as well. If you've been paying any attention at all you will have read that the government has already alerted troops along the Mexican border to defend us against seditious acts. Troops have also been deployed in various states to guard power plants and railroad bridges and reservoirs. We have to be alert! Citizens have to play a role, and here, where we're so close to the border and where the forest provides the perfect hiding place for criminals of all sorts, our responsibilities are doubled—we must be vigilant.

"I can't say more. Others will fill you in, when and if that becomes appropriate. But for now I simply wanted to explain why I need to be absent for some time, and to encourage you despite that to continue with your gatherings even as you're watching out for anything or anyone unusual."

As if, we thought, we'd stop because of him. As if we hadn't secretly wondered how much more pleasant our meetings would be without him.

"One more thing," Miles said, folding his sheet of newsprint. "I've arranged through a friend of mine who distributes films to have some special ones sent here, which I'm hoping will arrive in time for your next movie night. I trust you'll find them inspiring, or at least educational."

"But we have pictures picked out already!" Lydia protested.

Miles, folding the papers into his elegant calfskin briefcase—when had he started carrying that?—shook his head, leaving Naomi to reply.

"But don't you know?" she said to Lydia and the rest of us. "Our Mr. Fairchild is suddenly a very important man. So important he gets to order me to drive him around on his errands. Or change the pictures you see, or—"

"That's enough," Miles said sharply. "It's time to go, I have a meeting in the village."

We watched in amazement as he picked his way through the circle of chairs and across the floor, his excellent shoes going *tik*, *tik*, *tik* while behind his back Naomi rolled her eyes and made a face but followed him.

15

O N MAY 3, Miles wrote this to Dr. Petrie—

> *Forgive this note; I meant to speak with you alone after our session but I had to rush to another meeting, and in front of our entire group I couldn't explain. But I want you to know the truth. And I want your help. I want you to join a group of men—leading citizens, you can be proud to belong—who've volunteered to aid the war effort.*
>
> *My dear friend Edward, back home, has in the wake of the explosion of the Eddystone Ammunition plant bravely put aside his grief over Lawrence's death and organized a unit of the American Protective League. Hundreds of these groups have sprung up since March, charged to look for evidence of sabotage and espionage and to combat the threats to vital industries. Agents gather information and report to the police any suspicious activities on the part of alien residents, and I gladly gave Edward my permission to enroll my plant supervisor, Mr. Maskers, as one of his lieutenants.*
>
> *But of course that made me think about the grave danger we're in because of our location. Trains arriving daily from New York, Chicago, and*

Albany; the Canadian border so close by; a constantly changing population in the sanatoria and the cure cottages, some far from savory and a great many foreign-born: one could hardly imagine a situation more hospitable to spies and saboteurs of all kinds. Who knows who may be hiding among us even now? When I was asked to join the unit forming in Tamarack Lake, of course I said yes.

I've been meeting with policemen, local politicians, bank presidents, merchants, doctors, pharmacists, hotel managers, ministers, teachers. A number were previously involved in the preparedness campaign and have considerable experience. I can't reveal the names of our chief or the other captains; for security reasons we must strictly limit who knows what, but I can tell you that similar units have already been formed in Rochester, Syracuse, Utica, and Jamestown as well as New York. I'd like you to be one of my lieutenants.

Your duties would mostly consist of learning what you can about the doings of your foreign-born staff and patients at Tamarack State, the naturalized as well as un-naturalized and indeed anyone strongly connected to their German or Austrian heritage, also anyone known to have been engaged in labor union activities before arriving here. The police chief and his deputies are sworn to help us in any way possible and you can ask them for assistance. Mail can be inspected, telephones can be tapped; what we rely on you for is information. You may use anyone you think appropriate to help you gather this information, but should in no event tell them about this organization, or suggest who might belong to it.

This is a volunteer position—of course there is no salary—in fact many local leaders have already pledged fifty dollars a month to help defray our expenses, and if you see fit to contribute, any amount would be welcome. Please let me know at your earliest convenience if you are willing to accept this post and how much you can contribute. A badge awaits you (it costs seventy-five cents), and while you should generally keep it hidden it will ease your way with the authorities when you need assistance and also help convince those who might hesitate to give you information.

Please don't talk to anyone else on the staff about this; we'll contact other candidates separately. I imagine it goes without saying that you should not keep this letter, nor copies of any correspondence to me or others regarding this.

He never considered the possibility of Dr. Petrie refusing. He himself had said yes the instant he was approached, sure this was the right thing to do and the only way, given his illness and his exile from home, to use his talents. He'd been repelled by the pacifists marching through Washington, white tulips in their hands, on the day the president went to Congress to ask for a declaration of war; then furious at the handful of senators and representatives who'd voted against the resolution. Fortunately it had passed despite them, and Congress was already debating a proposal to draft a vast army. If he was too old and too frail to join up himself, at least he could help make sure that the draft went smoothly and that the new soldiers had everything they needed to fight.

Which meant, he knew, a tremendous amount of work as well as constant vigilance. Overnight, the declaration of war had turned nearly a million resident German aliens into potential agents of the kaiser. Some might conspire with the Mexicans to take over California. Those in New York might help German submarines planning to attack the city. Saboteurs might already have infiltrated munitions factories as well as plants that made steel or acetone, felt or tool dies, anything needed for the war. The government had sent soldiers to guard bridges, reservoirs, railroad tunnels—but they could only do so much, and if it had not been, Miles thought, for the efforts of himself and Edward and thousands of other like-minded businessmen, quietly recruiting and putting into place the squads of operatives who'd listen and watch for trouble, anything might happen.

Suddenly there was more to do than he could have handled even back when he was healthy. Six hours lost each day to his cure chair; no choice, then, but to make the most efficient use possible of every minute he was upright. No more walks for pleasure, no more movies or card games or reading that wasn't essential. No more Wednesday afternoons with us. Anyway he hadn't enjoyed our last few gatherings; what difference could Einstein's theory make when the country was at war? Now he focused solely on his new duties, pushing aside his grief over Lawrence's death. Lesser pains—Leo's thoughtless rejection of his offer; Dr. Petrie's dismissal of his feelings for Naomi and, now, his surprising refusal to join in this work—he pushed aside too, although Naomi herself still managed to hurt him freshly every day.

His own feelings were puzzling enough. As for hers—crucial hours disappeared, if he wasn't careful, into trying to understand why she acted like this. Looking back, it seemed perfectly clear that she'd approached *him* and was responsible for the way he felt: she'd offered, back in October, to drive him on Wednesdays to Tamarack State. She'd sought him out, brought him extra desserts, listened to his plans for us with apparent interest, and once he'd seen that, once he'd turned and really *seen* her, he hadn't been able to turn away. She'd held his hand after Lawrence's death, when no one else thought to comfort him. Yet now she seemed to enjoy wounding him. Not once had she worn the necklace he'd given her for Christmas; not once had he seen her reading the book. When he'd first asked her to drive him on his new rounds, she'd balked as sharply as if she had no interest in either his company or in contributing to the war effort. Mrs. Martin, whom he'd been forced to ask for help, had reminded him that Naomi was only eighteen and a little nervous, as any young woman might be, at the attention of a slightly older man as powerful and successful as himself. He told himself that once she saw the importance of his work, she'd be proud to be part of it. Perhaps their bond would even deepen now that they shared their tasks. For the moment, though, she was painfully abrupt with him and whatever ground he'd gained during the winter seemed to be slipping away.

Grumpily she drove him to the hotel where, in the ballroom, he and the other two unit captains gathered with the village leaders to talk about bond sales, medical inspections, registration of transients, new train schedules, what the newspaper editors should print and what they should omit. A hundred details and hardly any time. Miles made lists, wrote letters, carried orders from door to door. Already, thanks to those meetings, the shops sprouted flags and loops of bunting but always there was more to do. Often he was late returning to his porch for rest hours and Naomi, who might have been so helpful, offered nothing but transportation.

On the Wednesday after Miles wrote to Dr. Petrie, he had Naomi take him to the post office. "I have to stay here for a while," he said, getting out of the car. "To organize something. There's no sense in having you wait around while we do this—why don't you take an hour off, and come back and get me at three? If we're not done then, you can wait until we are."

"When *will* you be done?" She flicked her fingers against the steering wheel, refusing to look at him. Her white shirtwaist, he saw, closed with unusual buttons shaped like tiny silver pinecones. Weeks ago he'd seen her sewing these on and, remembering how often in the past few months she'd ornamented her everyday clothing with a sleek belt or a fresh embroidered collar, he told himself she did that for him and recovered his patience.

"I'm not sure," he said. "Not earlier than three, but perhaps a bit later than that."

"But you want me to show up anyway and *wait*?"

"If you would," he said firmly. "I'll be very late for my rest hours by then, and I'd like to get back to my porch as quickly as possible."

Inside, he found his two lieutenants near the loading dock. The mayor had taken him aside at their last meeting to whisper that, while the Selective Service Act was still being debated in Congress, the secretary of war, wanting registration to take place as soon as the bill passed, had secretly arranged the printing of the necessary forms. Forty million of them, he'd said, needed to register ten million men. The main post office buildings in Washington, where they were being stored, had overflowed before the printing was halfway done.

"So we've all been sent our share now," the mayor explained. "Every town, every city. Ours came on the dawn train but we're supposed to keep them hidden until registration day is announced. I can't ask anyone for help officially, since we don't want the newspapers to get wind of this until after the act is signed into law. But I thought perhaps you and your squad . . . ?"

"Say no more," Miles had responded. Pleasant to have a concrete task, after all the meetings and the long hours discussing reports on suspicious people.

On the loading dock, he found rows of canvas mailbags, each stuffed to the top with the freshly printed forms and waiting for him to take charge. He opened one, releasing an inky odor so sharp that one of his lieutenants, standing a few feet away, turned with a startled look and the other said, "We'll have to be careful where we store those." Together they went to look for a hiding place.

Discussions, measurements, more discussion; an argument over whether to unload the sacks or move them intact. By the time they'd arranged the forms in a small room on the second floor and installed a new padlock, Miles was feeling feverish. Down the stairs he went, looking forward to the sight of Naomi's face and the comfort of the car seat as they drove up the hill to her mother's house, but outside, there was no Naomi. He walked to one end of the block and peered down the cross street: nothing. Wearily he walked back and sat—why should he have to do this?—on the stone bench in front of the pharmacy. If she felt for him a trace of what he felt for her, she would never, he feared, keep him waiting like this.

WHILE HE FRETTED, she was busy in her room. In the days since Miles had disrupted Irene's second talk, since he and her mother had ignored her wishes and forced her into this full-time driving job, her body had obediently managed the Model T but her mind had been seething. Why was nothing up to her anymore? Because Miles decided he was too busy for the Wednesday afternoon gatherings, she was cut off from them. Because she couldn't get to our gatherings, she had no chance to talk to Leo. Because Eudora was working with Irene every spare minute, she couldn't ask Eudora for help; everywhere she turned she was blocked. Blocked, blocked, blocked, blocked, half her time and more this past week wasted driving Miles here and there, watching him open doors and vanish inside and pop out again a few minutes later, each time climbing back in the car with his head sticking out from his chest like a chicken's. How could a man look like both a sheep and a chicken? He did, though; it made her sick to imagine him fussing self-importantly with the other men too old or too weak to be soldiers. He'd claimed he needed her specifically, rather than a man hired at the garage, because he had to have someone he could trust. Amazing that he thought he could trust her.

She'd left him at the post office, driven home, gone straight up to his room and stolen a shirt and, from the top desk drawer, some money. Not all of it—he'd stashed so much he probably couldn't be sure what was missing—but enough to help her. As they'd been arguing, what she'd threatened idly, so many times before, suddenly seemed both easy and obvious: she *would* run away, in a few weeks or a month. But not alone. In her room, crouched in front of the long, low cabinet beneath her dormer window, she snipped the buttons from Miles's fawn chamois shirt and replaced them with handsome bone toggles. Then she wrote a note—another note; the one in *The Kill-Gloom Gazette* had indeed been hers—to Leo.

A movie night was scheduled for Friday at Tamarack State, she knew. Eudora would be safely off with Irene, occupied as she always was, while Miles had earlier mentioned that he had a meeting that night. He was expecting her to drive him, but that wasn't much of a problem. Swiftly she finished writing and addressed an envelope with Leo's name and room number, forgetting in her rush to add "Tamarack State Sanatorium"—an omission that would stall her letter for two days while an irritated postal clerk checked the registration lists of the several sanatoria. With a little brass key she then opened the cabinet door, bending at the same time to block the wave of paper spilling out. Drawings, her drawings—far more than anyone, even Eudora, knew about. Sometimes she forgot, herself, how many there were. Carefully she selected the best of them: Leo smiling, Leo dreaming, Leo thinking, speaking, reading. She stacked them on a piece of brown wrapping paper and then added the book Miles had given her, which she believed Leo might like, and the refurbished shirt.

Time was passing, Miles was waiting—he was walking down to the corner now, already looking for her—but still she contemplated the parcel. Her truest self, she thought, had been muffled by the Naomi who lied to her mother and the one who waited on Miles. That was fear. That was what fear could do. She'd been afraid that Leo could never learn to love her, and then Miles and her mother had arranged to keep her away from him. As soon as that happened, she could see that he already *did*—if not love her, exactly, then something close to that. If they were to head together for New York, his home, it wouldn't take long before she found a way to take care of him.

Before she could even propose this, though, she had to give back what she'd taken from him. She could see, now, that this was no way to start; everything had to be honest between them and she needed to bring it back and ask him to forgive her. Then she could give him her drawings, and the warm handsome shirt, along with something to read that he couldn't have afforded himself and that would signal how much she believed in him. In a week or two she'd propose her plan, and then . . . She added the pencil to the pile, folded the paper around it, and tied the parcel with a string. Knowing how late she was, but hoping that Miles would still be busy, she ran out to the car and drove back to the village.

At first she didn't see him. He wasn't on the steps or at the door; she ran inside but he wasn't there either. Quickly she pushed her letter into the mail slot and then ran outside again. To the left of the steps, beyond the door to the pharmacy, was a stone bench and there, as she paused at the bottom of the steps, she finally found him. Instead of yelling at her, as she'd feared, he rose stiffly and waited for her to bring the car alongside and open the passenger door.

"I'm sorry," she said. "Were you waiting long?"

He coughed and leaned his head back against the seat.

"Are you all right?"

"One hour," he said quietly. "One hour I've been here, when I should have been resting. Why do you *do* this to me?"

16

O N THAT FRIDAY night, May 11—it's not surprising we remember the date—we filled the dining hall. By "we" we mean, here, not just the group who'd been gathering on Wednesdays but all one hundred and twenty of us, less the seven—three women, four men—lying upstairs in the infirmary, and with the addition of a handful of the evening staff and doctors. Not until after eight o'clock, when the last daylight faded from the windows, could we hope to see the screen, which two of the maintenance crew had hung on the front wall. Outside the tree frogs were racketing and the air smelled green, while inside we were reveling in our rare freedom; only during holiday parties and these occasional movie nights were we allowed to break the rigid segregation of the men's and women's tables. Now the tables had been herded toward the walls and the chairs that usually surrounded them were curved in concentric rows facing the screen. Men and women might sit where they liked, with favored friends or cousins. Those of us who'd made dates with acquaintances we hoped might turn into cousins arrived early and scrambled for seats; women had put on lipstick and done their hair while men had ironed their shirts, and we wore shoes instead of slippers. The night began with the air of a party.

Leo, who had taken a pair of seats in the back row, near the third and last door to the corridor, was waiting nervously for Eudora. Nervous because she might not come; nervous because he wasn't sure what it would mean if she did, or how he'd explain her presence. It wasn't so uncommon for us to connect with the maids, the orderlies, or the nurses, and women among us sometimes had—why shouldn't we admit it?—powerful crushes on some of the resident doctors, but none of this was officially permitted and Eudora, Leo knew, might risk her job if their behavior was seen as more than friendly.

He paced back and forth near the door, in everyone's way. Bea and Polly smiled at each other when they saw him; they knew. Most of us had, like Irene, been aware of Leo's moony glances for some time. We went, according to our inclination, to the front seats where we could stretch out and see every detail of the pictures, or to the sides and back where, if we had better things to do, we wouldn't be observed. Once the main lights were out, there was only the glow from the screen and from the hooded lamps at the back of the room, which were placed, the staff said, for our safety, to help us see the doors and each other if we needed help—but which really served to let them keep watch on us.

It was 7:45, then 7:50, and still there was no Eudora; seats were swiftly disappearing and the two Leo had marked with newspapers would soon be claimed; she had never, he realized, had any intention of coming. She'd agreed only to placate him, so she could escape his questions that afternoon in the laboratory . . .

But here she was. A flowered dress, green leaves and red flowers— roses?—tumbling over a creamy background, light-colored stockings and shoes with a small curved heel and a strap across the instep; he'd never seen her unwrapped from the long, shapeless blue garment that all the maids wore to protect their clothes. Her hair, usually pulled back with two combs, hung softly around her face, framing her blue-gray eyes. In her heels she was nearly as tall as he was, and when he darted forward to greet her she drew back slightly, then laughed—at herself, he thought, not him—and touched his forearm.

"I'm so glad you came," he said. He hoped she couldn't see the tear in his collar, the only defect in the shirt he had, in anticipation of this evening, retrieved from the men's donation bag.

"I said I would."

"Yes, but—well, I'm glad. I saved us some seats here, near the door, where we won't feel so cramped."

What unusual coloring she had! That clear pale skin, flushed so smoothly over her cheeks that the top layers seemed transparent; he'd never seen anything like it. "Take the outside seat," he said. "You can stretch your legs."

Perhaps whole families up here looked like her? All he knew of the people in these mountains was what he saw of the staff. "I didn't think you'd come," he confessed as she sat and turned to him.

"I always like the movies."

The lights went out and the projector whirred.

For weeks we'd been looking forward to the feature, *20,000 Leagues Under the Sea*. Newspaper accounts had promised underwater photography and the spectacle of a submarine attacked by a giant octopus; the room would be dim for more than an hour and the background music—Kathleen, after her success demonstrating the work of Stravinsky, had been recruited to play, which was something new for us—would cover up other, subtler noises. Women, during the frightening moments, might reach for comfort; men might lean protectively. In our anticipation of those possibilities we'd managed to forget what Miles had said during his last Wednesday appearance. The whole audience groaned with disappointment when a different title flickered on the screen.

Mick, the power-plant mechanic who doubled as our projectionist, called out, "It wasn't *my* idea—don't kill the messenger!" The laugh sweeping over the room almost drowned the deep voice saying: "It was mine."

Dr. Richards, so often in New York raising money or in Albany talking to politicians, in Colorado Springs or Arizona inspecting other sanatoria, had joined us, a rare event. "A generous friend has arranged for us to see several short films instead," he added from his seat next to Dr. Petrie in the front row.

Miles, some of us remembered. We had Miles to thank for this.

"It's important that we keep up with events," Dr. Richards continued. "I hope you'll all pay appropriate attention."

We sighed and settled in. As the first reel began we saw, not actors and gorgeous sets but scenes of the fighting in France. War footage, but not a newsreel; the titles announced these as scenes from the great battles of the previous summer. The man who'd filmed them, an American traveling with the Canadian troops, must have been very brave, but even the most amazing sequences didn't impress us. Enormous guns belched enormous clouds, columns of men passed by on horses, men beat bells to signal approaching waves of gas. Kathleen played marching music over shots of battles and long waves of tangled wire; most of us, though, despite Dr. Richards' admonition, weren't watching very closely. We'd wanted the octopus and the leaden boots, something different to look at, some entertainment. Leo, distracted by Eudora's presence, studied her profile in the light reflected from the screen.

"Look at that," she whispered, tilting her face toward the sausage-shaped observation balloon, which tugged at the men who tethered it to the ground. "I didn't know they were so big."

"Huge," he agreed, wondering what she'd do if he reached for her hand.

The balloon, Eudora saw, pushed like flesh through the netted ropes.

Each scene was interesting in its own way; when the heavy artillery pieces were fired, the barrels moved like the plungers on hypodermic needles. Men ran through trenches, lay behind mounded sandbags, crossed open ground in great crowds, but never fell, were never shown wounded or dead although all around them—unless these scenes had been staged?— there must have been fallen soldiers. An illuminating torch drifted down from an airplane, lighting up the trenches below, but no men were caught in its beam. Miles Fairchild, she remembered, owned a factory that made cement, which went into concrete, from which bunkers were made.

The screen went blank at the end of the reel and Eudora started to say something to Leo about her latest experiment downstairs. But as the next reel started—ships attacked by submarines, sinking while passengers leapt into the ocean or scrabbled along an overturned hull—someone started coughing. The harshness, the compulsive quality, the desperation and wetness; before the overhead lights went on she'd already risen. Two figures rushed out the center door, supporting a figure between them. Those of us who'd leaned closer together straightened in the sudden cruel glare while Charlie and Zoltan, in the third row, righted the chairs that had been kicked over. *Myra*, we whispered, *that was Myra*. Although she'd been doing poorly the last few weeks, she particularly wanted to see the men walking on the ocean floor while fish swam past their helmets.

"A friend of yours?" Eudora asked Leo. By now she was looking expectantly toward the door.

He shook his head. The night nurse stepped in from the corridor, scanned the crowd, and then gestured toward Eudora.

"I have to go help," she told Leo. "I'll try to come back later."

He watched her pass into the brightly lit corridor. Somewhere Myra, whom he hadn't gotten to know, was being lowered onto a bed with ice packed over her chest to stop the bleeding; in a room or a corridor close to here was the mess she'd left behind, which Eudora was cleaning up. He slumped in his chair, watching the images flicker on the screen and trying to calculate how much longer was left on the reel, and what the chances were that he and Eudora might still have some time to talk between reels. When a hand fell on his shoulder he was so pleased that she was already back, so grateful that they still had part of the evening, that he forgot his need for caution and closed his fingers around hers. It took a second for his grasp to loosen when he heard the words, "You got my letter!"

Kathleen's accompaniment, crashing chords that punctuated the sinking ships and exploding torpedoes, muffled the words but still Leo recognized Naomi's voice before she sat in the empty chair beside him.

"What letter?" In the glow from the hooded lamps behind him he could see how carefully she'd arranged her hair. "What are you doing here?"

"The letter I sent you Wednesday," she said, reaching again for his hand. "I said I'd meet you here, and here you are. I was afraid you wouldn't come."

"I came to watch the *pictures*," Leo said. "I didn't get any letter."

"But you're here," Naomi said, swinging a large cloth bag onto her knees. "Where I asked you to be. And I brought back what I took from you—I'm sorry, I shouldn't have done that." She extracted from the bag a parcel wrapped in brown paper. "Open it."

Nan and Pietr, beside Leo, were peering his way, while Albert, in the next row, turned to see what was going on.

"Please?" Naomi said. When he crossed his arms over his chest and stared at the screen she said, "I can do it for you."

"Be *quiet*," he said, sure that some of us could hear despite Kathleen's vigorous playing. If not their words, then the great rustlings of paper.

"Here," Naomi said.

On his lap she placed a shirt—she was giving him clothes?—and a sheaf of papers. The sheet he tilted toward the nearest lamp might have been a clouded mirror. He lifted another, another: his eyes, his chin, his face from the front and from the side. "Why would you do this?" he whispered.

"I made them on Wednesdays," she said. Against his ear, her breath was unpleasantly warm.

He squared the pile of papers and inched his chair away. In the X-ray laboratory, when Eudora had told him about Naomi, he'd dismissed the idea: preposterous that someone should feel that way about him. He should, he saw now, have taken her warnings more seriously.

"It's just something I do," Naomi said. "I've always been good at capturing faces." He let that pass. "Say *something*."

Her hands, which she'd been squeezing together, separated. One headed for his knee and he flinched and pushed it away, gathering everything on his lap and stuffing it back in the bag she still held. Nan and Pietr looked over again at the rustling, catching the abrupt movement of Leo's left arm and the way Naomi leaned toward him. The rest of us saw almost nothing. Yet even if we'd understood what was happening, we wouldn't have interfered. These were the dramas of movie nights, also of holiday parties, secret walks in the woods, late night meetings. With so much time to brood and dream, great dramas, based on a single word or a tiny gesture, sometimes unfurled in our fantasies. Often the object of someone's deepest desires was unaware, or uninterested. Or incapable; we all hid secrets beneath our clothes.

Leo crossed his legs, raising his knees to prevent Naomi from giving him anything else. "You don't even know me," he said.

She clutched her bag. "I know how you look at me."

He spread his hands, palm up, miserably.

"You don't think I saw you writing about me? Pretending to be taking notes on those stupid talks . . ."

"I was taking notes," Leo said slowly, "*on what my friends were saying*. I'm sorry for the misunderstanding but that's what it is—a misunderstanding."

Once more the door to Leo's left opened and then closed.

LATER, EUDORA TOLD herself she'd had no way of knowing that Naomi had sneaked into the building and found Leo. No way of knowing that, when she returned and went to sit beside Leo once more, she'd find Naomi weeping at Leo's side. And no way of knowing that, when Leo saw her, he'd say to Naomi, "That's Eudora's seat you're in," reaching as he did for Eudora's hand.

As Eudora pulled her fingers guiltily from Leo's, she saw that Naomi was wearing a dress she'd made herself: a dark red cotton print, with a white piqué collar, cuffs, and square patch pockets, surprisingly stylish except for a puckered shoulder seam, where the sleeve hadn't set correctly. Perhaps she imagined that; the light from the hooded lamps was dim. But certainly she didn't imagine the look on Naomi's face, or her choked voice saying, "What are you doing here? Why aren't you with Irene?" Rising, Naomi caught her hem with one foot and nearly tipped over.

"I took a night off," Eudora said, while her friend righted herself. "I didn't think I needed your permission."

At home, putting on her second-best dress, she'd ascribed the jumpiness in her stomach to curiosity. Not only about what Leo would do, but what she'd do herself when they saw each other away from their normal routines. That, and perhaps also a sense that she was doing something underhanded. She'd wanted to believe she wasn't doing anything wrong, but it was more, she realized now, that she hadn't expected to be caught. Her own sense of betraying Naomi made her sound harsher than she'd intended. "What," she said, "are *you* doing here?"

By now those of us close enough to hear were eavesdropping with what, if we're completely honest, we'd have to call a kind of malicious pleasure. The short films had been only sporadically interesting, whereas this . . .

"But you *know*," Naomi said. Her voice rose, bewildered. "You know how I feel, you've known all along."

Eudora looked beyond her to Leo, wondering how she might ease the situation.

"You *told* him!" Naomi said, catching the glance Eudora and Leo exchanged.

She ran from the room, the bag dangling at her side. For a moment, as she threw open the door, her slight figure was outlined against the white rectangle of light. "Shut it!" someone called, and she banged it behind her. Myra's sudden hemorrhage had caused the usual speculations, but this—bad behavior without the excuse of illness—we found simply entertaining, something we could gossip about without feeling too cruel.

Have we said how bored we often were? How hungry for something to happen? Perhaps we didn't say enough, earlier, about the feuds and quarrels that used to be common here. The way we found scapegoats, broke into factions and groups, turned like jackals on those who tried to hold themselves apart or guard their privacy. It wasn't that we hoped for the worst or didn't like a happy ending, but we wanted to be included in the process.

The door closed. Leo sat, Eudora sat; the next reel offered aerial shots of two airplanes fighting. "This is terrible," Eudora whispered to Leo. "I have to go after her. Or maybe you should."

"I can't do anything without her misinterpreting it," Leo groaned. "She's so convinced . . ."

Eudora nodded and rose. "You're right," she said. "It's better if I go."

Again Leo watched the rectangle of light open up on the wall, this time silhouetting Eudora for an instant before the door shut again. Several of us saw her leave, although no one was with her as she stood looking right and left down the bright corridor, trying to imagine where Naomi might have headed.

A girl had been embarrassed, we thought, as we focused once more on the screen. It was nothing more than had happened to many of us, and she'd get over it. She was well, she was free to go wherever she wanted; what did she have, really, to complain about? Some of us looked with pity, others with amusement, at Leo, who now had his head in his hands. In the corridor Eudora turned right—she should have turned left—toward the walkway leading to the men's annex and Leo's room, where she thought that Naomi, trying to comfort herself by going where she was most forbidden, might have headed.

IN THE REEL we were watching by then, the dogfights happened as if they'd been scripted, so far away that they were tiny, almost toylike. When a plume of smoke went up it seemed no bigger than what might rise from a match, while a wing torn off and falling looked like the wing of a moth. We knew there were men inside those machines but we couldn't see them. We rustled in our seats, flirted with our neighbors, kissed our cousins if they would have us. We tuned out the Tchaikovsky Kathleen was playing, talking to anyone within range and feeling, although we wouldn't have admitted it, slightly bored, now that the drama between Leo and Naomi had played itself out.

Perhaps because of that, those of us in the back row, including Leo, turned toward the piano as soon as Kathleen started coughing. We were on our feet when, as the coughing grew more violent, her playing stuttered and stopped. Surely we couldn't have a repeat of Myra, not twice on the same evening? Four of us rose, took a few steps toward her, and in an instant, as something noxious filled our nostrils and mouths, began to cough along with Kathleen. Kathleen kicked over her bench and fell to the ground, a searing pain in her throat and lungs and then in ours; someone shrieked and someone else turned on the lights; those of us toward the rear of the room saw the thick yellowish brown smoke pouring out of the ducts along the back wall, while those toward the front saw, if not the smoke itself, the rest of us clutching our throats, bending double, falling down.

How fast does chaos arrive? Faster than we can say it. We heard a hissing sound, which seemed to come from beneath us, and then more smoke mushroomed through the ducts. The lights were still on but the room was dark; some of us squeezed toward the three doors opening into the corridor, pushing so hard that we might have killed each other if Otto, Albert, Ian, and Frank—they deserve much credit—hadn't seized chairs and hurled them through the windows running the length of the room. Through those jagged holes we poured, shredding our hands and faces and backs. Someone heaved Kathleen, already unconscious, out one opening; her arm broke when she landed. Dr. Richards and Dr. Petrie, handkerchiefs tied over their faces, crawled along the floor beneath the clouds, working toward the back and searching for those who'd already fallen, dragging them toward the windows and doors. The night watchman, walking the grounds, saw the smoke and rang the fire alarm, which sent Eudora, who by then was standing in Leo's empty room and wondering where next to search for Naomi, down the stairs at the end of the wing and outside. The moon was full and across the wide lawn she saw the crowd tumbled in the flower beds in front of the dining hall and the lobby, the figures stretched out on the circular driveway, a resident doctor herding those of us who could walk or be dragged into the raised garden that filled the center of the circle. We knelt and clutched our chests and choked, vomited and gasped and began to turn blue. Eudora ran in our direction, trying to grasp what was happening.

But this wasn't like any fire we'd known before; there were no flames shooting out the windows, no floors collapsing downward in the heat. Nothing that might, had the fire engines from the village been anywhere near us yet, have driven back the hoses. There was only the smoke, which, those of us less badly hurt were beginning to realize, was not so much smoke as a suffocating gas. Still it poured through the dining hall, which was empty by now, pushing through the corridors, the lobby, and the solarium, into the elevators and the stairwells of the administration building and then up, and up.

Jaroslav, who'd been sitting in the second row behind Dr. Petrie and Dr. Richards but who'd bolted before the bulk of the crowd, running into the lobby and throwing open the main entrance doors, was in better shape than many of us; he was the first to shout, "The infirmary!" and to remind us that seven people lay up there. In the center circle Nan and Polly were already counting, although they could barely breathe themselves. Twenty, forty, sixty, eighty; was everyone here, was everyone out of the dining hall? We knew how many of us had been present, but weren't sure how many staff had joined us, and the confusion over that distracted attention from the infirmary patients.

We weren't cruel, we weren't stupid; we were nearly dead. We had broken wrists and legs and ribs, wounds small and large from the broken glass (Zalmen was struggling to get a tourniquet around Belle's thigh, which was jetting blood), while even those without a scratch were coughing so hard tears ran from our eyes.

Our heads swam, our vision dimmed. But some of us looked up not long after Jaroslav called out, and then we saw that two of the fourth-floor windows had been opened and were leaking trails of smoke. Framed in the windows were five faces: Mary, Vivian, Morris, Pinkie, George. Still there were no fire engines. The building had no fire escapes; the stairwells were fireproofed, lined with gypsum block and tile, and we'd been instructed to avoid the elevators in an emergency and use these sturdy passages instead, which could never burn. Indeed they were not burning now.

"They'll have to jump," the night nurse, who'd rolled Myra out in a chair to the front lawn when the alarm sounded, said to Eudora.

"Onto what?" Eudora asked. Knowing the answer, refusing to think it, she continued to scan the crowd. By then she'd glimpsed Leo, Dr. Petrie, almost everyone she'd seen inside the dining hall. But where was Naomi?

The nurse looked down at Myra, whose eyes were closed and who was very pale. Then she turned her head at the sound of a motor and Eudora, following her gaze and hoping the sound signaled a fire engine approaching, instead glimpsed a Model T headed away from us, far down the hill but only just emerging from the curve that, for a long stretch, hid everyone approaching or leaving Tamarack State. Later, when Eudora could leave us for a moment (already she was bending over our bodies, encouraging one of us to breathe deeply, wiping another's foaming mouth, pressing a wadded shirt against a wound), she would check the parking lot for Mrs. Martin's car and feel relieved by its absence. But for now Eudora moved among us, trying to help everyone at once and realizing as she did so that she hadn't seen Irene. Irene hadn't been in the dining hall; perhaps she'd gone out for the evening, or perhaps she was still at work. Like the rest of us, she hadn't yet remembered what would seem obvious later: that Irene's domain was directly underneath the dining hall.

"Jump!" called one of the four orderlies who'd appeared beneath the infirmary windows, each holding one corner of a blanket. They moved together, like the legs of a horse, shifting the small scrap of safety right and left.

Instead of fading, the clouds pouring from the infirmary windows increased, and when the fire engines still didn't arrive (their ladders wouldn't have reached, but they had nets), all five patients did jump, one by one, onto that improvised device. Mary bounced off, hit the ground a glancing blow, and broke her collarbone, four ribs, and her shoulder. Vivian broke both legs. Pinkie was fine—except for his lungs he has always been lucky—while George broke only his wrist. Morris fell at an odd angle and died just a few minutes later; a rib had punctured his liver

and one lung. And in the excitement everyone who was still conscious—
not very many of us by then—forgot that not five but seven people had
been up there, and that two were still in their beds, where they remained.
Edith Weinstein, Denis Krajcovic: gone.

17

L ATER, WHEN SUCH things became possible, we placed these notices in our *Kill-Gloom Gazette:*

EDITH WEINSTEIN, b. 1881 in Brooklyn, New York. Daughter of Israel and Ida Weinstein; stepdaughter of Helen Graber Weinstein (first) and Louise Rubin Weinstein (second); beloved sister of Helena, Shmuel, Louis, Yudele, Esther, Leike, David, and Gabriel. First employed at age fourteen as a buttonhole-maker, Edith continued work in the garment industry until 1913, when she was diagnosed with tuberculosis. After a short stay at Bellevue Hospital and a period living in a roof-tent, she arrived at Tamarack State in March of 1915. An avid moving-picture fan, her reviews in *The Kill-Gloom Gazette* were much appreciated by those too ill to attend movie nights. She entered the infirmary only a week before the fire, after the onset of intractable intestinal symptoms, and on the night of her death had delegated two assistants to take notes as she was unable to attend herself. Her skill with a needle was legendary and many of us benefited from the alterations she made, without charge, to our clothes. Among her many friends here she is particularly missed by Hazel, Rosika, and Belle.

DENIS KRAJCOVIC, b. 1890 in Bukovina. Parents unknown; brother of Simon and others unknown; beloved husband of Karin and father of Thomas and Stephen. Immigrated to New York in 1902. First worked as a telegraph delivery boy; later as a pushcart vendor; then entered employment with a building firm where he specialized in the installation of ironwork, especially cornices and skylights. After a three-story fall, during which he broke a rib, Denis failed to recover as expected and was diagnosed eight months later with tuberculosis. In July of 1913 he was sent to Tamarack State and seemed through December of 1916 to be making a slow but steady recovery. In February of 1917 he suffered a series of hemorrhages and was confined to the infirmary. He is particularly missed by his former roommate Frank Turner; by his close friend David Yavarkorsky; and by Lydia Lasky.

MORRIS VIOLA, b. 1896 in Utica, New York. Only son of Sadie and Joseph Viola. In high school Morris was notable as a champion debater, two-time winner of the central New York spelling bee, and outstanding thespian, best remembered for his role as Brutus during his senior year. After graduating from high school in 1914 he enrolled at Cornell University but was taken ill before the end of his first semester. His father having suffered an accident at the slaughterhouse that year, and his mother much occupied in caring for his father, he was sent to Tamarack State in February of 1915. Released in April of 1916, he was sent back in July after a relapse; from November of that year until his death he was confined to the infirmary. Not well known among us generally, he was a particular favorite of Dr. Petrie's.

⁓

WE DON'T HAVE funerals here. When we die our bodies are taken away at night, to the village for an autopsy or directly to the undertaker's, returned either way in a plain pine box and buried quietly. The cemetery is a mile north of our central buildings, in a clearing on the other side of the hill, hidden by a border of white pines, never shown to visitors and not mentioned in our rule book. We learn where it is from each other. When, during an afternoon walk, one person shows another the clearing for the first time, it usually signals a new stage in the relationship. After that, we think differently about how long we've been here and what time we might have left.

Twice since the fire, all of us involved in the Wednesday gatherings have gone to the clearing as a group, to visit the three who, although they didn't join in those afternoons, were still tied to us. The hospital commission gives us modest grave markers rather than headstones, low oblongs twelve by four inches, set almost flush with the ground. Morris, Edith, and Denis lie at the western edge of an area about the size of a swimming pool, neatly paved.

18

EARLIER ON THE night of the fire, before anyone was dead, Miles had indeed made Naomi drive him to his meeting. They hadn't spoken during the journey. Beside him the hills slanted up and down, trees giving way to fields, but instead of enjoying the view he'd been looking at his notes, his concentration interrupted by Naomi's low, tuneless humming. When he asked her to stop she frowned, obeyed, and then a few seconds later started tapping her thumbs against the steering wheel, increasing the speed as they pulled up at the meeting place. As she jolted to a stop he said, "Please come back at ten o'clock." Then he stepped down from the car, one hand still on the door, and found himself surprised by the clear, soft, twilit sky.

He could hear but not see a flock of geese moving high overhead. The leaves in the trees, just opening, were small and sharp, lovely in this light, and for an instant he recognized that he should be outside, walking around the lake or lying on his porch, watching the stars appear in the darkening sky. Instead he was five miles west of Tamarack Lake and seven miles from us, about to enter the limestone hall where league members from across the county were meeting to discuss their most recent cases. He turned back to Naomi, who was smoothing the front of her dress—a new dress, he thought—and who said, "Whatever you'd like." Her voice was peculiarly flat.

"That's what I'd like," he said. "Ten it is, then." He peered in through the open window but her face revealed nothing.

"Naomi?" They'd argued over every drive this week.

"What would you do if I just stopped doing this?" she asked.

Cars were drawing up to the building in twos and threes; men, streaming up the steps, were nodding seriously. Miles said, "Please."

"You'd find someone else," Naomi said calmly. "In a day. It's not like I'm the only person capable of driving you, it's just that you *want* to make me miserable, you like forcing me."

"You *offered* . . ."

"Months ago. And I offered something different."

A Cadillac pulled up, disgorging three men in dark suits—all strangers to Miles but all, he saw with embarrassment, looking at him and Naomi; without meaning to, he'd opened the door of the Model T, craned his head inside, and raised his voice. Carefully he closed the door and stepped back. "Let's not have this argument again," he said. "I will expect you later."

Naomi drove off without answering him. Throughout the meeting, which was long and complicated, only the mass of business kept him from dwelling on her. Each of the sixteen lieutenants had reports from their operatives to present, and two cases had to be discussed in detail. A man known to be a dues-paying Socialist had been overheard in a library talking about the Socialist meeting held in St. Louis. The proclamation signed there had deemed participation in the war to be a capitalist ploy, both dishonorable and unjustifiable—and the man's tone, the agent reported, suggested that he approved and would have signed himself if he'd had the chance.

Miles's attention fluctuated during the discussion that followed, but he was alert enough to hear the motion delegating an agent to befriend the suspect and try to determine his true attitudes. The motion passed. Someone who worked for the electric company next volunteered to enter the suspect's house under the pretext of reading his electric meter, and to look through his mail and his private papers. That motion passed as well. Then it was Miles's turn to present the case of the Baums.

The Baums, he said—Sidonie and Martin—had in the nineties immigrated to Tamarack Lake from Germany and had long been solid citizens. Children took piano lessons from Mrs. Baum, who taught in the music studio attached to the back of their house. "You, Charles," he said to a man on his left, "—didn't you study with her?"

"Four years," Charles said. The man next to him chimed in, "I took for six."

Miles nodded. "It seems like half the village has taken lessons from her at one time or another. She has quite a number of students now from the high school. Including many boys."

Much as he'd stood before us during our early Wednesday gatherings, he faced the men in chairs and went on to describe Mr. Baum, whose fabric and notions store was familiar to everyone but who was also known as the director of the local choral society, the Mountain-aires. For years, anyone who could carry a tune had crowded into the church hall and sung what Mr. Baum directed. Some years, when they had a good soprano, the Mountain-aires had done very well, other years less so, but no one had found them controversial until, two weeks ago, at a rehearsal for the summer concert, several members had suggested politely that the Bach and Brahms selections be removed and replaced by English works.

"And this," Miles continued, "is where the problem arose. My agent reported to me that Mr. Baum called the member who'd suggested this an unpleasant name, in German. And then said that German music represented German culture, which in turn represented the highest level of human achievement. And that anyone who would turn their back on that culture because of a war, a war in which we had no business interfering, understood nothing."

A hand rose in the back; Miles called on its owner. "He said 'a war in which we had no business interfering'? Those words exactly?"

"So my agent reports," Miles answered. The fabric in Naomi's new dress, he thought, had probably come from Mr. Baum's shop.

Charles added, "My sister talked to Mr. Baum the next day. He said he loved America, which was like his wife. But that Germany was like his mother—and how could he fight his own mother?"

"Recommendations?" someone asked.

For half an hour they discussed the Baums, who, they all agreed, had an unusual degree of access to young people in general, young men subject to the upcoming draft in particular. Against the arguments that they'd been known for decades as good neighbors and good teachers, the men weighed Mr. Baum's outburst, the couple's background, and their potential for spreading harmful attitudes. Both should be watched, the group decided. And if necessary disciplined.

An agent from a village north of Tamarack Lake then proposed that they adopt a unified warning system using color-coded cards. "Something like these," he suggested, passing around samples.

The air was stuffy inside the hall, and the light so dim that, when the cards reached Miles, he had to move closer to the shaded bulb hanging over the table. The buff card read:

> You have been reported to your local committee of concerned citizens for unpatriotic
>
>   ACTIONS   or
>
>   SPEECH   *(circle one or both).*
>
> Please adjust your attitudes. This is your First Warning.
>
>   *(signed)*
>
>   Local Patriots

A blue card offered a Second Warning; a red card announced the visit of a committee member. Miles passed the cards on, listening as his companions discussed details of wording. Should the second-to-last line include the word "please," or should it be more abrupt? Should the committee identify itself by name? He felt his mind split in two as he listened, like a long sheet of newsprint torn lengthwise. On one side all the words he'd said and heard tonight appeared in columns, bordered by neat ruled lines: motions made and seconded and passed, rules approved, language adopted, money allocated. This was the world he'd known since childhood, orderly and businesslike. Hardworking men, whose chain of command was clear, disposed of tasks in a certain order; this was what meetings were for. The tasks might be trivial, the tasks might be crucial, but the method was the same either way, a calm discussion and assignment of duties, the items ticked off the list. The minutes ticked by, the agenda items came and went. The words continued to accumulate in one half of his mind. In the other was an image of Naomi.

HE WAITED OUTSIDE, after the meeting ended, as the doctors and lawyers and merchants drove away. The three men in the Cadillac drove away. The mayor of Tamarack Lake, whose little dog had waited patiently on his car seat throughout the meeting—"I renamed him," the mayor said, cradling the brown creature. "He's Fred, now. And he's not a dachshund, he's a liberty pup"—offered Miles a ride, but Miles assured him his own driver was coming and so the mayor drove away. A local man shut off the lights, locked the door, and talked for twenty minutes to one of the undertakers from Tamarack Lake. When the undertaker was ready to go, Miles finally accepted a ride with him.

Both furious and frightened, he greeted Mrs. Martin harshly when he got back to the boardinghouse. "Where is she?" he said. "I know it's late, but I want to talk to her."

"She's not here," Mrs. Martin said—looking, Miles thought, not half so concerned as he was himself. "She didn't pick you up?"

"Obviously not," Miles said. "If it hadn't been for Monty I couldn't have gotten home."

"Maybe she's doing something with Eudora, and lost track of time?"

As she said that, the powdered planes of her face shifted briefly and Miles saw something that might have been worry, or fear. Then it was gone, and she was once more wearing her pleasant, meaningless smile. At the Wednesday gatherings, he remembered, he'd often caught Naomi and Eudora whispering together. Slightly comforted, he said, "I want to speak to both of you, together, first thing in the morning."

Coming into town from the west, he'd missed the fire trucks going to Tamarack State, which had headed up the hill while he was at the meeting. All night long he tried to sleep, leaping to the window at each slight noise, hoping to hear the grate clack as the car pulled into the carriage house. Before breakfast, he paced his porch, peering at the windows and screens of the houses nearby as if Naomi might be hiding behind one.

He entered the dining room to a flurry of excited gossip about the fire. As the facts surfaced—there weren't many, yet, but it was clear that the damage was serious—his mind once more seemed to tear into two strips. This time he forced himself to ignore the one belonging to Naomi. His league work during the past weeks had put him in contact with every important person in the county; back at home he'd not only run his plant but had been on the boards of four different charitable organizations; who was better equipped to organize help for Tamarack State?

By ten o'clock he was already at work. His lack of a driver turned out not to be a problem; one call to the chief who'd recruited him produced, half an hour later, a weedy boy with a red cowlick, a shriveled left leg, and, on his left foot, a black shoe with a thickly built-up sole. He could never serve in the military, Miles saw at a glance. And was correspondingly eager to do what he could to help at home.

"Tyler," the boy said, introducing himself. "At your service." The Willys-Knight limousine he'd driven over was, he proudly claimed, on loan to Miles "for the duration" from the owner of the dealership. Throughout the day, as Miles moved through his long round of visits, Tyler was so useful that Miles once or twice wondered, guiltily, why he hadn't asked his chief for a car and driver from the start. The answer was too painful to consider. Hourly he checked in with Mrs. Martin, hoping for news of Naomi. Had she been in an accident? Simply gone to visit a friend? Late that night, when he finally returned to the boardinghouse after missing all three of his rest periods and several meals, Mrs. Martin set before him a warm plate, which she'd saved from dinner. "You won't last long if you don't take care of yourself," she said.

"Any word?" He tried not to wolf the scalloped potatoes.

"Not yet," she said, her voice as flat as Naomi's had been the previous night. "I think she's run away."

"Why would you think that?" Even as he spoke, he remembered Naomi's words—*What would you do if I just stopped doing this?*—and saw again her red dress with the crisp white collar, which now seemed too nice for an evening's duty driving. The baked ham he'd been enjoying suddenly seemed both dry and salty.

Looking down at a dish on which birds carrying bows of ribbon chased each other around the embossed rim, Mrs. Martin explained, never meeting his eyes, that some money, which at first she thought she'd lost, was missing from her purse.

UP ON OUR OWN hill, it didn't seem possible that we'd survive. The administration building was ruined, not destroyed exactly—it stands where it always stood—but blackened with soot and so saturated with toxic fumes that no one could enter without a mask. Lost with it were our X-ray facility, our kitchen, dining hall, and reception room, our library, the infirmary, the clinical laboratories, most of the staff offices, and the solarium where our little group had met on Wednesdays. Before the night of the fire, we'd already lost to the suddenly ravenous military a number of young doctors and orderlies and maintenance staff. Now there were fewer people to take care of us just when we needed more, and no place else to send us; every place was like Tamarack State, suddenly overcrowded and understaffed. And everyone was short of money, too; funds that might have been used for rebuilding went, instead, to construct hospitals for the war wounded who would soon enough return from overseas. We were on our own.

The officials who arrived to advise Dr. Richards pointed at the undamaged wings of the men's and women's annexes, separated from the ruined central building by the covered walkways. Combine the patients in a single wing, they said. Men on the top floor of the former men's annex, women on the ground floor, the middle floor split half-and-half. Four of us rather than two in each room; on the porches the dividing panels removed and the chairs crowded into long rows. All the functions of the central building could then be transferred into the former women's annex.

Doctors and nurses crowded in to help from other sanatoria in the village; housewives ferried in meals; grocers and druggists brought bread and bandages and medicines while our own maids and orderlies, Eudora included, worked double shifts moving us into our new quarters, making up beds, and carrying meals. A new infirmary was improvised on the second floor of the women's annex, a dining room wedged into what had been the women's lounge, offices and laboratories scattered here and there. Floors were reinforced to support the heavy stoves, new plumbing was installed and equipment moved for a new kitchen. Until that work was finished, our meals were cooked on the back lawn, in a sort of field kitchen.

We were lucky this had happened at the beginning of the summer. Tents, wooden platforms, canvas awnings; military cookers on wheels donated by the army training camp at Plattsburg; wood and coal stoves carted over from merchants in the village; finally we were grateful for Miles's managerial skills. Scrubbing and soaking restored the utensils and the big pots and pans, but our old familiar tables and chairs, which were made of wood, seemed to have sucked the fumes into their pores and couldn't be used without being sanded and repainted. Until then we ate our meals from trays in bed or on our cure chairs. Before, this wouldn't have been much of a hardship, but it made those early days, when many of us were still sick and all of us were getting used to our new, forced intimacy, more difficult. Rooms and porches that had been snug for two were crammed with four; we quarreled—we still quarrel—over lockers and sinks and toilets and our positions on the porches.

Both Dr. Richards and Dr. Petrie, healthy to begin with, recovered more quickly than the rest of us; on Dr. Richards' orders, Dr. Petrie began assembling notes and writing a preliminary report on the fire as soon as he was out of bed. Who was injured and how badly. Who had died so far: Morris, after his botched jump, and Edith and Denis, who'd been trapped in their beds. Who might yet die: Kathleen, who'd been exposed the longest; Janet, who'd been in the back row and who had only one functioning lung; Leo, who'd received a very large dose when he'd tried to help Kathleen. Naomi didn't appear on any of his lists; Eudora had seen what looked like Mrs. Martin's Model T spiraling down the hill long before the fire trucks arrived. He was far more worried about Irene, who was struggling to breathe and whose throat was still so swollen that she couldn't talk.

Piecing together where the fire had started and what had burned, he determined the nature of the brownish yellow clouds that had made us so sick. He wrote:

A fire of undetermined origin began in the X-ray facility at approximately 9 p.m. Concrete walls and floors retarded the spread of the flames and only moderate damage might have been done had not the fire heated the metal shelves along the walls of the facility, in which were stored several thousand radiographs. While the shelves did not catch fire they conducted heat, causing the sheets of film to melt and smolder.

The film stock, made of highly flammable nitrocellulose, gives off carbon monoxide and nitrous fumes as it decomposes. Ductwork extending from the basement area to the dining hall directly above it spread the toxic gases rapidly.

Within the respiratory tract, moisture converts nitrous fumes to nitric acid, with subsequent damage to the trachea, bronchi, and lungs. Alveolar rupture, pulmonary congestion, and pulmonary edema may result. The effects are not dissimilar to those I observed in France among soldiers exposed to poison gas. Worst affected are the radiographer, who apparently tried to rescue some of the films (she remains unable to speak, so we have no clear account of why she was in the vicinity), and those who were closest to the ductwork from which the gases poured into the dining hall.

As he wrote, stopping occasionally to rub a cramp from his hand, he was thinking about Edith and Denis and Morris, and about all his other failures. He might have recognized the first whiff of the fumes and rushed us out before anything worse could happen; if he were taller and stronger he might have pushed and carried from the hall more people than he had; if he hadn't succumbed to the fumes himself he might have taken better care of the sick in the first crucial days instead of lying in bed, wheezing and vomiting. And how had he failed to pry Irene away from her work that night? They often urged each other to take a break, and it had been his job to convince her. If he had, she might be back at her desk already, like him. Instead—she too might die, he thought. His pen paused at another repetition of the word "pulmonary"—suddenly the spelling looked very odd—and then stopped altogether. For the first time since his return from France, his job seemed like too much.

He stood, stretching his aching arm over his head and flexing his fingers until the soreness eased. How had the fire started? He could imagine Irene bent over her apparatus, so caught up in her work that she failed to notice the first signs until she was enveloped. Either she'd rushed from the room too late, her arms heaped with films, or, an even more upsetting thought, she'd fled promptly but then steeled herself to return and rescue what films she could. She'd been found on the back stairs leading to the service door, clutching to her chest an enormous stack of images of our lungs. The first investigators, masked and goggled, had followed a shining trail of radiographs from the spot where she'd collapsed all the way back to her desk.

Dr. Petrie shared his report with the fire department and the police, the commission from Albany and the other one from New York. More informally, he told us, so that we began to get a sense of what had happened. His partial information was better than what we got from the newspapers, which tried to link our fire to others of the recent past: at the Williamsburg tenements, the insurance building, the shirtwaist factory. Interspersed with their speculations were shots of our own faces, swollen and covered with soot, which eager local photographers had taken as we lay out on the lawns.

The investigators, after sorting through the evidence and taking statements from everyone able to speak, found nothing scandalous to feed those papers, though. No defects in the heating or the electrical systems, no mismanagement, nothing scanted in the building's design or maintenance, no evidence of shortcuts during construction, no sign of arson. An accident, the investigators said. A spark, perhaps, or a shorted wire from a piece of apparatus in the X-ray facility. The cause of the "smoke-related incident"—that was how they referred to it—remained mysterious, but the destruction would have been far worse and the fire spread more rapidly if the building hadn't been so well-designed and well-built. They particularly admired the central stairwell, recommending only that exterior fire stairs be added to the top floor of each dormitory wing.

⁓

DURING THE DAYS immediately after the fire, Eudora hardly left Tamarack State except to snatch a meal and a few hours of dreamless sleep. She knew, as the rest of us didn't, then, how upset Naomi had been to find her with Leo, and she blamed herself for Naomi's disappearance. Briefly she wondered if Miles might have helped her leave town, but when she saw him at Tamarack State, directing a line of volunteers carrying groceries, she didn't dare ask him. Mrs. Martin was useless; Eudora had glimpsed her at the pharmacist's, telling whoever would listen that her daughter had run away for no reason, taking the car that even now wasn't fully paid off and leaving her shorthanded. Perhaps, Eudora thought, Naomi had left some clue in her room.

She sacrificed her first morning off since the fire, bicycled over to Mrs. Martin's house, and went in through the service door. A young woman stringing beans greeted her as she walked past white walls fringed with Mrs. Martin's notes. New ones, about conserving food for the war: reminders about observing wheatless Mondays and Wednesdays and meatless Tuesdays, about using less sugar, eating more fish, saving cooking fats for soap and fruit pits for carbon that would go into gas masks to save soldiers' lives. *Eat Potatoes!* one card read. *Eat Oatmeal!* read another.

"What's all this?" Eudora asked the girl, whom she hadn't seen before.

"Mrs. Martin signed the food pledge," the girl said, pointing with her knife toward a larger placard hanging from a pin.

Eudora paused and said, "Sooner or later, I suppose everyone will have to sign."

"No doubt," said the girl. "But they won't all be so smug, will they? Or volunteer to head up the local women's drive to save food. All the time bragging that she keeps the best table in the village, and making everyone who works here suffer for it."

She chopped a pile of beans in half and added, in a high, mocking voice, "'There is no reason why we can't serve nutritious, delicious meals while still conserving to the utmost. We must be endlessly *creative* . . .' She's ten times worse now that she's got Mr. Fairchild egging her on. He overheard me complaining about trying to cook with so little butter and he accused me of being disloyal."

Taken aback by the girl's vehemence, Eudora pushed through the swinging door to the dining room and nearly bumped into Mrs. Martin, standing just a few feet away. She'd had her hair done recently, Eudora saw, a new style involving a complicated mat of gray braids clamped to the back of her head. Her apron, ruffled along the bodice, looked new as well, or at least freshly starched.

"How nice to see you," Mrs. Martin said, crossing her arms at her waist. "But why did you come to the kitchen door?"

"I didn't want to bother you," Eudora murmured, trying to look trustworthy.

Mrs. Martin proceeded to talk about the weather, the tragedy at Tamarack State, the difficulty of running a boardinghouse with the new wartime restrictions and how she'd nonetheless triumphantly adapted to them; about everything except Naomi. As if, by refusing to mention her daughter, she erased any grounds for worry. Five or six years ago, when Naomi had had a terrible case of bronchitis and a cough suggesting that she might have something worse, Eudora had seen Mrs. Martin wall off her fears in just this way, betrayed only by her rigid hands. As she rattled on now, the skin on her knuckles whitened.

"Was there something you wanted?" she finally asked.

"Just—to see how you were," Eudora answered, knowing she'd lost any hope of ducking into Naomi's room. "And to find out if there'd been any news."

"Nothing," Mrs. Martin said. "Too much trouble for her, I am sure. But as long as you're here, I know Mr. Fairchild wants to speak with you."

Before Eudora could protest Mrs. Martin had vanished up the stairs. A minute later Miles came down alone, his stiff collar buttoned and cinched by his tie.

Without any greeting, he asked the same question she wanted to ask him. "Have you heard from her?"

In this house, Eudora thought, "her" always meant Naomi. "No," she said. "Have you?"

His face crumpled, and then his body, depositing him on the broad bottom step. "I thought she told you everything," he said.

"If she had," Eudora replied, "I might know where she was." The top of his head, now at the level of her knees, had a bald spot she hadn't noticed. She tried to step back but his hand clutched her right shin through a handful of her skirt.

"She didn't mention leaving?"

"No," Eudora said. She held her breath, waiting for the obvious question: when had she last seen Naomi?

Instead he said, in an anguished tone, "There's money missing from my room. From her mother's purse as well. It disappeared the day she did. How could she not know that if she asked, I'd give her anything?"

He was so upset that Eudora didn't dare hint at Naomi's real feelings, or at her own. At movie night, the pang she'd felt when she'd returned to find Naomi sitting at Leo's side had shocked her.

"Really," she said to the top of Miles's head, "I have to go."

She left him on that bottom step, knowing as she fled the house that she wouldn't feel so guilty if Naomi's suspicions hadn't been true. In the weeks since the fire, she'd felt more and more strongly drawn to Leo each time she crept into the rough new infirmary and listened to him struggling to breathe.

19

I N OUR NEW infirmary, which was wedged into the second floor of
the former women's annex, Leo lay on a white bed resembling those
in which Edith and Denis had been trapped during the fire. He
didn't know that they were dead, nor did he know about Morris's fatal jump
or how badly Irene had been injured. Although many of us had recovered
from our exposure to the fumes, he'd developed pneumonia in both lungs,
with a fever so high he felt like flames were licking at his sheets. Often he
was unconscious when Eudora visited him, and even when he was awake
he didn't always recognize her behind the mask Dr. Petrie made her wear.
Watching the muscles at the base of his neck tighten and hollow as he
struggled for breath, sometimes she couldn't recognize him either. For the
ten minutes Dr. Petrie allowed, she sat next to him silently, now and then
stroking the smooth web of skin between his index finger and his thumb.

Afterwards, she took off her mask and crossed the hall to the wom-
en's section where Kathleen, Janet, and Irene were laid out in identical
beds. Kathleen and Janet remained very weak while Irene, whose face

was heavily bandaged, still couldn't talk. The fumes pouring through the basement had swollen her windpipe shut and she'd already stopped breathing by the time the firemen brought her up the basement stairs. Dr. Petrie had saved her life—a few of us had seen his arm swoop down, the scalpel glittering in the moonlight before it pierced her neck—but in the process damaged her larynx. No one knew how long she'd lain there before the firemen fetched her, and Eudora worried that her brain might be damaged as well. She might speak again, or she might not; might work again, or not. All Eudora could do was visit each day, deliver the news and gossip in a cheerful tone, and then—she knew that Irene didn't want anyone else to touch her hand—change the cotton inside her violet glove. The glove itself was clean and fresh, replaced from the box in Irene's room.

When she finished her visits, she went back to work with a sense of relief. For fifteen hours a day she worked without a pause, falling asleep at home as soon as she reached her bed. In between those states, the bicycle ride that should have relaxed her became a kind of torture. Pedaling up the hill at dawn, or flying down in the last bit of twilight, she couldn't help thinking selfishly of all she'd lost. Who, if not Irene, would sympathize with her complicated feelings for Leo? Who but Leo could understand her uneasiness over not telling Miles that she'd seen Naomi the night of the fire? Who but Naomi could understand how lonely she felt with all of them absent—but her loneliness wasn't all of it. She'd lied, she'd betrayed her friend, she'd made a mess of everything, and still she was selfish enough to grieve over what she'd lost in the basement.

Both the new X-ray apparatus and the old one she'd restored had been destroyed. The gas tubes, the darkroom, the lead-shielded stand were gone; also the notebooks in which she'd kept the record of her experiments, the films she'd taken of Irene's chest and of Leo's, and her father's old specimens. Gone too were the images from her first clumsy experiments with bits of leather and wood, buttons of bone and vulcanite and glass. The data she'd collected, at first only out of a sense of duty, had revealed a great delight: simple rules were useless. The best images required a subtler tinkering, which she realized, now that she was separated from any hope of doing more, she had loved.

LEO, DELIRIOUS WITH fever, confused the X-ray laboratory with his old classroom, his old life and his new; well into June, nothing made sense to him. He missed the rearrangement of his room—Otto tucked into Ephraim's old spot, next to Leo's empty bed; Arkady and Abe wedged in as well—and he missed the arguments the rest of us had as we were shifted similarly. When his fever spiked he relived the fire, batting the gas from his face while he tried frantically to parse the rules of this combustion. When his fever dipped, he wandered through his past.

While he floated outside Grodno, watching a sleigh move down one hill and up another, rain washed the residue of the fumes from the walls of our ruined central building, turning it into acid that singed the surrounding lawn. Leo saw, not that burned brown oval, but the dark and beautiful forest where he'd spent summers with his mother's relatives; he was with his mother, crossing a field of sugar beets as they walked home from the creek. In an office he stood, his head no higher than the desks, listening with wonder as his father spoke Russian to the tax collector, Polish to a foreman, German to a friend. Then he was older, thirteen or fourteen, wandering the streets like a wolf and later trying to please the Odessa merchant who'd rescued him and paid his fees at the polytechnic institute. In the closet off the pantry where the merchant had let him sleep, two mice visited him each night and ate sunflower seeds from his hand. At the institute, an Armenian friend gave him a soft felt hat while another diagrammed the reaction of sodium chloride and sulfuric acid to yield hydrochloric acid, which could in turn yield chlorine gas. In New York, not long after he arrived, he fell in love with the fourth of his landlord's six daughters, whose father promptly married her to a Jew from their old village. After her there'd been other girls but no one, until Eudora, who had the power to change his life.

Days passed in a dream for him, while those of us who'd recovered watched the burned grass melt into the dirt and the building walls, once a soft brick red, streak and darken. Blackflies plagued us on the porches as we continued to trade hypotheses about the fire and then to share them with the men from Albany and New York who came to question us. They treated us like immigrants just off the boat. Miles we saw hardly at all, glimpsing him only as he flicked past to talk to some of the staff or—this was new—to Dr. Richards. Rumors zigzagged down the porches. We thought we'd known him, his tidy suits and excellent shoes, his boring talks; at the Wednesday session now marked forever as our last, his comments about sabotage and spies had sounded like someone else speaking and we'd assumed the Miles we knew would soon return. If we'd had more evidence, we might have guessed how much he worried about Naomi, or how, thinking she'd left the village directly after their quarrel, he blamed himself. But Miles never gathered us together, as he would have in the old days; he never spoke to us as a group, and he never asked what we thought about Naomi's disappearance. We didn't learn how deeply he'd changed until he appeared unexpectedly in Dr. Petrie's new office.

They hadn't spoken easily together since Dr. Petrie had declined to join his league, and Dr. Petrie was surprised to see him. More surprised when Miles dropped into the wooden chair substituting for the one in which, before the fire, he'd sat while pouring out his passion for Naomi. His hair was too long, his nails were chipped, his shoes lacked their usual polish; in the aftermath of the fire, even he was still disheveled. What had brought him back? Perhaps, Dr. Petrie thought, simply the fact that he'd been Miles's earliest confidant.

Without introduction, Miles said, "I got your report."

"I'm sorry?" Dr. Petrie said. He looked around at the papers littering his desk. "If I was supposed to send you something—"

"Your report on the fire," Miles said. "Dr. Richards sent it to me. As you might have expected."

"Ah," Dr. Petrie said, struggling to control his voice. Of course Miles had asked Dr. Richards to join his league; of course Dr. Richards had accepted. Of course nothing he submitted to Dr. Richards was confidential anymore. How had he mistaken Miles for someone ineffectual?

"I would have come to talk to you sooner," Miles said, "but I had to put aside everything for Registration Day."

"You were involved with that?"

"In the background," said Miles. He'd organized all the volunteers and donations necessary to restore something like order to Tamarack State, while at the same time keeping an eye on every aspect of the draft registration, but in both cases he'd acted somewhere between anonymously and secretly. Now his reward was Dr. Petrie's surprised, suspicious glance. Either one of those tasks would have been plenty for a healthy young man. But for him, middle-aged and sick, worried about a girl who'd run away and who might be hurt, or worse—only by the most rigid discipline could he hold himself together. He straightened his back. He smoothed down a wisp of hair. He pressed his eyeeteeth against his bottom teeth, a trick he'd learned to keep his face from trembling. He added, coolly, "In case men had questions, or had some thought of failing to register, or were in danger of being swayed by someone with Socialist or anticonscription tendencies."

"Really," Dr. Petrie said, his hand smoothing a piece of paper that already lay perfectly flat. "I hadn't realized that was part of your volunteer work."

And it was true that most of us had hardly noticed the events of June 5, coming so soon after the fire. We were already wards of the state, sent here by our local Boards of Health, and our backgrounds and identities had been documented to perfection. We couldn't have altered our birth dates or lied about our naturalization status if we'd wanted; anyway our illness exempted us from serving. But in Tamarack Lake the situation had been different. In the high school auditorium, every man in the village between the ages of twenty-one and thirty-one had been required to appear and fill out a form. Later, we heard that the high school band had played at intervals all day. That the Boy Scouts formed an escort for the truck that carried the registration forms from the post office to the high school. That the Mountain-aires—now led by Mr. Harries, hastily recruited after Mr. Baum's dismissal—sang at 7 a.m., when the polling place opened, and again at 7 p.m., when it closed, in between passing out miniature American flags for the young men to wear on their chests.

"We had agents at the main doors, and out back, and at both ends of town," Miles admitted, wanting someone to know how carefully he'd arranged things. "One man at the train station, in case someone got the idea to leave that way, and one parked on each of the main roads. We could have used you—I still feel uneasy about the population here."

"There's nothing here for me to help with," Dr. Petrie said. "The male patients aren't eligible to serve. And I'm sure the men who work here registered. Though what we'll do if the army starts to take them . . ."

As he spoke, he tried not to scratch at the crusty red bubbles erupting on his left forearm. Not poison ivy, not shingles; some sort of reaction, perhaps, to the fumes: but then why did only he have them? He forced himself to look away from his arm and at Miles, whose face was unpleasantly pale. "Aren't you concerned about your *own* health? You shouldn't be working such hours—you shouldn't be working at all."

Miles rose and began to pace in front of the desk. "You've been here so long that you don't see, anymore, what's happening out in the world."

"Yet *I* was the one who went to France, I notice," Dr. Petrie said. "Not you."

"Thank you," Miles said bitterly, "for reminding me of my failures with Lawrence. As if I ever forget."

Dr. Petrie murmured an apology, considering at the same time the truth of Miles's accusation. Twenty years ago, when he'd arrived with patched socks and single suitcase, his mind whirling with a thousand ideas gained in the clinics of Baltimore, he was sure he could turn Tamarack State into a model institution. Since then he'd worked so hard that he seldom traveled or read anything not directly related to his work. His visit to France had been the one great exception.

"If *I* had gone," Miles said, "I would have come back with some new ideas. Didn't what you saw make you curious? Didn't it make you wonder about how we'd handle raising an army here? All you seem to think about are the patients right in front of you, but what's going on is so much larger—Socialists are preaching draft resistance. Pro-German elements are spreading rumors everywhere. Young men are going to Mexico and Canada, and lying about their ages, and producing forged birth certificates and claiming to be married when they're not. And that's just the tip of what's happening. I don't have time to worry about myself."

"I read the same newspapers you do," Dr. Petrie said. "I'm perfectly well aware of what's going on."

"You don't see the league reports from the other districts, though. Which you might have, had you joined when I asked you—why don't you want to help?"

"Here's a story I heard," Dr. Petrie said, abruptly pushing aside a huge stack of files. "I heard that in Boston, a member of the American Protective League brought in a white carrier pigeon that he suspected of being used in German spy work because it had spots inside its wings. Tiny black lines and spots that to him looked like dots and dashes. Since he didn't know how to read Morse code, he called in someone from the Signal Corps, who called someone from military intelligence. Everyone got excited until a boy figured out that the specks were clumps of bird lice."

"Anyone can suffer from an excess of zeal," Miles said. As if to tease him, a pigeon flew past the window, wings mottled in shades of gray. "It doesn't mean the other cases aren't important."

"I'm not criticizing your work," Dr. Petrie said. "I just don't feel that I can be of much help. I've been as busy as you these past weeks, and anyway it sounds as if you have plenty of men to train and supervise already. Maybe you should be giving *them* your Wednesday afternoons."

"The two have nothing in common," Miles said angrily. "The men I'm working with now are different, they're men like me. I simply coordinate their activities." He opened the door, turning back to ask, "Why are you being so thickheaded? You have a huge problem staring you in the face. That fire . . ."

"If you read the report," Dr. Petrie said, "then you saw my explanation. The fumes came from the racks of stored films. A simple chemical reaction, which could have been predicted."

"All well and good—but you explained nothing about how the fire started in the first place," Miles said. "Do you think I didn't notice that? The state investigators can say 'accident' as many times as they want, but something still seems wrong to me. Why aren't you taking this more seriously?"

ABE AND ARKADY AND OTTO, crowded together in Leo's old room as Leo struggled in the new infirmary, were trying as hard as they could *not* to take their situation seriously. If they had, they would have given up, or fought so bitterly that their friendship would have shattered. After rooming together for more than a year, Abe and Arkady had grown used to each other's snores and squeaks, Abe's way of paring his nails with a knife, Arkady's habit of snorting through each nostril twice, once gently and once more firmly, each time he blew his nose: the thousand little irritations of sharing close quarters. But Otto, who before the fire had roomed with Sean, cleared his throat every two or three minutes, spoke with food trapped in his overlapping teeth, and read sentences from the newspaper out loud. It took everything Abe and Arkady had learned in their time at Tamarack State not to band together and turn against him for what were, really, only their new roommate's natural ways. Otto, in turn, missed Sean, who whispered when he read but at night fell into a sleep like death, never rolling or stirring a limb until dawn. In the early morning hours, lying awake miserably while Abe and Arkady snored in concert and Abe flopped from side to side like a seal, he sometimes imagined mashing pillows over their faces.

But they'd been through this before—we all had, though never to this extent—and during their first weeks together they learned to joke about their resentments. In Leo's absence, they used his bed as a couch and tried to enjoy that scrap of extra space. All three of them liked Leo, but as a way of deflecting their own discomforts, they took turns making fun of him.

Abe did a perfect imitation of Leo's most common gesture, right hand raised to push a wing of his hair behind his ear; Otto and Arkady both found that hilarious. Otto mocked the hours Leo spent in the library, poring so earnestly over books and papers. Arkady popped his eyes and made moony glances that were, he claimed, exactly how Leo had looked at Eudora during our Wednesday sessions, and Abe said, "Did you see the way he was with her, the night of the fire?" Then Otto, who was stretched out on Leo's bed, picked up the two green volumes Leo had left lying on the white-topped table.

"I can't believe this is what he reads for pleasure," he said, turning the first one over in his hand. "It's no wonder he was the only one paying attention during some of Miles Fairchild's early talks. *The Principles of Chemistry*—"

"Read some," Arkady said, egging him on. One thing that made Otto bearable, even likable, was his ability to turn the driest material into something funny.

Otto flipped a couple of pages before clearing his throat and pursing his lips, assuming what he imagined was a professor's demeanor. "Listen to this." Reading swiftly, he began:

INTRODUCTION

The study of natural science, whose rapid development dates from the days of Galileo and Newton, and its closer application to the external universe led to the separation of Chemistry as a particular branch of natural philosophy, not only owing to the increasing store of observations and experiments relating to the mutual transformations of substances, but also, and more especially, because in addition to gravity, cohesion, height, light, and electricity it became necessary to recognize the existence of particular internal forces in the ultimate parts of all substances, forces which make themselves manifest in the transformations of substances into one another, but remain hidden (latent) under ordinary circumstances, and whose existence cannot therefore be directly apprehended, and so for a long time remained unrecognized.

He ran out of breath as Abe asked, "That wasn't all one sentence?"

"It was," Otto said, flipping the page. "You couldn't make this stuff up if you tried."

"More, more," pled Arkady, who'd been laughing throughout Otto's high-speed recitation.

Otto obliged.

The primary object of chemistry is the study of the homogeneous substances of which all the objects of the universe are made up, with the transformations of these substances into each other, and with the phenomena which accompany such transformations. Every chemical change or reaction, as it is called, can only take place under a condition of most intimate and close contact of the re-acting substances, and is determined by the forces proper to the smallest invisible particles (molecules) of matter.

He shook his head in disbelief. "It's all like this. Except the footnotes, which are worse. The tiniest type, page after page . . ."

"Let me see," Abe demanded. Otto handed over the book.

"Well," Arkady said, wiping his eyes, "but if Leo likes it, it must be good for something. It's not his fault he's still trying to make himself into who he was in the old country. I felt like that too, the afternoon I was talking about the history of communes. Those Wednesdays made it easy to think we might have a chance."

"Might have, *then*," Abe said, setting the volume back on the table. "Not now. We should leave his things alone, I suppose."

Otto shrugged and set the other volume down. Elsewhere the rest of us had our own irritations with the new living arrangements, which we were trying to work through room by room. We tried not to hear what we couldn't help overhearing, tried not to see what was better left hidden; everything we knew about inventing our own privacy had to be doubled after the fire. Belle said, later, that she tried to imagine a wall of glass bricks surrounding her bed, which let in light but blurred any sights and shut out sound entirely. When she imagined that most fully, she said, she could lie in her bed, with Pearl and Bea and Sophie just a few feet from her, and not hear Bea crying or see Pearl examining the ulcer on her thigh. Pietr said that when he wanted to feel separate from Ian, Frank, and Albert, he re-created the night sky in his mind, complete with all the constellations about which he'd once talked to us, and then imagined himself moving among them like a shooting star.

All of us took refuge in conversations about the outside world, which some days seemed like the best way to ignore the difficulties here. Once the delivery of our newspapers started up again we seized on them eagerly, gathering what news we could about the world and the war. When the draft lottery came around in July, we were settled enough in our new lives to read with interest the story of how a general, in Washington, stood above a glass bowl filled with black capsules, each of which concealed a numbered slip, which he tumbled with a wooden stick until a blindfolded man reached in and chose one. Another man opened the capsule and read the number, which was flashed by way of a telegraph operator to all the local draft boards, to be chalked on a wall or pasted in a post office window. Although it touched us only indirectly, we considered for days how in our village, in any village, the man who held that number might cheer, or he might turn pale and stare down at the street. How in Washington a group of men too old to fight stood watching another number rise from the capsules moving like fish in their huge glass bowl. Lying in our cure chairs, while nine million men in other places waited for their numbers to come up, we read letters in the newspapers complaining that we were fed and housed at the state's expense. Some people, we were reminded, resented every penny spent on keeping us alive.

Inside our own fishbowl, we longed to talk with more than our roommates about what we'd seen and felt. We're not sure who started the message moving down the crammed porches and passing from one chair to the next, skipping some and landing at others, crossing floors to reach those of us who'd been in the habit of meeting on Wednesdays—but someone did, the message moved. Not long after the lottery we began to meet outside, under the pavilion at the nearest pond, at our traditional time and also on Saturday afternoons.

Without a leader or a formal plan we stood knotted under the cedar roof, talking awkwardly, our old ease hard to muster. At first we talked about the fire itself and about those who'd been killed or hurt. Morris,

Edith, and Denis, of course, although we had not yet made, then, our first visit to the clearing. George, whom we saw in the dining hall, eating with his left hand as his right was still in a cast, and Vivian, confined to a wheelchair while her broken legs healed. We talked about Janet and Kathleen, who'd finally been released from the infirmary; about Irene, who had also been released but who still, worryingly, couldn't talk at all; and about Leo, recovering very slowly. Then about what Dr. Petrie and Eudora, who were busy working, had hurriedly passed along to us in the hallways. His reports, her worries about Naomi. We spent much of one cloudy afternoon discussing Naomi's continued absence and the gossip concerning Mrs. Martin's swift, apparently casual acceptance of it. While we struggled to piece together what we knew regarding Naomi—why had we noticed so little about her?—the mist blanketing the hill beyond the pavilion dropped down to the level of the field. Twenty minutes later we were drenched, but what was rain to us? Any weather seemed like a blessing and we were grateful to be there to get wet.

20

I T WAS RAINING on the day, toward the end of July, when the three investigators working for Miles crept through our crowded rooms at the sanatorium, asking questions and writing in their notebooks. *Tell us what happened,* they demanded. *Tell us again, in your own words.*

Once more, wearily, we told our stories. But this time, for the first time, several people mentioned that the door at the back of the dining hall had opened and closed a few times on the night of the fire. One of the agents noted that detail, and then another wondered if a patient could have slipped from the dining hall during the movies before sneaking back. The third, a tall man with lumpy skin, passed that suggestion on to Miles, who showed up two days later with his new driver and asked to speak with all the patients at once.

Those of us involved in the Wednesday sessions gathered, along with everyone else, in the cramped new dining room. We sat, Miles stood, as if in mockery of the learning circle he'd started so optimistically. His slight figure was draped in a new suit, his hair freshly trimmed and his league badge glittering on his vest each time a gesture parted his jacket. He was only a few inches taller than Dr. Petrie and we'd never found him impressive. But the recent excitement seemed to have improved his health, and as he summarized what he'd heard about the opening and closing door in the back of the dining hall—those three men who'd talked to us, he said smoothly, worked for him—his voice took on a crisp authority. He read from notes, neatly organized; those sitting near the front could see the hand-drawn arrows marking his main points. From the interviews his agents had just conducted, along with data from the other, earlier reports, he'd assembled a single chronology, which he now reviewed with us.

At 8:15 the first reel had started and at 8:16 Mick had made a joking comment in answer to our groan of disappointment. At 8:30 the screen had gone blank while Mick switched from the short film about the fighting in France to the one about the ships attacked by submarines; we had talked a lot during that pause. At 8:34 the second reel had started. Myra started coughing at 8:36 and the overhead lights went on as Stephen and Gloria rushed her out. Charlie and Zoltan then righted the fallen chairs; the night nurse entered from the corridor and summoned Eudora to help; the lights went out again.

No later than 8:40 Mick resumed showing the second reel in the darkened room. Somewhere between 8:43 and 8:46 many of us saw, for the first time, the tall rectangle of light in the wall as the door to the corridor opened and then closed again. Some whispering followed, and also other noises; there were several reports of an argument. At about 8:55 the door to the corridor opened again, and swiftly closed—but within two minutes it reopened. At that point someone, annoyed at the interruptions, had called out, "Shut it!" Just after the door closed—at 8:58—Mick had switched reels again. By 9:02 the film showing aerial combat was running and by 9:04 the tall white rectangle appeared in the wall for the fourth and final time. At 9:16 Kathleen started coughing . . .

"The rest you know," Miles said.

And indeed we did—but still, for the sake of completeness, he marched us through the moments when Kathleen had lifted her hands from the piano and risen, and when Jaroslav had thrown open the main entrance doors, and when Albert, Otto, Ian, and Frank had starting smashing the windows to free us. Every event he pinned to his timeline, asking us at each point to show, by raising our hands, how many agreed.

We gaped at the numbers, so strangely precise, but mostly we did agree: not because we were sure he was right but because already, ten weeks after the fire, the details were jumbled in our memories. Belle remembered the feel of her thigh sliding along the rim of the window, a sensation of cold rather than pain; then the surprise as she saw her own blood pouring out—but had that been before, or after, she'd seen someone crawling along the floor with a napkin tied over his nose? Sophie remembered watching the fumes slide toward her like dirty water and then, as they reached the chairs, gather and rise into clouds that engulfed her even as she saw that transformation. Agnew remembered the sound of his own ribs cracking as Dr. Richards, pulling him from the room, paused just long enough for Ian, who tripped on Frank, to fall on top of him. Each of us remembered a few brilliant images, and the fear, the smells, the sounds, the panic: but the mundane minutes before the fire, what had happened when and in what order—how could we be sure? We did our best.

"I'd like," Miles said, "to try to amplify just a few points." He looked down at his timeline, now heavily annotated. "Most of you seem to agree that the door at the rear opened four times once the room was darkened again after Myra's departure: between 8:43 and 8:46; at 8:55 and again either one or two minutes later; the final time at 9:04. Do any of you remember who you saw *near* the door?"

Five minutes here, five minutes there—who knew? "Eudora was sitting there for a little while. And Leo," said Nan, who'd been near them.

Engrossed in trying to fit her own memories within the boundaries of that obdurate timeline, she didn't grasp the point of Miles's questions. Polly and Pietr, similarly preoccupied, murmured their agreement before any of us had absorbed the implications.

"Leo Marburg?" Miles asked. As if we had more than one Leo.

"Leo, *Leo*," Albert responded impatiently. The long wound down his right arm had inflamed a nerve, and the pain made him testy. "The one your other chauffeur has such a crush on. She was there too, they were having some sort of fight."

Miles drew his lips together. "Naomi was *here* that night?"

We could see from his face that this upset him, but we didn't understand why. A different voice added, "She brought a package for Leo."

"For *Leo*?" Miles said. His gaze moved over Vivian, and then over the scars on Frank's hands, but he didn't seem to be seeing us. "When did she get here?"

No one knew; we'd noticed the argument, but nothing before it. But Leo, insisted someone—it might have been Belle—had been there the whole time. How else could he have been poisoned so badly? And much of the time, Arkady added, it was Eudora to whom Leo had been whispering. She'd left, Frank said, to help clean up after Myra had her hemorrhage.

"That's one of the times the door opened?" Miles interrupted.

"I think so," someone said.

"And you think Leo was there all the rest of the time? While the door kept opening and closing?"

"We were watching the movies," someone else said. "But he must have been there. How else could he have gone to help Kathleen?"

～

IN THE OLD BUILDING, Dr. Petrie's office had been on the second floor, not far from the library, while Dr. Richards' suite of four rooms had been on the ground floor, opposite the reception desk and within easy reach of important visitors. In their new quarters in the women's annex they were squeezed into adjacent rooms, separated only by the flimsy walls and doors deemed sufficient when these were our bedrooms. Miles walked into Dr. Petrie's office again, this time without knocking and without even looking at the chair. What, he asked, without sitting down, did Dr. Petrie know about a connection between Naomi and Leo Marburg?

"I hardly know Naomi," Dr. Petrie said cautiously. "She never confided in me. But once or twice I did see her talking with Leo. And they had some sort of argument the night of the fire. She was gone before the trouble started, though."

"Did you see her leave?"

"Someone did. Eudora, I think."

"Did Leo go with her?"

Dr. Petrie spread his hands. "How would I know? It was dark before the fire started, and once it did—all I know is that I found him by Kathleen, both of them unconscious."

Miles nodded and moved on to Dr. Richards' office. The walls were so thin that Dr. Petrie could hear their voices, Dr. Richards remaining calm despite Miles's increasing intensity. He heard Miles saying, *We must, we must*, before they left the office together, still talking earnestly.

⁓

THAT WEEK, we had just begun to use the rough kitchen and the new dining room reconstructed in the women's annex. Our old tables were gone—stripping and refinishing them had turned out to be too much work—and at each of the new rectangular tables a dozen of us now sat elbow to elbow, men and women separated only by a narrow surface: the sole good change. We could look into each other's faces, sit side by side and talk; apparently, given our new housing arrangements, separating us at meals no longer had a point. On the last day of July, while we were eating our midday dinner in each other's company, the men who worked for Miles returned. After dinner, Abe, Arkady, and Otto stepped through the doorway to their room and found the three agents looking in the nightstands and under the beds, lifting the sheets and the blankets and peering at the books.

"Excuse me," Arkady said. "What are you doing?"

He retrieved his own pillow from one of the men. The agent took it back and tried to explain, even as Abe clutched his slippers to his chest.

"It's come to this?" Otto said, sitting down heavily on his bed.

The second agent grimaced. "Dr. Richards' orders," he said. "Don't make a fuss."

"Everyone's room?" Arkady asked. "Or just us?"

"Just you," the third agent said calmly.

Arkady and Abe sat down on either side of Otto then, glaring at the strangers. It was an outrage, Otto thought. Ridiculous, thought Abe. But it would be over, Arkady thought, in a minute; they'd done nothing wrong. The third agent opened Leo's locker, which was also now Otto's—we'd all had to double up—and, after examining the shoes on the floor and the clothes on the hooks, found under Leo's jacket the little tin box Eudora and Naomi had held.

"Yours?" the agent said to Otto.

"I've never seen it," Otto said truthfully.

"Then it belongs to Leo Marburg?"

"How would I know?" Otto said.

The agent returned to the empty bed and pointed at the white-topped table beside it. "Leo's?" he asked Abe.

"Obviously," Abe said.

The agent picked up the two green volumes, which he must have already looked at once; they sat squarely in the center of the table, not open as Otto had left them. Now Arkady watched the agent reinspect them with disturbing eagerness. "We should take these," he said to his two companions. "*The Principles of Chemistry*—wouldn't you like to know what he learned from *these*?" The three men nodded at each other and one went off to notify Dr. Richards.

We are nothing if not efficient and the news spread instantly; the rest of us knew what had happened, and what was in the box, even before Dr. Richards returned an hour later with Miles. When we saw him arrive in his sleek new machine, we clammed up. No one had to tell Arkady, Otto, and Abe not to speak further while Dr. Richards and Miles searched the locker again, checking for anything the agents might have missed.

"You three," Miles said. "What do you know about this box?"

Nothing, they said; nothing, nothing. They'd never seen the box or its contents before. In the midst of their protestations, Dr. Petrie, who'd just heard what was going on, skidded into the room.

"What's this about?" he asked indignantly.

Miles showed him the contents of the box. "Otto claims it isn't his," he said. "Which makes it Leo's. I've seen drawings of these in the papers and I suspect you have too. What possible reason could Leo have for owning such things, unless he had a plan to burn the place down?"

Something like pleasure rushed through Miles's veins as he spoke. Earlier, piecing together the chronology of movie night, he'd found that although the details themselves were painful, their accretion into an orderly structure was as satisfying as mapping out a fossil skeleton dispersed in rough ground. As he'd explained the chronology, substituting for our chaotic and contradictory memories one clean narrative of the night, he'd felt sure that this work would yield similar rewards. Already it had uncovered three new shards of truth: Naomi had been here that night; Leo had lured her here; Leo was a liar. When he thought of Naomi, forced to run away because of something Leo had said or done to her, he wanted to throw the bedside table through the wall.

"Leo wouldn't hurt a fly," Dr. Petrie said.

But with the box in his hand, the intact pencil-that-wasn't-a-pencil exposed along with the pieces of another and the diagram showing how the pieces went back together, Miles could see that his own intuitions had been right. A perfect structure rose before him, the last bones ready to lock into place.

"That's Leo's handwriting," he said triumphantly. "Look how he shapes the r's—I've seen that on his notes." Perhaps it was over this very diagram that Naomi and Leo had quarreled; no wonder her voice had been raised, no wonder people had noticed them arguing! If she had only come to him when she first suspected trouble, he might have prevented everything.

The diagram did look bad, Dr. Petrie admitted to himself. So clear, so careful. But to Miles he said, "You're talking about a man who risked his own life to save that of another patient."

In answer, Miles held out the volumes his agents had plucked from Leo's table. "Since when do patients have books like this?" he asked. "We could have another Dr. Scheele on our hands. That druggist, in Brooklyn—a German chemist, from a family of chemists, who was sent here by the German government as an undercover agent."

"The Scheele cigar bomb," Dr. Petrie murmured, appalled at the connections Miles was making. He'd seen the diagrams in the newspaper, a little metal tube a few inches long, separated by a thin tin partition into two compartments. Some chemical filled one compartment, a corrosive acid the other, needing only a sailor or a stoker willing to plant the tube in the bowels of the ship. Out at sea, a few days later, the acid would eat its way through the tin and combine with the chemical to start a fire. Ships had burned to the waterline.

"How is this different, really, from those cigar bombs?" Miles asked. "Even you can see the resemblance. And here we have another chemist, also with a German name, and another device in close proximity to a fire . . ."

"It's true that Leo has an interest in chemistry," Dr. Petrie said, "but we all knew that. Irene *gave* him those books, and she loaned him others. I loaned him some, myself."

His stomach rolled and burned and his ears were ringing. Was he going to faint? He'd been working too hard since the fire, seldom sleeping, eating poorly, cut off until recently from the comfort of talking with Irene.

To Miles he said, "His interests don't make him a criminal. I'm sure there's a good explanation for the box—if you have a question, go ask him. He's still weak, but he's well enough to talk."

"You *would* defend him," Miles said. He closed the box and tucked it carefully under his arm. "I'm going back to town, I have to check something and I need to make some telephone calls." *I have to talk to Eudora,* he thought. "But I'll be back tomorrow," he said.

EUDORA HE FOUND on the ground floor of the men's annex, bent over a bucket in her blue wrapper, disinfecting the baseboards along the main hall. He was so angry that he nearly slipped on the damp linoleum as he rushed toward her. Clearly she knew far more than she'd let on weeks ago at Mrs. Martin's house, when she'd evaded his question about Naomi's disappearance. Perhaps she'd been lying all along, about everything.

But before he could ask her where, exactly, she'd been during the fire, and what she knew about Leo and Naomi, she straightened up, a wet rag in her hand, and said, "What gave you the right to search Leo's *room*?"

"The law," Miles said, surprised at her boldness. "The new laws give me every right; I would have been remiss if I hadn't looked. Just as you were remiss not to tell me what he was studying. Those books Irene supposedly gave him: you knew about those?"

Drops of water darkened Eudora's wrapper as she squeezed her rag. She already knew what his agents had found—news does travel fast here—but she hadn't realized how he might interpret it. Without knowing she was repeating Dr. Petrie's words, she said, "Studying chemistry doesn't make Leo a criminal. I—"

"It's not just the chemistry books," he interrupted. "Not even the books combined with what's in here." He tapped the box tucked under his elbow. "It's everything, every aspect of his behavior. No one's thinking clearly. Not you, not Dr. Petrie. Not even me. We have to look at this rationally—I'm upset, of course I'm upset. That doesn't mean I can ignore the facts. And you—why didn't you tell me that Naomi was here the night of the fire? Why didn't you tell me before about Leo's interest in Naomi?"

"What's between them is private," she said indignantly, ignoring the first part of his question. "And what does that have to do with—"

"I'm trying to find out the *truth*," he said, interrupting her yet again. "Which is more than I can say for you—you've made a fool out of me. Naomi visiting Leo, at his invitation I'm sure; Leo quarreling with her on the very night of the fire. You hid this from me. All of you did."

"There wasn't any *hiding*," she said. "It wasn't your business. And Leo doesn't care for her. He never has."

As she spoke, Miles's new chauffeur appeared at the far end of the hall, his left shoe with its built-up sole clumping heavily. "There's a message!" Tyler called, his face shining with eagerness.

"Stop," Miles said. "Wait for me right there." He turned back to Eudora. "How do you know Leo's *not* interested in her?" he asked.

"Because . . ." It was awful to have to say it out loud, but she couldn't think how else to turn his attention away from Leo. "Because he's in love with me." How had she let everything grow so confused?

"But if that's true," he said, "if that's true . . ." His fingers moved as if he longed to be holding a pencil, noting on a sheet of paper this new piece of data, which needed to be fitted in among all the others. "Then what was Naomi doing here at movie night?"

"You'd have to ask Naomi that."

Miles looked at her suspiciously. "You're still hiding something."

"I'm not," Eudora said. "Just saying that what's private is private."

Forty feet down the corridor, Tyler bounced in place and gestured at his watch but, obedient to Miles, approached no closer. Before Miles could ask her anything else, Eudora dropped her rag and stalked away, brushing past Tyler as if he were a potted plant. She went home, went straight to bed, and slept for ten hours, comforted only by the knowledge that she had the next day off. In the morning—this was August 1—she opened her closet before she'd even had breakfast and pulled out the drawings that Naomi, over the years, had given her. Her own face, her parents, her brothers; the elegant house with a large front garden that once had been Naomi's home and now was occupied by strangers; all vibrated with life and none offered a clue as to what had happened to her.

If she could find Naomi, she thought. If Naomi would only call or write, she could apologize. She stared at the drawings for a few minutes longer before carefully packing them up again. Since the time they'd met, Naomi had been threatening to run away; finally she'd carried out what had often seemed like no more than an idle threat. Too clever to signal her intentions, she'd taken only the Model T and the money she'd stolen from Miles and her mother: all she needed, really, to speed her trip. Eudora couldn't figure out, though, whether she'd meant all along to leave that night and had stopped at Tamarack State to say goodbye to Leo—perhaps even to convince him to come with her?—or whether she'd left on an impulse. When Leo had reached for Eudora's hand, Naomi had looked as stricken as Miles had yesterday, in the corridor. My fault, Eudora thought: both times. If only Irene were well enough to advise her.

21

LATE ON THAT afternoon of August 1, Leo sat, propped up by a mound of pillows, looking at the wall. The new infirmary was smaller than the old, as the new beds were shorter, and he was alone in the dark and narrow room. Kathleen, Irene, and Janet had all been released and no one new had come to fill the beds. He'd missed the announcement that intake had been halted, as he'd missed so much else; everything since the fire was hazed by his fever. Vaguely he remembered Eudora's visits, her beautiful skin obscured behind a mask, and Irene sitting by his bed, silently pressing his hand. Except for them his only company had been Dr. Petrie, who, perhaps sensing his loneliness, had come by almost daily. Lately, as he'd begun to eat again and to recover some of his lost strength, his isolation had felt like actual pain.

Dr. Petrie's new office was close by and at the sound of footsteps coming down the hall Leo straightened himself against the pillows, hoping the doctor might stop by for a minute. Then he slumped down again: two sets of steps, a disappointment. Orderlies, perhaps. He'd already begun to turn away when Dr. Richards and Miles Fairchild marched into the ward.

Their faces were drawn and Miles's cheeks were flushed, but Leo had no chance to wonder why. Dr. Richards held out, opened, and then closed again the little tin box that Ephraim had left behind. Leo was so bewildered by his accusations and by Miles, yapping like a dog, that at first he couldn't understand what either of them were saying.

"We found this in your *locker*," Dr. Richards repeated.

Miles was barking words like "traitor" and "spy" while Dr. Richards, obviously upset, seemed to be weighing two stories. In one, Leo had done everything Miles accused him of doing—plotted cunningly, planned carefully, obtained and concealed a secret weapon, attempted to destroy an institution of the state—while in the other, there was a different explanation for the presence, in his locker, of this box. No point, Leo saw, addressing Miles. He turned toward Dr. Richards.

"The box isn't mine, and neither is anything in it," he said. "It was never mine."

"So how did it get in your locker?"

He opened his mouth and then closed it, registering what he'd glimpsed when Dr. Richards had opened the lid: one of the little fire-wands was missing. Ephraim, he thought at first. In his occasional notes from Ovid, Ephraim had described his daughter's slow recovery, his own brief relapse, and then, cheerfully, his increasing strength throughout the spring. Perhaps he'd taken one of the pencils before he left—but he couldn't have, Leo realized then. All three pencils had been in the box when he'd dissected one and made the diagram. Then someone here had nosed around in his locker? Almost he groaned out loud. He'd kept the box when he knew he shouldn't, he'd left it where anyone might find it; if the missing pencil had anything to do with the fire, then he was at least partially to blame.

"I was taking care of it for someone," was all he would admit. We give him high marks for this, even though we wish he and Ephraim had told the rest of us, back when it happened, how it got here.

"We found your books," Miles said. "We know what you've been studying, we *know* you have a background in chemistry." He reached over, opened the box in Dr. Richards' hands, and extracted the sketch showing the instrument's design. "So don't pretend you don't understand exactly how these work. Or that you didn't make this diagram. Isn't this your handwriting?"

Again Leo sat helplessly. Of course it was. But nothing seemed safe to say; any comment would lead to other questions and then to lies.

And indeed Miles was already saying, as he rattled the paper in his hand, "Are you going to lie right to my face?"

The sun, blazing through the window, cast a bright shaft across the room, truncating Dr. Richards' legs and cutting Miles in two. Leo let himself slide an inch or two down the bed, and then an inch or two more, into a posture that often bothered him. As he slipped into the pool of sun, he began to cough. At first the racking croaks that had accompanied his pneumonia, and then something deeper, something wet and bubbling he hadn't felt in months. He coughed and coughed, his face burning, the bed shaking, half lost but still aware of Miles and Dr. Richards stepping back and of their expressions when, after a few minutes, he pressed a napkin to his lips and was able to pull it away spotted with blood.

NEWS OF THAT scene spread quickly, and some damage was already done by the next day, when Dr. Petrie was called into Dr. Richards' office for yet another discussion. There he found Dr. Richards struggling, as were the rest of us, between his own knowledge of Leo's character and what, he said, was Miles's fierce conviction that Leo had somehow caused the fire.

"If you had seen Leo yesterday," Dr. Richards said, "the way he went silent—"

"I *did* see him," Dr. Petrie said. "Last night, when I went to check on him." On the corner of Dr. Richards' desk lay the confiscated copy of *The Principles of Chemistry*. Months ago, before the fire, Dr. Petrie had paused in his rounds while Leo read to him a sentence from one of those green volumes: *Knowing how contented, free, and joyful is life in the realm of science, one fervently wishes that many would enter its portals.* They'd laughed like hyenas, agreeing that science as they knew it was endlessly interesting, even engrossing—but never free, not here.

To Dr. Richards, he said, "I was getting ready to release him to his room, but now—he's taken a big step backwards."

"His health has to come first," said Dr. Richards, tugging at his ear. "Still, even you might admit that the evidence Miles has gathered is more than troubling." He gestured toward the books. "If those belonged to one of us, it would be different. But for someone like Leo to have them, along with that box, and then to offer such a feeble excuse . . ."

"But he has a perfectly good reason for having those books," Dr. Petrie said wearily, repeating what he'd already told Miles. What, exactly, did Dr. Richards mean by "one of us?" "Irene gave them to him, so he could study. Give him a little time to explain himself."

"I don't think we have much. Miles wants me to go to the Board of Overseers and see about a new official investigation. Or, failing that, that we let him organize one himself through his committee. He took the box as evidence." Dr. Richards plucked his ear again. "We're supposed to keep this secret, but I think you know already—I'm on that committee too, now. Along with quite a few people you know. Miles reports to someone at the Secret Service and I think it's going to matter, later, who joined and who didn't."

Dr. Petrie stared at the mounds of paper surrounding the green volumes, aware that even his silence cast him as Leo's champion. Whatever evidence Miles had uncovered, he wouldn't get to see it; Miles would tell him nothing more now. If he'd joined the league, Miles might have spoken more openly—but how could he have done that? The letter of invitation had burned his hands like poison. He'd dropped it, tossed a newspaper over it, failed to answer it for a week, and finally responded with a one-line note. All he could do now was try to delay Miles and Dr. Richards until Leo was ready to explain himself. Baffled, he said, "I have work to do. Would you excuse me?"

At least, Dr. Petrie thought as he left, Leo had friends: by that he meant us. Back in his own office, he pushed aside a pile of papers and then, exasperated by the chaos on his desk—how could he work, how could he *think*, with these tongues of paper lapping from stack to stack, stray sheets wandering from one report into another?—he swept the whole array into a single mass and heaped it on the floor. One project on his desk at a time, which he could then work on unimpeded. For the moment he wanted only to think about Leo and Miles. If Miles really wanted to push matters, he'd be supported by the rest of his league and maybe even by Dr. Richards. On the other hand, Leo would be supported by all of us. So many companions, willing to testify about Leo's good character, must be worth something. Calmed slightly by that realization, he began pulling sheets from the pile.

OVER THE NEXT FEW DAYS, what Dr. Petrie sensed as he made his rounds among us shocked him as much as if we'd all sprouted tails. We were so cold-blooded we shocked ourselves. From the moment Miles's agents searched Leo's room, something swept through the sanatorium that we're still ashamed to admit, and that we still don't completely understand. On the night of the search, it spread from the cluster of Abe, Arkady, and Otto through the second-floor porch in both directions. *The chemist*, we muttered among ourselves: as if we didn't know Leo, as if we didn't know better. *Of course. Who else?* From that row of densely packed chairs, the judgment we were so quick to pass seeped up to the women on the third-floor porch, down to the men on the first-floor porch, voices rising as the conversation took hold. Leo had shown no one the little tin box; why was that? We hadn't seen the diagram, and we knew nothing then about Ephraim's visitor; why had Leo been so secretive? And what had he said to Naomi that had so upset her on the night of the fire?

He kept secrets, we felt. He always had—and now, as news spread of Leo's well-timed coughing fit and his failure to answer Miles's questions, we discovered that we'd all resented that. Who'd given him the right to keep himself to himself? By the end of the second day, our suspicions had painted a portrait of Leo about as close to his true self as Eudora's X-ray portrait was to his living, breathing lungs. Dr. Petrie and Eudora both found, over those two days, that each time they moved toward a group of us we'd break up and slip away, no one saying anything, everyone avoiding any mention of Leo. Dr. Petrie, so sure he understood us that he often assumed he *was* one of us, could not believe what he was seeing. When it registered, he went to Irene.

During Irene's stay in the new infirmary, he'd visited her daily, reading aloud to her or simply chatting into the silence. Leo, so glad for Dr. Petrie's visits, didn't know that she was the one who'd really drawn Dr. Petrie there; he'd stopped by to see Leo only after seeing her. He brought her tidbits from the newspapers and news about the latest conception of atoms and their structure. Astonishing, he said, the reverse of common sense. Instead of seeing the atom as a solar system, electrons whirling like planets around a dense nucleus, now we were to imagine that each atom possessed a certain number of possible shells which the electrons might inhabit.

Irene, her throat bandaged, her face scarred, had listened intently, comforted as no one else would be by his blundering explanation of atomic structure. Her mind, he'd seen then to his huge relief, was as keen as ever. Now, as he knocked at the door of her room in the women's staff cottage, he felt sure that she'd be able to make some sense of Miles's accusations, Leo's reticence—he felt sure Leo had willed his collapse, as a way of gaining time—and our disturbing behavior.

Her room, which had only one window, still seemed cheerful and bright and Dr. Petrie sank with relief into her blue upholstered chair. Resting his feet on the ottoman, he explained the events of the last three days as Irene, still unable to speak, listened closely, nodding now and then. She'd already heard about the search.

"The worst of it," Dr. Petrie said, "is what's driving Miles to pursue this. He told both Dr. Richards and his own agents that Leo's background makes him particularly suspicious. Russian, Jewish, German—there's not a part of him Miles trusts. But we both know the real reason. Apparently someone hinted at Naomi Martin's feelings for Leo, and once that happened . . ."

Irene, her mouth compressed, reached for her pad of paper. *Why are the patients acting like such sheep?* she wrote. Us, she meant.

"They're frightened," Dr. Petrie said with a shrug.

But not of Leo, she wrote. *Surely not of him. I should have told them why he was studying, this is partly my fault—*

"Not at all!" Dr. Petrie protested. "We were trying to help."

Still, she wrote. *I don't understand how he got that box.*

"I don't either," Dr. Petrie said. "I was hoping you might."

But let's be logical, she wrote. *I had a good reason for giving him those books. So let's assume someone else gave him the box for a similarly good reason. Also that he has a good reason not to tell us what that is.*

"Rather a leap," Dr. Petrie said. "Very generous; probably correct. But not convincing."

There are also other factors, she wrote, tearing off that sheet and turning it over.

For another half hour they continued their conversation, Dr. Petrie rising once to close the window. Although the afternoon had been hot, the night was beautifully cool and the room had slowly chilled. This was the weather that convinced people to cure in the Adirondacks: this antiseptic pine-scented breeze, these stars brilliant in a dense black sky, owls and nighthawks speaking in the dark. The noise Dr. Petrie heard was unfamiliar, though, a gentle, low-pitched wave of sound that rose and fell, rose and fell, wordless but still signaling emotion. It took him a few minutes to realize that he was hearing our porches humming, fifty feet away.

⸻

IRENE HEARD THAT noise as well, and the sound stayed with her through the next day, as she wrote to Dr. Richards in defense of Leo.

> *I first got to know Leo Marburg through the Wednesday meetings organized by Miles Fairchild,* she wrote. *Since then, I have helped him with his studies in chemistry—he was* trained *as a chemist, as was I. He's an intelligent and honorable man, eager to learn and to further his education, and I gave him those two books, which he wanted purely for his intellectual pursuits. They were mine before they were his; there is nothing the least bit dangerous in them, in the right hands.*

She paused for a moment, remembering the look on Leo's face when she'd given him the green volumes. The swiftness with which he'd learned, the intensity with which he'd worked; she'd been hoping to offer him an apprenticeship that might someday, after his discharge, lead to a job as satisfying as her own. If she hadn't immigrated here with money in her pocket, a married sister to greet her, and a brother-in-law willing to help fund her studies, she might easily have ended up no better off than Leo was. Firmly, she continued:

I don't know how Leo came by that box and its contents, but I'm sure there's a perfectly reasonable explanation; he's a person of sterling character and I would vouch for him in any situation. In any event, there's no link between those objects and the fire, which I know for a fact that he couldn't have started. I was in the X-ray facility that evening; at no point was there any sign of him. The one person who visited me was Miles Fairchild's young driver, Naomi Martin.

We had a discussion. She was upset about something when she came to see me, and still upset when she ran out. Because I was worried about her, I went after her, but before I could catch her, she pushed through the service door and ran away. On my way back to the X-ray facility I smelled something odd, which when I think about it now makes me wonder if we didn't have a short in the transformer, or a failure in the main electric line. When I opened the door the room was already filling up with smoke and so I brought my smock up over my face and rushed into the back.

With one hand, she realized, she was clutching at her throat, her body returning before she could stop it to the fire itself. What that had felt like, which she could never write down. She dreamed, still, of expressing some confused version of this out loud, an easier task than shaping a single version on the page. She would have preferred to write nothing, waiting until her voice returned—but Dr. Petrie had said that Leo's situation was urgent, and it was possible that she wouldn't speak again. She couldn't remember breathing through the bit of tubing Dr. Petrie had pushed into the slit in her throat, but when she closed her eyes, she could still see the scalpel glitter in the moonlight. She turned to the letter again.

I couldn't find where the fire was coming from and couldn't put it out, although I did save some of our films. At no point was Leo or anyone other than Naomi in the room with me.

She folded the pages, wondering at the same time how Leo was. If she could have seen him alone in the empty ward, hearing the troubled hum from the porches as we turned against him, our ill will emanating through the corridor where not one friendly set of footsteps echoed; if she could have known how alone he felt, she would have risen despite her own exhaustion and gone to stand silently next to him.

22

ILES VISITED THE sanatorium several times during the first two weeks after Leo's relapse, but Dr. Petrie refused to let him see Leo; an emotional upset might, he claimed, make his condition worse, and Leo had to be spared any stress. The hay was mowed in the fields while Miles came and went and came again; the hay was dried in rows and then it was baled. The creeks dried up and the locusts buzzed as day after day the sky shone imperturbably blue. In the garden the pansies wilted and we did too, in our over-crowded rooms. The rough new kitchen wasn't ventilated well, and so our densely packed dining room smelled of cooking and, on the hottest days, of us; Miles avoided that place. But everywhere else at Tamarack State continued to seem like his fair territory. Our improvised mail-room, where he looked at what came in and went out; our pitiful library, reconstituted in a former bedroom in the women's annex and reduced from its already shameful state when, after Miles's inspection, his agents removed any books by Germans, or in German, or about Germany or the

Austro-Hungarian empire. We don't know if he bullied Dr. Richards into this or if Dr. Richards freely agreed, nor do we know how he arranged to have our shipments of newspapers from New York City stopped. We do know that he considered a plan to enlist the national headquarters of the American Protective League, perhaps aided by the Department of Labor, in the deportation of Leo Marburg—a plan he might have followed through on had it not been for Irene's letter and Dr. Petrie's maneuvers.

To Dr. Petrie's surprise and then dismay, Dr. Richards hadn't been convinced by Irene's letter. What seemed so obvious to him, the argument that, as he gently reminded Dr. Richards, not only supported what he himself had said about the presence of the chemistry books in Leo's room, but also made it almost impossible that Leo could have had anything to do with the fire, was for Dr. Richards apparently only one facet of something more complex.

"If you trust Irene," Dr. Petrie had pointed out, "then you have to believe what she wrote. Which means Leo didn't do anything. He couldn't have."

"I know that seems true," Dr. Richards said, obviously troubled, "and I know I was the one who pushed to hire Irene; I've *always* trusted her. But Miles has raised other points."

Whatever those were, they were enough, Dr. Petrie saw, to pressure Dr. Richards into continuing to let Miles interfere in our daily business, and to make Dr. Richards so nervous that he asked Dr. Petrie not to tell us about Irene's letter. Because Dr. Petrie honored that request, and perhaps because Irene was confined to her room in the staff cottage and still unable to talk, our information-gathering failed this once and her letter didn't immediately become public knowledge. For a little while longer, then, we were left in our uncertainty. In the new infirmary the nurses checked on Leo every few hours but refused—Dr. Petrie's orders, they said—to talk to him about Miles's investigations. Dr. Petrie himself came by twice a day but, wanting Leo to heal as quickly as possible, also said nothing about Miles or the shifting moods inside Tamarack State. Rest, he said, echoing the instructions Leo had received almost a year ago. Think only of resting.

Lying there alone, Leo tried to convince himself that the situation with Miles would heal itself quietly, gradually, in the same fashion that his lung was healing. He'd insulted Miles, he saw now. Back in March, when he'd turned down Miles's generous offer to move him to Mrs. Martin's house, he should have been more delicate; he might have expected that his refusal would make Miles feel like the outsider he was. Now Miles, obviously angry about more than just the box, was paying him back for his clumsiness. He'd apologize, Leo thought, and explain why he'd wanted to stay here. Although even if that worked, it wouldn't fix what was going on with us. Until he'd heard that humming from our porches, he'd always assumed that here—up in the mountains, far from the crowds; here, where the air was clear—he was safe from the poison of his last weeks in New York, when everyone had turned from him.

Much of what happened to him then had stemmed, he thought, from his bad luck in falling ill when another disease was raging through his neighborhood, and when his landlady was already so worried about her children. The streets along which he walked to work had fallen strangely silent soon after the first cases of infantile paralysis were diagnosed. The pool had closed, then the movie house, and then the ball field had emptied; men came and shot the dogs and cats in the alleys, to keep them from spreading the disease. Silenced, the days had felt like nights. In the shops, people turned away from each other, fingering the little bags of camphor and garlic hanging from their necks and embarrassed—had they been embarrassed?—not to be able to help each other for fear of infecting their own children. Everything had seemed infected. Bricks leapt from the roof of a building struck by lightning and hit the children walking below; a hammer glancing off a pipe at the oil plant in Greenpoint set off an explosion; a subway excavation caved in and buried twenty workers.

In Williamsburg, mothers carried into the clinics screaming babies who could no longer wave their arms or hold their bottles, while others hid from the nurses who knocked on doors. Rumors spread: that the doctors got a bonus for each child captured and taken to the hospital. That the children got sick from eating ice cream, which chilled their stomachs, and that stores sold them ice cream anyway. That gasoline fumes spread the disease (why were automobiles still allowed on the streets?), or commercial laundries (the germs moved in the sheets). That the mothers of stricken children shook their sleeves over the cans of purified milk at the milk stations, hoping other children might sicken as well.

He'd found those rumors terrifying. He knew what happened when they spread, and he knew how the solitary were punished. During his last year at the refinery, after he began working as Karl's assistant, he'd been neither a salaried employee nor quite one of the regular laborers. Upstairs, where the magma spun in the centrifuges and the raw-sugar crystals, separated from the syrup, tumbled into the melter, he was alone when he tested the liquor's acidity, adding milk of lime until the proteins coagulated and then telling the foreman when to release the fluid into the cloth filters packed with diatomaceous earth. Alone at the other end of the line, he tested the final product; alone on the dock, he sampled the loads of raw sugar. Only by a freakish bit of bad luck had a stranger seen him cough blood onto the crystals, and then he'd had no friend to lie for him.

The two refinery workers who brought him home and helped him up to the flat told Rachel and Tobias exactly what had happened. Rachel, whose sister had died of tuberculosis, wanted to evict him from the apartment immediately, but Tobias reminded her of how much they needed the rent. After the tuberculosis nurse made her visit, Rachel had added her own refinements to the nurse's advice. She washed Leo's plate and utensils separately and stored them in a cardboard box kept out on the fire escape, where she made him eat his meals. Her children ran, holding their breath, when they had to pass his cot to get to their own. The four other boarders, after watching this, hung a spare sheet from the ceiling between his cot and theirs. He'd learned, then, what it really meant to have no family. Not having kin here, and not having roots in a single village or city, had set him apart more than he'd understood. When the nurse found him a spot at the tuberculosis day camp, he'd been glad to go.

Sometimes he'd glimpsed men on the lower deck of the old ferryboat moored at the recreation pier, but until he was sent there he'd never known what they were doing. The boat had looked like a hulk being stripped for salvage, but instead, he learned, it salvaged consumptives, who took their daily cure behind heavy nets that screened them from passersby. Among the deck chairs he found Meyer, a man he'd once known at the char house and who, having been there for two months already, helped him settle into his new routine.

He rose when Meyer told him to, so that he could drink glasses of milk or eat boiled eggs, sit down at one o'clock to the enormous dinners somehow produced in the boat's tiny kitchen, later drink milk again. In the mornings, well-meaning women brought them stacks of newly sewn shirt collars, still inside out; each collar had to be turned, the collar points poked out with a small smooth dowel and the seams aligned to be pressed. They worked for two hours: earning their keep, said the camp director sternly. After dinner they rested until a nurse came by and took temperatures and pulses. Once a week the doctor tapped and listened to their backs and chests, looked down their throats and in their ears.

And that was it, not bad at all; the routine passed the time. The most difficult part was returning each night to Rachel's domain and the glare of all those nervous eyes. Meyer, cared for at night by the three cousins, the aunt, and the grandmother with whom he shared an apartment, couldn't understand why Leo lived like that.

"But you have countrymen," he'd said. "People from your home, who'd be glad to welcome you; a *landsmanschaft*, surely? I belong to the Young Men of Poniewiez and they've helped me with everything. They help my family, and they're making arrangements to get me into a Jewish sanatorium. Someplace where the doctors speak Yiddish. And where the food is more what I'm used to."

When Leo explained, yet again, that he didn't speak Yiddish and that he was an atheist, Meyer said, "You Russians who aren't Jews—how do you live?"

During his third week on the boat, the polio epidemic spread to New Rochelle, carried, or so the newspapers claimed, by four Italian families. On Long Island, Boy Scouts went house to house, searching for children visiting from New York and, with the help of their parents, driving them back beyond the city line—and still, Leo had imagined that he'd be returning to work as soon as his coughing stopped. On the ferryboat, a social worker told him that she could get him a place at the Municipal Sanatorium in the Catskills but Leo said he'd prefer to stay in Williamsburg—learning only then that the Board of Health could send him wherever they chose, that he'd never been free to leave, and that the refinery would never take him back.

That night, when he returned to his cot in the small apartment, Rachel refused to wash his clothes although this was included in his weekly rent. On Sunday Tobias, speaking from the door of his and Rachel's room, finally told him that they'd done what they could and that he had to find someplace else to live. By the end of July he'd been out of money, out of work, and about to lose his lodging. Just in time, his placement up here had come through.

On his last night in Williamsburg, he'd slipped outside after everyone was asleep. Where the streets should have been packed with people trying to catch a breeze, the fire escapes carpeted with children lying on folded blankets, the rooftops covered with older people trying to sleep and younger ones hoping to find some privacy, instead he'd found almost no one. A few young men were drinking; piano music rose from the bars. By the waterfront he saw the flare of matches, three or four people sitting out on the wharves to fish and smoke cigarettes, and although it was nearly two in the morning he'd walked that way, through the gentle breeze, to the water. His last night, as he remembered it, of freedom.

HE MULLED OVER those experiences during his first, solitary week. Midway through the second week, after his temperature had come back down, he was allowed his first visitor: not Miles, thankfully, but Eudora. From his bed he saw her pause in the doorway, looking up and down the corridor as if to make sure she was unobserved. As she turned her head, a moth detached itself from the lampshade and drifted her way, passing so close to her neck that he could feel the touch on his own skin.

"How are you feeling?" she asked. "Better?"

"Better," he agreed. When she smiled he felt, at first, only the pleasure of seeing her. Then he saw that she held one hand pressed over the side pocket of her blue wrapper, as if she had a pain there. Still working double shifts, six days a week—suppose she was getting sick? He said, "But how are *you*?"

She shrugged, looking back toward the door. "Busy," she said, "but fine. I was very relieved when Dr. Petrie said yesterday that you could have visitors." With her hand flattened along the top of her thigh, she continued, "It's not as if this is my first time—I came to see you a lot when you were first sick. Don't you remember?"

"Not exactly." He sat up a little straighter, smoothing the front of the white shift required in the infirmary. Beneath the blanket, his legs were humiliatingly bare. "I couldn't always tell what I was dreaming and what was real. But I thought I remembered you sitting next to me, wearing a mask."

She nodded. "I stopped by most days to see you and Irene. She still can't talk, but she's doing much better."

"I heard."

He waited for a moment, wondering when she'd ask him about what Miles had found, hoping she'd leap into the silence. Instead she looked around again and then drew from her wrapper pocket an oblong tin. "For you," she said.

A smaller, more delicate version of the box Miles had taken from his locker—for a second, he wondered if she was mocking him. As he pried at the lid, she said, "I baked them."

"Cookies," he said, wonderingly.

She made a wry face. "I hope they're all right; I'm not much of a baker but I wanted to make you something."

He nibbled the edge of a tawny disk: gritty, buttery, not too sweet, scented with vanilla. Something like shortbread but not as rich. In another life, in another century, his mother had made a treat with ground almonds that had tasted faintly like this and had a similar sandy texture. His mouth watered, and then his eyes.

"Then you don't believe what Miles has been saying about me?" he asked. After all, his relapse had been worth something. The moth flapped slowly back into the room, found a column of sunlight, and began spiraling up toward the ceiling, spacing its turns as closely as if it were moving through the coils of a still.

Eudora looked down at the tin. "No," she said, more slowly than he would have wished. From that he knew he'd been right to fear the hum from our porches.

"The box belongs to a friend of Ephraim's," he said, sketching the story of Felix's visit—but not, we have to note, telling her that the box had once held three pencils rather than two. On the other hand, she'd never admitted to him that she'd seen the box at all—and she didn't admit that now. All she said, when he was finished, was, "I knew there was an explanation. Can I tell the others?"

He shook his head. "It's too risky, the way Miles is acting. He has contacts all over the state. Maybe all over the country—I don't want anything to happen to Ephraim or his family. And you know what it's like here: tell one person, and everyone else knows in an hour. People here know me well enough; they ought to just trust me. You did."

"But I'm not a patient here," she said, startling him.

~

MILES COULDN'T PROVE anything, especially since he couldn't question Leo further. But at both Tamarack State and throughout the village he voiced his suspicions. He told anyone who'd listen about Leo's refusal of a room at Mrs. Martin's house—some of us were indeed baffled by that, and others annoyed; no one offered *us* such things—and he harped on the box and its contents.

Finally, after Dr. Petrie found Miles discussing Leo with the milk delivery man, he asked Miles for a private meeting, much as Miles had once asked him. First Miles said he was too busy; then, relenting a bit, said he might be able to spare a few minutes but that he couldn't come to his office. "In the village, then," Dr. Petrie said. "Tomorrow, or the next day?"

"Tomorrow," Miles said. "At Mrs. Martin's house."

"Not there," Dr. Petrie said. They compromised on the picnic area at the lake's east end, not exactly convenient but easy enough for both to reach.

It was raining that Wednesday, without a breath of breeze and still very warm; Dr. Petrie, arriving first, chose a bench and covered his end with half the piece of oilcloth he'd carried down the hill. Then he sat beneath the shelter of his old umbrella, carefully keeping the rest of the cloth dry. When Miles arrived, five minutes late, he unrolled the rest of the cloth and watched, bemused, as Miles perched at the farthest end of the bench and hid under his own umbrella. Briefly the ribs of the two umbrellas clashed, so that Dr. Petrie was forced another inch away.

"What is it you want?" asked Miles, looking straight ahead. "I have another meeting in less than an hour."

"I want you to stop bothering Leo Marburg," Dr. Petrie said. Out on the lake young gulls, speckled like eggs, were floating in groups of three and four, apparently more interesting to Miles than anything he himself said. "I'm asking you as one professional man to another," he went on, trying to keep his tone calm, "to do what you know is right. You've seen Irene's letter. Both Dr. Richards and I have explained the situation to you, as we understand it. Your accusations are based on nothing but your own anger."

Beneath the umbrella's scalloped edge, he could see only part of Miles's profile: earlobe, nostril, mouth and chin, the lips drawn tight. Still, in the most annoying way, he kept staring at the seagulls.

"Miles?" Dr. Petrie said.

"You might," Miles said distantly, "want to be a little more careful about how you talk to me."

Dr. Petrie lowered and furled his umbrella so that the rain, falling more gently now, might cool his head. For this he needed calmness, clarity. He took two slow breaths, gripped his umbrella in both hands, and said, "You refer, I know, to your powerful friends, and to your committee. Then let me refer to them as well. What would they think if they knew you'd hired Naomi Martin as a driver only because of your infatuation? And that you kept her on—that you let her drive you to the most sensitive meetings, where she could see exactly who was present and even overhear certain things—long past the point when you knew she was untrustworthy?"

Miles's umbrella dropped another two inches, obscuring everything but his chin. "They'd say nothing. Because that's not true."

"It *is* true," Dr. Petrie said. On the lake a group of gulls drifted quietly toward the grass at the foot of the park. "How many times did you insist on telling me exactly how you feel about her? And the patients who attended the Wednesday sessions know how you feel, as well—did you think they didn't notice? They talk about everything."

A faint noise, which might have been a groan, emerged from the umbrella.

"And now," Dr. Petrie continued—here he took a huge, intuitive leap at which he would later marvel—"now that we know what she took before she left . . ."

The umbrella rose, sending all the gulls into the air as Miles's head swiveled toward Dr. Petrie. "What do you know about that?"

Fascinated, Dr. Petrie continued to press at the same spot. "Certain things are missing from the X-ray laboratory. From other places too. I'm sure the members of your organization would find that interesting, given the access Naomi had to your room and your papers."

Miles furled his umbrella and stood up. Instantly the rain began to dampen his hair, so that it flattened against his skull. "You would blackmail me?"

"A request, let's say. Leave Leo alone. You know he didn't do anything."

"Why go to such extremes to protect him, if he's not guilty?"

Dr. Petrie rose, folding the oilcloth twice along its length before rolling it into a tidy cylinder. "Because someone," he said, "has to put a stop to this."

⌒

NONE OF US, including Leo, learned of that discussion until much later. In the infirmary Leo had been dreading the arrival of Miles every day since the restriction on visitors was lifted, but no one came except Eudora. That Thursday, Dr. Petrie completed his examination of Leo's chest, pronounced him much improved, and then said, offhandedly, that he could return to his room tomorrow, and that Miles had finished his investigation and withdrawn his accusations.

"Has he figured out what started the fire, then?"

"Not that I know of," Dr. Petrie said. "I still think Irene's idea—that a piece of equipment shorted out down there—seems most likely."

"I do, too," Leo said, even as the image of the missing pencil flashed before him. For the first time he began to think seriously about how it might have disappeared, and if it might have been involved in the fire. Even to Dr. Petrie, though, he couldn't suggest this. Instead, keeping the focus of their conversation on Miles, he said, "Maybe he just needed some time to reconsider."

He coughed twice and sipped at the glass of water near his bed, antici-pating his release. His own room, at last. His old routines, however those might have been changed by the fire. He hadn't seen the new dining room, the sealed-off central building, the curving dirt path hastily cut to provide a detour between the single, combined dormitory wing and the wing where he lay now. He imagined our days were essentially the same, except that our quarters were slightly more crowded.

"Maybe that helped," Dr. Petrie said, fiddling with his stethoscope. "And also Irene wrote a very kind letter on your behalf."

He said nothing about his own intervention, summarizing, instead, what Irene had written. Leo listened, amazed. Once, perhaps, one of his teachers might have done such a thing for him, or the Odessa merchant who'd sent him to school. But no one since. That Irene, still almost a stranger, could be so kind, and that her kindness could defuse Miles's heated accusations, made him think that perhaps he hadn't made such a bad decision seven years ago, when he'd crossed the ocean to come here.

That Friday, when he left the infirmary, his cough was gone, his fever was down, and Miles was nowhere in sight. Making his way through the corridors of the women's annex and then across the new dirt path—the central building looked terrible, he noted, and the garden was trampled—he felt almost hopeful despite the humming he'd heard from the porches. The covered walkway leading to the men's annex looked as it always had, and so did the stairs and the second-floor corridor. He stood before the door to his old room, delaying for a moment the pleasure of returning to the place he'd known before the fire, which he'd been used to thinking of as home. The instant he crossed the threshold, he saw that it now belonged to Arkady, Otto, and Abe.

Politely, as they might have received a guest, they made room for him. His bed was perfectly made; the clothes in his locker neatly arranged. His precious books had vanished from his bedside table, which was clean. Every other surface was covered with his roommates' belongings, as every molecule of air seemed saturated with their smells and sounds. They were patient with him, courteous, but even on the first night he sensed that they made only small talk in his presence, saving any real conversation for the times when they were alone.

At his first breakfast in the new dining room, he felt the same thing on a larger scale. Not since the night of the fire had he eaten with all of us; we might have applauded when he came in, we might have roared our approval or at least stopped what we were doing to welcome him. Instead, we carried on as if we'd never missed him. He waved across the cramped space at Kathleen, who looked remarkably well; smiled at Vivian, now walking with crutches; wedged himself into one of the tightly spaced chairs. Over our dishes of oatmeal with dried fruit and heavy cream, of eggs scrambled and heaped on toast, we nodded as he passed, said hello when he greeted us, asked politely after his health. But nothing more. No one, not even Kathleen, whose life he'd saved, came over, wrapped an arm around his shoulder, and said, "We know you haven't done anything." No one mocked Miles, his agents, or his league, as we would have done—had done—until the moment we'd learned about the box and what was in it.

It was no surprise that Miles remained suspicious of Leo even after he dropped the investigation. The surprise was that we remained suspicious too. After Dr. Petrie released Leo, he'd finally let some of us know the contents of Irene's letter; from that we knew that Leo couldn't have started the fire directly. Still, the letter didn't make us forget the horrors of that night, or bring Edith and Morris and Denis back from the clearing. The letter didn't restore our lives as we had known them, which had been far from perfect but which were at least ours. Everything familiar had vanished in the fire, which had laid bare the real nature of our confinement and still seemed related to Leo. In his secrecy, in the way he'd been so absorbed in his studies, in the way he'd stopped confiding in any of us after Ephraim left, we couldn't help feeling that he was guilty of something.

Dinner that day was the same, and so was supper. When Leo walked into the library, five or six of us were there; fifteen minutes later he was alone and he knew this was no accident. That night, when he went out to the porch and found his chair squeezed between Arkady's and Sean's, the partitions torn down and the line of bodies, stretching in both directions to the ends of the annex, so tightly formed that we looked ready to leap the railing together at the sound of a whistle, he was startled to hear himself apologize as he wedged himself into position. By nine o'clock he began to hear the humming sound, first from the porch above and the one below, finally spreading to the far ends of his own rank. Once in a while, he caught the sound of his own name.

23

FTER HIS MEETING with Dr. Petrie, Miles had skipped dinner and spent a long night out on his porch, inspecting the wreckage of the plans he'd made a year ago. Bad enough that everything he'd hoped to do at Tamarack State had been destroyed by the fire and by Leo. But that his crucial war work was threatened and his feelings for Naomi cast into doubt made him so angry he thought his heart might burst. This from Dr. Petrie, whom he'd once counted as a friend. A little, little man after all, as small in spirit as he was in stature, who'd used Miles's feelings against him and twisted what Miles knew was a generous impulse toward a troubled young woman until it seemed like a weakness.

He couldn't stop his daily round of meetings—indeed he was busier than ever—but for the rest of the week he avoided anything to do with Leo or Dr. Petrie. When he had to pass the east end of the lake, he turned his face from the benches. At Tamarack State, where he still had duties, he timed his visits for hours when he knew Dr. Petrie was making rounds and we were on our porches. To Dr. Richards, who seemed puzzled but relieved, he explained that Irene's letter, while not completely satisfactory, had along with a lack of sufficient resources reluctantly convinced him not to pursue his investigation further. The night after he told that lie, he had such savage stomach pains that Mrs. Martin had to call in his private physician.

He was an invalid, he reminded himself then. Nowhere near as strong as he pretended, and useless to everyone if he didn't take better care of his health. He had responsibilities to the other members of his committee and he had to balance the work that only he could do with the rest his cure demanded. Mrs. Martin, ever thoughtful, put him on a special diet and guarded his rest hours fiercely, answering the telephone herself and taking messages for him. On Saturday, when he was feeling a little better, he decided in return to help her with one small task.

In preparation for their outing, she had one of the new kitchen helpers—since May there'd been five—bring him a pot of tea. From the first sip, he could tell it had been made from water that wasn't quite boiling. The girl who brought it had a long braid of brown hair that swung sullenly against her back and an expression that seemed to dare him to complain. The one before her had had grubby hands, another had flirted outrageously with several boarders, although not with him; they came, stayed for a couple of weeks, bungled their tasks, and then left. Around him were other signs that Naomi might have had more to do with the household's smooth functioning than he'd suspected. A stain on the carpet, an unrepaired tear in the dining room curtain. Also a disconcerting influx of mail: letters from booksellers, complaining that payments he knew he'd left to be mailed had never arrived; from clothing stores in Philadelphia wondering why they hadn't received his usual order for shirts and vests. In Naomi's continued absence, nothing seemed to work. He tried not to think about her, and thought about her all the time.

To the list of things for which he blamed Leo, he added this: Leo had driven Naomi away. He blamed Eudora for failing to stop her, Mrs. Martin for overburdening her here at the house, Irene for whatever clumsiness she'd committed the night of the fire, when Naomi came looking for consolation. Dr. Richards had shown him Irene's letter, from which he remembered this: *She was upset about something when she came to see me, and still upset when she ran out.* The line made him want to weep. How was it that Irene, old enough to be Naomi's mother, supposedly so resourceful and sympathetic, had failed to comfort her?

How had he? Sometimes, as when he looked up now to see Tyler in the doorway, so eager to drive him that he was bouncing gently on his built-up shoe, he also blamed himself. Long before Naomi left he could, he saw, have freed her and hired his own permanent car and driver. Except that he had wanted her next to him. Except that he had wanted to be able to study her features in a place where, with her eyes fixed on the road before her, she wouldn't be able to turn away. Except that, worst of all, he had enjoyed making her do what he wanted. During their last weeks together, when he'd ordered her to take him somewhere and she'd curled her lip and looked down at her shoes for a second before looking back up and saying, "Of course"—that feeling moving through his veins had been pleasure.

He set down the unsatisfactory cup of tea and rose just as Mrs. Martin entered the parlor. "Ready?" he asked her.

"Ready," she said, patting her bag. "I have my notes, I know what I want to say—really this is *so* kind of you."

Miles nodded to Tyler, who clopped ahead to the limousine. Mrs. Martin, who hadn't ridden in it before, settled into the back seat as if she belonged there, running her hand slowly over the smooth leather upholstery. All week long she'd been talking about this meeting, which she'd organized herself. Gathering together other directors of cure cottages, along with the women who worked in the hotel kitchens and the hospital dining rooms, she planned a brisk half-hour speech, complete with diagrams, of how they might most effectively conserve food and cooking fuel. Before she started, though, Miles was to give a brief talk on the sacrifices being made by the drafted soldiers, and how every scrap saved here would directly help our men.

As they drove the short distance to the hotel, she prattled, Tyler responded attentively, and Miles, listening to their eagerness and good-will, their obvious delight in finding a purpose, felt his own spirits plummet. How worthy both of them were, and how tiresome! Mrs. Martin with her meticulous lists and the mat of carefully plaited hair clamped to the back of her head like a trivet; Tyler with his sweaty hands and his way of brushing off the seat with a handkerchief before Miles sat down. They agreed with him on every point and anticipated most of his requests. He didn't care for either of them.

Except for the days he'd shared with Edward and Lawrence in Doylestown and their blissful summer digging fossils in Canada, he some-times felt that he'd spent most of his life with people he didn't really like. The ones who drew him magnetically always moved just beyond his reach, living lives that seemed much more interesting and joyful than his own. They danced past, talked gaily together, burst into laughter, and then dis-appeared. Meanwhile he dutifully worked with the earnest ones. This, per-haps, he'd shared with Dr. Petrie; which made the betrayal worse.

"Shall I wait?" Tyler said as he parked in front of the hotel. The moon was full, illuminating the leaves swaying on the basswoods, the soft shad-ows of the shrubs and the darker ones of the buildings on the street. Lights were on here and there, linked by scallops of bunting strung across the façades, and porches glowed on the cure cottages marching up the hill. In some he could see figures lying on their chairs, where he'd once been. Where he should be.

"Come in and listen," Mrs. Martin urged Tyler. "I promise it will be interesting."

He could engage a private detective, Miles reflected as he helped

Mrs. Martin from the limousine. Not for any further investigation of Leo—Dr. Petrie had closed that route—but as a way of trying to find Naomi. Several detectives, even, in different cities; one young woman with modest resources couldn't be that difficult to find. But even if he found her—what then? She didn't care for him, she never had. Let her mother find her, let her mother sort out what had happened. Already, he knew, Mrs. Martin had circulated inquiries through the web of her professional acquaintances, cure cottages here connected to boardinghouses in the Catskills, home economics instructors on Long Island in touch with hospital administrators in Vermont and far beyond.

He straightened his narrow shoulders. His job tonight was to inspire the audience so that they would all adopt, enthusiastically, Mrs. Martin's recommendations. More tasks loomed tomorrow, and the next day, and the next. Work in the village, work for the league, work related to Tamarack State; fortunate that he knew how to husband his energies. At home in Doylestown—*home*, he thought, seeing the pale, well-ordered rooms of his house, the ranks of machinery in his plant, each piece tended by his well-trained employees—other work awaited him, which only he could do. Would do, as soon as he was cured. Everyone, he thought, must do his duty.

IT WAS ON A Wednesday that Dr. Petrie met with Miles; Leo returned to his room on Friday, the same day Miles told Dr. Richards he'd completed his investigation. On Saturday Miles went to the meeting with Mrs. Martin, after which nothing changed. Sunday, Monday, Tuesday passed, during which the news of Miles's retreat spread throughout Tamarack State. We might have welcomed Leo back then: but still nothing changed. He confided in no one; he told none of us the story he'd told Eudora about Ephraim's visitor and the box he'd left behind. Twice he walked to the clearing by himself, looking over the new stones that marked where Morris and Edith and Denis lay, and this seemed to us to signal something suspicious. By then, perhaps it wouldn't have mattered what he'd done. We no longer trusted him.

None of us slept during our afternoon rest hours that next Wednesday, the balconies so hot beneath the canvas awnings that we could feel ourselves shriveling, and when four o'clock arrived we leapt from our cure chairs and headed toward the pavilion. Even here there was only the smallest breeze, but this, combined with the shade of the pavilion roof, the smell of the cedar shakes, and the sight of the creek emptying sluggishly into the weedy mouth of the nearest pond, was still a relief. No one was feeling well. Six patients were in the infirmary Leo had so recently left; there'd been three dramatic hemorrhages in the last four days and no one had any appetite. Twice the afternoon milk had curdled. Our hearts seemed curdled as well. We sat on the pavilion benches or the balcony rails, fanning ourselves with copies of *The Kill-Gloom Gazette* while Leo paced slowly back and forth between the willow tree at the top of the pond and the three larches clustered at the first bend in the creek.

He looked, Polly remarked, as if he were attached to a pendulum. Back and forth, back and forth, thinking intently while we drooped in the shade. How long would he do this? Ian wondered. And what was he thinking about?

Us, we knew. We'd been behaving badly. Overhead a swarm of sparrows pulled tightly together only to scatter, as if even they were too warm to be near each other.

He felt, he was thinking as a larch cone crunched beneath his feet, like a stranger. A stranger to us. In the dining room he felt more alone than he had a year ago, when, during a similar heat wave, Ephraim had first wheeled him through the door of the old hall. Then we had welcomed him; now we were polite. Always, but only, polite. We never accused him of anything. Yet if he walked up to Pietr and Zalmen and Lydia and Bea and tried to join their conversation, he felt his words slide into nothingness as he spoke. If he suggested to Abe and Ian that they read a book together and discuss it, they smiled, spoke vaguely of being busy, and moved away. David and Pearl and Celia had separately offered excuses when he'd proposed walks to them; even Kathleen turned from him, although she blushed as she did. We'd all evaded him, our eyelids lowered and our real thoughts shrouded. None of us offered more than courtesy demanded and no one would say—we could not, exactly, have said—what he'd done wrong. We thought of the library books Miles's agents had earlier carried away in boxes, and of the orders to darn worn sheets instead of replacing them, change the linens less often, reuse rags that should have been burned. *It's our duty to economize,* Dr. Richards had told both the staff and us: but we sensed Miles behind the new directives. Miles, reaching for Leo, punishing us.

As Leo paced, a young fox popped up from the grass, snapping at a butterfly that lifted effortlessly just out of reach. He stopped, watched, and then watched us watching the fox, while ignoring him. If he'd known for sure how Eudora felt, perhaps he wouldn't have panicked, but he'd seen little of her since leaving the infirmary. He couldn't read her intentions any more clearly than he could read ours, and he wondered, now, if she'd really heard what he was saying when he'd asked her to the movies. He wasn't sure anymore why she'd come that night, or what might have happened between them without the fire. Apparently they were going to have to start all over again.

A handful of sparrows, one missing a foot, landed on the dusty path, and he glanced over at us again. Clumsily, obdurately, we looked away while Otto, feeling guilty because of Naomi's letter, turned his back completely. For more than a month that letter, stalled at first by her careless address and then by the chaos after the fire, had lain in the village post office with the other mail meant for here. Once the sacks were finally delivered and all the mail was sorted through, Otto had seen the envelope addressed to Leo and, well-intentioned then, had taken it back to their shared room, to deliver when Leo returned. After the humming started, though, he'd hidden it on purpose. "Not my fault," he'd said blandly, when he finally decided to deliver it: already that line embarrassed him. "I stuck it in a book and then forgot about it." And so it was only on the night before we gathered at the pavilion that Leo had read:

May 9, 1917

Leo—

I don't know why I've been so stupid. You were doing everything possible to let me know and still I missed all the signs. In your room that afternoon, you signaled me again—I saw the way you avoided my face so carefully. The way you closed the door behind us, your right hand wrapped around the edge, showing me your fingers until the last minute. Your shirt collar opened so I could see the pulse at the base of your throat—

I used to think I knew what longing was but I was wrong. You're with me everywhere, all the time. The birds are you, the foxes are you, the plants pushing up beneath the trees and the trees themselves, trunks and branches, from the smallest needle to the roots spreading through the ground. The curtains in my mother's house and the silverware in the drawers. Everything. What we feel for each other, the way we're intertwined—I can feel everything you mean to say to me, you don't need to say a word. It means nothing that you are sick. Nothing. You'll be well as soon as we're together, away from here; I'm healthy enough for both of us and my strength will flow into you.

Meet me this Friday at the movies. Sit near the back and wait for me, I have to take Miles someplace but then I'll come to you. I have something to give you, something of yours, which I've been holding on to for too long; that was my mistake, but I know you'll forgive me and then we can make a plan. I have the car, I know a place where we can stay. I have money enough for our journey. All we need to do is pick the day and we can leave our old lives behind.

Love, Naomi

He remembered Eudora's trusting glance the afternoon she'd been in his room, and the way she'd looked toward him for help. He'd hardly noticed Naomi and yet she'd apparently studied his every move. The idea of her drawing his face again and again, and then writing that letter and sitting beside him, made his skin crawl as if insects were marching up and down in rows. He gazed longingly across the meadow at the staff cottages. Irene, who lived in one of them, might have helped him sort through his confusion. But she'd already done so much by writing to Dr. Richards on his behalf that he felt ashamed to trouble her again.

In the west clouds were gathering, weather moving in from Canada. We turned our faces to the breeze and saw Leo, perhaps unconsciously, turn his head as well. He stopped in the middle of his circuit, halfway between the clump of larches—larch, we'd learned years ago, was another name for tamarack—and the willow. Miles, he was thinking, didn't really believe that he was innocent; he was pushing the rest of us as a way of getting at him. In fact as that breeze touched our faces we were discussing another of Miles's intrusions: the arrival, that Monday night, of our own personal Four-Minute Man. Everywhere else in the country, Miles claimed, these volunteers were giving pep talks in theaters and churches, inspiring audiences to buy Liberty Bonds, plant victory gardens, conserve food, work longer hours, economize on coal. Surely we needed this more than most; why not set aside a dinnertime slot once a week, and let a series of these punchy speakers inspire us while we ate? Dr. Richards had agreed, perhaps to placate him, and so along with our baked macaroni and cheese we'd been served with a barrel-chested man, standing on a chair and chattering at auction speed for the time it would have taken to change reels, if we'd been watching a film.

His topic had been the importance of following the rules of our sanatorium even more rigorously than usual: the harder we worked, the faster we'd heal. *One of the most encouraging features of the war against tuberculosis is that it requires few new weapons or strange and complicated ammunition for*

the rank and file of the army, he said. Did we look like an army? *Our weapons are food, fresh air, and sleep. If you do what you are told, and do it well, you
will cut days from your cures. And each day cut saves vital funds for our effort
overseas.*

We could feel the knife. The harder Miles pushed, the further we
pulled away from Leo—who from his place between the willow and the
larches saw that he might have to leave. There was nothing here, there
had never been anything here but our community, which the fire had
destroyed. He hated the room he'd once shared with Ephraim; he hated
his slot on the porch. He hated the chaotic new dining room where,
although his tray clattered against our trays and his elbows banged ours
at the crowded table, we talked across and around him. He had no friend
and yet he was never alone. If he'd been alone, away from the whispers
and night noises of Otto, Arkady, and Abe, he might have been able to
sleep, which might have allowed him to think. He'd barely slept since
moving back among us and now the whole place seemed to him diseased.

The warning bell for supper rang, six strokes thudding through the
air. We turned at once, we turned as a group, and Leo saw how we'd file
inside together, find our places together, whisper about him together in
the few minutes it would take him to follow. When he walked through the
dining room door alone we'd turn together to look at him, or together
ignore him: unbearable, either way. He had to leave. He wouldn't go back
to the city, though; he'd never go to a city again. He wanted a place where
no one resembled him, where no one spoke Russian or German, no one
remembered crossing the ocean or slept six and eight to a room and pretended that was a reasonable way to live. He wanted fresh air, animals,
open land; people one or two at a time but never in groups: Ephraim's
place in Ovid, near the Finger Lakes. Ephraim, his friend.

At the door to the dining room the roar of all of us talking at once rose
like a concrete wall. He told the nurse on duty that he was feeling poorly
and then turned and went to his room and fetched his bag. He wrote a

quick note to Dr. Petrie, thanking him for his help. He wrote another to Irene, thanking her for the gift of the books and for her confidence in him; also for her letter, which he hadn't seen. Then he wrote Eudora's name on a third envelope, put Naomi's letter inside it, and added a note of his own. *I am leaving,* he wrote. *I am starting over; I don't want to say where but I'm sure you know. My health is very much on the mend and that last incident meant nothing. I wish you would join me when you feel ready. I love you. Leo Marburg.*

HE LEFT US with hardly more than what he'd brought to Tamarack State. That night, carrying one small bag with a change of clothes and the little box Eudora had given him, he caught a ride down the hill with Roger, our night watchman, who'd been called up and knew he'd be leaving soon. Sympathetic to anyone wanting to get away, Roger dropped Leo off at the lake. There Leo spent an hour on the bench where Miles and Dr. Petrie had talked. When dawn came he walked to the village station, which he hadn't seen before. Red brick, a square tower capped with a skylight, a stone arch over the door rimmed with green tiles. In the stone were chiseled the words that would have greeted him had he arrived by choice, with money in his pocket, headed for a place like Mrs. Martin's house: *Welcome, Health-seekers!* He took the first train headed south.

24

I F WE FELT ashamed of ourselves—Otto, Abe, and Arkady especially; if we worried about the ways we'd failed Leo, we were comforted by the way, almost immediately, the tension here eased. Still the Four-Minute Man came to lecture us; still Miles came several times each week to consult with Dr. Richards. But our routine settled down after Leo vanished, as if Miles wasn't interested enough in the rest of us to continue constricting our lives. Curiosity about our own behavior would come to us later; what we had at first was a continued curiosity about the fire and its causes, and also about what had happened to Naomi. Any information, we knew, would come to us from Eudora—but Eudora, after Leo left, didn't spend much time with us. She worked extra shifts, still; she performed her duties carefully and was always pleasant when cleaning our rooms. But she left as soon as her tasks were done, and although she never said anything about Leo's sudden departure, we knew she judged us.

To Irene, her only real companion after Leo left, she admitted how angry she was with us (we expected that) and also, more surprisingly, how angry she was that Leo had bolted without talking to her. That he'd finally state his feelings not in person but in a note: how was she supposed to respond to that? Something delicate and interesting had arisen between them in the X-ray room, which was one of the reasons she'd agreed to meet him at movie night—and which, after all that had happened, still hung unresolved. A blunt line, at the end of a note, only served to hide everything worth talking about. And she was further distracted by his first paragraph, which explained how, after all this time, he'd finally received Naomi's letter.

That letter itself she read with a terrible pang. Naomi's feelings had developed in front of her as steadily and clearly as a photographic plate, but she'd acted as if, because Leo didn't share them, they meant nothing. When she'd suggested that Naomi should let Leo know how she felt, she'd imagined a few words, perhaps a warm glance at the end of a Wednesday session—never a letter like that. But she also hadn't imagined that Naomi would sneak into the movies on a night when she was driving Miles. All their walks and talks and bicycle rides, the confidences they'd exchanged, the times they'd skated on the frozen lake with their arms linked and the moon rising over the mountains, counted for nothing against the moment when Naomi had caught the look she and Leo exchanged. Naomi had left without a word, without even a hint. Now the letter made Eudora suspect she'd never hear from Naomi again.

When she did get news of Naomi, it came indirectly, in late September. In Irene's tidy room, which Eudora visited each week and which was slowly filling with the books Dr. Petrie begged from friends to replace the collection destroyed in the basement, she flipped through a radiography manual. She glanced at a formula for mixing a developing solution—already, this was out of date—and then she told Irene that her brother Ernest had seen Naomi in New York.

Irene reached for her pad and pencil. Still, then, she hadn't regained her voice. *I didn't know they were even friends,* she wrote.

"I didn't either, really," Eudora said. "She used to see him at our house, but I never thought of them as *close.* Ernest wrote that she'd gotten in some trouble during her first few weeks in New York—I guess that's where she went from here—and then she looked him up."

She's all right, then?

"So Ernest says."

You must be relieved.

"Ernest didn't know how she got to the city, or what she did when she first arrived. But he said she showed up at his room one night—he has a tiny place in an attic, near Central Park—and stayed for a couple of months. Then one day she told him she'd found work in Brooklyn, and the next day she left."

Irene, who still hadn't admitted to Eudora, or to the rest of us, all that had happened between her and Naomi, wrote, *What kind of work?*

"As a trolley conductor," Eudora answered, wondering why this would matter. "Maybe being so good with her mother's car helped." While Irene drew a jagged border in the margin of her writing pad, she added, "But the important thing is that she's in one piece."

Eudora had found a fresh glove for Irene after the fire, changed the cotton inside the fingers, later wrapped the ugly wound on her neck with a bright printed scarf. In all ways she'd been an excellent assistant and it would have been nice to spare her feelings. Still, Irene had to ask, *Do you know why Naomi left?*

"I'm not sure," Eudora said.

Irene waited, her pencil motionless.

"She saw Leo and me together, at the movies," Eudora admitted. When Irene nodded, Eudora continued, "She was upset. We were all upset. But it's worse than I knew. She . . ." Eudora paused and looked out the window—it was lovely outside, the leaves just beginning to turn color on the trees near the pond and the swallows eagerly darting—before taking two folded sheets of paper from her pocket. "I've been wanting to show you these."

Irene read Naomi's letter, and then Leo's. Then Naomi's again. She wrote, *What did she have that belonged to Leo?* Leo's name she underlined twice.

"She had a bag with her that night. I saw some drawings in it. Drawings of him."

Irene nodded. *She showed them to me as well.*

"Did she?" Eudora asked. For a minute they looked at each other. "She might have meant those."

She might, Irene wrote. She turned her gaze to the swallows while she decided what she'd keep to herself. Then she added, *What will you do now?*

—

WE WEREN'T SURPRISED to hear that Eudora had decided to leave us; with the X-ray laboratory destroyed and Irene unable to work, she didn't have much reason to stay. Irene and Dr. Petrie helped her apply to a nurses' training school in Jamestown, where she might get certified quickly as an aide. She planned to head overseas when she was done, with whatever organization would take her. Once she was in France she could find a place helping with a mobile X-ray unit or assisting a radiographer in a field station. At worst, she could work in a base hospital. *Three months*, she told Leo, when she'd forgiven him enough to write. *I'll let you know where I'm posted as soon as I hear.*

From Miles, who caught her one afternoon on the lawn near the men's annex, she hid both her own plans and Leo's whereabouts. Nor did she tell him what she'd learned from her brother about Naomi. Behind his good manners was not, she thought, the meek creature Naomi had thought she could manipulate so casually. She avoided Miles when she could, now, and concealed anything important when she couldn't.

"I suppose Leo's gone to be with Naomi," Miles said bitterly. The wind, blowing from the west, carried with it the smell of a thousand miles of pine. "They're probably in the same place. What have you heard?"

"Not a thing." She turned and headed toward the annex.

From right behind her, crowding her heels, he said, "Why do I ask you anything? You thought he was in love with *you*."

"I've been wrong about quite a few things," she replied. Including, she thought, her own feelings for Leo. Packing up her few belongings, explaining to her distraught parents why she had to do this, her anger at Leo had faded. She liked Leo enormously, she realized. She longed to touch him, take care of him, sleep next to him—was that love? She couldn't imagine joining him now, when she'd still accomplished nothing and been nowhere, but she could imagine returning to him.

WINTER SET IN not long after Eudora left, the coldest winter anyone could remember. The lakes surrounding us froze quickly, their surfaces so glossy that from our porches we could see them gleaming like mirrors between the hills and hear the runners' whisk as the iceboats flew from shore to shore. In New York, the Hudson River locked up partway into the bay, allowing astonished men to walk from Staten Island to New Jersey but stopping all traffic between there and Albany. Families froze to death in tenements as wood and coal grew scarce. Men who'd been drafted in July and shipped to army camps thrown up from wood and canvas shivered next to each other on cots without blankets, trained without woolen socks or overcoats; whole regiments came down with pneumonia. There were investigations, hearings, newspaper articles condemning the ill treatment of our new soldiers. Once the revolutionary government in Russia signed an armistice with Germany, the war news became even worse, and that, in a way, was a blessing for us: suddenly no one had time for us anymore, and we were left alone.

In January one blizzard after another marched over us and then on to the East Coast cities. The wind blew, the snow fell. The snow fell and fell and fell and no one could get anywhere, but we didn't care: we had nowhere to go. There were Bolsheviks in the Bronx, we heard; no longer admirable fighters for freedom and peace but traitors. We ignored the cold, we ignored the news. (Although we paused at that word "traitors": was that what *we* were?) Clinging to what was left of our weekly gatherings, beginning at the same time to realize what we'd done, we went to work. No single person, we thought, had done anything so terrible. Yet together, without noticing exactly what was happening, we'd contributed to destroying our own world. We wanted to understand how we'd done that, or how we'd failed to prevent it.

Even as our time on the crowded porches grew more bitter, our hands stiffer, our faces more frozen, we continued to sift and sort our recollections. We've made more progress than we might have thought. By February, we'd looked at the various letters and at Dr. Petrie's reports, and also at the drawings Eudora left with us, which deepened our sense of Naomi's desperate attachment to Leo. We looked at the green volumes Irene tried to give to Leo, which Dr. Petrie retrieved and which taught us something about scientific proof. The last piece of the puzzle came from Irene herself, though, when she regained a whisper of her voice.

She's completely one of us now that she can't work, a patient again as she was in her youth. She was, as she's admitted, unwilling at first to rejoin us, disappointed by our cowardice, our pettiness, the misplaced sense of clannishness that drove us to cling together and push Leo away. But eventually, she also began to remember some of what she'd seen in us during our Wednesday sessions. Our hopefulness, our eagerness to learn. Our belief that, sick and inadequate as we were, we might help each other. One night, finally—we had gathered in the kitchen, completely against the rules—she told us what she'd omitted from her letter to Dr. Richards and also withheld from Eudora.

On the Friday evening of the fire, she'd been sorting radiographs, looking for images that Dr. Petrie might find useful. Later she meant to go upstairs to the movies, but she was behind in her filing and the work went slowly. Images of the dead she laid to her right, images of the living to her left. Through the door, which she'd left open to air out the musty room, she heard footsteps pounding down the stairs and rushing past before stopping, walking back, and tentatively entering the lab.

She rose from her desk in the back, which was behind a dividing wall lined with shelves, and walked into the area nearest the corridor. In the pale light of her desk lamp, she could see a young woman huddled on the couch. Her head was in her arms and she was weeping.

"Are you all right?" Irene asked gently. The woman raised her head and Irene recognized Miles's driver. Despite the Wednesday afternoon sessions they'd shared, Irene didn't feel she knew her well. Naomi sulked, and had a biting tongue; sometimes she drew Eudora away from her work; otherwise Irene couldn't figure her out. Still, she couldn't work with Naomi sitting alone in the gloom. Lowering herself into a chair, she asked why Naomi was so upset.

"*Because*," Naomi said, flinging her hands dramatically.

She leapt from the couch and began circling the room, touching the walls, trailing her fingers against the edges of the gray paper envelopes holding each patient's films. We were all there, arranged alphabetically, our folders thicker or thinner depending on when we'd been admitted and what crises we'd had: lungs before, during, after, lungs scarred or healed or dense with fluid and deposits. Naomi circled counterclockwise, her right arm outstretched, fingers clicking over the edges of the folders and making a sound like a stick rubbing down a washboard, which at first Irene could only envy: it had been years since she could imagine doing something so harsh to her own scabby, truncated hands.

"What can I do?" Irene asked. In the kitchen where we listened to this, the radiators popped and hissed and we drew closer together, as if the anxiety Irene had felt, listening to Naomi, had made its way across the months to us.

A cloth bag hung from Naomi's left shoulder, Irene said. The bag—some of us remembered seeing it—swayed back and forth as she moved. Her head was down, her arm was out, her dress was red and had a crisp white collar. Her fingers clicked against the films as she began to speak. Disjointed phrases, disjointed feelings. Her yearning for Leo and the signs he'd sent her, so surreptitiously, all through the winter and spring. His secret intention to meet her and watch the movies together, and the letter she'd sent him, which he pretended not to have seen. Eudora had tricked her, lied to her . . .

"Eudora would never do anything to hurt you," Irene said. "If she deceived you at all, it would only have been to keep you from being hurt."

"You *would* take her side," Naomi said. "You've done everything you could to come between us, you *took* her. You took my friend."

"That's not true," said Irene. *Click click click click click*, went the nails against the folders.

"Leo loves me," Naomi said, "the way I love him. I see the way he watches me, I *know*. I made the mistake of telling Eudora and now she's trying to take him for herself, just the way you took her. The way you two take everything."

Irene drew a breath. How terrible, she thought, not to be able to see what was real. Gently—she wondered if she'd ever misread a person so badly—she said, "Leo has been mooning over Eudora for months now. He was watching *her*, not you. He's told Eudora how he feels. And I think she's beginning to have feelings for him as well. I don't approve, I think she should keep her mind on her work, but—"

Naomi glared at her and then set her bag firmly on the floor. "Why are women like you so stupid?" she said. "You, my mother—both of you too old and dried-up to understand how *anyone* feels."

Reaching down, she pulled a handful of papers from her bag and waved them at Irene. Chins, ears, noses, eyes; at first Irene wasn't sure what she was looking at. Eventually, she made out Leo's face.

"*This* is what's real," Naomi said scornfully. "The way I feel about Leo. Not that you'd know what it's like to look at someone's mouth and feel it on you, or to know how his hands would touch you . . ."

For a second, Irene wanted to slap her. Of course she knew: when she and her husband were first married, the sound of his footsteps coming toward her in the dark could make her heart race like a greyhound's. He used to tease her by holding his right hand over her breast, so close he was nearly touching it, hovering until she lifted her body to meet him. And then years later, after he'd died and she'd moved to Colorado and thought she was past all of that, she'd been startled by the fierce charge that leapt between her and her brother-in-law when they were first experimenting with the Roentgen rays. She'd taken the job Dr. Richards offered as a way of saving her sister; she was here because of just those feelings. How upsetting that, to someone Naomi's age, she looked as if she'd always been old.

She calmed herself and raised her good hand to Naomi's shoulder. "I do understand," she said: sympathetically, she hoped. "I'm fond of Leo myself and I can see why you'd be drawn to him. His intelligence, and his desire to learn; it's touching. He told me once that in Odessa he earned money for his laboratory fees by cleaning out latrines. You work hard yourself, I know. You must feel like that's a bond between you."

Naomi shoved the drawings back into her bag. "When," she said—her hands were trembling—"when did he live in Odessa?"

"Before he moved here," Irene said. "After his mother died and he left Grodno." All those drawings, and yet Naomi seemed to know nothing essential about him; not even, perhaps, that he'd meant to be a chemist. "He told Eudora that during the first winter after he ran away from home, he slept on the floor in someone's pantry."

In response, Naomi burst into tears, heaved the bag at Irene, and ran from the room. Papers, and something that looked like part of a garment, fluttered past Irene's shoulder. She had an instant to be grateful that the bag had missed her; there was something heavy inside, a book perhaps, which made a thudding sound as the bag hit the floor below the shelves.

We think the thudding sound was made by the antique fossil book given by Edward Hazelius as a Christmas present to Miles, which Miles then gave to Naomi and which Naomi must have wanted to give Leo. The stolen shirt lay on top of the book, along with the heap of drawings. Below it, we think, lay the third pencil. In the letters Eudora had started writing once she was over in France and working in the hospital, she'd tried to explain to Irene, and to herself, the evolution of her feelings for Leo. Without understanding the implications, she described the afternoon she'd found Naomi rummaging through Leo's locker. *I was ready to hit her, when I saw her there. I should have known then how I felt about Leo.*

I should have known, Irene would tell us later, as we leaned against the kitchen counters and nibbled the sunflower seeds she'd brought. But on that May night all she knew was that Naomi was crying. She followed Naomi into the corridor, leaving the bag where it fell. Behind her, we hypothesize, the pencil crushed between the book and the floor let out a little spurt of exceptionally hot flame.

—

WE HAVE THE LETTER from Eudora's brother; based on that we imagine Naomi's life in New York. Probably, we think, she is fine. Upset, perhaps; grieving over the loss of Leo—but for all that basically fine. Unaware of what she has done, what she has caused. If she saw a report about the fire in the newspapers, did she figure out her own role? We think not; she paid no attention to anything but her own feelings, and it wouldn't have occurred to her that her actions might affect other people. We imagine her dressed in a streetcar conductor's uniform, collecting fares and smiling at passengers as the car traverses a stretch of Brooklyn, perhaps flirting with a young man who looks like Leo. A girl, still; not quite twenty years old. In time someone else will catch her eye. Who knows what will happen then? She doesn't know that Leo was forced to leave, that Irene will always whisper, or that the clearing has expanded by three stones.

What she knows is that she escaped. Leo escaped as well, which seems lucky given the climate these days. When he left, he couldn't imagine how he'd make his next life. He went to Ephraim, whom he trusted, but soon he found that Ovid didn't suit him. Too much family, he wrote Dr. Petrie, all those cousins speaking Yiddish: exactly what he didn't want. One of Ephraim's friends found him work not far away, at a winery in Hammondsport. *A pretty village, beautiful hills,* he wrote to Irene. (He writes to Irene and to Dr. Petrie; not, so far, to the rest of us.) *A chance to work once more with grapes and the chemistry of fermentation, as I did long ago in Russia. I have my own laboratory.*

He felt safe sending letters through the mail, knowing that Miles, to everyone's great relief, wasn't here to intercept them. In January, against the advice of his doctor, Miles left Tamarack Lake. No one, he supposedly said, could produce cement like he could, and so he went back to run his plant: his contribution to the war. When he left, it was like a patch of bad weather blowing out. The tops of the trees reappeared, and the tops of the mountains. The stars above the mountains, and the moon. We could see each other. We could see where we lived, what we had done, and what we still had left.

How innocent we seem to ourselves, now, when we look back at our first Wednesday afternoons! Gathering to learn about fossils, poison gas, the communal settlement at Ovid, about Stravinsky and Chekhov, trade unions and moving pictures and the relative nature of time, when we could have learned what we needed about the world and the war simply by observing our own actions and desires. We lived as if we were already dead, as if we'd died when we were diagnosed and nothing we did after that mattered. We lived as if nothing was important.

Despite the cold—it is ten below zero on this February day—we've walked through the snow to the garden behind our old solarium, the place where we were first joined. Around the fountain, shut off for the winter, we draw together as Abe begins to read the pages we have made. Once we built ships and towers from the pieces of an Erector set. Now we build hypotheses. About what Naomi did, and how Miles felt, and who said what to whom. About how the pencil that disappeared from Leo's locker ended up being used, almost accidentally—more and more, we think it started the fire—in Irene's laboratory. And about how all of us are to blame.

Abe reads, then Pietr reads, then Sophie, and then the rest; the sparrows perched on Hygeia's shoulders rise; words mingle in the air. If the voice we've made to represent all of us seems to speak from above, or from the grave, and pretends to know what we can't, exactly, know—what Miles was thinking, what Naomi meant—that's our way of doing penance. Singly, we failed to shelter Leo. Singly, then, we've forbidden ourselves to speak. *This is what happened*, we say together. *This—this!—is what we did.*

AUTHOR'S NOTE

I'm grateful to the Dorothy and Lewis B. Cullman Center for Scholars and Writers of the New York Public Library, for a fellowship that made possible much of the research for this novel, and to the John D. and Catherine T. MacArthur Foundation, for a fellowship that enabled me to write it. Numerous libraries large and small were helpful, but I'm especially grateful to the Saranac Lake Free Library. Rich Remsberg uncovered marvelous photographs that inspired me and provided crucial details. Ellen Bryant Voigt's wise counsel led me to the title. Jim Shepard and Karen Shepard offered sympathetic, truly helpful readings of the final draft, while Margot Livesey's brilliant comments on many drafts along the way improved the book immensely; the failures are mine alone.

Although this novel is set in and around an Adirondack village that resembles Saranac Lake, New York, the village of Tamarack Lake and all its inhabitants are invented, as is the institution of Tamarack State. Mendeleeff's book is real, though; Leo and I used the same edition.

THE FAMILIES

IRELAND

Michael Kynd = *Pegeen*

DETROIT

Francis MacEachern = *Nora*
b. 1825   b. 1825

Denis
b. 1833

Ned
b. 1835

ENGLAND

Max Vigne = *Clara*
b. 1835 b. 1837

CROOKED
LAKE

*Henrietta
Atkins*
b. 1852

TAMARACK
LAKE

Andrew = *Elizabeth*   *Gillian* = *Michael MacEachern*
b. 1861   b. 1863   b. 1825

TAMARACK
LAKE

Mary Roberta Martin

RUSSIA

Helen   *Eugene*   *Ernest*   *Sally*   *Eudora* = *Leo Marburg*
b. 1887 b. 1889 b. 1891 b. 1894 b. 1896   b. 1890

Naomi   *Thomas*
b. 1897   b. 1903

KEY

= Marriage

| Child

  Strong tie
  beyond blood
  or marriage

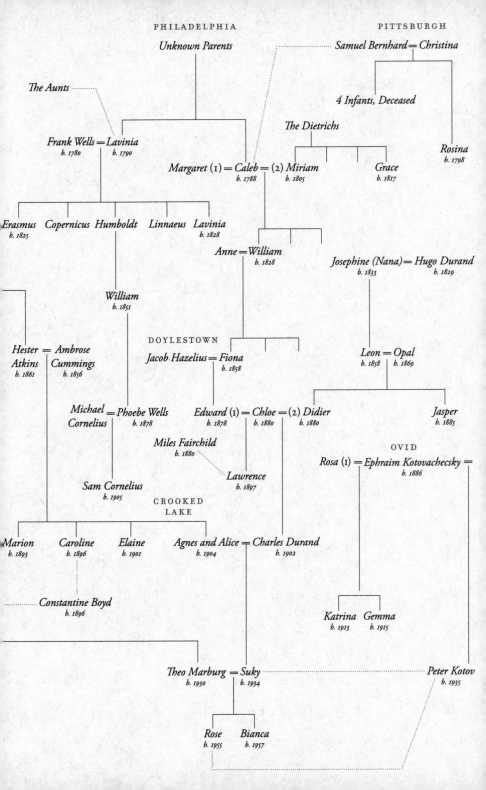

THE AIR
WE BREATHE

Andrea Barrett

READING GROUP GUIDE

THE AIR WE BREATHE

Andrea Barrett

Although the action of *The Air We Breathe* is confined to a tuberculosis sanatorium, the novel is also very much concerned with American attitudes toward the war raging across the ocean. Andrea Barrett's characteristic fascination with the history of science and technology—in this case, early twentieth-century developments in chemical and biological weapons, changing theories of atomic structure, and the use of X-ray images as diagnostic tools—helps connect aspects of that war to the patients' isolated situation. Through their Wednesday discussion groups we can share their growing knowledge, but we also know things they *can't* know—what, for instance, resulted from "the war to end all war." The appearance of places and families familiar from Barrett's earlier work further helps expand the novel's resonance, as we fit our knowledge of some of the characters' relatives into what we learn about them here.

"I've written about the northern Adirondack Mountains before," Barrett says, "especially in a story from *Servants of the Map* called 'The Cure,' which is about two women—Eudora's aunt and one of her grandmothers—running private boarding cottages for people with tuberculosis in the late nineteenth century. Working on that, I grew curious about the large public institutions caring for patients, often immigrants, who had neither money nor family. And I started wondering what it would have been like to be confined inside one of these big, prison-like buildings that once dotted not only the Adirondacks but also the rest of upstate New York and northern New England.

"At first I imagined a kind of low-rent, democratic version of Thomas Mann's *The Magic Mountain*. As the setting was transposed to America, so the rich patients would be transposed to impoverished immigrants in a public sanatorium. As *The Magic Mountain* takes place just before the outbreak of World War I in Europe, so I thought this might be set in analogous time, 1916 and 1917, just before the American entry into the war. But the initial conception changed a great deal, even before I started writing.

"First, the intertwined family of characters I've been working with for some time barged their way in. *The Air We Breathe* was particularly altered by connections to characters who first came to life in the stories of *Ship Fever*: the sisters Rose and Bianca Marburg, and siblings Ned and Nora Kynd, who emigrated from Ireland during the height of the great famine. Together they've generated a dense web of connections and relations that continues to influence what I write now. 'The Families,' a version of the family tree I've been keeping over the past decade, is meant to help interested readers follow these relationships.

"The novel changed even more during the year I spent in New York. As it happened, my first day at the New York Public Library, where I'd been lucky enough to get a fellowship meant to help me research the background of some of my characters, was on September 10, 2001. The experiences of the following days and months made me think differently about the meaning and subject matter of the novel, even though the characters and the setting remained the same. Suddenly I was thinking less about the medical aspects of the situation and more about the war taking place offstage. About the way both communicable diseases and the threat of outside attack tend to make us clump together and blame 'outsiders' for whatever's wrong; and the way wars induce prejudice against immigrants; and the way, during the course of a war, it's easy to toss certain liberties overboard. About the way, in a climate like that, it becomes easy for us to betray one another."

DISCUSSION QUESTIONS

1. Who betrays whom over the course of the novel? How do those betrayals and underlying conflicts mirror what's going on in the larger world? Can you connect those betrayals to the novel's unusual narrative voice?

2. The two opening chapters explicitly contrast conditions at the public sanatorium of Tamarack State, inhabited largely by impoverished immigrants, and the cure cottages of Tamarack Lake, inhabited by wealthy patients. Discuss the role class differences play in the novel.

3. The novel's plot turns, in part, on a triangle of misplaced attractions: Miles is drawn to Naomi, who's drawn to Leo, who in turn is drawn to Eudora. What do you think keeps each of these characters from perceiving the reality of the situation? Why, for instance, is Naomi so attracted to Leo, and why might she believe so deeply that the attraction is reciprocal?

4. What analogies do you see between the characters' misconceptions of one another and the way the patients as a whole are perceived by their families and by politicians? Between the way the healthy perceive the patients and the way they perceive immigrants?

5. Leo Marburg, who enters Tamarack State as the novel opens, catalyzes much of the action. How do you account for his effect on others? Do you view him as a romantic figure? And what role does his love for chemistry play? Elsewhere in Barrett's work, he appears as the elderly grandfather of Rose and Bianca Marburg, both of whom learn to love science because of him. Does that knowledge affect your understanding of Leo here, as a young man?

6. Dr. Petrie's attitude toward both his patients and his coworkers, especially Irene, seems quite sane and balanced; he's also responsive, at first, to Miles Fairchild. How do you view the conflict that ultimately develops between them? What role does Dr. Petrie play in the group's reaction to Leo after the fire?

7. Irene, who listens sympathetically to the patients while she takes "roentgenograms" of their chests, hides from them the wounds caused by her experiments with the X-rays. Dr. Petrie at first conceals, and then reveals, some of the effects of the first uses of gas warfare in France. Discuss how they and other characters are affected by the explosion of new technologies, and their relative degrees of knowledge about them. Do some seem to profit from the American entry into the war?

8. In an essay about working on this novel ("The Sea of Information," *The Best American Essays 2005*) Barrett wrote: "The more I learned about the First World War, the more I saw how much it had in common with what was known at the time as the 'War Against Tuberculosis.' Those wars overlap exactly in time—but also, more importantly, in their uses of propaganda and corrupted public language. The militaristic, and yet at the same time euphemistic, language of the 'War Against Tuberculosis' is very like that found in the documents used to whip up American support for entry into the war. The sound of that language interests me a good deal—it's a sound that's becoming familiar again." How do various forms of propaganda affect characters in this novel? How would you compare the language used then to language you see now in print and television journalism?

9. Tuberculosis, nearly eradicated at one point, has become a serious problem again with the advent of an extensively drug-resistant strain (XDR-TB). For the first time in decades, public health officials have quarantined patients positive for this. What would you do if you, or someone you loved, developed XDR-TB? How would you want to be treated?

10. What associations does the title have for you? How do you interpret the two epigraphs, drawing from sources written more than a century apart?

For a complete list of Norton's works with reading group guides, please go to wwnorton.com/reading-guides.

Meghan Kenny	*The Driest Season*
Nicole Krauss	*The History of Love*
Don Lee	*The Collective*
Amy Liptrot	*The Outrun: A Memoir*
Donna M. Lucey	*Sargent's Women*
Bernard MacLaverty	*Midwinter Break*
Maaza Mengiste	*Beneath the Lion's Gaze*
Claire Messud	*The Burning Girl*
	When the World Was Steady
Liz Moore	*Heft*
	The Unseen World
Neel Mukherjee	*The Lives of Others*
	A State of Freedom
Janice P. Nimura	*Daughters of the Samurai*
Rachel Pearson	*No Apparent Distress*
Richard Powers	*Orfeo*
Kirstin Valdez Quade	*Night at the Fiestas*
Jean Rhys	*Wide Sargasso Sea*
Mary Roach	*Packing for Mars*
Somini Sengupta	*The End of Karma*
Akhil Sharma	*Family Life*
	A Life of Adventure and Delight
Joan Silber	*Fools*
Johanna Skibsrud	*Quartet for the End of Time*
Mark Slouka	*Brewster*
Kate Southwood	*Evensong*
Manil Suri	*The City of Devi*
	The Age of Shiva
Madeleine Thien	*Do Not Say We Have Nothing*
	Dogs at the Perimeter
Vu Tran	*Dragonfish*
Rose Tremain	*The American Lover*
	The Gustav Sonata
Brady Udall	*The Lonely Polygamist*
Brad Watson	*Miss Jane*
Constance Fenimore Woolson	*Miss Grief and Other Stories*

Don't miss other titles by National Book Award–winning author

ANDREA BARRETT

ANDREA-BARRETT.COM

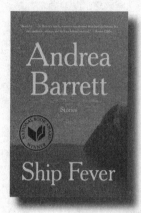

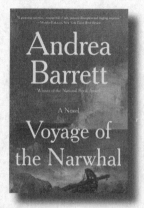

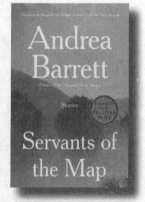

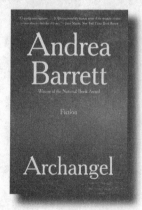

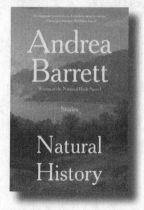